WHITE LIES

WHITE LIES

A NOVEL BY
JULIE SALAMON

Hill & Company, Publishers • Boston

■■■■■■■■■■■■■■■■■■■■■■■■■■■■■■■■

Library of Congress Cataloging-in-Publication Data

Salamon, Julie.
  White lies.

  I. Title.
PS3569.A4583W4 1987   813'.54   87-8634
ISBN   0-940595-08-7

Designed by Milton Glaser, Inc.
Printed in the United States of America

■■■■■■■■■■■■■■■■■■■■■■■■■■■■■■■■

The characters in WHITE LIES
are fictitious.
Any resemblance to persons living or
dead is coincidental.

To Sanyi, Szimi and Suzy

The centipede was happy quite
  Until a toad in fun
Said, "Pray, which leg goes after which?"
That worked her mind to such a pitch,
She lay distracted in a ditch,
  Considering how to run.
            Mrs. Edward Craster, Pinafore Poems

WHITE LIES

The Dreamer

It had gone like clockwork tonight.

She'd hopped on the train at Thirty-fourth Street and skedaddled right for the front car. The train was long and silver and sleek, wearing the war paint of the young city savages. Her mission had been to guide this coach into the station. The deed had been accomplished.

Jamaica Just smiled in her sleep. Even when she was dreaming, she liked to keep a schedule.

She saw herself standing there, a grown woman, gripping the handle of the soot-splattered door, her feet positioned two feet apart so she could ride with the bumps and grinds as the train galloped down the tracks. She had rocked back and forth, swaying to the accelerating rhythm of the Big "D" running through the dark. The train's lights illuminated this cavernous universe, empty save for the silvery tracks, bits of garbage, a rat.

"Holy shit," she marveled. "I could ride this train forever, night and day, day and night, allowing the bumps to lift me, flowing with the tide, running with the grain. Now this is poetry. Forget soliloquies to the eyes of lovers, lyric ballads to pastoral scenes, songs of praise for rushing streams and rivers falling over rocks and mountains."

Though she knew she was starting to talk aloud, she couldn't help it. Besides, who could hear her? Waking or sleeping, she loved the speed, the dark terror, the beauty, and the fearsome noise. Her mother might have reason to fear the trains, but not Jamaica, not now.

Jamaica realized she didn't seem peculiar at all until she was asked to name what she loved most about New York. "The subway," she would answer. Oh, she loved other things too. Like people—never herself—sitting down to eat Chinese food in restaurants at 1 A.M. But the subway promised and often delivered what she had come to the big city for: adventure, pathos, the titillation of pressing up close to exotic people. And what a haven from the cruelties of nature! On freezing days, the subway air was always warm. When the city sweltered, the subway was fresh and icy, if the air conditioning worked, or a hothouse for romance as tropical air blew in the windows, fanning carloads of fevered brows.

"I sing a hymn to the city, a song of praise, a cantata. Let me tell you of my affection for the life and spirit and movement and clash of people and smells and vibrancy. I am in paradise," she intoned into the din.

Paradise jerked to a stop at West Fourth Street, knocking the poetry out of Jamaica. She stumbled through the open doors onto the deserted subway platform.

She strutted awkwardly through the dimly lit subway station with what she hoped looked like conviction. She felt—well—peculiar, and to compensate, she remembered what she'd read recently in a *New York Times* article—that women who walk "with conviction" are less likely to get mugged than women who walk without it. Unfortunately, the author had neglected to describe what conviction looked like.

Jamaica didn't know either, but she could feel her mother's thumbs pressing against her protruding backbone until her young shoulders snapped to painful attention. "Don't walk like a schlump, darling," her mother was saying cheerily. "You want people to think, 'Now *there's* a girl with somewhere to go, things to do. She's obviously got things on her mind. Important things on her mind.' Shoulders back, chest out."

Stiffening into cautionary good posture even as her mother's voice faded, Jamaica realized something—she wasn't sure what—was amiss the second she stepped off the train. Yes, the map was still obscured by graffiti. The smell of urine diffused by industrial strength cleaner hadn't evaporated. Jamaica lifted her hand discreetly to her nose to filter the foul air through the gray wool of her mitten while she searched for clues. She did this discreetly because the inability to stroll nonchalantly through the cloud of ammonia that seemed to rise up from the concrete floors might be taken as a sign of weakness. A lack of conviction.

Peering from above the fuzzy mitten clasping her nose, she saw what TV newscasters call "a gang of youths" strolling toward her. Suddenly, she wanted very much to wake up.

She dropped her hand as the smell of urine was subsumed by a much more powerful smell, and it was emanating from *her,* pushing its noxious way through the layers of undershirt, sweater, lined tweed coat. The notion that emotions could take on physical characteristics, such as smell or taste, had always struck her as somewhat fanciful, the delicately wrought product of overheated imaginations. But she was dreaming, wasn't she? Wasn't she? No time to muse. There it was, unmistakably: the odor of fear.

As she often did when an unpleasant situation presented itself, she ignored it. She refused to acknowledge the steamy stench now liquefying under her arms, beneath her breasts, in the pores on her nose. This was her own kind of practical metaphysics. Make believe the thugs aren't there—they'll go away.

"Hey, pretty mama," one of the miscreants snarled. "Why don't you just hand me over your bag and maybe you won't get hurt."

Jamaica swallowed the quick curse ready to fly off her tongue. Instead, she rubbed her ear, which had developed a sharp pain. She laughed. A smile would be her umbrella.

These creeps didn't know the lyrics. Or maybe her smile was too insincere. They grabbed for her purse, pushed her. This incredible rudeness jarred her out of numbness. She began to scream and kick, aiming with hurtful if not deadly precision at what she presumed to be the source of their aggressive behavior. Thrashing about, she imagined herself trouncing all four or five of them (who could count at a time like this?).

Then she felt her confidence waning. She was starting to feel tired and lethargic, even though seconds before she'd felt she would emerge from this battle victorious. Now, all she wanted to do was go to sleep. She was cold. And she'd always thought fear would feel hot, if it could be felt at all. She moaned.

What happened next wasn't clear. She was slumped in the back seat of a stretch limousine, headed for the mayor's office to collect a citation for bravery. A camera's lights kept flashing. A *New York Post* photographer had managed to finagle his way into her limousine. Although she despised him and the tabloid that printed his pictures, she stared directly at him; her profile was lousy. She felt achy, but excited. She couldn't wait to hear the mayor's speech . . .

Real Life

. . . WINS news time, 7:40. Good morning, this February 7. This is Paul J. Smith with the news. Get ready to bundle up, New Yorkers. The thermometer shows 11 degrees Fahrenheit in the city, 5 degrees in the outlying areas . . . The mayor refused to comment on the guilt or innocence of Ernest Arnheim, the subway vigilante, who goes before a grand jury today in Manhattan . . . A Queens mother denies throwing her baby off the roof of their apartment building . . . Twenty thousand homeless people crowd city shelters as record-breaking temperatures continue to chill the Northeast . . . Tammy Jones, the nine-year-old schoolgirl from Columbus, Ohio, returns from Peking and pronounces the Chinese "real nice" . . . This is 1010 WINS Action News Radio. Give us twenty-two minutes and we'll give you the world . . .

Jamaica pulled her face up from the comfort of her extra-fine down pillow. "Sammy," she screamed. "I'm bleeding to death." She waited a beat. Another beat. Finally, a thick voice from another room offered reassurance.

"No, you're not. You had your period last week."

Off flew the comforter, the three blankets, the percale sheet. Jamaica, still clutching her pillow, marched into the bathroom.

"Hey, give a guy a little privacy," Sammy said, as if it had been somebody else who had scolded Jamaica years ago for her habit of locking the bathroom door.

"Look at this," she demanded, pointing to the patch of blood dried

7

brown and ugly against the red and white striped lines of her pillow-case. "I am bleeding to death. And I had another weird dream."

"I would love to hear about your dream." Sammy had a great deal of dignity for a man whose eyes were dusty with sleep and who was squatting on a toilet, his pajama bottoms piled around his feet.

He folded the paper on top of his bare thighs and squinted at Jamaica. "I'd say those drips of blood most likely spilled from that scratch on your ear." He squinted some more. "The scratch looks like the paw work of your cat."

Satisfied that he'd done his duty, Sammy reopened the *Times*. "I'm not trying to shake the drama from your life, but worrying about death at your age and excellent state of health is cheap," he said, studying the headlines. "I expect more than that of you."

Jamaica nodded as she let her pillow drop onto the hairy, dusty tiles of the bathroom floor. She shuffled into the kitchen. There she dropped herself onto the floor and stared at the patterned tin ceiling, basking in the tropical steam heat filling the room, drying her skin. Light filtered in through the room's only window, which offered a view of the sooty building next door, clotheslines hanging limp and empty.

It was winter and she felt tired, worn out by the steady progression toward Valentine's Day. For all its tacky commercialism, this contrived holiday never failed to make Jamaica feel as though she were missing something. In fact, what she missed on this and every holiday was what she still thought of as home, her childhood home where she'd had a front-row seat for the most heart-stirring drama of her life. Her parents raged at life, and loved it, and made their children feel that their time together was incalculable and therefore precious. She and her big sister, Geneva, would spring out of bed on cold Valentine's Day mornings and race into the dining room. Their father would have preceded them and covered the table with flowers for their mother, heart-shaped chocolates wrapped in red tinfoil for the girls. Jamaica copied the way Geneva would carefully peel back the corners of the tinfoil and break off a tiny bit of those hollow chocolate hearts. As their mouths and throats filled with the rich, bittersweet flavor, their parents would join them to open cards and hug them and smile for the dozens of pictures shot to memorialize these moments.

Jamaica closed her eyes and thought of all those photographs stored somewhere, packed tight in albums, pages and pages filled with beaming faces, overflowing with emotion. She felt empty.

It had all started yesterday, when she'd spent two hours standing in front of the pink and red display at Reflections, the card shop. She wondered if the shop's owners were being deliberately ironic. Surely they must suspect that people who purchase prescripted cards can't reflect too much on the messages they send for birthdays, anniversaries, Valentine's Day, Grandparent's Day. They want Snoopy, or uninspired sentimentality, pictures of silhouetted lovers kissing against gauzy skies.

But then, isn't that precisely what she had wanted as she stood there, glaring at For Mother cards covered with intricate patterns of roses, pictures of pink young mothers cooing at powdered babies? What did those gentle creatures have to do with her mother, a sturdy little fireball who would never pause to coo? Still, the images were so soft and warm, Jamaica longed to snuggle onto the shelf and fall asleep there to the sound of soothing verses, the Valium of vapidity. "Disgusting," she had muttered as she bought two of them.

As she lay on the kitchen floor, she wondered when she would have to mail the cards to her mother for them to arrive on time.

"Sammy, what day is it today?" she yelled, wincing at the sound of her own voice, waiting for Mrs. Castelli across the hall to answer, as she often did.

"The seventh," he yelled in return, having settled in for his morning read of the *Times*, so rudely interrupted earlier.

There it was, yet another reason for this morning's anxiety. It was her father's birthday. She used to worry about it, the fact that everyone else in her immediate family had been born on days that could be divided by lucky sevens. Her father had been born on the seventh; her sister on the fourteenth; her mother the twenty-eighth. Poor Jamaica, born on the thirteenth and a Friday's child, loving and giving. Who would love her, give to her?

Lying there, listening to the Sunday morning bells of Saint Anthony's next door, and the little second-generation Ant'ny's playing on the streets, she daydreamed about home. As she scratched the cat, who had climbed onto her belly, she imagined her father sitting at a red Formica kitchen table. He was wearing a long-sleeved white shirt, a dark blue cardigan vest, a dark tie. Even though her imagined picture revealed only a torso, she knew the trousers beneath the table were black and baggy. Long-fingered delicate hands, covered with a fine layer of black hair, were clasped together on top of the table.

Her focus shifted to the face and she wept quietly. It wasn't that she was overwhelmed by the face's beauty, although no movie star ever touched her the way old photographs of him did. She had only old photographs since he had died when she was still too young to do much more than to worship and to fear him. The face in the portrait her memory was drawing was structurally deficient. Even in her nos-

9

talgic reverie she could see that the bone structure was too wide and the eyebrows so black and bushy that they cast a shadow over the deep-set brown eyes. She could see how stern and authoritative that threatening brow seemed. Yet she could also imagine how those troubled eyes, viewed in isolation from the magnificent brows, revealed an understanding of the terrors that confronted his children daily.

A wide expanse of forehead unrolled above the eyebrows. This wasn't the barren skin left in the wake of a receding hairline, but an expressive surface that would pucker fearsomely when the eyebrows drew together to signify disapproval or confusion. Sometimes she thought God had broadened the forehead as a way of protecting those who came into contact with this saint from the power of those eyes and eyebrows.

His hair was thick and black. "You've got your father's hair," Jamaica's mother would say as she tried to brush the wild brown tangles her daughter brought home at the end of the day.

The mouth was quite nice, except when anger would pull it in a tight line that strained all the face's other features, pulling them toward those squeezed lips. In pictures, which were all she had now, the mouth was always laughing, saying "Cheese," preparing to blow out birthday candles. It was February 7, so she was remembering those birthdays, the ceremonial reading of the cards, all arranged late at night so he'd find them on the kitchen table in the morning. There would be a cake and flowers. Before the dispersal to work and to school, he'd read the printed messages aloud. The private messages, the ones that usually contained apologies or resolutions or both, he had the grace to read silently.

She felt a sudden pain in her side.

"Jamaica, why are you lying on the floor?" Sammy had brushed his wavy hair and gargled—his voice was clear. She stared up at him, then at the plaid slippper on his foot, nudging her ribs. At that moment, the plaid slipper seemed to be the most endearing article of clothing conceivable. She grabbed his foot and hugged it tightly.

"I love you," she said. After all these years, she still felt as though the words were escaping her lips at considerable risk.

"Are you thinking about your father?" Sammy leaned down to stroke her eyebrow. He'd never met Jamaica's father, but had spent many hours listening to the legend. On their first date, only weeks after her father's death, he heard the first verse of Jamaica's lament. He would always say it was evident to him then that he would fall in love with this girl, with the patch on her unstylishly short blue jeans:

"War is not healthy for children and other living things." A sorrowful Pollyanna, so needy.

"Let's have breakfast," said Jamaica, pulling herself to her feet, using Sammy's leg as a crutch. Her mournful reveries generally climaxed in unseemly cravings—for frozen bagels on which she would gnaw for hours, for carrots dipped in preserves. Jamaica reasoned that the contemplation of spiritual matters and the internal meanderings that followed must burn up a lot of calories. This explanation for her ravenous behavior was easier for her to swallow than the alternative possibility that she was merely shallow. Mourn awhile, snack awhile.

She and Sammy managed to put up a pot of coffee, cut a bran muffin in half, and divide a grapefruit into bite-sized portions. They ate the same breakfast every day between November and June. (In June, they exchanged grapefruit segments for cantaloupe.) As they poured and sliced, Jamaica gave Sammy the details of her subway dream, her conquering of fear, her heroism.

"I think it means you are terrified of your driving lust for fame," Sammy teased, baiting his wife, who tended to assign noble interpretations to her dreams. Ambition, she felt, wasn't noble.

Jamaica ignored him, and idly sucked a grapefruit section off her spoon. "Can you believe this?" she spluttered, as she stared at the newspaper propped on the kitchen table. "There's an article here that says our nitwit senator is afraid to take the subway without a bodyguard. What a creep! Pandering to the vigilantes who want to idolize the Subway Avenger is bad enough, but discussing something he knows nothing about is outrageous. He admits that he never rides the subway. He's from Staten Island, for God's sake. Boy, do I feel vindicated. I've always suspected that the general level of ignorance in Washington depends on the absence of human experience. Here it is. Confirmation. Right here on page two."

Sammy grunted and glanced up from the Travel section. Although he'd heard variations on this speech before, he still was curious to know where it would segue.

"Want a heater, Sammy?"

"Um, no, I'm fine." He sipped some coffee to confirm.

"Good. Well, just the other day I was riding the "E" train heading uptown." Jamaica became wistful.

"Don't you just love to imagine the subway crawling up the map, knowing that you are underneath the street and that above you traffic hums, dogs take a dump, muggers mug, hearts are broken. Huh, Sammy? Are you interested in this?"

11

Reluctantly, Sammy peeled his gaze from the news summary. "Of course I'm interested, Jamaica. Keep talking. I'm just not quite awake yet."

Barely pausing, Jamaica resumed her tale in earnest. "Anyway, next to me I see a young guy, artfully dressed. What I mean is, his socks are bright red. He is almost deaf. I say almost because he is wearing a hearing aid and he laughs and mutters with the clarity of someone who knows what sound is. He's chattering away with his hands at a young guy sitting across from him, whose hands are chattering right back."

Jamaica began wiggling her fingers and bouncing in her chair. Now she had Sammy's attention. She could tell because he set the paper aside. "Anyway, they seem pretty lucky to me because they don't have to decide whether to ignore what is about to happen. They can't hear. What happened was this. A man standing near the doors says, 'Excuse me, ladies and gentlemen.'"

She jumped up from the table, and continued. "The train is pretty crowded and the ride's pretty smooth, so no one pays much attention. But he doesn't give up," She began to demonstrate the beggar's limp, to ape his plea.

"I'm sorry to interrupt your ride, but I was just released from Beth Israel Hospital last week," she muttered. "I don't have work and can't work or I wouldn't be bothering you. I'd appreciate your quarters or dimes or whatever you can spare." She bowed slightly. "Thank you for your attention."

She could see from the worried look on Sammy's face that her performance was effective. She knew he sometimes wondered if one day he would find his wife huddled on some street corner surrounded by shopping bags overflowing with the leavings of other people's lives. Jamaica was a compulsive collector, dragging home old books, odd people, small containers of jam from restaurants. Her drawers were stuffed with letters from people she'd forgotten, delinquent payment notices.

"Are you listening, Sammy? I'm trying to tell you about this guy." Jamaica hobbled rapidly around the table until she was standing right next to Sammy. She leaned down so her mouth was right next to his ear and her voice dropped to a whisper.

"His glassy blue eyes looked to me like burned-out flashcubes, although you could barely see them beneath his eyelids. They were all droopy like an old hound dog's. He limped through the car, but he wasn't carrying a cup and he never stopped, not even in front of people who looked ready to pull some change out of their pockets."

"I said to him, 'This is no way to make a living.' Does he pay any attention? What do you think? Of course not. I figure I have to get through to this guy. So I touched his arm. Just like this." She gently placed her fingers on Sammy's forearm. "What does he do?" she shrieked. "He shudders."

Jamaica grabbed Sammy by the chin and turned his face toward her. "This is what I wanted to do. Grab him and ask him, 'Have you thought of playing an instrument? The fat black man who plays the steel drums on the trains seems to collect a lot of dough. Or look at the guy with the saxophone who pretends he's from outer space. He screeches out sounds on his horns that set everyone's fillings on fire with pain. People pay him just to stop.'"

Sammy played along with a nod.

Jamaica snickered and let go of Sammy's chin. "You nod. That's because you aren't crazy. This guy stared at me like I was speaking Hindi. 'Do you get what I'm saying?' I asked him, with all good intentions. You know that."

Slowly, Jamaica walked around to her side of the table and sank into her chair. Her cheeks were pink and moist with sweat. "Well, you know what he did? He backed away from me as though it was me who didn't smell so nice. The doors opened and he hobbled out fast. I couldn't believe it."

"Well," said Sammy. "That's some story."

"You bet," Jamaica said triumphantly. She held out her cup. "Could I have some more coffee?"

A few minutes later she felt Sammy staring at her.

"What's the matter?" she asked.

Sammy shook his head. "You know, not everyone wants you to save them."

Jamaica ignored him and began thumbing through the *Daily News*. At times like these, she felt as though the only rational people left in the world were her and Jules Marlin.

Actually, she didn't think that Jules Marlin was rational. Not in the sense that rationality meant approaching events as they unfolded in life or on the news with a certain measure of objectivity and calm.

What she meant but hated to admit, especially to herself, was that sometimes she felt as though the only people left in the world who *cared* were her and Jules Marlin. Of course, she recognized the absurdity of this feeling. She knew she had only to finger her way through the Yellow Pages, and she would discover the existence of dozens of agencies devoted to the bureaucracy of caring. Office buildings containing payrolls, water coolers, and IBM Selectrics were filled with people, staffs, whose lives were devoted to compiling mailing lists and arranging parties in hotel ballrooms to solicit money for worthy causes.

All that, however, was abstract. Jules Marlin was specific. Here he was today, speaking his mind in a letter to the editor of the *Daily News*. Jamaica had followed his letter-writing career for some time; once she'd even seen his picture, a fuzzy mug shot of a startled-looking elderly man. That was his "My Turn" column in Newsweek. She'd never seen a Marlin letter in the *Times*; his *vox* was too *populi*, no doubt. What words came from his pen, though: the wail of indigestion, a man choking on the puree whipped up daily by the processors of news. She imagined him locked in his apartment in Kew Gardens, Queens, listening to reports of violence and moral decay. He would switch from channel to channel, searching for still another update on the arms race, murder, inflation, the changing weather pattern, child molesters. Periodically the information he gorged on would erupt in letters, missives splattered with the honest outrage of confusion. These passionate outpourings appeared in print with surprising regularity, considering his apparent lack of notoriety or connections.

After breakfast Jamaica clipped Jules Marlin's commentary on the Subway Avenger, the meek computer jock who'd gunned down four black kids on the subway and become a hero for fighting back. Liberals, who publicly denounced the Avenger, secretly admitted they sympathized with the guy. In a stroke of populism over procedure, the grand jury snorted at the prosecutor's attempt to charge the Avenger with attempted homicide.

This was how Marlin's letter appeared in the *News,* part of a two-page spread on reader reaction:

Serves 'em right!

Kew Gardens, Queens: The whole criminal justice system is kaput in America. I remember living on Parsons Boulevard 35 years ago and at 10:30 at night my sister, who was pregnant, was ready to go to the hospital. Her husband was working so she told me I'd have to take her to the hospital. Lebanon Hospital in the Bronx.

It didn't occur to us to be afraid. We took the subway, changed trains twice. At midnight we got there. I stayed around an hour until her husband came and I could go home. Today you've got to have a machine gun to go to the Bronx on the subway.

I feel bad that just one of those muggers was paralyzed from the waist down after he got shot. I wish all four were paralyzed. I wouldn't be afraid to be with them on the subway. **Jules Marlin**

Jamaica dropped this letter into her file. By now she'd gathered several pieces of information about Jules from his letters. He was a Holocaust survivor: this from a condemnation of bilingual education in public schools ("If you want to speak Puerto Rican stay in Puerto Rico. If you want to live in this country, learn to speak English. Did they offer American history in Hungarian when I moved to the United States after Hitler?"). He wasn't married: this from a complaint about women smoking too much at singles' dances ("No wonder these women can't find a husband. They ruin these dances for everyone, sitting there like human chimneys. Disgraceful"). He believed in abortion: this from an endorsement of welfare allocations for abortion ("There are too many poor people as it is. If they want to take responsibility for themselves, the government would be doing us all a favor by helping them out"). He was a news junkie: this from an attack on the rescheduling of the network morning news program ("You'll be making a mistake, putting 'Breakfast A.M.' against 'News with Norm.' There are a lot of us out there who don't like to miss a trick. I guess you could say that I am a news junkie").

Sammy couldn't object to Jamaica's interest in Jules. He, too, clipped and filed. Their newspapers and magazines resembled Shredded Wheat by the time they were discarded. Sammy sliced out tales of oddballs and freaks, filler items. Stories like the one about the husband and wife, two psychiatrists, who slashed each other to ribbons the night they met at their apartment to discuss their divorce settlement. He collected rapists confined to wheelchairs, vengeful neighbors, unexplained decapitations.

Mostly, though, he clipped reports on the latest census data and housing trends. Sammy was an urban planner, a specialist in mass transportation. Nothing pleased him more than the sight of chaos waiting to be organized. After a few frustrating years of apprenticeship with the city, he'd just joined a private consulting firm and was eager to make his mark.

Jamaica respected Sammy's orderly mind, though she didn't understand it. When relaying information to friends, she often referred to Sammy as her source. Lately, though, there had been a marked increase in her attributions to Jules. "According to Jules Marlin," she would preface some sweeping generalization about crime, about elections, about Central America. Jamaica's conversation was generally littered with attribution, an occupational hazard for a reporter. She worked for a big daily paper, where her beat was breeze: features, amusing snatches of life, poignant tales of woe. She'd started out in news but soon tired of scooping up information and wrapping it up in "significance" that would change as new facts came in. Packaging tragedy into tidbits for mass consumption wasn't for her. Information was power; information overload was powerlessness. Jamaica opted for escapism. Give 'em a chuckle over breakfast, or a tear. Let Dan Rather overwhelm them, terrify them. Break her heart. Terrify her.

3

Under the Boardwalk

It was 32 degrees and damp, according to the AccuWeather forecast. Jamaica and Sammy were on their way to work, walking up Sixth Avenue, carrying on parallel conversations. He was holding up his end of an intelligent analysis of the Off-Broadway play they'd seen the night before, exactly the kind of post-theater repartee Jamaica always nagged him to deliver. They had a tendency, which she decided was unhealthy, to telescope their reactions to movies, to the theater, to life into grunts. Ever on the lookout for self-improvement, she'd gotten Sammy to agree to reject "mmmh" as acceptable conversation. They would speak in sentences. To oblige her, Sammy was figuring out, in sentences, why they'd liked this play, even though its central character was a paraplegic and they usually hated the Theater of Cripples. Physical infirmity as a moving plot force had been overdone in the past year. They'd suffered through too many plays that depended on deafness, blindness, stuttering, and strokes to produce emotion.

Jamaica wasn't listening. "Do you know that when Rebecca West was my age she'd already written a novel? And what would Edward R. Murrow do if he had to report about the world today? Do you think he'd be covering New Wave fashion? I have these great ideas, see. I understand the world's problems. But am I a teacher? Am I a doctor? And even if I were a doctor, all I'd worry about is medical malpractice, not curing cancer. This guy wrote me a letter the other day. He wants to marry me on the basis of the article I wrote about women weightlifters."

Sammy interrupted. "That's great, Jamaica. Look how people respond to your writing. It's fantastic."

"It is?" Jamaica looked at Sammy's smooth, cheery face. "I'm sorry. I wasn't paying attention to you. What were you talking about?"

"The play."

"The play?"

Sammy laughed. "I was just trying to hold up my end."

Jamaica slapped him on the back. "You're right, Sammy."

"I am?"

"Yeah, about my life. I'm cheerful and upright. I'm sensitive. I'm not falling apart most of the time." She paused. "I'm married." She began walking briskly.

"And to a wonderful guy, too," teased Sammy. "Don't forget that."

Jamaica ran ahead. "You know what Joanne Robbins said to me at lunch yesterday? She and her best friend were making lists of all the men they'd slept with. They stopped when they got to the men whose names they couldn't remember." Waiting for Sammy to catch up, she dipped her toe in a puddle.

When they were even, she looked up into his eyes. "I can remember the name of every man who's ever touched me." She clutched his arm.

Sammy shook her hand loose. "And what's wrong with that?"

Jamaica didn't answer. She was dragging again. All of it seemed to be settling there in her boots—the immensity of the city, the disintegration of art and civilization, the cold. "I'd like to go to sleep right there," she said, pointing dramatically at the wet pavement where yesterday's snow was rapidly melting into filmy slush.

Sammy grabbed her hand and twirled her around. "Let's dance."

He stood still, his baggy tweed coat flapping in the wind, and held her hand high in the air. She slid her hand back, so only their fingers touched, and began to spin, faster and faster. She was dazzled by the blur of pedestrians, the silvery beacon of the Empire State Building to the north, the cool white towers of the World Trade Center to the south, the glint of the wet pavement, the cars hurtling up Sixth Avenue. Her breath shortened as she flung herself around, the motion clearing her mind. Finally, grasping Sammy's shoulders, she hung limp, empty, happy.

He hugged her so hard her ribs ached through all her layers of clothing. "Well," he said. "A thrill a minute. Now, can we go? I want to pick up some fruit to take to work and I'm late already."

Jamaica was giddy. "I think you are absolutely right about the effectiveness of leaving the deformed child onstage during almost the entire performance," she gasped. "Somehow that constant, morbid reminder of life's senseless pain made the laughs come easier."

"Huh?" said Sammy.

"The play," she said. "Remember?"

"Oh, yeah, right."

Jamaica still felt a little vulnerable, a little sad, especially when she noticed the restaurant they were standing in front of, at the corner of Bleecker Street. A succession of immigrants of different types moved in and out of this particular location every few months. The new owners would rearrange the chairs, paint the walls, and hang out "Grand Opening" pennants. There had been Luis's Empanadas; Hunan Village West; Dimitri's Mediterranean; the Bagel Emporium; and Moshe's Felafel and Frozen Yogurt. This time the motif was fish. The new occupants had painted over the mural depicting the Wailing Wall and effected an underwater cave out of plaster molded to resemble crumbling sand castles. Every day she and Sammy stopped to stare at the fish in the window. They would discuss the menu posted there and agree the prices were reasonable. By evening, though, they'd forget and go to the Napoli for baked ziti. Already Jamaica felt personally culpable for the fish restaurant's inevitable failure.

She and Sammy moved on to the fruit store next door. While Sammy selected oranges, Jamaica noticed a young man swipe a pear from the bin. As he slid past her, heading for the door, she pointed at him and said loudly: "Look at that man. He stole a pear." Sammy poked her so hard he nearly knocked her over. "Don't be such a Girl Scout," he hissed.

Outside, he apologized. "You never know who's carrying a gun these days. Now, let's go, so you can collect some news I can use."

"News You Can Use." That was the motto of the *Observer,* the paper Jamaica worked for. She often wondered how readers were going to use the information she gathered, like the story she'd written the week before about the man who had completed a scientific study of why dollar bills are so dirty. He was a retired officer of the Federal Reserve Bank of New York, and he'd come up with an elaborate theory to explain, as he put it, "why lucre is so filthy." It had to do with the high rate of inflation in the seventies, the substitution of machines for human dirt spotters, and the inroads that acid rain was making into the ozone layer. Jamaica dutifully installed all this in her notebook, then collected "color" by spending an afternoon in the mock Gothic fortress near Wall Street that housed the Federal Reserve, watching machines pluck dirty dollars from an assembly line full of money.

As she and Sammy waited in line to buy tokens, she shook her head vigorously, setting loose a spray of cold water. The snow melting above ground was dripping into the subway.

"News you can use," she murmured. "Let's see. How can you, Sammy Fein, use the latest Geneva summit talks between the superpowers?"

He played along. "Hey, hon, my feet sure are cold and the heat doesn't work. Do you think Star Wars will take care of it?"

They reached the token window and bought a ten-pack. Jamaica tore open the little plastic bag, took out a token, and darted through the turnstile.

"Jamaica, wait a second," Sammy called out. "I want to buy a paper."

"I'll run on ahead. Meet me downstairs on the lower platform." Jamaica knew it annoyed Sammy when she left him behind, but she couldn't wait to see what adventure might be waiting down below. She realized it was childish, this game she played, but the subway gave her a sense of adventure, the chance to peer into the lives of strangers she wasn't likely ever to see again. Even unpleasant encounters—perhaps especially unpleasant encounters—provided welcome diversion from what passed for life above ground.

She skipped down the stairs, tensing slightly as she always did as she approached the vast, empty tomb that separated the Eighth Avenue trains that pulled into the upper level of the station from the lower-level Sixth Avenue trains. No matter how crowded the station was, and it wasn't very crowded this morning, this midway point always seemed deserted.

As she started to turn the corner to reach the stairs leading to the station's lower bowel, she was stopped by a frightening wail.

"Fuck you, I'll kill you!" A loose-limbed man—a smelly scarecrow—stood in front of her, his fists flailing at some invisible target. His skinny legs wobbled inside the big work boots that seemed too heavy for his bony, exposed ankles; he wore no socks. He dangled like a puppet held by invisible strings. "Stop bothering me, you shit."

Jamaica stood quite still, afraid that movement would attract his attention and that he might confuse her with the object of his frustration. She barely breathed as she watched him mutter and spar furiously with the air. Only when someone grabbed her arm from behind did terror set in. "Let go," she said, barely able to force the words through her constricted throat.

"Jamaica, it's me." Sammy guided her past the man whirling and cursing in the shadows; together they descended the stairs.

"God, that poor guy up there. Do you think there's anything we can do for him?"

Sammy tightened his grip on her arm. "If I hadn't come along, you would have started talking to that guy, wouldn't you? Every time I see you make eye contact with drunks and strike up conversations with demented maniacs, I get terrified thinking of you wandering around by yourself. I hate to tell you this: sainthood is not automatically conferred on the down and out."

She started to respond, then shushed herself. Something lovely was in the air. *Under the boardwalk, out of the sun . . .*

Both she and Sammy turned their attention to the young black man singing a cappella, and a great old Drifters tune to boot. He sang so clearly, with such a sweet smile, Jamaica wanted to touch his cheek. *He sang, He sang, He sang so sweet, along came Jamie and kissed him on the cheek.*

Glancing around the station, which was grayer than ever as puddles formed with drips—from where? They were fifty, maybe seventy-five feet underground, another platform was above them—she noticed three other women who she could tell felt the way she did. They were blushing as they listened to the ballad. The singer's smile widened, as he noticed the effect his melody was having on his audience, their lowered lashes. "Sing along now," he called out, not missing a beat. His hips swayed, gently, as though he were wearing loose-fitting cotton pants, a white shirt open at the neck, rolled up at the sleeves, his toes curled in the sand of some imaginary beach. No matter that he was wearing blue jeans and a blue down jacket, his toes curling inside brand-name running shoes against damp concrete. His magic was working.

He swayed and crooned just a few feet from a bench where two dressed-for-success women sat. The black one wore a prim dark suit, underpinned by a ruffled, high-collared blouse, all wrapped up in a trench coat with a red lining. Her hands were folded protectively over the oxblood leather briefcase, initialed, resting on her lap. Her legs were crossed at the ankles next to her Lord & Taylor shopping bag. She giggled and whispered to the blonde sitting next to her. The blonde had creamy skin, a sculpted bob of hair, and oversized glasses, the kind meant to indicate that she was a serious person, not merely attractive. She was staring at the *Wall Street Journal,* mouthing the lyrics to "Under the Boardwalk."

Jamaica leaned against one of the girders running along the edge of the platform by the track, her gaze wandering contentedly between the women on the bench and the singer. An oversized black leather coat approached her and the woman in it asked her what train stopped at this station. The two women glanced at the subterranean troubadour and exchanged what Jamaica felt were poignant smiles. She knew hers was. She resisted the urge to ask this pleasant-looking stranger with the dirty-blond hair and kindly face what memories the song was dredging up for her. Were real-life events attached to those words? Had she been "having some fun" under the boardwalk, fallen in love, felt the sexy warmth of sunburned flesh pressing against hers? Not really enjoying the gritty sand scratches but willing to accept small discomforts for the exhilaration of the moment. Had it ever happened?

Sammy had already lost interest in the impromptu concert. He began to pace between the girders that made up the subway's skeleton. "You know, the Sixth Avenue line was the toughest one to put in," he said absently. "They didn't finish it until 1940. Can you imagine the problems at Herald Square, all those underground tunnels and pipes to avoid? Plus traffic. Plus a humungous water main that went off to Jersey, I think. What a great project."

Jamaica was usually a ready audience for Sammy's subway lore. But, enthralled by the music bouncing off the tiled walls and cement roof, she fell into a meditation on her journey to New York from a tiny town in Ohio by way of a little New England college. Like thousands of small-town Ohio girls before her, she had come to invent herself, although she would never have put it that way. Often she felt as hollow as the vast underground cathedral of the subway, reverberating with the lives of those passing through. Sometimes she joked that she didn't think she had a soul. That's why she became a journalist. Not to save the world or to become famous. She was simply collecting material to fill up the space where her soul was supposed to be. She had ears, a big heart, enough brains, but no soul. She began to expound this theory, especially after a few drinks, after years of sympathetically watching her friends search their souls, often in groups. She never had much to say on these occasions, and one day she came up with slick reason, a clever enough response: "Oh, I'm not talking because I believe I don't have a soul." Sometimes she more than half-believed this.

Otherwise, how could she cheerfully putter around the park with Sammy just mintues after she'd read about a twenty-five-year-old man in Phoenix who'd put a gun to the head of a TV newsman and ordered him to read the following on the evening news:

A platoon of purple ants from the planet Uranus will be invading Earth on Tuesday. It isn't clear what their mission is, but everyone in the Tucson-Phoenix axis should be on the alert.

Or how about the story last night on the news about the six clean-cut young men who'd cleared the smoke and talk from a late-night restaurant in Long Island by ordering the seventy-five people eating there to remove their clothes and jewelry? Even though everyone obeyed, these citizens killed two men and raped a woman. If she started thinking about what that meant—deep in her soul, if she had one—how could she stand there calmly waiting for the train?

She watched a young woman pull her small daughter close as a group of loud young men brushed by. Sunday's newspaper had carried a copy of a comic book in which a superhero warned children against molesters by admitting his own painful childhood sexual mistreatment. Later, she had heard on the news that the comics were delivered to one million homes in Sunday supplements. She felt relieved that her parents were spared that, at least. She didn't have to protect them from that.

On shaky days, Jamaica was fairly convinced that all of this information should frighten her into paralysis, and would if she had a soul, or at least a functioning memory. On such days, she felt as though she were floating through life in a bubble. She saw pain and confusion. She wanted to help. Really she did. But before she could act, her bubble drifted on.

"Jamaica, snap back to earth. The train's here." Sammy pulled her into the waiting "D" train just as the doors were closing.

4

All Work, No Play

Jamaica's phone was ringing as she walked into her cubicle at work. It was Henry Frank, her editor.

"Good morning, Jamaica," he said in the overly bright voice he assumed when he was about to tell reporters something they didn't want to hear.

"Hi, Henry, what can I do for you?" she said wearily.

"Jamaica, a little enthusiasm, please. I've been thinking we ought to do more stories with a business angle. It's the new world. People want the inside skinny on things, how the deal got made."

"All right, Henry. What *is* the deal?" She pulled out a piece of paper.

"There's this guy called Abraham Palermo, a commodities trader who made a bundle of money in stock index futures. You know, where you bet money on which way the market's going? Never mind. It doesn't matter. His accountant had convinced him to invest in movies as a tax shelter. Palermo produced a hit, a rags-to-riches story about a guy who trades in pork belly futures. It was a rock musical called *The Pits*. Now he's got a three-picture deal with Paramount. I want you to do a piece on him as an example of the new movie entrepreneurs."

Jamaica had never heard Henry express any interest in futures trading or the movies. "Where did you come up with this one, Henry?"

"Boy, are you suspicious." A pause. "Okay, I met this guy at a party."

"Oh, yeah?"

"All right. I met his press agent at a party."

"Who is she?"

"How did you know it was a she?" Henry laughed sheepishly. "All right. It's a she. Do me a favor. Call her up and have her arrange a meeting. Then you decide. Okay?"

Jamaica sighed. "Okay. I'll call her later."

Immediately after she put the phone back onto the receiver, it rang again.

"Hello, this is Maggie Saxton, Abraham Palermo's public relations counsel." Jamaica recoiled from the aggressive cooing of the professional flack. "Henry told me you're doing a story about Abe. I'm just delighted. I've arranged to have a limo pick you up next Tuesday at noon in front of your office. I'm so glad that you'll be doing the story. I so admire your work, Jane. Ciao."

Jamaica slumped in her chair, then angrily punched Henry's extension.

"Henry, how could you do this to me?"

He wheedled. "Come on, Jamaica, it'll be fun. The next one will be something to sink your teeth into. I promise."

Later, Jamaica had to admit, grudgingly, that Henry was right. The Palermo story turned out to be fun. Palermo had a quick wit and an agreeable lack of pretension; he seemed more embarrassed to be riding around in the limo Maggie Saxton had hired than Jamaica was. Maybe because he was so chubby, he seemed to lack the edge that made most Hollywood people Jamaica had met so frightening. He was bright, amiable, quotable. The interview was, as Henry liked to say, a no-painer.

Henry could be a man of his word, when it suited his purposes. Not too long after Jamaica had turned in her sprightly piece on the new movie moguls, he called her into his office. Leaning back in the chair behind his desk, he gave her a warm smile and motioned for her to sit down.

"Nice job on Palermo," he said, smiling persistently.

Jamaica sat straight in her chair. "Thanks, Henry. What's up?"

"Nothing, nothing. I just wanted to fill you in on what's going on at the paper."

"Really?"

"Yes, I like our top reporters to feel involved."

Jamaica waited tensely.

"Listen, at the editors' meeting today Leonard Butler—you know him, runs the op-ed page?—told us he's putting together a series of articles focused by the debate over New York's proposed Holocaust

Memorial. It sounds terrific. Lots of diversity, complexity, significance."

"That's nice," said Jamaica warily. "But what's that got to do with the news department?"

"Hold on a minute. He's already lined up lots of experts. He's commissioned pieces from an architectural writer, a city planner, an important Jew from one of the organizations. The only thing he needs now is something personal, something *moving* from a writer who hasn't already made the Holocaust a personal trademark. He wants a fresh look at horror."

Jamaica rested her elbow on Henry's desk and rested her head—shaking no—on her clenched fist.

"Now, just hear me out, Jamaica. The managing editor has been pushing us to cooperate more with the editorial side. So naturally I said to Butler, 'Leonard, I have somebody who's just perfect.'" Henry scowled at Jamaica. "And I meant it."

"Henry," said Jamaica. "I don't want to have anything to do with it."

"Fine, Jamaica, don't do it." Henry lowered his voice. "But don't you feel some sort of obligation?"

Jamaica loathed much about Henry, but nothing more than his almost perfect sense of manipulation, which was especially remarkable in a man who was otherwise almost perfectly insensitive. She also regarded him as a renegade, knowing as she did that his father had been a manufacturer of ladies underpants in Queens and a Jew, one of the many details of Henry's life that he'd deleted from his curriculum vitae. He would deliberately look quizzical when somebody said "Oy." To hear him tell it, his life began the day he'd graduated (completely without distinction) from Princeton, streamlined and Waspy, as though losing the baby fat built on his mother's matzo balls was the last triumphant separation from his past. Now in his early forties, Henry was slightly chubby again, his healthy appetite unleashed too frequently by too much Scotch. His elegantly tailored suits were pulled out of shape by the pressure exerted by the rapid expansion of his fleshy butt. Jamaica couldn't help noticing the outline of his bikini underwear whenever he walked by her desk.

Henry was the kind of man one couldn't imagine as a child, innocently pitching a ball or playing hide-and-seek. Born with an instinct for plotting and scheming, he had demonstrated at an early age a notable proclivity for lying, sniveling, snobbery, bigotry, and lechery—all of which he perfected as he got older. His sense of humor, however, was stunted. At parties, if he'd drunk more than his usual significant allotment of Johnnie Walker Red, he would drop his lumpish body onto the floor and flail his arms and legs, shouting, "Gator! Gator!"

Henry was unfailingly canny. He knew that Jamaica would feel compelled to oblige him if he pressed just a little, because she had made the mistake of revealing to him that her parents had survived the camps where her grandparents died. While other kids' parents were shyly not telling them about sex, her parents were studiously not telling her about surviving death. She would feel compelled because she wanted to forget but it was her birthright to remember. Lucky her, Chosen of the Chosen.

"What are we talking about here, Henry?"

"You know, just an essay on what it was like to grow up as the child of Holocaust survivors. I mean, what you people went through was so sad, so *tragic,* hon. It'll be good for you to write it out, work it through your system." Henry's mustache was quivering with sincerity, his dark eyes glistening with tears. This was a man who liked to make his emotions work for him. Jamaica had found that out when, shortly after he became her boss, he'd invited her out for drinks at Windows on the World.

She'd been flattered. It hadn't occurred to her that this wasn't an appropriate setting for a business meeting, the lights twinkling more than a hundred stories below them, the insinuating piano music. Or maybe it did occur to her and she chose to ignore whatever apprehension she may have felt. Her new boss was handsome, in a studiously conventional sort of way, with his curly graying hair, well-trimmed mustache, and small, even features. A neatly folded handkerchief always peeped out from his breast pocket. He always wore tie bars; moreover, they were always monogrammed, discreetly. And he seemed so interested in her career, where she'd come from, her hopes, her dreams, the usual palaver. He ordered what he assured her would be "a delightful little drink"—Kir Royale, champagne mixed with cassis liqueur—after she'd warned him that sparkling drinks destroyed her equilibrium.

He won her confidence with a confession. Leaning close so she could feel his body heat without actually touching him, he told her about the last bitter days of his first marriage.

Shortly before his divorce, his wife had looked at him in disgust and asked, "Henry, have you ever felt anything other than smug about anything?"

He admitted to Jamaica that this had struck him as a curious question, but rudeness was not part of Henry's code of ethics. He'd felt some final duty, so he replied, as honestly as he could.

"The last time I felt bad, I guess one could say guilty, about something was back in college. Within a two-month period I managed to get three girls pregnant. That was in the sixties and abortion was illegal so I had to raise the money, which I did, naturally. I went through two of these things, took the train into New York with the girls, waited for them, and paid the tab.

"This third girl was really freaked out by the whole thing, getting pregnant. I was exhausted from the first two and couldn't face the thought of watching this girl freak out. I just knew she would, she was so neurotic, unsophisticated. So I simply didn't do anything."

Henry thoughtfully stroked his gold tie bar and looked out into space.

"As predicted, she freaked out. Checked into some kind of high-class loony bin for a while. That disturbed me, though I must say, I can't say I'm entirely sorry I kept out of it."

He fell silent. Jamaica asked softly, "What did your wife say?"

Henry looked at her blankly, as though he'd forgotten who she was. Then he gave a short, bitter laugh, the most sincere sound Jamaica would ever hear him utter.

"As I recall the exact quote," he said, "it was short and to the point. She looked at me and whispered, 'You shit.' Then she made her exit."

Jamaica felt guilty about encouraging this humiliating revelation. Lulled by the alcohol, she began to feel warmer and warmer toward her increasingly out-of-focus companion. She found herself babbling about her dead father, the Holocaust, her bottomless insecurity. Foolishly, she wanted the person she worked for to know who she really was, to love her, to understand that she was a phoenix child, rising out of the ashes of death and destruction.

"There, there," he murmured, sincerity oozing from the top of his head to the tips of his fingertips, which, to Jamaica's dim surprise, were fondling the inside of her thigh. No one had ever accused Henry of being an imaginative character.

"Excuse me, Mr. Frank. Don't you know I'm married?" Jamaica was too tipsy to feel truly annoyed, not so much with Henry's uninvited familiarity as with the clichéd setting of this scene. This little seduction was insultingly dull, an episode out of some schoolboy's wet dream.

"Yes, hon, but do you really believe in the institution of marriage? I'm getting my second divorce right now and I find it hard to believe anyone can take the whole thing seriously." Henry's eyes took on the mournful sincerity of a cow in bad need of milking.

Jamaica weighed the pleasure of critiquing Henry's performance against the possibility of getting fired. Sighing, she settled on practicality. "You know I was just married a month ago, right before I started work?"

"Really?" he asked, as he motioned for the check. Later Jamaica realized that experience had taught Henry that new brides were particularly vulnerable to his charms, particularly young career women who were concerned that marriage was going to throw them off track. They were ripe for seduction and too guilt ridden to blame him for their indiscretion.

"Well, Jamaica, don't think badly of me." Henry made a neat recovery. "You're a talented woman; I'm sure we'll work just fine together."

And so they did, largely because Henry's callousness was matched only by his ambition. He was the sort of talentless man who rose to the top of organizations by making himself the middleman between his superiors and his underlings, whom he consistently relieved of the responsibility of bearing full credit for their work. His superiors liked Jamaica's writing, and Henry was glad to reinforce their admiration, always carefully pointing out his indispensable role in the final product. In other words, his relationship with his reporters was the usual symbiosis between employer and employee: polite cooperation motivated by mutual need and faint distrust.

Usually Jamaica carried out Henry's orders without much protest; they came infrequently enough, since he was not a man brimming with ideas. She loathed the prospect of writing about the Holocaust, however, the pop metaphor for evil. Television producers had learned that genocide made for instant pathos. (She could imagine story conferences: "Hey, Leo, I've got a great idea! Make the victim a Holocaust survivor. Double the pain, double the gain when you catch the perpetrator. Get it?") At Holocaust conventions she had witnessed slightly dazed elderly people wandering around vast auditoriums wearing "I survived Auschwitz" T-shirts.

Even as these thoughts made her cringe, they also quickened her blood, invigorated her rhetorical juices. She, too, wanted to join the wailing minions of Holocaust memorializers, to scream from the tops of skyscrapers: "Never forget!" She wanted to provoke tears of remembrance, even though she knew nothing she could write could ever compete with the photographs she'd seen on the news the other night, recently unearthed color shots of skeletons with skin the color of flesh, survivors peering out from bony skulls with *blue* eyes. She wanted to write this piece even though she knew the point of it was to sell advertising, to further Henry's career and probably her own.

"Okay, Henry, I'll do it. I'll need some time, though."

"Hon, too much time isn't good for something like this. We're not talking reporting here. You've just got to breathe. Reach deep down. You know the kind of thing we need." He glanced at his watch. "Hey, I gotta run. Catch you later."

Jamaica snorted at his back as he strolled away whistling. She knew what he had to accomplish that afternoon; she'd overheard his secretary complaining in the restroom. Henry's Princeton class reunion was coming up, and he had volunteered to put together an updated yearbook. His poor secretary had been working on it for weeks, and there were some loose ends he wanted to tie up before his five o'clock squash game at the club.

She called out after him, "Henry, you didn't give me the deadline."

"You've got plenty of time," he said, just as he was about to turn the corner and disappear. "We don't need the piece until end of day tomorrow."

For a very long time after she returned from her session with Henry, Jamaica sat trembling in front of her word processor.

Exposed

Breathe, Henry had said. Why did she feel as though she were choking? Wasn't she always complaining about the triviality of her work? Why wasn't she elated? Hadn't she spent years anguishing over this pivotal event of her life, and the fact that it had taken place before she'd been born? Her alienation was complete, separated as she was even from other Jews who were made uncomfortable by the ugly scar on her past. Even from Sammy. Here was her chance to tell the world what had happened to her.

But nothing had happened to her, really. What were her memories of the Holocaust? None of her emotions about it felt reliable. Her parents hadn't belonged to the Jules Marlin survivors' school, with the clearly defined "Never Forget!" as their rallying cry. Her parents—especially Jamaica's mother—were curiously flexible in their view of the past. They preferred to look at it from a certain remove, when they could bear to look at it at all.

Try to settle down, she told herself. What is it that Henry always says? Start with the little picture that tells the big story. Start small, then look at the whole. If only she knew what the whole was, or what it could possibly be. Well, there she was, an out-of-context American Jew. She and Sammy had always told themselves that they had so remarkably much in common: close families, energy, and, perhaps above all, Jewishness, a shared heritage. They both knew the story of Abraham and Isaac, and what mezuzahs are. But being a Jew meant one thing to Sammy, and something entirely different to Jamaica.

Thinking about the difference gave her the beginning of an idea, a little story, enough to get started. She began to write:

(holocaust memories/just, jamaica/ny) My husband, Sammy's, parents spent most of World War II on a U.S. Air Force base in Texas. They were newlyweds. She was just out of high school. He was an engineer, a captain. The recollections of those years they passed on to their three sons were reminiscent of Hollywood service comedies. One such memory: the laundry once failed to return the soldiers' dress pants, and the entire barracks posed for pictures in their undershorts. Big ears, baggy drawers, barrel of laughs.

I was amazed when I first heard these stories. For most of my childhood it seemed to me that all parents of Jewish children spent World War II in concentration camps or in hiding. I mean, I knew other Jews existed. I'd read Philip Roth, Saul Bellow. I just didn't know them, those American Jews. I was brought up in a tiny town in Ohio, where my family was the only Jewish one for miles. The only Jews I knew were my immediate family and my cousins and aunts, most of whom lived in New York. Nearly everyone of my parents' generation had spent some time in a concentration camp.

I explain all this because I was asked to write how my life is different because my parents survived the Holocaust. I don't know, of course, because I don't know what it would have been like otherwise. However, from the time we were small children, my sister and I were aware of the Holocaust. For us, "the war" always meant World War II, as though we'd been born a generation earlier. I don't remember a particular moment when I "learned" about the Holocaust. It was one of those vague facts we knew about our parents, like the fact that our mother grew up in an unknowable—and unspellable—place called Berecszacz.

Jamaica snapped off the computer in frustration. She was doing it again, arranging the facts for public consumption in a way that didn't begin to convey what had happened. It would help if she knew herself, and her best source of information—her mother, Eva—was far more skillful than her daughter at tailoring truths to fit the listener.

Jamaica kept asking Eva, how did Holocaust survivors end up living in a small, Gentile town in Ohio? The last time she'd asked, quite recently, Eva had announced that television drove the Just family to Ohio. It was the 1950s and she'd seen a program describing New York as a postnuclear wasteland. "I'd lived through one war," she said. "I didn't want to live through another." Like many of Mrs. Just's historical bombshells, this shrapnel of trivia exploded without warning, in the middle of a telephone call to remind her daughter not to forget Uncle Zollie's birthday.

This new piece of data had surprised Jamaica simply because she could have sworn Eva used to say they'd moved because she'd always wanted to raise her children in the country. Then again, sometimes she said they'd moved because her husband couldn't make a living in New York. Once she'd said they'd been on their way to an Indian reservation in Arizona but got sidetracked in Ohio.

Eva Just wasn't a liar. She was a woman of imagination and impulse whose avocations were embellishment, commerce, and geography. She was a great practitioner of spontaneity. Midsniffle in some tragic story about the murder of her brother, she would jump up and telephone her stockbroker. She stunned her husband when she blithely identified their surname to immigration officials as Just, the town he came from. (The fact that Just wasn't a Jewish name like Pearlman, she swore, had nothing to do with it. Just, in English, carried with it such noble meaning. What a good name for her children to live up to, when she had them. Besides, the name would remind her of home, never mind that she had said she never wanted to be reminded of home again.) Then there was the way she had named her daughters. Her first daughter was born in New York, but Eva was certain she'd been conceived during a stopover in Switzerland. According to Mrs. Just's interpretation of Jewish law, her child's name must begin with G, to honor her dead grandmother, Gizi. So, with due deference to tradition and geography, Geneva Just was named.

Some years later, a second daughter was conceived in transit and born in Ohio. She was named in honor of her grandmother Jolie and Jamaica, Queens.

At least, that was the way Jamaica remembered the stories. She and Geneva had spent hours trying to match the pieces they'd gathered separately over the years. The most frequently corroborated story had the newly married Justs arriving in New York in 1949, having given up on postwar Czechoslovakia, feeling ill at ease in Switzerland. Eva's Uncle Zollie had paid for their boat trip and signed their affidavits.

Jamaica tried to pick up the story there, with Uncle Zollie.

My parents were luckier than most. My mother's uncle, Zoltan Finkel, had left Europe long before Hitler's rise to power. He'd arrived in America in 1924, just before the immigration laws were tightened. He was an American success story. By the time World War II was over, he was a rich man, rich enough to guarantee that my parents wouldn't become wards of the state. We were always grateful to him, both for what he did and for what he symbolized: America was truly the land of opportunity.

She groaned. "Is that how it was?" She set her cursor at the top of the paragraph and slowly moved it down the screen. She pressed "delete." The screen was blank again. It was time to go home.

America *had* been good to Uncle Zollie, but not until the war came along to demonstrate capitalism at its finest. Life in the New World was tough for the first fifteen years after he had immigrated with his wife, Irma, who was built like Mae West and talked like Jimmy Cagney with a Hungarian accent. They hired themselves out as a maid and butler, then tried to repair radios, and otherwise failed at a dozen different schemes. One day Irma picked up some used refrigerators from a man who owed them money. The war had started, and refrigerator factories were making arms. "Hot summers without refrigerators were like hot summers without love," Uncle Zollie would chuckle. The used-refrigerator business boomed. Zollie and Irma bought real estate with their profits. While their famlies were being slaughtered in Europe, they were making a killing in America.

"What a bad thing, very bad, very bad," Uncle Zollie would mutter to Jamaica when the Just family visited Miami Beach at Christmas, as she allowed him to cheat at chess, hoping he would tell her the real story about the early days. He'd chew on the cigars she never saw him light, a pink man with icy blue eyes, his face a dead ringer for President Eisenhower's, his body slight, much slighter than Ike's.

"They lost everything, poor kids. We didn't know nothing about what was happening over there. I didn't know your mother, see, until she wrote to me after the war. She wasn't born yet when I left the old country over there. We made it here pretty good, heh? Pretty good. Poor kids. But they made out all right for themselves here. Out there in, what's that town? Harmony. Yeah. They made out for themselves."

Zollie and Irma didn't have children. They had buildings and houses and clothes and country club memberships in Miami Beach and on Long Island. Uncle Zollie's closet, as big as the bedroom Jamaica and Geneva shared at home, was packed tight with suits and shoes and hats. Aunt Irma's closet was filled with styrofoam heads. All they did was hold her wigs, but they always reminded Jamaica of death.

The Just family visited Uncle Zollie and Aunt Irma with decreasing frequency over the years—at Christmas, for a couple of days in the summers during the family's annual trip to New York. They were exotic, foreign, even to two little girls accustomed to hearing foreign accents. He spent his days chewing cigars, playing tennis and golf, then he would slip into white suits and Panama hats and go to night-clubs or the jai alai, ignoring the jackhammer voice of his wife. She wasn't fond of her husband's greatnieces, whom he'd insist on bring-ing along. One year he invited them for Thanksgiving, when Geneva and Jamaica were still in grammar school. He took them to the Foun-tainbleau, where the girls gaped at the women dancing topless while the turkey and cranberry sauce were served. They were suspicious of Uncle Zollie. Their father worked all day, wore dark suits, and smoked one cigarette daily—and that one at night as he and their mother watched the evening news after the children had gone to sleep and couldn't see them.

Eva admitted to her daughters that she recognized the deficiencies in her aunt and uncle, but they had bought her and her husband and all his surviving relatives tickets to life and that was enough for her. And, she knew that, inasmuch as her Uncle Zollie was aware of any-one, he was aware of her, even admired her. She liked to be admired.

Jamaica was in awe of Eva, a pistol of a woman apparently so unmarked by her proximity to death and degradation at an early age that sometimes even Jamaica could hardly believe it had happened. Suffused with shame at her inability to grapple with her parents' ex-perience—and, yes, by a weird form of jealousy—she turned back to the computer the next morning:

None of our home-town friends knew about the Holocaust. Most of them tended to confuse World War II with World War I, and we didn't blame them. History was poorly taught, and on Veterans Day and Memorial Day the dead were honored in speeches that seemed to blur the Big Ones together. Later, though, when I met Jewish kids who didn't seem to know or care that my grandparents were killed because they were Jewish, I fairly shook with moral outrage.

When I went to college and first read Jerzy Kosinski's The Painted Bird, *I almost gagged when I read about "the Jews going to slaugh-ter." Just writing those words—"the Jews going to slaughter"—still makes my throat tighten. Those Jews aren't nameless, pitiable beings to me, yesterday's swollen bellies, a 40-year-old newsmagazine cover. They are my mother, my father, my uncles, my aunts, my cousins. They are me.*

I read Exodus *for the first time when I was a girl of nine. I didn't analyze the quality of the prose, and I was confused by words like "whore." What I lingered over were Leon Uris's detailed descriptions of torture, concentration camp style. Night after night my dreams filled up with visions of mangled and bloodied Jewish bodies. Every night I screamed for Mommy and Daddy, whose faces stared at me blankly from the vast piles of corpses. They didn't seem to recognize me, and this hurt my feelings until I realized that they were dead. In the mornings my father would tease me for being a crybaby. I was ashamed to tell him the source of my tears.*

I became virulently anti-German. Everything that was evil was held together by bolts manufactured in Bonn. I refused to eat German chocolate cake, even when my mother pointed out that all the ingredients were made in the U.S.A. except for the chocolate, which was Swiss and neutral.

I felt that I wore some kind of badge of honor because my parents had suffered and survived. My fastidious father—how did he endure the stench and rot of human decay in cattle cars? It's hard to picture my mother, who carries her own toilet paper when she travels, squatting over an open latrine where privacy was something to dream about.

A loud ringing interrupted her. She got up and bought a Cherry Coke from the coffee cart making the morning rounds. She stuck a straw into the can. Slowly blowing bubbles into her soda, she read what she'd written, and continued:

My father already had a medical diploma when he checked into Dachau. To pass the time, he took an advanced degree in irony. It was completed after he watched his brother survive Dachau just long enough to be killed accidentally by the British. The conquering heroes were horrified by the skeletons who greeted them, their mouths hanging open. The survivors looked like pathetic, featherless chicks, squawking weakly for food, so I'm told. The soldiers meant well, our father explained to us. He wanted us to believe in heroes, I guess. So I do, when I'm able to forget about those liberators feeding fatty pork into those shrunken Jewish bellies, killing them with kindness. At least they died free, although it seems a little cruel that their last supper wasn't even kosher.

My mother was eighteen years old when she matriculated at Auschwitz. Her wardrobe consisted of a blue dress, no underwear, no shoes; Auschwitz is not located in the tropics. When people's toes turned black with cold in cruel Polish winters, the toes were not amputated. They were kept fastened to their owners, who were gassed. My mother learned new ideas about hygiene at Auschwitz, which was a clean camp. The Nazis shaved her head to keep out the lice. She learned how to sleep compatibly on a bunk, night after night, with twelve women. It was a tight fit, so if the third woman from the end got an urge to roll over, everyone rolled with her. I used to think of that when, as children, my friends and I used to chant: "There were five in the bed and the little one said, 'Roll over, roll over.' So they all rolled over and one fell out, there were four in the bed and the little one said, 'Roll over, roll over.' So they all rolled over and one fell out . . ."

Though she wasn't sure about her father, Jamaica knew she was miscasting Eva as a victim. But to make her point, to explain the horror, she needed pathos, didn't she? There was nothing pathetic about Eva in Jamaica's eyes. Her mother was a force of nature, a small container of heat and energy, a heroine, an optimist, a jaunty dame like the Hollywood stars she'd idolized as a child growing up in Berecszacz. When her children would run to her, disappointed, heartbroken about misplaced affection, a loss, she would draw herself to her full five feet of height and sigh, "Remember, darling, what Scarlett O'Hara said at the end of *Gone With the Wind*: 'Tomorrow is another day.'"

Uncle Zollie told Jamaica and Geneva about the five years Eva and her husband had lived in a two-room apartment in one of his, Uncle Zollie's, tenements in Queens. ("My niece did all right," he would say admiringly. "Her husband is a doctor, an educated man—a handsome and educated man.") The rent was cheap, but life was hard. Though there was plenty to eat, everything else seemed meager. The girls could tell. Like everyone else, Uncle Zollie didn't divulge much about life back in Europe, but they gleaned bits of information here and there. They learned that their father had been Dr. Pearlman back then, and had changed his name in honor of his home town. This didn't seem unusual to them, no more unusual than anything else Uncle Zollie told them: that their father had been a surgeon, the only man in town who owned a car, a small-town Jew with a medical degree from Charles University in Prague. The youngest of seven children, he was the pride of his family—uneducated dirt farmers, Uncle Zollie reminded them—and the toast of whatever town he happened to pass through. Their great-uncle explained that their father was the kind of good-looking man who gathers respect and awe by knowing how to remain silent, to reserve his smile.

The girls had heard about how on Tuesday, Thursday, and Saturday nights, Dr. and Mrs. Just went to the movies—to learn English, Eva would explain to the cousins, the remnants of her husband's unwieldy extended family who arrived in New York, frail and startled as newborns. She felt she had to explain why they were spending the money, not spending the time at Olga's or Tibor's, playing cards and smoking cigarettes, not talking about what it meant to be alive. "Dr. Just must learn enough to pass the medical boards," she'd say, though no one asked. No one ever questioned Eva or Dr. Just, who was always referred to with the honorific "Doctor," even by his family. It was, after all, Eva's Uncle Zollie who'd arranged affidavits for everyone (as he never failed to remind them). And Dr. Just was beyond reproach: he was a doctor. So they were excused from the family gatherings to go to the movies three times a week, and that explained why, years later, Eva's conversation would be decorated with Hungarian embroidery and gangster-picture slang.

"I think she's his moll," she would whisper about an acquaintance's lady friend.

During the New York years Eva was young, in her twenties, and she was happy to have a child, a handsome and respected husband, enough relatives to provide occasional company, an apartment. She always presented that early period in America to her daughters as a montage of images: the young couple wheeling a baby stroller through a park, a crowd of wistful-looking greenhorns grinning at a camera, the same group clustered around a child propped up in front of a birthday cake. There they were again at Coney Island, on the beach. Conversations were very specific: "How's the baby?" "What are you making for dinner tonight?" "Did Dr. Just hear anything from that doctor in the Bronx?" It was as though they had all been born yesterday, been created on the spot in New York, speaking pidgin English, bearing numbers on their arms like forceps marks. None of them spoke of their dreams or confessed to having any—not to each other.

But that isn't what Jamaica wanted to tell the world. These are the dreams she gave her family, in print:

But our parents didn't fill our heads with nightmares. They filled our heads with dreams. "In this country, you can be anything you want," my father used to tell us. Though he'd lived here for years by the time my sister applied for college, he found the fact that there were no quotas on Jewish students something of a miracle. When I put on my formal for the Junior-Senior prom, I remember my mother saying, "You look like a dream."

Eva had been pleased to see Jamaica wearing something besides jeans. That much was true. But she hadn't kept her dreams from her daughters; in fact, when they asked her about the war, she'd tell them what she dreamed and dreamed. They were always the same two dreams, whose significance would be evident to any university student who'd taken Psychology 101, but which eluded Eva, who firmly believed that "overanalyzing," as she called it, was destructive behavior and to be avoided.

In one of her dreams, she was riding a train in almost complete darkness. No moon lit the sky. The windows reflected only blackness, and just barely; the interior lighting was dim. She was frightened and certain that she was being pursued. At the same time, she felt distinctly alone. Running fiercely, panting, she glanced back, terrified, again and again. Her pursuer remained out of her sight, taunting her with silence, invisibility. The train whistle screamed, clashing with the crescendo of steel screeching against steel, almost deafening Eva. She felt her strength being sapped. Through the windows the darkness lifted somewhat, and she could see shadowy figures hovering near the tracks; the train sped by them so quickly, however, they might have been illusions, shrubs. She was quite definitely alone—desperately, sadly, finally alone.

In the other dream—Jamaica had replayed her mother's nightmares so many times they seemed to be her own—Eva huddled in the bottom of a giant pit that she sensed might be filled at any moment with giant spiders. Huge craggy rocks sprang up all around her, a ladder to the sky, to freedom. No matter how vigorously she climbed, she was trapped down below, doomed to wait for the spiders that never came. Mornings she would wake up, short of breath and exhausted, one of her small legs thrown across her husband's back.

It isn't accurate to imply that none of them, the survivors, had ever talked about the war. Each of them had told his story, her story, once, to a husband, a wife, usually right before they married, right before they emigrated. I was here, my father was there, this happened to us. They gave the facts, simply and with finality. It would be years before any of them would lay out those facts again. They had families to create, wages to earn, lives to get on with. These were survivors. The manic-depressives, the introspectives, they were dead.

The movies did the trick, Eva used to say. Dr. Just learned enough English to pass his boards. Later, she confessed, the movies only helped; he also took an English course designed to prep immigrant doctors for the test. He worked hard, at a hospital in Brooklyn, then at a private office in Manhattan. But no matter how hard he worked, he couldn't make a living. Forget prestige, hero worship. He couldn't afford a car, a decent apartment. Every summer, he would quit whatever job he had and spend the summer as a resort doctor in the Catskills, with Eva and Geneva. In the mountains there wasn't any pressure, he wasn't thirty-six, thirty-seven, thirty-eight and no one special, another refugee, another doctor. The money he earned held them until the next job, the next summer. What did he feel? His wife didn't know. His wife didn't ask.

One day he showed her an advertisement he'd clipped out of a medical journal. A town in Ohio called Hamersville needed a doctor. They wrote to a friend in Chicago, a doctor from home. Ohio was nice, fine, good, clean, he wrote back. This was another upbeat survivor, a cockeyed optimist, a man who no doubt wept at sad movies. He'd driven through Ohio on his way to Illinois. In the southern part of the state there were hills and trees. He'd heard that in the cities, Cleveland and Cincinnati, there were Jews.

Dr. Just answered the ad. Then he persuaded Eva to hock their nice things so they could buy a car, an Oldsmobile with a light blue body and a dark green roof. His cousins and nieces and nephews would have thought he was crazy if he'd been someone else, but they had designated him the brilliant one, the one with the education and promise. He and his pregnant wife and their five-year-old daughter drove west, the first time any of them had been anywhere in America besides New York. They already had a sense of the country's beauty. They'd been to the Catskills. Still, they were awed by the sweeping green of Pennsylvania, the spanking clean motels, the cleverly painted barns ("Chew Mail Pouch Tobacco"), the damp smell of spring in Ohio.

On their way to Hamersville, they rolled into a town that looked familiar. Eva was certain they'd seen those one-story brick stores, the ramshackle wooden railroad depot before, in a John Ford Western. Her sense of geography was more romantic than accurate; after three days of driving she felt certain they must be in the Wild West, no matter what the Triple-A map unfolded on her lap indicated. They were lost and needed gas.

"You folks ain't from around here, eh?" asked Gus Daniels, proprietor of Gus's Gas Station.

"No, we are on our way to Hamersville. Do you know where that is?" responded Eva, who was in charge of directions and casual conversation.

"Why do you want to go there, if you don't mind my askin'?"

"My husband is a doctor and the people there have advertised for a doctor. Is it far from here?"

"Ma'am, would you mind just waiting here for a few minutes? I know someone who would like to talk to you folks. Just hold on one minute, all right?"

The Justs didn't mind the chance to stretch their legs a bit, and they were curious to look around this town, easily observed from end to end as they stood right there at Gus's. The gas station rested in the right angle formed where two roads met and created a town. Actually, the town was born a bit up the road at the railroad station, built on a plot of land donated by a man called John Harmon in 1835. In exchange for his generosity, he asked only to be remembered as a barely noticeable dot on a map. There was a dry goods store, a drugstore, a machinery repair store, a post office, a grocery store, a hardware store, a barber shop, and a lumber mill—all within view right there at Gus's. What the Justs couldn't see was the Frostee Freeze, which was around the bend, and the schoolhouse and the eight churches competing for Harmony's eight hundred souls. They couldn't see the tree-lined streets, the cow pastures that backed right up into the city limits, the train that came through twice every twenty-four hours, hooting into the silent night. They couldn't see the twenty years that they would spend in this friendly, sniveling, upright, sanctimonious stretch of Ohio backwater.

Eva would later tell the girls how fine the air felt on that day in May, warm and moist. She remembered sniffing the gasoline fumes wafting out of Gus's tanks, and waiting. Within minutes Gus reappeared, clutching the elbow of a burly man, all grins and handshakes and fast talk.

"Hi there, folks. My name is Burl Opel and I'm the mayor here in town. Well, sometimes I'm the mayor, when we've got business to tend to." He paused to gasp loudly with great sucking noises that the Justs eventually realized were laughter. Although they didn't get the joke, they smiled.

"Most of the time I run my barbershop, over there, down the road. You see it? I've got me a nice red and white pole out front and . . . that's not what I want to talk to you about. Gus here tells me you're thinking about going over to Hamersville. They've already got a doctor over t'Iris, which is only five miles from Hamersville, and another one over to Lawshorn, ten miles the other way. It seems just plain ridiculous to me to set up an office so close."

The words seemed to pour out of Mr. Opel's mouth, as though his generous proportions were filled with sentences and he'd been given a big squeeze. The Justs didn't quite catch the meaning of all he was saying, but they were drawn by the force of the attention he was paying to them. For the first time since they'd arrived in America, they were made to feel singular, identifiable, not like homogeneous particles of historical fallout.

Mr. Opel hung his thick arm across Dr. Just's shoulders. "We lost old Doc Clary here five years back and this town—this whole area—is dying for a doctor."

He put the other arm around Eva. "Why, in this whole county there's only four doctors and the nearest one is ten miles away. If you wait here an hour, I can get some of the town council together. There's an empty bakery up the street that would make a fine office for you, and we could help you add on a house."

Turning to face the couple, he lay his hands on them, as though to bless them. They hadn't said a word.

"What's your name, by the way?" Mr. Opel asked. "Are you from Cincinnati or where?"

And so the Justs found Harmony.

Jamaica started to chuckle, as she sat there imagining Mr. Opel glad-handing her parents. At that moment they shed their raggedy refugee robes and became the town's glamorous oddballs. She sighed, and turned back to her story, wrapping it up with a last oratorical gust.

I want my children, when I have them, to know what happened during World War II. I don't want them to think their birthright is privilege and ease. I hope they have those things. I have. But I want them to know that such things are a matter of luck and circumstance and should be appreciated. My mother, too, was a child of privilege for the first eighteen years of her life. I guess I will make my children feel guilty, even though that isn't my intent.

I want them to learn what I think I've learned. I make an effort to be decent because I have some understanding of what happens when decency doesn't exist. I try to keep aware of what the government is doing because I have some understanding of what happens when governments turn evil. I try to be good to my family and friends because I have some understanding of what it's like to have family and friends taken away. Most of all, I understand that I have only some understanding of these things, which is quite different from experience.

She could barely look at what she'd written, all those quivering nerves laid bare on the page. She was sure Henry would love it, which made her feel all the worse.

She was right. The article was published, barely edited, the following week, the capper for the Holocaust series. It was framed by a thick black border, Henry's idea, his signal to readers: "Get out your handkerchiefs. This one's a guaranteed tear-jerker. It's personal. It's real." He calculated correctly. Readers responded. Granted much of the response came from Jewish organizations, many of them soliciting contributions of money or time. But there was response. The Holocaust hadn't lost its stuff.

Jamaica, who never destroyed anything, threw all the letters away except for two.

Dear Miss Just,

I just wanted to write to tell you I read your beautiful article in the paper today. I personally went through the Holocaust myself and am definitely in favor of telling the world about what those Nazi butchers did to us. Your family must be proud of you. That's all I wanted to tell you. You did a beautiful job.

Sincerely,
Jules Marlin
Kew Garden, Queens

Dear Ms. Just,

You should be fired from your newspaper, writing a lot of opinionated personal trash. If I were you, I wouldn't be talking very much about how your parents survived the Holocaust. Hitler was pretty efficient and managed to get rid of most of the whining Jews like you. So you figure out how anyone survived. By lying, cheating or turning on their own, that's how, I'll tell you right now. If you want to do your parents a favor, don't tell anyone that they survived.

One more thing. I work for a big advertising agency and we do a lot of public opinion polls and research studies. Our data show that people are sick and tired of all this Holocaust crap and all this whining. My advice to you, honey: CLAM UP.

Regards,
A reader

"What is wrong with you?" Sammy asked, when Jamaica showed him the anonymous letter. "You tell me you got dozens of nice letters and this is the one you save. A letter from a schmuck who doesn't even have the balls to sign his name."

"I'm sure it's from a woman," replied Jamaica. "Look at the handwriting, so even and fine. It's from a woman with nice handwriting. Sammy, did I do something wrong?"

6

The Best of Intentions

How could Jamaica expect Sammy to understand her reaction to those letters? He'd been taught at an early age to turn missteps into triumphs. When he was only twelve years old, he stood nearly six feet tall and seemed a shoo-in for the junior high basketball team. His two older brothers were sports legends at their suburban Kansas City school. It was expected that Sammy would continue the Fein tradition of athletic achievement in high school, followed by academic excellence in college and graduate school, preferably medical school. Both his brothers became doctors.

Sammy, however, had neither the natural talent of his brother Wayne nor the manic drive of his brother Paul. He dutifully showed up at basketball practice every day and tried his best to keep from displaying the bewilderment he felt as he watched the ball flying around him. Occasionally one of his desperate tosses toward the basket would miraculously slip through the net and he would shake with gratitude.

Four weeks into the semester, the coach posted the list of those who had made the team.

Sammy often told Jamaica how miserable he had felt, having to go home and tell his mother the disappointing news. When she asked him how it went, he began to cry.

Mrs. Fein, who would always describe herself as a "take-charge kind of person," quickly responded, "What do you care about that silly old game for anyway? Didn't you win the science fair competition for your skyscraper model? What good is basketball anyway? You'll be an architect."

That was the explanation Sammy always gave Jamaica for his choice of professions. (His early interest in architecture led him to urban planning. Though his parents never quite understood what he did, they were very proud of him.) Jamaica wondered sometimes if Sammy would have become a doctor had he made the basketball team.

The thing that amazed her was how Sammy seemed to know his place in the universe; moreover, he didn't doubt his right to occupy it. He was hardly a simpleton. He looked out at the world around him and saw good and evil. It was just that he preferred to think of the glass as half-full, not half-empty, a way of thinking that wouldn't hurt Jamaica, he kept reminding her, always gently.

It kept occurring to Jamaica, though, that if she started sipping from a half-full glass, she'd tip the balance. She tried to explain this to Sammy, that the world was hopelessly off-kilter and so, possibly, was she. But looking into his eyes, she saw that even half-full, she seemed to be enough for him.

Jamaica, however, was never satisfied. So she spent her days discovering and publishing small details about life in the metropolitan area and managed to convince herself she was somehow furthering the larger debate about the human condition. A few weeks after the Holocaust piece was published, she was assigned a story whose social significance seemed unassailable; it was about the poor, who in Jamaica's mind were always worthy. The sixties had been her favorite television program when she was a child in Harmony. There were good guys and bad guys, the warmongers versus the peace lovers, the racists versus the humanitarians. By the time she came east in the seventies, the protests were finished. Students had resumed the humdrum of studying and preparing for careers as doctors and lawyers. Abortion was legal. Lunchrooms in the South were integrated. Blue jeans had designer labels and jogging had become a matter for serious discussion. Jamaica was all fired up to do battle for truth and justice, but the war was over. Defiantly she sewed messages of peace and love onto the legs and seats of her carefully ripped jeans and wrote earnest papers about the difficulty of living anachronistically in an age of conformity (these would receive A's from appreciative professors, the only long-hairs left on campus).

The idea had come from Henry of all people, a man who had volunteered for duty in the paper's Bonn bureau during the sixties, where he became something of an expert on German wine. Politics, Henry liked to say, wasn't his thing. Yet he'd come back from his

Princeton reunion aroused by a conversation he'd had with a woman he'd met there who ran the urban problems division of one of the big foundations. He'd listened raptly while this crisp, beautiful creature earnestly described the project her group was funding. She was delighted to give him her business card *and* her home phone number after he'd said he thought he should assign one of his reporters to do a story on the project.

"I want a lengthy piece describing the lives of three generations of a welfare family," Henry explained. "Almost twenty years have passed since the Great Society was born, and welfare has become a way of life for millions of people, not just temporary help. The idea would be to show how welfare has become a trap, especially for teenagers, who are producing babies at an unprecedented rate." He glanced at the notebook where he'd scrawled notes during his follow-up conversation with Miranda ("Call me Mindy") Airendale, whom he was taking for drinks at Windows on the World that evening.

"Meanwhile, the government, having created this underclass, now wants to end the cycle of dependency. Several administrations have come and gone; the Age of Aquarius had long given way to the New Conservatism and renewed emphasis on individual achievement," he recited.

Jamaica was fascinated by the subject and by Henry's ability to describe it with such sincerity, given his complete lack of interest in social trends that hadn't appeared on the cover of *New York* magazine. Mindy must be a hot number. Jamaica stared earnestly at Henry and nodded.

"The question is," summed up Henry, "how is the elimination of day care centers and job-training programs going to transform welfare recipients into useful citizens?"

That evening Jamaica told Sammy, "This will be a wonderful story. I can write something that may actually help someone, change the world a little bit. This could be a story that will get noticed."

Absently she added, "And it isn't about me."

"Just be careful, Jamaica," Sammy said.

"Careful of what?"

"Harlem, for starters." Sammy shrugged. "And . . . I don't know. Just be careful." He grabbed her nose between his forefinger and middle finger, and tugged her toward him. She giggled.

Later, after they had tenderly licked and sucked and clutched their way to mutual satisfaction, Sammy flopped onto his belly and touched Jamaica's damp cheek.

"Why are you crying?"

"Sex makes me feel so alone. Don't you feel alone and frightened?"

"No." he mumbled into his pillow. "I'm not alone. I'm with you."

Finally, long after Sammy's breath became deep and even, Jamaica drifted off to sleep. Her rest was short-lived. She jerked awake in the middle of the night, sweating, fearful that her dream had been an omen, and ashamed of her fear. She could remember only part of the complicated scenario. She'd been in Harlem with a group of people at a restaurant, ordering a meal. The waiters hovering about were cordial, but seemed wary, preoccupied.

Jamaica took her time choosing what to eat. Finally, she asked for a felafel sandwich. Two of the waiters whispered to each other, then told her to pick up her order several blocks away, somewhere in deepest Harlem. A friend put her in touch with the head of the local vice squad, a jowly, swarthy character. He told her to make the felafel pickup; she had unwittingly become involved, a pawn in a drug bust.

A cab delivered her to the designated address, where she found a giant K-mart, in Harlem! The slums had miraculously been cleared to make room for a giant parking lot and a gleaming new discount center. From outside she could see a group of skinny punks, glistening with danger, their teeth, their hair all slick in the reflection of the fluorescent lights. They sprawled around the check-out counter near the sliding glass doors, smirking at her as she nervously entered the store and headed for the manager's office. The manager was really a plainclothes policeman. Fat, his T-shirt riding up his white, hairy belly, he glared at Jamaica while he talked on the telephone.

"C'mon," she screamed at him, grabbing the telephone from his ear. "They're getting away."

The two of them huffed after the youths. Jamaica dragged the bulbous cop by his overstuffed arm. In the dark confusion, she could see a man, silhouetted, yank open the door of a car parked in front. Overhead lights flashed on for no apparent reason except to illuminate the gun he was jovially pointing at Jamaica.

That's when she woke up and began to worry about her reporting trip to Harlem the next day.

She lay there awake, furious at Sammy for sleeping so peacefully after stirring up her subconscious with his warnings. She wasn't afraid of going to Harlem, and she was looking forward to this story. She had it all mapped out already. So why did she feel so uneasy?

As they often did on those frequent sleepless nights, Jamaica's thoughts went back to Harmony. Jamaica always wanted Sammy to believe, as she did, that the Holocaust was just a tragic footnote to an otherwise golden past. Indeed there were many bright, vivid moments that were wonderfully plain: the sight of Eva vigorously bending and straightening as she hung out clothes to dry in the back yard, even after the arrival of the automatic dryer. She was convinced that the fresh air penetrating the material of the clothes they wore and the sheets they slept on warded off illness. Summers, before the girls were big enough to take over the job, Eva would run behind their large lawn mower. The machine seemed to have its own agenda as it roared up and down their long, narrow back yard, chased by a small woman dressed in bright yellow baggy shorts, laughing uproariously. Winters, she tucked the girls beneath enormous feather quilts to protect them from the chill night air pouring through open windows—more of Eva's fresh air theory. As they talked late into the night, small clouds would float above their beds as their warm young breath blew out from their quilted haven.

Their father was a shadowy figure, working long hours in the office attached to their house. He would dart into the living room for a few minutes each evening, as though making sure they still were there. He rarely socialized with the townfolk, except for the brief, uncomfortable public appearance each week at basketball games to watch Geneva, then Jamaica, play in the marching band at half time. Eva would always show up in some sort of outlandish turban and her fake leopard-skin jacket. Dr. Just wore his somber suits and white shirts; his hat stayed on his head for the entire fifteen-minute performance. They sat stiffly at the edge of the bleachers. Around them milled the farmers and the townies, mostly dressed in jeans and flannel shirts, discussing the game, drinking pop and eating hot dogs—nodding their respects to "Doc" and "Doc's wife" from a distance. Jamaica would panic when she glanced up from the gym floor and didn't see her parents, yet when they arrived—and they always did—she felt slightly mortified.

Although she had her share of friends, Jamaica preferred her own company. By the age of ten she was a regular at the Bookmobile, which rolled into town every six weeks; she persuaded the head librarian to allow her to take books from the adult shelf. For a long while her favorites were historical novels and biographies; these fed her already wild-eyed notions about life's possibilities. After reading alone for hours, she would slip out of the house and head off down one of the roads leading into the country, looking for adventure. She would mimic scenes she'd read about in her children's books; wade through brooks by the side of the road, skip rocks in ponds, stare at birds preparing their flight south for the winter. Yet none of these tiny adventures caught her imagination the way similar escapades did in books. She would invent imaginary war games and crawl on her stomach through wheat fields, pretending she was being pursued by Germans. But she was never fooled by her own fakery.

Her parents seemed oblivious to their daughter's prolonged absences, so long as she was home in time for supper. Her wanderings continued as she grew older; one day she finally found the adventure she'd been looking for.

It happened the summer she turned sixteen. Jamaica radiated the glow of a young woman aware enough of her feminine attributes to display them by means of the shortest shorts and skimpiest T-shirts, but innocent of what the impact of that exposed, tan flesh might have on less-than-honorable men. The summer days seemed to last forever back then. On days when she wasn't doing chores for Eva, or occasional field work on friends' farms, Jamaica would languish in the sun, reading, her foot drumming to the beat of the Top 40. Or she'd hop on her bike for aimless rides out into the countryside.

Although Kentuckians were the butt of jokes in Harmony, the best thing about Smith County was its proximity to the Blue Grass State. The lovely hills rolling back from the Ohio River were the only rich thing in the county. They used to say around Harmony and other Smith County towns that in Ohio the roads got better and better the closer you got to Columbus, the state capital—and Smith County was as far south of Columbus as you could get without spilling over into Kentucky. Harmony was connected to neighboring hamlets by a network of roads whose quality was measured by whether the potholes sank into asphalt or gravel. The roads were rough, the farming rougher. The scenery, however, was grand. One could ride for long stretches without meeting a car, or seeing much of anything besides small patches of woods and fields tucked between hills sparkling with wildflowers.

One hot August day Jamaica couldn't bear the thought of sweltering in the sun, particularly after reading an article in the beauty parlor that said wrinkles could start developing in unheedful sixte-year-olds.

"Mom, I'm going for a bike ride," she shouted into the empty kitchen, then mounted her blue three-speed. Whizzing down Blue Ridge Road, she felt the sweat drying on her neck, freed from the weight of her pigtails billowing behind her. The potent bouquet of fresh tar smacked her in the face. She screeched to a stop and laid her bike by the side of the road while she squatted by the sticky black patch and punctured tar bubbles with her forefinger. At that moment the fleeting preciousness of her country life struck her; she submerged all her fingers in that comforting hot goo, in hopes perhaps of cementing herself forever to childhood.

Hearing the rumble of a car engine in the distance, she extricated herself from the tar, wiped her hands clean on the grass by the road, and headed deeper into the hills on roads she'd never traveled before. The lulling pleasure of the bike's motion and the warm, yeasty smell of the baking fields kept her from noticing the temperature climbing into the low 90s until she found herself far down a gravel road facing a steep climb. The moment she stopped she almost keeled over, she was so parched and flushed. Her heart seemed to have sprouted throbbing tentacles that were pounding throughout her body.

"You jerk," she muttered to herself, realizing how long it had been since she'd spotted a farmhouse or a tractor in the fields. "Well, come on." Righting her bicycle, which she pushed while she walked, she began to whistle "When You Walk Through a Storm," one of her mother's recommended cures for nearly everything.

Only a few minutes passed before a beat-up pickup truck came wheezing and crunching its way up the road. Jamaica's bike fell to the ground as she raised her arms to flag down her would-be rescuers.

"All right! I knew someone could come along!" she shouted into the air as she waited for the truck to draw closer.

She wasn't at all perturbed by the dirty, unshaven, and slightly cockeyed appearance of the truck's two occupants. This was farming country, and men who looked like unwashed vagabonds by day, when they were eking an honest living from the soil, could be quite handsome at night when the dirt was washed away and overalls removed to reveal gleaming tans and robust bodies. She wasn't worried when the driver doddered out of the truck cabin, or when she could barely understand the words falling out from his gummy smile. Many of her father's patients were impoverished and inarticulate. They always treated her with kindness.

"Kin I hep you, little missis?" he slurred, kicking the gravel with one foot onto the other.

Jamaica turned around, giving him a chance to inspect the fringes of her short shorts as she learned over to pick up her bike.

"Would you mind giving me a lift to the main road or anywhere near Harmony, if you're going that way?" she asked. "You don't know how glad I am to see you. I'm boiling hot." She patted the wet strands of hair clinging to her neck. Only then did she take note of the rotten smell coming from her Prince Charming, who seemed more wobbly on his feet than she was.

Without a word he grabbed her bike and heaved it onto the back of his truck. He opened the door on the driver's side and took off his cap, with which he motioned her inside. Jamaica could have sworn she felt a hand on her backside as she swung up into the cab. But she was so relieved to collapse onto the torn leather seat, she didn't dwell on it.

Only after the driver settled in next to her did she begin to comprehend her situation. The sour, fermenting odor she'd noticed outside was augmented tenfold inside, and the two empty six-packs of beer clattering next to her right foot gave her an accurate clue as to its origin.

"My name's Frank," said the driver, his tongue hanging limply outside his mouth, like a dog's tail on a hot afternoon. "That's Ned over there."

Jamaica glanced to her right and the presence of Ned sank in, along with the realization that she might be in trouble. It would be generous to say that Ned was not entirely in control of his senses. In fact, he was stinking drunk and possibly crazy. Hot as it was, he was wearing a thick wool shirt over a T-shirt, and a leather hat with ear flaps that were pulled down below his lobes. He seemed unaware of Jamaica, engrossed as he was in the empty beer bottles on the floor.

Since tugging at her shorts seemed a hopeless and perhaps inflammatory gesture, Jamaica instead clasped her hands in her lap and clenched her knees together.

"What's your name?"

"Jamaica Just," Jamaica said firmly. "Doc Just's daughter."

Frank did not radiate the expected spark of recognition.

"That's a funny name," he said. "I'll call you darlin' instead." He hooted until a belch silenced him.

They bounced along the road for several minutes in a fog of dust and heat. Jamaica relaxed somewhat, and began to chide herself for her uncharitable thoughts toward her rescuers.

"Darlin'?"

"Yes, Frank?"

"Why don't you give Frank a little kiss?" He leered as best he could with a mouth so toothless it resembled a Halloween pumpkin.

"Oh, Frank, I don't think that would be a good idea," Jamaica said with remarkable calm.

"C'mon," he wheedled. "Give Frank a little kiss." Ned's concen-

THE BEST OF INTENTIONS

tration on the beer bottles was undisturbed by his companions' repartee.

"Frank," Jamaica said sternly. "I have a boyfriend."

"All I want is a little kiss," he whined, as he placed his moist hand on her bare thigh.

Jamaica started. Until that moment she'd almost been savoring this adventure; it was so much more vital than the ones she had played out by herself. But Frank's touch was alarmingly real.

"Frank, I feel like I need some exercise and I'm not very hot anymore," she said. "Could you please stop the truck and let me out?"

"Don't git sore, darlin'," he said. "Look, we're almost to the main road. I'll let you out there."

The "main" road was just as narrow and deserted as the gravel road, but it was paved. As promised, Frank brought his vehicle to a rattling stop, then sat impassively with Jamaica trapped between him and Ned. Without waiting to see what might happen next, Jamaica reached across Ned's immobile form, yanked his door open, and quickly crawled across his lap and hopped onto the ground. She walked to the back of the truck, balanced herself on the fender, and pulled down her bike. No sooner had it landed on the ground than a by-now familiar hand jerked the bike away from her.

"Give me a little kiss, darlin', and I'll give you your bike," Frank sang out softly. In Jamaica's eyes his dumb, friendly pumpkin face had taken on the monstrous proportions of a Frankenstein monster, hollow eyed and mad.

"You give me my bike, Frank," she hissed, wondering how long she could go on before her tough facade would crack.

"Give me a little kiss, darlin'." He repeated his chant in a sing-song voice.

"Take the lousy bike, Frank," Jamaica cried. "I'm going home." She turned and started to march down the road, quickening her pace as she heard heavy footsteps behind her. "I can't believe he can run," she thought, as she felt Frank's arms encircling her waist and pulling her to the ground. His hold grew stronger as she tried to jerk away. She felt like a fish impaling herself more solidly onto a hook as she tried to wriggle free. With a solid kick to her captor's shin, she shook loose. He tackled her again, and the two of them rolled down the slight incline by the roadside, disappearing from the view of anyone who might drive along.

Every repeated touch of Frank's groping hands renewed Jamaica's vigor. She kicked and punched and scratched and wiggled silently except for grunts and moans until she heard the sound of a car approaching up on the road. Then she screamed, as long as it took for Frank to jam his dusty index finger deep into her throat. Reflexively, Jamaica chomped down hard and almost gagged on the blood and dirt clogging her mouth. There wasn't any indication that the car's passengers had heard her. She felt an alarming wave of lethargy sweep through her. Frank sensed her weakness and propped himself on top of her, his knees straddling her torso.

He cackled, and sucked his bloody finger. "Now, darlin', maybe you'll give Frank a little kiss."

Jamaica closed her eyes. Her body went slack.

Suddenly she felt cool and light. She opened her eyes and saw the sky instead of Frank's silhouette. In the distance she heard voices.

"Miss, miss, are you all right?"

Jamaica got to her feet and stared up at the road. Two men were holding Frank and a third was calling to her. They'd heard her screams faintly as they'd driven by, and it had taken them a minute or two to connect the sound of her voice with the anomaly of the parked truck and its dazed passenger, and the girl's bike lying twisted on the ground.

The men were efficient, taking down Frank's license number, depositing Jamaica's bike in the trunk of their car, wiping her face with a moist towelette one of them pulled from a packet in the glove compartment. Jamaica watched all this activity with dry eyes, and quietly gave them her address. Neither of them asked her questions. They regarded her solicitously and asked about the weather.

When they reached the Justs', the parking lot that surrounded the brick ranch house and office annex was empty. Her father's morning hours were finished; he'd left for the hospital for his afternoon rounds. The men walked Jamaica around to the back door, past the arbor of yellow roses Eva tended so carefully. While Jamaica washed up and changed clothes, she heard their muffled voices telling Eva what had happened, as far as they could tell, and she heard her mother thank them for taking down the man's license number and for bringing her daughter home. And, no, that was more than enough.

Jamaica waited until they were gone to face Eva.

"What is the matter with you? Why would you get into a truck with a stranger?" Eva was yelling. "I could kill you."

"I'm sorry, Mommy." Jamaica began to weep.

Eva grabbed Jamaica by the elbow and pulled her into the living room.

"Are you all right, darling? Tell me what happened."

The two of them sat side by side on the couch while Jamaica gave her account. Afterward, Eva pulled the paper with Frank's license number on it from her pocket and ripped it into pieces.

"Aren't you going to call the sheriff, Mommy?" Jamaica was astonished.

Eva turned and hugged her daughter. "No, dear. You'll be more careful now. Believe me, it's better if we keep this between us. Daddy mustn't ever know."

"Why shouldn't Daddy know?" Jamaica sounded irritable. "I could have been killed or something."

"Shh," said Eva. "I don't know what he'd do. He might kill that man."

Jamaica grew sarcastic. "Maybe you think he'll kill me for being a jerk."

Eva's face darkened. "Don't ever say such a thing."

Mother and daughter squinted at each other. They were partly obscured from each other by the haze of sunlight filtering in through the translucent curtains. Suddenly, the furniture began to rattle, startling Jamaica. A pounding noise penetrated the moist dullness that lay over Harmony in summer, muffling nearly every sound except the insistent scream of crickets at night. Eva's Rosenthal figurines began to rock on the living room shelf as jackhammers beat outside, creating a commotion equal to that of an army of crickets. Jamaica stopped cowering when she remembered where the noise was coming from: Harmony was finally getting a sewer system.

Jamaica clutched the edge of the vibrating couch and stared at her big toe peeping out from a hole in her right sneaker. A chill curdled the sweat on the back of her neck as she regurgitated the vulgar sensation of Frank's dirty finger in her mouth, the metallic taste of his blood. Goose pimples rose from the faint stubble on her legs. She burned with icy shame at her stupidity for getting lost and her laziness, and realized how right her mother was not to give her father still more evidence of her general lack of competence.

"Daddy wouldn't really kill Frank, would he, Mommy?" Jamaica twisted her pigtail into a knot.

"Jamaica, darling, don't be ridiculous. Your father is a doctor. He wouldn't kill anyone. Even if he wanted to. He couldn't." Eva sprang up impatiently from the couch. "*Nu.* I have a lot of work to do, and thank God, you're fine. Why don't you go read outside? Drink some juice first."

She leaned over and kissed Jamaica's eyelid. As she dashed out of the living room, she muttered, more to herself than to Jamaica: "I just don't want to bother him. I don't want him to worry."

Jamaica was worried, though, when she got on the train for Harlem the next morning.

A magician is riding on the subway with a newcomer to town. "You wanna watch all the white people disappear?" the magician asks.

He waits until the train pulls into the Fifty-ninth Street station and claps his hands. All the white people get off the train. The trick, of course, was knowing that the next stop was Harlem.

Jamaica kept replaying that scene from John Sayles's *Brother from Another Planet* all the way up to Lenox Avenue. Her ride was uneventful, although she felt somewhat lost without the anonymity that usually made the subways so restful. (She was the only white in a car full of people.) As she got off the train at Lenox Avenue, a young man lifted the earpiece from his Walkman and asked her if she was lost.

"No," Jamaica replied. "Thank you." She walked upstairs to the street.

She had barely begun to edge toward the high school that was her destination, when a blue station wagon screeched up against the nearby curb. An acne-scarred white man leaped out and raced toward her.

"What a joke," Jamaica thought. "I have bad dreams about Harlem and I'm going to be kidnapped by a white man."

The man reached into his pocket. "Are you looking for Columbia, miss?"

Jamaica looked at the ground.

He pulled his wallet out and waved it in front of her. "We're police. A lot of Columbia kids get off at the wrong stop and end up on the wrong side of Morningside Park in Harlem."

Jamaica was annoyed rather than relieved. "I know where I am," she said huffily. "Thanks."

In fact, she would never know where she was in Harlem, even though she would visit this street and other nearby streets many times over the next few weeks.

7

Hell to Pay

For a time she would think she understood what lay behind the boarded-up windows, what the men and women huddled in groups on corners were thinking about. She would forget that she was just another do-gooder dropping in for a dose of conscience, clucking at the sideshow of misery and then feeling better for having made the excursion. She was merely taking fortification from the self-deception all journalists must gulp down like vitamins in order to practice their trade. From the moment she stepped out of the subway station onto Lenox Avenue, the truth would become the world as it appeared through the despairing lens of her story.

She had decided to find one family to exemplify the generational transfer of welfare dependency. Once again, trying to squeeze the big story into a little picture.

The most important piece of her story, she felt—after some gentle steering from Mindy, whom Jamaica liked despite the woman's inexplicable attraction to Henry—would be the second generation. She wanted to find a teen-ager who had been raised on welfare, who had had a baby, and who very much desired to remove herself and her child from the welfare rolls. Jamaica felt herself to be alarmingly apolitical for someone of her generation, but she disliked unfairness. Poverty clearly was unfair, and the way the government fiddled around with it in unconstructive ways only made things worse. She wanted to write about someone bravely trying to fight the system.

Mindy's project at the Atlas Foundation, a privately funded organization that conducted social experiments with live subjects, was attempting, through education, to offset the harm done by cutbacks in government programs. The foundation had hand-picked several hundred teen-age welfare mothers in five cities around the country. For a small stipend, these girls agreed to attend sex education classes, finish high school, and learn skills that would enable them to earn a living. The foundation hoped to prove that, with training and day care, these young women would prefer working to the dole.

Mindy arranged for Jamaica to sit in on a sex education class where she might find the girl she was looking for. She entered the vast concrete building that seemed no more or less forbidding than other aging institutional structures she had visited, mostly as a student. The smell in the hallway was immediately familiar: the swampy cologne of stale food and sweat almost always found lingering in aging high schools. The handful of after-school stragglers paid little attention to the white woman walking by.

She made her way to a classroom, where she was studiously ignored by a dozen or so young black women—girls, really. They all had taken great care in putting together their outfits. There were many feet shod in colorful flat shoes, several pairs of ankle-length pants, and many loose-fitting sweatshirts that were that season's rage. Except for the four toddlers crawling about and the obviously pregnant bellies protruding from five of the girls, this appeared to be as normal a group as one could hope for among high school girls. There was much giggling and munching of corn chips and pretzels, and they sneaked glances at Jamaica and waited for Miss Green to arrive.

At precisely four o'clock, Miss Green came striding through the door. She was a striking, tall black woman who moved and spoke efficiently. The moment she entered the classroom, the girls became quiet and slumped into their seats, assuming a familiar posture of bored defiance. Miss Green got them to sit up in their seats by placing on each of their desks a plastic speculum and launching matter-of-factly into an explicit lecture on venereal disease.

"The first thing you girls might do," she suggested, "is stop referring to your vaginas as 'downstairs' and 'pee-pees.' You are mothers, or about to become mothers, and it might be helpful to your future sexual activity to think about your bodies in an adult fashion."

She explained how to use the speculum, frowning at a couple of girls in the corner who were amusing themselves by pretending the devices for vaginal self-exploration were alligator jaws. Then, she asked if anyone had any questions.

By now the girls had stopped giggling and casting sly peeks at Jamaica. She, too, had taken great care dressing that morning, choosing a black skirt, a white blouse with tuxedo pleats down the front, a gray sweater with padded shoulders. She wanted to look as nondescript as possible without appearing deliberately unstylish. She wanted to seem approachable but not as if she were trying to establish herself as a buddy.

A chubby girl with a perpetually extended lower lip and two earrings stuck in her right ear tentatively raised her hand. Her child, a dazed-looking little boy in a blue jogging outfit, crawled on the floor by her leg.

"Yes, Yvette?" said Miss Green, snapping her head in the girl's direction.

"Can you get pregnant if you do it standing up?"

Miss Green ignored the explosion of giggles. Jamaica sputtered a bit, and scribbled gibberish in her notebook. She didn't want to be expelled from class.

"If you don't use the proper birth control methods, you certainly can," replied Miss Green. Her unflappability remained intact throughout the onslaught of questions.

"Can you get pregnant the first time?"

"Can you get pregnant if you do it when you're at that time of the month?"

"Where do you get those diseases they're always talking about on the news, that AIDS?"

This offered Miss Green the opportunity to lead a discussion on venereal disease and to hand out pamphlets. A girl who was so skinny that she appeared to be a maze of jagged angles pushed her tortoise-rimmed glasses up her nose. Her cleverness was apparent from her deliberately poor posture and bored grin. She had been observing the proceedings with more than a little amusement.

"I don't let nobody stick his thing in me unless I look it over real good," she declared, having waited for the chatter to subside. "I've got enough worries to mess with without having to be bothering with dis-ease." She rolled the word off her tongue with such knowing disgust, the other girls squirmed in their seats.

"Thank you, Edith," said Miss Green, who, for the first time during the session, appeared on the verge of smiling.

And for the first time, the tall, slender girl sitting silently next to Jamaica seemed to come awake. She looked at Jamaica, grinned, and shrugged her shoulders. Jamaica noticed how calm and sad she seemed, compared with the other girls. After the class was over, she asked the girl her name.

"Lonnie." The girl glanced at Jamaica's notebook. "What you writing in there?"

"I'm a reporter and I'm taking some notes."

"Are you going to do a story about this class? Like on TV?"

"Well, I'm going to do a story about the class, but mostly about one of the girls and her family."

Lonnie kept staring at Jamaica's notebook. "I wish I could talk to you some more, but I gotta go. My mother's taking care of my baby and I said I'd be home right after class. What's your name?"

"Jamaica."

"Good-bye, Jamaica." Lonnie said softly. "Maybe I'll be seeing you."

Jamaica felt a little apprehensive about her after-class meeting with Miss Green. She always felt shy and fumbling around assertive women like her, women who could speak directly to teen-agers and who had dedicated their lives to the betterment of others.

Miss Green encouraged her to choose Edith, the smart, skinny girl with the sassy mouth. She was on the verge of getting her high school diploma, could type ninety words a minute without mistakes, and had her two-year-old enrolled in a church-sponsored day care program. She was articulate, funny, and a vessel of optimism, good p.r. for the foundation's program and an example for other girls in her situation.

Jamaica saw Miss Green's point.

"What about that quiet girl in the back, Lonnie?"

"Lonnie? Well, I'm not sure you want Lonnie. She's a sweet girl and all, but she's a hard one to get to know. Quiet, mumbles a little. She's trying hard but it's a struggle for her. Her mother's a southern woman, tries to help out. Why, are you thinking about Lonnie?"

For the next few weeks, Jamaica would think of little besides Lonnie.

On her way home from that first venture to Harlem, Jamaica stopped to sit on one of the benches in Father Demo Park. It wasn't much of a park, a bricked-over triangular road divider shoved off to one side of Sixth Avenue. But she liked to sit and watch the Village *alter kockers* engage themselves in endless discussions about God knows what, feed the pigeons, scold the pigeon feeders for propagating the species.

She needed a few minutes to decompress. As she sat there, she noticed two well-dressed black men, about forty, standing by the curb on Sixth Avenue, waving their arms at taxis passing by.

Without realizing what she was doing, she wandered over to where they were standing and stared at the two of them. The cabs kept slowing down, then swooshing by. Some of the cabbies flicked on their "Off-Duty" signs as they accelerated. Jamaica felt suspended in time, as though she and these two men were the only people left alive in Greenwich Village, as though her hand could pass through the apparitions that appeared to be moving around them in cars and on sidewalks, pushing hot dog carts and sketching chalk portraits of tourists.

"Excuse me." She looked around to see who had spoken, then noticed that the two men had stopped waving for taxis and were looking at her. She had their attention whether she wanted it or not.

"Why are you having such a hard time getting a cab? Is it because you are black?"

"Lady, where have you been?" The man shook his head.

A taxi whose driver was black slowed down, then sped up.

"Fuck you, too," the man cried at the taillights.

His friend said, "C'mon. Let's take the subway."

He turned to Jamaica. "Don't worry about it. This is a fact of life. Sometimes it gets me down. But what can you do?"

As she ambled home, her head bent, hands shoved way down in her pockets, Jamaica thought, with the foolish optimism of inexperience: "File charges. Get their medallions revoked. That's what you can do."

There had been no blacks in Harmony when Jamaica was growing up. She had been taught about racism, however, at an early age. One evening, about dusk, shortly before the Just family would convene for dinner, Geneva ran panting through the door, her face and arms covered with soot. Jamaica, who was about five years old at the time, was already inside with her parents. The thought occurred to her that this was the first time she could remember in her brief life that she was clean, tidy, and where she was supposed to be while her elder sister was dirty, disheveled, and late. Her parents seemed alarmingly oblivious to the anomaly.

"Look at Geneva," squealed Jamaica. "She's so dirty she looks like a nigger." She cocked her head in the direction of her parents, expecting . . . she didn't know what. Laughter? A spanking for the sister she worshipped?

Dr. Just simply looked away. Mrs. Just was on her feet, moving with a will and speed Jamaica knew well. "Don't you ever use that word again," hissed Mrs. Just as her hand met her child's bottom with some force. And so Jamaica received her early liberal training.

As far as Jamaica could tell, Lonnie had received very little training of any kind. After meeting with Miss Green that first day, Jamaica arranged a rendezvous with Lonnie and her mother at their apartment. If they seemed to fit the requirements of Jamaica's story, she had agreed to discuss the project with Lonnie's social worker, who would in turn make sure the family understood and approved what they would be submitting themselves to.

Jamaica called Lonnie at the number Miss Green had provided.

"H'lo?" someone mumbled.

"Hi, this is Jamaica Just. Is Lonnie there?"

There was silence. Then, "Hmm-hmmm. Umm. I am Lonnie."

"Hi, Lonnie. Do you remember me from Miss Green's class?"

"Mmmmm." A giggle.

Jamaica was starting to feel some concern. How was she going to draw poignant anecdotes, pithy quotes out of this halting speech pattern? Then again, this was the phone, she was a stranger, Lonnie was a teen-ager. Let's have a little perseverance, she thought.

"I was wondering if I could come visit you at home to chat with you and your mother about using your family for the story I told you about." Jamaica disliked the pitch of her voice; she was speaking a full tone lower than usual with the mannered cheeriness of the official interviewer. When had she started doing that? she wondered.

"Okay," Lonnie said, almost whispering. Jamaica took the shortness of the pause preceding the "okay" as an affirmative sign. Several monosyllables later, she had obtained an address, arranged a time for the following afternoon.

She was starting to enjoy her subway rides to Harlem, especially when she realized that she was probably the safest person on the train. A white woman traveling alone that far uptown must be a social worker or a cop.

Lonnie's street appeared at first to be a pleasant block of low-rise tenement buildings, not very different from the ones on Jamaica's street. Closer inspection revealed the concrete blocking many doorways. Jamaica walked by a small white building; a hand-painted sign over the entrance said, "Jesus Saves." She felt vulnerable to the stares directed her way by a group of small children gathered around the tenement steps next to the Church of Zion; her back ached from being continually straightened.

When she arrived at the number Lonnie had given her, she felt ashamed of her response. She was comforted to see that the front was unpainted and impoverished, that the stairs leading to the front door were broken and dangerous, and that the entryway was dark and reeked of spilled beer and damp plaster. It smelled the way the hill shanties she used to visit with her father on house calls smelled. The smell didn't come from dirt. It was the smell of settled-in poverty, a smell that neither detergent nor social workers could wash away.

Jamaica recorded the details in her notebook ("smelly plaster, hole in wall, dark, murky, POOR") and pushed the buzzer to Lonnie's mother's apartment. Nothing happened. She pushed the door leading inside. It wasn't locked. She stepped into the dark hallway and called out, "Lonnie?"

"Who is there?" answered a woman's voice from down the hall.

The voice came from a woman whose body and face had gone slack, as though all her fluids had been pumped out. A rumpled blue pullover barely met the top of her worn black pants. She wasn't wearing socks. She moved like an old woman, yet Jamaica knew from Miss Green that Camille, Lonnie's mother, was thirty-five years old. Closer inspection contradicted the impression that she gave of being elderly. The shape of her face and features belonged to an attractive woman. She wasn't wrinkled. What stood between this used-up frump and someone vital was as simple as straight posture and a new hairdo and as complicated as an entire social system.

Jamaica didn't think of all these things as she stood there peering into the darkness. They occurred to her gradually, over the next three hours, as she sat talking to Mrs. Williams about Lonnie, about living on welfare.

The apartment, which had five small rooms, was tidy but suffused with the depressing smell of damp plaster. There were leaks all over, Mrs. Williams explained, as she pointed to the mottled plasterboard walls. The living room was cluttered with lumpy, shabby furniture and dominated by a large television set with a cable hook-up. The place was dimly lit by a few naked light bulbs. This dreary light accentuated the suffocating closeness, the sense of hopelessness that hung over the apartment like spiritual pollution.

Later, before she looked at her copious notes, Jamaica could remember very little about that first afternoon with Mrs. Williams except that she, Jamaica, had felt overwhelmed by fatigue and compassion while she conducted the interview. What struck her was how often court came up in conversation. In the middle-class circles in which she moved, no one ever brought up court except lawyers or disgruntled recipients of jury notices. "Court" had kicked Lonnie's father out of their house. "Court" was where Lonnie's sister and the sister's boy-friend had spent a great deal of time after the boyfriend had ended an argument by pulling a pistol. "Court" had summoned Mrs. Williams for an appearance on Tuesday because Lonnie's little brother had been caught sucking subway tokens out of turnstiles and selling them.

It was agreed. The Williams family would be the subject of Jamaica's story, with the proviso that their surname would not appear in print. Pumped up from the dangerous combination of earnestness and diligence, Jamaica set about the business of collecting the ingredients for her piece. She was equipped for the task; she was an industrious, sensitive reporter. She knew what worked and how to get it, the specific examples of misery, of children bearing children against the sordid backdrop of relentless poverty and monotonous violence.

With Lonnie, she found the best interviewing technique was simply to follow the girl around. Lonnie actually enjoyed talking; her shyness and slight speech impediment silenced her most frequently when she was asked a question. Her terrible shyness both attracted and puzzled Jamaica. It was hard to imagine this timid, prudish girl doing what needed to be done to conceive the baby she now adored, James. On the other hand, Lonnie seemed to have no curiosity. She never asked Jamaica a question. One day, Jamaica accompanied Lonnie to the day care center in the housing projects behind Lincoln Center, that imposing complex of buildings, plaza, and fountains, its whiteness broken by the joyful shriek of the bright Chagall windows. As part of the foundation's program, Lonnie worked there twice a week as a teacher's aide.

On the subway, Jamaica asked Lonnie if she'd ever peeked inside the grand buildings at Lincoln Center.

"What's that?" Lonnie asked.

"You know, those big buildings across the street from where you work. You *must* see them when you come up out of the subway."

"No, I ain't never seen them."

For six months, twice a week, Lonnie had walked from the subway entrance to the corner and turned toward the housing projects without looking up once. Jamaica took her to lunch in a restaurant that faced Lincoln Center. Lonnie stared across the street at the gleaming white buildings throughout the entire meal. When she got up, she thanked Jamaica and said, "When my baby, James, is a grown up he will be rich. He'll be a businessman and I will go there with him, across the street there."

Jamaica was feeling more and more like a miracle worker. She followed Lonnie to her prep course for the high school equivalency degree, to a church where a young black leader exhorted her and other teen-agers to improve themselves because no one else would, to the hospital where she took James for a checkup.

"He be sick all the time," Lonnie said one day, staring at her shoes. She and Jamaica were sitting on a bench at the upper reaches of Central Park. "Maybe I'm jinxed. You know, I got myself pregnant on the very first time I ever did it. That baby, he's all I got, and as hard as I try, sometimes I think he's got a one-in-a-million chance of doing better than his momma did."

Nodding sympathetically, Jamaica scribbled in her notebook, surrounding this pulse-quickening quote with red stars.

Over the succeeding days Jamaica's own life receded until it seemed to her like a shadow as she absorbed the details of Lonnie's life. She learned about the older brother, the family hero, who was in the army and the younger brother, the token thief. She met the sister with the gun-toting boyfriend. Yvonne was even prettier than Lonnie and smarter, more street wise. She lived in her own apartment, a room five floors above a liquor store where drugs were dealt after hours. Without removing her eyes from the soap opera flickering on her tiny black-and-white television set, Yvonne blew smoke rings and told Jamaica that she spent her nights in clubs or on the streets because otherwise she would go crazy. She had a three year-old-daughter. Yvonne was eighteen years old and the most matter-of-factly hopeless person Jamaica had ever met. Her baby's father had been ordered to leave after he had pulled a gun. She'd responded with a knife. The police had come.

"Some life, right, miss?" she said to Jamaica. "Maybe Lonnie's got a chance."

Lonnie's various instructors and social workers were less sanguine. They never quite looked at Jamaica directly during interviews and would respond to specific questions like this: "She's very responsibile. She tries so hard. But it's a rough world out there and I'm afraid for Lonnie. She tries so hard."

Jamaica and Lonnie ate pizza and window-shopped together. Although she suspected she was violating journalistic ethics, Jamaica bought clothes and toys for Lonnie's little boy. On Lonnie's birthday, she brought a cake and a new shirt.

"That's the only present I got," Lonnie said, crying.

"It was the only present she got," Jamaica told Sammy, crying.

"Jamaica," said Sammy.

"What?" she sniffed.

He paused. "I don't know," he said.

One day Lonnie asked Jamaica, "When you gonna write my story, about how I'm working to get off of welfare and all?"

Jamaica looked at that hopeful face. "You know, Lonnie," she said slowly, "the story won't be a fairy tale. Your life isn't easy and I'm going to try and tell about all of it, the good with the bad. Do you understand?"

"Oh, sure. I understand. When you gonna write it?"

Jamaica wrote it, all right, a woeful, "sensitive" chronicle of the cycle of dependency. "Welfare Begets Welfare," the headline read. The story rippled with potent data about the rise in teen-age pregnancies, particularly among welfare recipients. Expert voices were brought in to comment on how the deck was stacked against welfare mothers, how society had failed them. She portrayed Lonnie's family as decent people struggling against formidable odds. She ended with that quote from Lonnie: "My baby has a one-in-a-million chance of doing better than his momma."

Henry's response was predictable.

"That was a highly readable story." He beamed. By then, he and Mindy were sleeping together regularly. Jamaica won a publisher's award. But she didn't hear from Lonnie. Every day she'd check her mailbox when she arrived at the office for the message that didn't come. Then the letters started arriving. As she yanked out the first batch, she flushed, craving praise to mitigate the uneasiness born of Lonnie's silence.

Eagerly she riffled through the letters as though they were a box of chocolates and she was trying to guess which one would have the most delectable filling. Finally she chose an envelope made of good-quality stock, neatly typed. Sitting at her desk, she smoothed the letter's thick pages and noted with pleasure that the salutation was friendly. She gave a quick glance at the signer's name; he was a physician.

Happily she read his opening remarks, commending her for her "excellent discussion of teen-age pregnancy and related problems." She arched her back, as though receiving a pat, as she read how good it was that she'd "exposed these issues to the American public so we can develop more enlightened policies to deal with them."

But as she continued to read, her shoulders drooped; she began to realize that this fan wasn't an enlightened creature at all. Her foot began to tap convulsively as the author droned on and on about how the United States had lost its competitive drive, finally circling in on his point.

I believe the reason for our country's decline is our overproduction of the mentally and culturally handicapped, and the decline in production of our more gifted people. In the long run, the race goes to the strong.

Jamaica groaned. "Sieg heil," she muttered.

A cheery voice sailed over her partition. "Did you say something, Jamaica?"

Jamaica cleared her throat. "Joanne? No. I was just . . . no, nothing. Sorry."

She returned to the letter, taking care to remain silent, though she felt herself bursting with rage, and something else, perhaps fear.

We should consider the possibility of euthanasia for those children of unwed mothers showing undesirable mental or physical handicaps. We should consider setting up special camps in our more underpopulated states such as Wyoming or Montana, where noncontributing segments of the population can perform useful work. . . . The nations that successfully reduce the numbers of their nonproductive citizens are the ones that will succeed in the world of tomorrow.

I look forward to more of your articles on how to deal with these interrelated problems.

Jamaica shoved the stack of letters away and stumbled out of her cubicle.

"You look awfully pale," said the receptionist. "Are you ill?"

Jamaica pulled on her coat. "I think I have to leave," she said.

The receptionist nodded sympathetically. "You run on home, Jamaica dear. You look run down. Just crawl into bed and take it easy, hon."

"Thank you so much," Jamaica sobbed, leaving the bewildered receptionist behind. Instead of going home she went to the movies; the junky comedy cheered her up more than she would have expected. By evening she'd perked up enough to surprise Sammy with a big pot of homemade vegetable soup—his favorite—and to convince herself that the letter from the Hitlerian doctor was a fluke.

She was wrong. The letters kept coming. It became a game for her, trying to guess which ones would be friendly, which ones hateful. A self-described feminist from New Rochelle complimented her for revealing "the callous effects of male sexual irresponsibility." A Wall Street lawyer wrote to tell her he had no sympathy for welfare mothers.

As viewed from the other, presumably greener, side of the line, I can assure you it is impossible to obtain the services of a competent housekeeper. Your article implies these people want employment. This is not the case.

Jamaica dragged the letters home, presenting them to Sammy along with varying manifestations of guilt: hysteria, sarcasm, self-pity, anger.

Every night she brought home a new packet, a new test; after pacing in front of her husband, examining his reaction as he read, she would explode, "Well, aren't you infuriated?" If Sammy's response wasn't precisely what she was looking for—and that, too, changed from night to night—she would pile on layers of Sammy's sweatshirts and storm out of the apartment.

But the message she was waiting for didn't come. As the days went by, she would start to call Lonnie, then Miss Green, then Lonnie again. She always interrupted herself, though, because it had sunk in that she'd lied to Lonnie. The lie had been her niceness, the fiction she'd created of Jamaica the Fairy Godmother. Some fairy godmother, presenting her ward her very own copy of "This Is Your (Hopeless) Life."

One day the phone rang with an unexpected message from Miss Green: "The Williams family wants to sue your paper, and to sue you."

All Jamaica could manage was a barely audible "What?"

Calmly, as though she were discussing vaginitis with a classroom of pregnant teen-agers, Miss Green explained. "They are furious. They think you misrepresented them and what you were doing." She added, "They think you made them sound poor and cheap."

"Can I talk to them?"

"I don't think it's a good idea right now." Miss Green dropped the all-business tone. "Look, Ms. Just. For what it's worth, I think you told it like it is. We're trying to calm the family down on this end. Maybe we can arrange a meeting later."

Sammy had been raised by fairly observant Jewish parents so he was not unfamiliar with guilt. Nothing, however, not even Jamaica's reaction to the letters, prepared him for the highly visible and audible way she suffered from her conversation with Miss Green. That evening, after silently pacing around their apartment, Jamaica left suddenly; Sammy followed her, murmuring platitudes. "Please come home, Jamaica. Everything will be all right. I promise."

"You don't understand anything! Leave me alone. I want to die," Jamaica yelled over her shoulder as she ran through the streets. Finally, at the corner of Cornelia and West Fourth Streets, Sammy caught up with her and pinned her against the side of a building.

"Now stop it," he demanded. "Jamaica, you got a publisher's award for the story. Henry loved it. You are probably going to get a raise. It was a good story."

Jamaica glared at his exasperated face and wished she could believe he was right. "I'm so sorry, Sammy." She sat on the corner curb; her backside immediately felt cold and wet. "I just wanted to help."

She laughed abruptly. "What did I think I was doing for Lonnie? Am I an idiot? You don't have to answer. I am an idiot. Do you know in my heart of hearts I *identified* with her? I thought we were the same."

Sammy looked puzzled.

She drew her knees to her chest and looked at the street. "It's hard to explain. I guess I have this image of myself as a martyr once removed, that somehow I've been victimized by the Holocaust even though that was my parents' show, not mine. In a weird way, I guess I 'related' to Lonnie, stuck where she is because of her parents."

She stood up and wiped the bits of gravel sticking to the seat of her jeans. "Gee, I'm really profound tonight, huh? Kiddie-Freud. Lonnie is a lot smarter than I am. She saw me for the fake and cheat that I am. No wonder she doesn't want to talk to me."

Sammy didn't say anything. They prowled the streets until dawn, strolling past the punks, the crack dealers, the hiply dressed hopefuls lined up outside Manhattan's late-night clubs. They climbed the stairs to their apartment as daylight was just filtering in the windows. Before they fell into bed to catch a couple of hours of sleep before work, Jamaica threw her cache of letters into the trash. For the next few days her nights—and Sammy's—were peaceful.

Then a national feature service reprinted her welfare mother piece in syndication. It appeared in two hundred papers around the country and was given prominent display in fifty. This time the letters came from all over. Bigoted and self-righteous readers, sympathetic ones, mean-spirited ones all had opinions, which the syndicate forwarded to Jamaica. Her contact there also sent her, "as a courtesy," assorted letters to the editor that had been printed in various newspapers.

"You are so lucky," Joanne Robbins sighed, when she dropped by Jamaica's cubicle one morning. "No one ever writes to me."

"You're an editor, Joanne," Jamaica said wearily. "No one writes to editors. They don't know who you are. Believe me, if they did, they would."

"If you don't want to talk, just say so," Joanne answered huffily. "I don't want to talk."

What she wanted to do instead was to read and reread the tortured, often hateful prose contained in the mail strewn across her desk. "You dumb liberal shit," was the salutation on one letter rife with misspelling and bad puns. "Here's my ode to you liberal shits. Phallus Erectus, Nigger Vincit!" She tried to imagine the writer, lying on a couch somewhere in a drunken stupor, laughing hysterically at his own dim wit. She couldn't tell which ones she hated more, the out-and-out lunatics or the people whose agenda was "doing good."

It was with cynicism that she greeted a Florida businessman's confession that her story had inspired tears of compassion "for welfare mothers and for troubled families, executives under stress, drugs, alcoholism, you name it." He continued:

There is an answer. You as a newspaperwoman must take a greater leadership role for good and I mean, for God. Try and give hope to those poor people by showing them the success of God's solutions. Do a major series on groups like Teen Challenge, the Fellowship of Christian Athletes, the Value of the Person, the Campus Crusade, or dozens of others I could name.

In a word, uplift, inspire and build. Be part of the solution, not the problem.

"Yeah, buddy, that's what I thought I was doing." Jamaica tore the letter in half. She dropped the pieces into the waste can, where they settled next to this fragment: ". . . and so, Jamaica Just, you'd better wake up to reality. The plot to destroy middle class America is well on its way, the fire lit by people like you!"

Once a week Jamaica checked with Miss Green to see if Lonnie was ready to talk. Finally Miss Green arranged a meeting, in the schoolroom where Jamaica had first met Lonnie. The two of them, Mrs. Williams, a couple of people from the foundation, and Miss Green sat around a conference table. No one said anything. Everyone looked upward or downward for quite a while, forever.

Jamaica heard herself talking. "Lonnie, Mrs. Williams, I don't know what you hated about the story. I'm sorry if I hurt you in any way, but I thought we understood one another. I realize that when you spend a lot of time with someone over a period of time, it's hard to remember everything that was said, but I have notes on everything."

Mrs. Williams had cooled off by then and had come to the meeting only because Lonnie insisted. "Yes, I guess I know what you are saying." She looked even more tired than usual.

"I thought we were friends and you were going to tell my story," burst out Lonnie, surprising everyone—not least herself, to judge from her expression—with her vehemence. "You wrote about our furniture. You called our house "shabby" and said it didn't smell good. You didn't say you were going to write about the furniture. Why did you write about the furniture?"

"Lonnie, I told you I wasn't writing a fairy tale but a story about your life, how brave you are, how tough things are for you. Didn't I tell you I thought your story might help out other girls who got into your predicament, help change things?"

"Yeah, but you got me birthday presents. You didn't laugh when I told you 'bout my dreams. You wrote all of it down, I saw you, and then you made me look like some poor, no'count girl."

"Lonnie—"

"Don't talk to me no more. I don't want to hear your voice or see your face never ever again." Lonnie had not looked at Jamaica throughout the meeting. She continued not to look at her as she stood up and walked out the door.

Healing

During the early spring evening following that awful meeting, snow began to drop, thick and fast, padding the city streets. There was lightning and thunder. It was a night in which anything seemed possible, one of those rare nights when the miracle of nature asserted itself in the city with a force powerful enough to make the cynics and the smartasses take notice of exterior storms. It was a night on which bad poetry would be written. It was a night for remembering.

Jamaica was prepared for a night of wallowing. She hoisted herself up the stairs by the bannister, ready to collapse on the couch with Sammy. The cat greeted her at the door, a note tied to its collar with a red bow.

J, Tried to call you at the office, but you'd left. We're having an all-weekend session down in Atlanta about the interlink project. Your mom called. Why don't you go out to Connecticut for the weekend? You can reach me at the Marriott Marquis. Love, S.

Not many years after Jamaica's father died, Eva Just had followed her daughters east, taking up residence midway between them in an airy house on the Connecticut shore. She grew geraniums that were six feet tall in giant pots by the endless picture windows and delighted her New England neighbors with her generous dispensation of warm strudel and sensible advice on subjects as diverse as child rearing and the stock market. She mourned the death of soap opera heroes and continued to greet with shock new evidence that there was cruelty in the world.

Gazing at the snow falling outside, Jamaica thought how calm and smooth the Long Island Sound appeared from her mother's living room. Soon the yard, now probably blanketed by snow, would blossom with tulips and azaleas.

She hesitated, then dialed.

"What's the matter?" Eva's accent was distinctly Hungarian, the language spoken in her native sector of Czechoslovakia, though her English was colloquial and varied.

Jamaica immediately took on the defensiveness of a teen-ager. "Nothing."

"Are you still upset about that girl?"

"Yes, I'm still upset about that girl." Jamaica mimicked her mother's accent.

"Why do you do that? Look, darling, you wrote a beautiful story, and if that girl didn't understand it, well, someday maybe she will. These aren't the best-educated people in the world."

"What do you mean, *these* people?" The sneer was involuntary; Jamaica wanted comfort, not a fight.

Her mother ignored the slight. "Maybe she'll make something of herself now. This could be an inspiration."

"Mom . . ."

"Oh, by the way. Did I tell you about what I did yesterday? I got the best bargain at Shopper's World. They were selling cereal, normally $1.59 a box, for 99 cents! Can you imagine that? I bought ten boxes. Jamaica, could I call you back? I want to check with Singer, the stockbroker, to see how I did in the market today." She giggled. "I lost $10,000 yesterday, so I want to see what happened today. If I made it back, maybe I'll go shopping. Clothes at Cost is having a big sale. Don't go away. I'll call you back."

The dead phone hung from Jamaica's hand. She leaned over and stroked the cat with the receiver. "Why do I call my mother about serious things? I've betrayed the trust of an innocent girl and she talks to me about cereal." The cat rubbed her head against Jamaica's hand.

"You know what else? I'll bet you a million dollars she's going to offer to send me another package of underwear. Do you know, I'm over thirty years old and I've never bought myself a pair of underpants?"

The phone rang.

"Hi, it's me again. Do you know today is *Yizkor*? It's the last day of Passover and you have to say a prayer for your father."

"Oh, sure. I have a prayerbook here somewhere," Jamaica lied. "Mom? How big a disappointment am I?"

"Where do you come up with these ideas? Where is Sammy?"

Thus, Jamaica was given an opportunity to wangle an invitation from her mother. Within an hour she'd settled in her seat on the nearly empty Amtrak train, the Chopin nocturnes on her Walkman mournfully echoing in her head. How did her mother keep track of all the dates for Yizkor, the memorial service? Absently, she chanted the Mourner's Kaddish, the prayer for the dead, as she stared out into the darkness rushing by: "Yit'ga'dal v'yit'ka'dash she'mei ra'ba . . ."

"Ah, Daddy," thought Jamaica. "We had lots of things to talk about. Religion, for example. You used to talk to us about why there must be a God, about how somebody had to set the wheels in motion, set the planets in their orbital spheres, draw the moral lines for folks to follow. Geneva's shrink thinks you must have felt ambivalent, though. Why else would you have deliberately set out to be a stranger in a strange land, a Jew in Harmony?

"A great person, a fine doctor, everyone said, and they must have been right. Your office was packed. You insisted that we come home for dinner every night at 5:30 sharp and encouraged Mommy to light the candles on Friday nights so our Presbyterian surroundings wouldn't obliterate the yellow stars engraved on our souls. You kissed us good night every single night and never failed to stand at the door, waving, as we walked off to school.

"You loved me dearly, I'm sure of that." Her thumb rested just inches from her mouth as she settled into her self-induced reverie.

Her eyes popped open, momentarily. "Didn't you?"

As the train rumbled along, her memory brought her back to Ohio, and she was, maybe, ten or eleven years old. She was accompanying Dr. Just on a house call, up into the hills of Shutter Creek, the poorest area of a county that considered 25 percent unemployment about right. Scared as she was, she was thrilled to be speeding along back roads with her father in his custom-painted Oldsmobile with the light blue body and earth-green roof. In the straight stretches Dr. Just accelerated to 80, 90 miles an hour, sitting soldier straight, the two fingers of his left hand resting on the steering wheel, his right hand pressed flat against the seat next to him. He'd lurch and screech around the hairpin turns, glancing sideways to make sure Jamaica hadn't banged up against the dashboard. Cows, rolling fields, all that bucolic splendor would flash right by; the wind pouring in the open windows pushed her thick hair and her father's straight up. They didn't talk much. Jamaica liked to recall these outings as moments of shared adventure.

Dr. Just was stopping in on old Mrs. Hartley, who had been old so long that "old" had become part of her name. Throughout Smith

County similar little old ladies waited for visits from this handsome stranger, whom they greeted with cups of tea and boxes of divinity candy.

The Oldsmobile heaved and sighed along the crunchy gravel road that wound its way back to Mrs. Hartley's clapboard house. It badly needed a paint job and, like its owner, sagged everywhere. As doctor and daughter disembarked, Jamaica shrieked, "Daddy, there's a snake in the driveway!"

"Run over there," Dr. Just cried, waving toward the side of the house. Jamaica, who had shrieked merely for effect, was starting to feel terrified, even though she was sure that the snake curled lazily in the driveway was of the garden variety. Transfixed, she watched her father yank open the car door and gun the engine. The Oldsmobile lunged at the snake. Gravel and dust flew as the car ground back and forth like some big crazed bull lanced by picadors. Finally the car stopped and the air was silent except for the buzzing of flies attracted by the fresh blood. Dr. Just emerged from the car, tan and erect, his white shirt clinging to the sweat on his back.

"I'll just be a few minutes," he said, without looking at Jamaica.

After that, he never asked her to go on a house call with him again.

The conductor broke Jamaica's reverie. "Pretty out there, isn't it?" He nodded at the ghostly film of snow blowing around the train. She pressed her nose against the cold glass before she nodded, and gave him her ticket. The steady hum of the wheels lulled her back to Harmony.

Jamaica liked to tell Sammy about how, when she was born, Dr. Just sent a dozen roses to his wife's room. A card was attached on which he had scrawled, "Thank you for this wonderful gift."

Sammy loved this story and always remembered to send Jamaica red roses on her birthday.

What Jamaica forgot to tell Sammy was how, for the eighteen months that followed her birth, Dr. Just had refused to pick up his younger daughter.

She knew he had his reasons. Eva had explained, after all. "He didn't want Geneva to be jealous."

Eva hadn't meant to let this anecdote escape from her repository of secrets. She was tricked into it by Jamaica, who persistently asked questions about her childhood, swearing that she could remember almost none of it.

"You had a wonderful childhood," Eva would tell Jamaica. "You had your little friends to play with, and trees and fresh air. You had a dog, rabbits, a pet hen, a pet duck, and three guinea pigs. We took you with us on trips, and we ate supper together every night as a family. You knew we loved you very much."

In moments of anger, her daughters thought their mother was conspiring continually to make them feel guilty. How dare they worry about not making the cheerleading squad, pimples, flab? Had they been in concentration camps? Had their parents been murdered? Why didn't anyone ask them these questions so they wouldn't have to ask them of themselves?

The subject never came up in Harmony—at least not directly. Not long after the Justs moved there, neighbors started to drop by and casually mention church. Everyone but the Baptists wanted the prestige of having the town doctor in the congregation. The Baptists figured the Justs were up to no good with their odd accents and strange eating habits; everyone in town knew that Mrs. Just fed her family green peppers, food fit only for pigs.

One day Miss Sarah came over. Her real name was Mrs. Prince, but she was always referred to as Miss Sarah because she hadn't married until she was forty and had been given up for spinsterhood.

"Why don't you want to join the Presbyterian church? We have the most modern ideas and the nicest building. I think it would be the best for educated people like yourselves," she said. Eva liked Miss Sarah, a straightforward, sensible elderly woman whose husband had died just a few months before the Justs arrived in town.

Miss Sarah was one of Dr. Just's first regular patients; nothing much was ever wrong with her, but she stopped by every month to visit first with the handsome doctor and then with his wife. When she and Eva had settled into a comfortable routine, the reticent Miss Sarah revealed a bit about her own past.

"My Homer was a fine man who brooked no nonsense from anyone, and I agreed with that outlook on life," she told Eva over one of their coffee klatches. What she meant was this: Homer had been married for several years before he fell in love with Miss Sarah Bennett, who had comfortably settled in with the notion that she was too strong and too smart for any man she was likely to meet around Harmony— or anywhere else in 1935 for that matter. She had lived in Cincinnati and traveled to Cuba in the twenties with a schoolteacher friend. The two of them had dined with strangers and drunk rum and after that Miss Sarah returned to Harmony, where she expected the rest of her life to be as dry and lifeless as her home town. Harmony, literally a "dry" town, has yet to acknowledge the end of Prohibition.

Then she met Homer and became the corespondent in *Prince* v. *Prince,* Homer's messy divorce trial. With its unusually vivid testimony and startling notions—the idea of middle-aged lovers caught up in swoony, dewey-eyed, irrational love—*Prince* v. *Prince* was considered interesting enough to be memorialized in Ohio's law school texts, where mention of the case can still be found.

Miss Sarah didn't tell Eva all this on the day she asked the Justs to align themselves with the Presbyterians, yet she seemed trustworthy anyway.

Eva decided to explain. "We're Jewish."

"Oh, my dear, well why didn't you say so?" said Miss Sarah. "Oh, you poor dear," she said, when she realized why Eva might not have said so. Miss Sarah and her darling Homer had taken a keen interest in the Second World War and what had happened to the Jews, having unintentionally become outcasts themselves.

Miss Sarah spread the word, but not fast enough for Earl Young, the meek meat cutter at Stern's grocery, who came to life Wednesday evenings and Sunday mornings when he metamorphosed into a spirited if ineloquent preacher at the Congregational church. Earl's following was the smallest in town—the church had only fifty members—but it was the noisiest. The Methodist and Presbyterian kids would sit across the street from the converted grange hall the Congregationalists met in and wait for the show. Women, especially, would burst out of the small, rectangular whitewashed church and race around the building dancing and screaming, "Lord! Lord!" displaying the kind of wild enthusiasm that was generally discouraged in town unless it was being displayed at a basketball game. Because Earl trimmed meat so nicely and never raised his voice except within the confines of the church, he was tolerated, even though he had moved to Harmony from Kentucky.

Earl and his wife and two daughters lived across the street from the Justs. One day this mousy man of God tapped on the Justs' screen door.

"Howdy, ma'am," he said, afraid to look directly at this strange, pretty woman with her red lipstick.

"Why, how-dee," said Mrs. Just. "Come on in, Earl. Are you looking for Doc?" Pushing the screen door open with her toe, she grabbed Earl's hand to shake it and pull him inside. She didn't understand why he seemed so flustered. Americans always were shaking hands in the movies.

Staring at the red nail polish on the toes peeking out from Mrs. Just's high-heeled sandals, Earl mumbled, "We was wondering over at the church why you folks was taking so long to join up with anyone and I wanted to tell you we'd be honored to have you up our way."

Eva was surprised he hadn't heard yet. She'd tipped Miss Sarah off the day before, plenty of time for the fact of their Jewishness to have circulated throughout town.

"Well, Earl, the problem is . . . it isn't a problem really. We're Jewish."

"Jewish?" Earl scratched his close-cropped head and sneaked a glance at Eva's face. "That ain't like Catholic is it?"

"Like Catholic?" Eva inspected Earl's smooth face, his guileless brown eyes and realized that he wasn't teasing. Clearly, the worst thing he could imagine would be for them to be Catholics, with their masses and mysteries. Jews simply didn't register.

"No, it's about as different from Catholic as you can imagine."

"That's fine, then. Okay, then. I best be going. I'll see you downtown, most likely."

Shortly after he left, Eva picked up the telephone.

"Miss Sarah? This is Eva Just, Doc's wife. I want to enroll Geneva in your Sunday school class."

Geneva, and later Jamaica, learned about the Old Testament from Miss Sarah. They loved walking up Main Street in their matching dresses, tipping their hats with bows at the town's Sunday-starched denizens, skipping a bit in their white anklets and black patent leather shoes. There was something grand and solemn about the red brick church set back just a little from the volunteer fire station. Inside, the benches were smooth and shiny, and the stained glass windows with their sad and lovely depiction of the Crucifixion stirred their young, impressionable hearts. They went to Bible camp at the local school in the summer until Jamaica was in second grade and the Supreme Court said they couldn't have Bible classes in school anymore.

Her Presbyterian education ended not long afterward and just as abruptly. Dr. Just came into the house from his attached office and heard Jamaica singing. She was sitting on the Oriental rug in the living room, tracing the pattern with her hand.

> *Jesus loves the little children.*
> *All the children of the world.*
> *Be they yellow, black, or white,*
> *They are precious in his sight.*
> *Jesus loves the little children of the world.*

"Hi, Daddy," she said, when she noticed him standing there. "Do you know this song? We learned that in Sunday school last week, and next week we're going to learn about the disciples."

Dr. Just went back into the office without saying anything.

A week later the girls found a package in their bedroom. While

Geneva picked at the tape, Jamaica ripped the paper. Inside they found two versions of the Old Testament—a fat comic book and a double record album. From then on, instead of walking up Main Street to church on Sunday mornings like all their friends, they listened to records. For them the Book of Exodus was forever summed up neatly by the song they replayed again and again:

> *Moses, little Moses.*
> *Little baby, you know why you were born.*
> *To take your people, set them free,*
> *Lead them from captivity.*
> *Across the land and through the sea*
> *To lead your people on.*

In the fifth grade, Jamaica learned about genealogy from Mrs. Worth, an old bag whose bras were in perpetual need of adjustment; she was forever tugging and yanking on various straps and wires beneath her shapeless dresses, and one day she horrified her students by unwittingly allowing a small patch of bare breast to show for a brief moment. Jamaica hated Mrs. Worth, not for her slovenly appearance but because the teacher never failed to call on her only Jewish student right before major holidays and ask in a saccharine voice, "And how do *your* people celebrate Easter, Jamaica?" (Mrs. Worth was only partly anti-Semitic. She also disliked Jamaica because she'd heard it was the Just child who had tagged her "Old Worthless.")

Mrs. Worth had gone to the trouble of tracing her family back five generations, four of them in Harmony. Her flabby white arms flew up and down the blackboard as she excitedly presented this information, these disembodied names. The students regarded her chalky tree with some interest only because they had never seen the dreary Mrs. Worth so awake and alert. Her pale blue hair glowed.

"Now children, I want you to interview your parents and bring in your own trees tomorrow," she rasped, at the end of class.

Jamaica couldn't afford to bollix this assignment. She knew Mrs. Worth would love to wrap her bony fingers around Jamaica's smooth young neck and squeeze the sass out of her. Her teacher hadn't found it amusing when she'd explained that she'd set off the school fire alarm "to test it out." She always scowled at Jamaica during class, as though she could see the novel Jamaica had propped up in front of her general science text. Mrs. Worth had actually raised her hand at Jamaica after she'd kicked a little boy off the merry-go-round when he'd expressed his affection for her.

Her roster of petty crimes had reached a critical juncture; one more and her parents would be notified.

After supper, though, Eva rushed off to a P.T.A. meeting. "Ask Daddy, dear," she called over her shoulder.

When Dr. Just ducked into the house for the seven o'clock news, Jamaica sat next to him on the couch, waiting patiently for the commercial.

"Can I ask you something for school?" she said during the pitch for General Electric. "We're doing a project where we have to make up a family tree and draw all the cousins and aunts and uncles, you know? back a lot of generations and stuff so we can have lots of branches."

Dr. Just sighed as he watched the man on television open a stove and point inside. He seemed to be thinking very hard about something, some secret irony, a joke perhaps. The girls never seemed to understand his jokes, so he would tickle their feet when he delivered a punch line. He looked at this chubby little American girl sitting next to him so expectantly and his face darkened as though in pain. Later, Jamaica would imagine he was wishing he could love her more. How could he tell her that too much had happened that he didn't understand? In Harmony it was easy to believe that the rest of the world existed only in dreams, on television, until Jamaica would pop up with one of her how's or why's. Later, she would imagine that as he stared at her sitting there so attentively, he felt more burdened than usual by the gift of a second life. It cost too dearly. Didn't he always tell his daughters that they were Americans first, Jews second, deliberately lying to repay an unwritten debt? Later, when the girls started dating, he would press money into their hands and tell them to pay their own way because he didn't want them to owe anybody anything. He didn't want the world to forget what had happened to him, but it seemed that he didn't want his children to know.

"Daddy?" Jamaica asked, nervously glancing at the television set, knowing that once the news resumed she'd have to wait for another commercial. "What about our family tree?"

Finally, Dr. Just spoke. "Ours has been pruned." He kissed Jamaica on the forehead and went back to his patients.

That evening, Jamaica laboriously sketched a broad-trunked tree. Not sure what to do next ("Ours has been pruned" would not do for Mrs. Worth, she felt sure), she idly colored the side of the tree with a green crayon, to represent moss. Pleased with her own cleverness, she examined the copy she'd made of Mrs. Worth's family tree and drew a series of similar branches and leaves from her mossy trunk. She began printing names inside the leaves, and when she couldn't invent any more, she dragged books from her shelf and borrowed some names. It was a beautiful tree, thick and leafy with ancestry, much better than Mrs. Worth's. Jamaica didn't understand why, when her mother came to kiss her good night and Jamaica proudly showed her the tree, Eva began to cry.

Jamaica meant to ask her mother if she remembered that tree, but somehow the subject didn't come up. The Connecticut weekend passed quietly and quickly. Jamaica and Eva replenished Jamaica's supply of underwear, curled up on the couch, and watched movies on TV—*The Guns of Navarone* and *Lover Come Back,* two favorites. They called Geneva in Boston; mostly Jamaica read and went for long walks by the sound. Yet she returned from this retreat feeling more morose than when she had left, though she was momentarily cheered by the dinner Sammy had waiting for her Sunday evening.

That week she walked around in a fog, checking her horoscope in four newspapers daily, poised to find the meaning of life in the slightest symbolic gesture. For example, the ceilings in Jamaica and Sammy's narrow tenement apartment were twelve feet high; to take advantage of the height, they had built shelves all the way up. No matter how she tried to array her important possessions—her books, her photo albums, her papers—Jamaica was always jumping up, crawling onto cabinets, knocking things onto the floor.

"Our apartment," she told Sammy, "is a metaphor for my life. I know what I want and where it is, but it's all slightly out of reach."

Sammy bought her a ladder.

"An angel, not a man," was the way her mother described Sammy to her friends. "I don't know how he puts up with my *meshuggeneh* daughter."

Jamaica couldn't resist the urge to toy with Sammy's halo. Complacency came too naturally to him. She had willingly made it part of her spousal responsibility to keep him from succumbing to the cloud of self-satisfaction that hovered over his head. It wasn't his fault that his great-grandparents on both his mother's and his father's side had been born in Kansas City and that he was considered a renegade merely for having abandoned the Feins' comfortably extended nest and moving to New York. His cousins, his brothers, and all their many children lived within twenty minutes of one another. There had been no suicides, marriages outside the faith, or divorces—except for cousin Richie, who everyone agreed was crazy anyway. In other words, Sammy's family was so normal, healthy, and unneurotic that it was unnatural.

Almost everyone she knew besides Sammy was a victim of something, although none of them could top her. Who else had the glamour of the Holocaust? Why not be the best? The most victimized?

At college she would sit back smugly during bull sessions when scared, fresh-faced youngsters trying to prove just how interesting they were would reduce tragedy to headlines. The point was to startle, not inform. The litany was endless: parents who divorced the instant their youngest left the house; mothers who forced their sons to track down their fathers' love affairs and testify against them in court; wives left widowed by their husbands' suicides, leaving them no choice but to pack up their children and impose on relatives; fathers who died leaving their children in the hands of evil stepfathers; parents who hadn't talked in twenty years; mothers who slept around and felt compelled to "share" the information with their children.

Jamaica would nod sympathetically. Because she seemed to listen so well, she became everybody's best friend; people mistook her silent glow of moral superiority for shyness. They didn't know what she was thinking: Had any of them, their parents, been tattooed and shaved, turned spooked and deranged? Were their grandparents murdered? Did their mothers talk cheerily about girlhood chums they went to camp with and mean Auschwitz? Go on. Top that.

Jamaica couldn't. She couldn't even match it.

When Sammy and Jamaica had been dating for more than a year, he told her he wanted to visit Harmony. Jamaica had made it sound so wonderful, the kind of small-town upbringing children of the suburbs found so very romantic. Jamaica had flown out to Kansas City the previous summer for the July Fourth weekend to meet the Feins. She was impressed by their house—its size, the meticulousness of its decorator-picked furnishings, the monogrammed towels in the bathroom—and she was startled by the friendly, casual conversation that passed between Sammy and his parents.

Her trip was a success. At dinner she amused the Feins with stories about Harmony, her folksy tales. Later, she lowered her eyes and mentioned that her parents had been in Europe during the war, and saw from the Feins' sympathetic nods that they understood the code. Brightening, she revealed that her father had been a successful doctor (they knew this from Sammy), and how zany yet business minded her mother was. Soon it became evident to her they would love her because she was the daughter of a Jewish professional whose family, against great odds, had come to America to try to accommodate themselves to the world the Feins had been born into.

The weekend passed without a hitch, although Jamaica did make one mistake. One evening Mr. Fein's brother Eddie brought wine to dinner, and Jamaica drank quite a lot of it. After dinner she helped clear the dishes, then sleepily wandered into the living room off the main entryway. She shuffled across the ivory carpet and sat on the edge of a fragile chair. Dimly she noticed how perfect, how untouched the room was. Even the magazines on the glossy coffee table were lined up in a neat row. Exhausted from the wine and conversation, she curled up in the delicate, uncomfortable chair and fell asleep.

A few minutes later, she felt Sammy shake her and drag her out of the room. Still groggy, she stood in the foyer and watched him as he tiptoed back across the carpet. He squatted into starting position for a sprint, his hands flat on the floor. As he backed carefully out of the room, he began smoothing away the imprint of Jamaica's footprints from the plush pile.

"What are you doing, Sammy?" she mumbled.

He pressed his lips into a sheepish grin. "Oh, Mom likes this room to look nice. It's the first thing you see when you walk into the house."

"Oh," she said.

Jamaica waited a couple of years—they were only in college after all—before she took Sammy to Harmony for Thanksgiving. Eva and Geneva picked them up at the airport. Jamaica proudly pointed out the rolling hills of southern Ohio as though she'd personally sculpted them. During the two-hour drive, Eva kept pulling small pieces of cake wrapped in foil from her bag and handing them to Sammy, who accepted them graciously.

Harmony appeared withered to Jamaica when they rolled into town. Sammy seemed to think it was all fine. "This really is a little town," he said with admiration as they drove past the dozen or so ramshackle buildings of downtown Harmony. "I didn't think places like this still existed."

After they'd dropped off their suitcases and freshened up, Jamaica took Sammy for a long walk down Burnt Cabin Road, her favorite, and showed him the old graveyard where she and Poochie used to picnic and the bushes where blackberries grew wild in early summer. They went to the Frostee Freeze, and even though it was cold, not chilly, they ate what were known in Harmony as Boston shakes, extra thick milkshakes with sundaes right on top.

"Do you like it, Sammy?" Jamaica was anxious.

Sammy nodded. "I'm jealous," he said, throwing his arm around Jamaica. "What am I? Another Jewish kid from the 'burbs. You've got the ghetto and Tom Sawyer, too."

They tramped through the woods behind the Justs' house for several hours, occasionally interrupting the silence with memories from when they were children. Sammy confessed that he'd enjoyed his suburban upbringing—it was quite a confession from a college boy, particularly in the seventies, a time when rebelling was still the thing to do.

He pushed Jamaica into the pile of leaves they'd kicked together with their hiking boots and plopped down next to her. "I always liked fall," he said. "We'd have class elections, and my brothers and me were great at them. Dad always helped out. He wasn't much for tossing a ball, but he was great with speeches."

Jamaica propped herself up on an elbow. "What kind of speeches?"

"You know, running for class president, or student council."

"You did that?" Her tone was both admiring and suspicious.

He laughed. "Yeah, we had all kinds of corny tricks we used. I remember in ninth grade, I had a big heavy speech about leadership. Then Dad had this great idea on how to wake the audience up at the end. I told them, 'Now, before I finish, I'd like you to all stand up.' And sure enough, they did! I had my punch line all ready. 'Now, that's leadership.'"

Jamaica covered his face with dead leaves. "That's awful. Did you win?"

Sammy brushed the leaves from his face and leaned over to kiss her gently. "Of course I won."

There were other guests at Thanksgiving dinner. Dr. Just's niece, Muncy, had flown in from New York to keep Eva company; at that time it had been only a couple of years since Dr. Just had died. The other guests, Dr. Vilnar and his wife, Ruth, had driven from Cincinnati. Originally from Eva's hometown of Berecszacz, they'd left before the war.

Sammy was slightly taken aback by the clutter at the Justs', almost as startled as Jamaica had been by the Feins' fastidiousness. Mrs. Fein, for example, would set the table for festive dinners at least three days in advance, the napkins carefully fanning out from water glasses.

Eva, on the other hand, went into action about three hours before the guests arrived, and could never understand why the turkey was undercooked. She enlisted Sammy and the girls to shove the papers strewn around the dining room into drawers and closets. That accomplished, she stuck a rag and a water sprayer into Sammy's hand. "Go, dear, clean the dust off the plants in the living room."

"Mom," wailed Jamaica.

"Glad to do it," Sammy said.

Jamaica's mortification grew when they sat at the table and she began to see their version of Thanksgiving dinner through Sammy's eyes. There was turkey and dressing and sweet potatoes, which Eva served without enthusiasm. "Save room for the cabbage and chicken paprikash and noodle kugel," she urged Sammy.

"This is delicious," said Sammy, who had filled his plate with a little of everything.

Everyone ate and chattered aimlessly about school, the weather. Jamaica relaxed.

Then Muncy paused with her fork in midair. "Eva, you always have the best food. Even in camp you managed to get the potato peels."

Jamaica fixed her gaze on Sammy, who continued to plow through the mass of food on his plate.

Mrs. Vilnar clucked her tongue. "Where were you, Muncy?"

Muncy held up her hand while she swallowed some sweet potatoes and wiped a bit of marshmallow dangling from the corner of her mouth.

"Auschwitz." She laughed bitterly. "I shouldn't even be here today."

"Why's that?" Sammy asked politely.

Muncy was a solidly built woman of forty-five or so, attractive despite the deep lines etched into her face from years of setting her mouth very tight. Never married, she'd lived with Dr. Just and Eva in New York when Geneva was small.

Muncy forced a big smile and reached across the table to pat Sammy's hand. "Well, you see, Sammy, I was a little girl when they took me and my mother there. They asked my mother how old I was and she lied, she said I was sixteen when I was only thirteen. They sent her to be gassed and they let me live."

Sammy nodded.

Her hand still resting on Sammy's, Muncy kept talking. "We walked toward the showers where they would shave us. Above us we saw a tower and flames and soldiers swinging bodies by their hair. Long hair. I screamed. We all screamed. We wouldn't move. They told us we were only getting bathed. They took two girls and shaved them and bathed them and dressed them in gray stripes and showed them to us. 'You see?' they said."

Eva interrupted. "Sammy, dear, would you like more turkey?"

He swallowed. "No, no. I'm set for now.

Eva glanced approvingly at his progress. "You have a good appetite. Girls, you need anything? Dr. Vilnar? Ruth? Jamaica, why aren't you eating?"

Jamaica stared at her plate.

Geneva turned to Muncy sympathetically. "That must have been awful for you, you were so young."

Eva broke in. "But she was so lucky. Muncy and I, we have nine lives, right?"

The two women began to laugh heartily. The Vilnars kept eating.

Sammy put his fork down and ventured into the conversation. "That's what my grandfather used to say. 'I've got nine lives and they get me through *tsuris*.'"

Eva reached across the table to caress Sammy's cheek. "Isn't he a nice boy?"

Muncy nodded. "Sometimes I think I would be happy to settle for just *tsuris*. I feel like I'm *oyf kapores*."

"What's that?" Jamaica's curiosity momentarily overtook her anxiety.

Dr. Vilnar answered. "You know, the offering for sins. In the old country the rabbis would sacrifice a chicken before Yom Kippur— maybe asking God to take the chicken instead of them."

Giggling, Eva said. "Maybe we could get God to take the leftover turkey."

"Mommy, why do you always laugh it off?" Geneva's soft voice cut through the dinner noises.

Eva looked at her elder daughter with surprise. "What do you mean?"

Geneva leaned back in her chair. A slight, freckled woman who would look like a teen-ager well into her thirties, she always drew back from confrontations. Though the sight of blood didn't faze her, outside the lab she was tentative. She recognized her own frailties and often joked that her shoes never wore out because she trod so lightly.

"Nothing." She smiled and held out her plate. "Everying is wonderful, Mommy."

"It would be more wonderful if you got married already," said Eva. "What happened to that nice Steven you were going out with?"

Geneva answered with a tight voice. "Look at Daddy. He didn't get married until he was over thirty. I've got a way to go."

Eva's face darkened briefly. Then, sprightly again, she said, "You're right, dear. Finish medical school first."

Sammy squeezed Jamaica's hand under the table. She pushed her chair away and excused herself. Sammy started to follow. Eva waved at him to stay put. The Vilnars and Muncy chattered vigorously in Hungarian. Eva winked at Sammy.

"She'll be out in a couple of minutes," Eva said. "I don't know where these moods come from."

"You're telling me," Sammy said. "I guess it's best just to let them pass."

"Absolutely," Eva agreed.

"So," said Sammy, turning to Geneva. "How's medical school?"

Her shyness dropped as she told him about the first time she had dissected a cadaver, how surprised she was at her ability to calmly slice into human carcasses. By the time Jamaica returned to the table, Sammy and Geneva were engaged in a spirited discussion of structures—human and architectural.

Later, after dessert, Sammy called his parents from Eva's bedroom to wish them a happy Thanksgiving. Jamaica paused outside the door and listened.

". . . I'm having a great time. It's wonderful here. They're so warm and . . . yep. Turkey, dressing, the works. I feel right at home. They're just like us."

Sammy wasn't going for irony. He was simply telling his mother what she wanted to hear and what he wanted to believe. He didn't realize then the task he was undertaking, trying to nurture Jamaica. He couldn't see himself ten years later, still trying to revive her, to convince her that she wasn't a dismal failure.

Shortly after Jamaica returned from Connecticut, the *New York Times* reported a footnote to the Atlas Foundation's experiment with welfare mothers. Jamaica was buried deep in Section B of the Sunday paper, studying the wedding announcements and brief concert reviews, when she noticed the headline: "Program Succeeds in Curbing Pregnancies, but Effects Wear Off After a Year."

She pushed her way through the article's hefty crop of statistics. While the foundation paid the girls to come to classes, 75 percent stayed in school, compared with 51 percent of the control group, she read. In comparisons made after the foundation cut off funds, however, the two groups had the same number of unwanted pregnancies and the same number of high school dropouts. Mindy Airendale was quoted as saying a longer program was needed, more research was required.

Jamaica called Miss Green to see if the social worker could tell her anything about Lonnie. Miss Green, she was told, had left the agency. She was working at Citibank.

Though Jamaica continued to work, the cumulative effect of the Holocaust story and welfare mother piece had been to drive her into a kind of permanent depression. Her face was pinched; her hip bones spiked Sammy when she clung to him at night. She read and reread *The War Against the Jews,* and rejected Sammy's suggestion that she see a psychiatrist. Geneva's shrink, she explained, was already trying to ruin their happy childhood. Sammy pretended there was nothing unusual going on when he overheard her confirming reservations she'd made on flights to Sydney, Tokyo, Rome.

He took action, though, the day he came home and found her curled up in the bottom of a closet, hidden behind the long winter coats. She'd spent the day there, taking refuge much the way she had done when she was a child and her parents would fight.

Those fights were horrible, thunderous affairs. She remembered her father coming in from the office and asking her mother something in Hungarian. Within minutes, a stream of words would be flying back and forth, all incomprehensible except for the odd Hungarian word Jamaica understood, or the bits of English her parents tossed in for flavor.

Shuddering in the dark, she'd hear a long burst of babble, punctuated by "hospital!" or "the girls" or "Where were you?" One day the door burst open and her father unwittingly yanked her out of the closet; she'd been clutching the bottom of his wool coat.

His eyebrows drawn together fearsomely, he looked as though he might hit her. Then he leaned over and asked, gently, "Why are you on the floor?"

"I'm sorry, Daddy," Jamaica cried.

His eyes misted over. "You have nothing to feel sorry for. Come here." He pulled her up off the floor and hugged her.

"Jamaica, get out of that closet." Sammy's tone indicated that he'd had enough. He walked away and left her sitting there.

The next morning, as he leafed through the paper, Sammy asked casually: "Say, Jamaica, did you ever hear from Jules Marlin again? I haven't heard you mention him in awhile."

"He's a jerk." She didn't look up from her book. "Did you know that in 1939 there were 90,000 Jews in Bohemia and Moravia and that only 10,000 survived? It was worse in Slovakia. Only 10,000 left out of 135,000."

A few minutes later she raised her head suspiciously. "Why?"

"I dunno. I thought maybe it would be fun for you to do a piece on inveterate letter writers, people like Jules who get their jollies jerking off in newspapers. I've always wondered about it myself."

Jamaica tilted her head, a sure sign that she was interested. "That's a dumb idea," she growled.

"Just an idea," Sammy said. He gave her a big, dimpled smile, as though he could tell he'd hooked her.

Jamaica put her book down. "Would you like to go to the movies?"

Before they left, Sammy pulled out their new ladder and put *The War Against the Jews* on the highest shelf.

9

Keep It Light

"Good morning, Joanne." Jamaica cheerily settled in her cubicle, affectionately referred to by management as her "work station."

"Jamaica?"

"Who'd you think it was, the tooth fairy?"

"Well, yes. You haven't exactly been Miss Personality around here the last few weeks. I've missed you, when I haven't been mad at you."

This conversation took place through the cloth partition that separated the two young women's work stations, which had been designed to permit the free passage of the smallest whisper while blocking all light and air. This arrangement gave the newsroom the appearance of a rabbit warren, dark and filled with unconnected rustling sounds.

Mottled gray carpet, mauve walls, and dim fluorescent lights created a "work environment" so purposefully monotonous that in contrast their work could only seem exciting and meaningful. The offices had been designed for the large insurance company that had occupied the building before the newspaper moved uptown, and management had been too cheap and insensitive to redecorate. Instead of hiding this embarrassment—after all, did anyone publicly discuss the publisher's unfortunate toupee?—company officials brazenly discussed it in their annual report to stockholders. Under glossy photographs of wood-grained Formica tables and stiff metal chairs standing cool and functional in the middle of cubicles formed by short, collapsible walls, the caption explained: "The newsroom of tomorrow is at the *Observer* today." The text cited psychological studies extolling the benefits of the desensitized workplace.

"Lunch?"

"Great. Twelve-thirtyish?"

Jamaica surveyed her office and its evidence of her accumulated gloom. Weeks had gone by since she'd thrown away a newspaper or a press release. There were piles of black-and-white glossies, many of them autographed, and print-outs of the silly little interview pieces she'd been producing almost by rote. She dug out the giant trash bags the cleaning women had rather unsubtly been leaving on her desk and began to clean up, pausing only to transmit a note to Henry by computer:

Henry,

A story suggestion: Ever wondered about who the people are who write to newspapers? I don't mean the occasional letter writer, the once-in-a-dozen-years guy with a specific beef about something. I'm talking about the folks who are virtually unpaid columnists.

The story would take a look at who these people are and why they do what they do. I'd round up the usual gang of suspects—the shrinks and the sociologists, of course, for a take on what this says about us as a society, media overload, and all that. What do you think?

Cheers,
Just, Jamaica

By lunch time, her office was tidy. Her mother would have been proud of her. Eva was a stickler for accomplishment, although her definition of it often confused her daughters. Cleaning their room always elicited praise; the straight A's they brought home drew a blank. Though Eva was herself an astute businesswoman and hardly a conventional homebody, she wanted tangible evidence that her girls could succeed at everyday life. The rest she took for granted. So Geneva, a rising young cardiac specialist, hadn't accomplished anything significant, her mother felt, because she wasn't married. Jamaica, however, had accomplished Sammy.

"I'm kind of sympathetic to your mother's point of view," Joanne said as they waited for their grilled Swiss on rye at the Sunset Coffee Shop. This restaurant, situated below ground midway between the street and the subway, was Jamaica's favorite. Throughout lunch she could feel the comforting rumble of the trains.

Joanne was continually debating whether to marry the man she'd been involved with for six years. Their relationship had to be described in this awkward way because they kept separate apartments, were free to date other people, yet maintained a scheduled form of fidelity. Mondays, Wednesdays, and weekends were reserved for each other, with time off on Tuesdays and Thursdays.

Jamaica was slightly awed by Joanne's assortment of casual lovers and her endless self-analysis. Joanne's father was a professor who did consulting on the side, which allowed him to raise his children in an atmosphere of academic rigor and upper-middle-class comfort. Joanne was equally conversant in Yeats and Ann Taylor. Jamaica admired that, too, since her own clothes never quite fit. Everything seemed to stretch out of shape the minute she put it on. Sleeves drooped over her hands, shirts bunched in the middle where belts fruitlessly grasped at saggy waistlines. Sammy's mother kept sending her packages of trim, tailored things—"funny little shirts," Mrs. Fein called them—with good labels sewn in the back. Jamaica kept these packages stacked on the top shelves in the closet, to keep them neat until the Feins came to visit. Worse, strangers were always rumpling her hair. This especially horrified Jamaica, who didn't like to be touched by anyone she didn't trust, and, despite appearances, she was stingy with that trust.

"I feel guilty about Matthew," Joanne said. "He's faithful, good and true, boring. You're lucky to have Sammy, to be so devoted." The source of Joanne's guilt this time was an editor she'd met at a publishing convention the week before.

"C'mon, Joanne. In the parking lot?" Jamaica wouldn't have believed it if she hadn't known that Joanne had had sex on an airplane. Joanne wasn't a locker-room Larry, exactly; she'd told about the airplane only after Jamaica had run into her cubicle one day to read a juicy passage from a pulp novel she was reading.

"I mean, c'mon, Joanne, do you know anyone in real life who's done it on an airplane?" Jamaica had asked, incredulously.

"Yes, Jamaica, I do. Me. And I'll tell you why," Joanne had said. "I figure I'm already thirty and I could die in fifteen years, breast cancer or something. That's my philosophy of life."

Jamaica didn't have a philosophy of life. She improvised. At one time or another, she had ruined almost every one of her favorite books and movies by imagining new endings. After Scarlett murmured, "Tomorrow is another day," she'd have a fadeout of Rhett and Scarlett dreamily wandering across Tara, arm in arm, as the credits roll. Ingrid and Humphrey would be sipping champagne on the Champs-Elysée. Ethan Frome's wife would have died and Mattie would be miraculously cured. Peachy and Danny, in *The Man Who Would Be King*, would escape with a couple of rubies, or maybe rule forever. Charlotte

Brontë had cheated, hadn't she, in a burst of empathy over artistry? Didn't she allow Mr. Rochester to see again?

"So tell me, Jamaica. Have you ever imagined Sammy dying? I mean, that you just walk in the door one day and boom. Sammy's dead? I often imagine that scene with Matthew, and you know what really bothers me? It doesn't bother me at all. I just step over his poor dead body, gather my things, and go home."

Jamaica had never imagined Sammy dead. Sometimes she had a hard time imagining him at all. It wasn't that she didn't love him. She did. Their marriage was perfect. Everybody said so. They worked hard, saved the money they didn't spend on the ballet, theater, movies, charity, and dinner, and treated each other with respect and tenderness. They managed to feel genuinely astonished each year at the surprise birthday parties they threw for each other. Sammy had answers for all of Jamaica's questions except the ones she couldn't ask anyone, not even herself—especially not herself.

"Of course not. Maybe you and Matthew should break up."

"Of course we should break up. That isn't the point."

These lunches with Joanne inevitably left Jamaica with the unpleasant task of considering her own relations with men. Instead, she told Joanne about her letter-writers idea, and Joanne suggested she go see Sherley Thompson, who handled the *Observer*'s letters page.

After lunch Jamaica wandered down to the letters department. It was odd that in the six years she'd worked at the paper, she had never gotten off the elevator at three, or bothered to find out who it was who sent her photocopies of the letters to the editor that came in response to her stories. She was usually so careful about these things, the protocol of making everyone feel warm and loved. It was the least she could do.

"Well, hello there, Miss Justice for All," the guard said, winking at her.

"Oh, hello there." She was disturbed that she didn't know his name. Unwittingly, she practiced reverse snobbery, remembering the name and marital status of secretaries and security guards all over the city, forgetting those of bank presidents and movie producers. Her selective memory loss was genuine; she was forever introducing herself for the fifth or sixth time to people who knew quite well who she was, if for no other reason than that they'd met her so many times before.

"I'm looking for Sherley Thompson," Jamaica said.

"Go right on back through that hall, there, Miss Justice," the guard said, howling at his own cleverness.

A cadaverous creature, his face drained of color except for his unnaturally bright red lips, sat hunched over the desk in the office marked S. Thompson. He started when Jamaica stuck her head in the door.

"Excuse me. Is Ms. Thompson here?" she asked.

"Why, my pretty darling, I am Sherley Thompson," this waxwork phantom said as he lifted himself to a half-bow. "My mother was English, you know, and she adored the name Shirley for some odd reason and decided to bestow the name on her daughter. Well, she had me instead, and so I became Sherley with an *e* instead of an *i*. Isn't that peculiar? And who, may I ask, are you?"

"I work upstairs in the news department. I do features."

"Your name, my dear," said Sherley, who had clasped her hand with his two clammy ones. He had walked around the desk, offering her a full view of his white-cuffed paisley shirt, the likes of which Jamaica hadn't seen since junior high school. In fact, his entire look was Sixties Mod, right down to his silver Beatles haircut.

"Jamaica Just."

"Ooh," he squealed. "Why, Jamaica Just, I adore your columns. You have such a refreshing approach to things, as you seem to understand the great joke life is playing on all of us."

His round eyes grew rounder. "Most of you news people are so dreadfully solemn, you know. That's why I stay off the newsroom floor. I can't remember the last time I was up on seven. Oh, my dear, not since I started working here . . . oh, my dear, I can't . . . ten—can you believe it?—ten years ago. I was in the theater myself, but I had this slight operation"—he waved at the air around his head—"and lost my coordination."

"Oh, I'm so sorry," Jamaica said, as she tried to pull loose from Sherley, who still grasped her hand tightly with his nongesticulating fingers.

"Don't be alarmed, my dear. It's nothing, really nothing t'all. Why, look at me. I'm fit as a fiddle-dee-dee." He tossed her hand aside and began to shuffle around the room, humming in a thin, quavery voice. He seemed unnerved yet exhilarated by the arrival of his unexpected guest.

Sherley's breath came in such fierce bursts his brittle skin seemed in danger of cracking open. He and Jamaica stood listening to the rasp of Sherley's wind, the thump of his pixilated heart. She hoped this strange little man wasn't dying.

Sherley held up his hand, indicating he was all right. "Excuse me if I seem a bit overexcited, my dear," he said. "I don't get many visitors. I'm *so* glad to see you here!" Without warning, he pressed his face up close to hers and spread his lips, plump and drippy as a split tomato, across her cheek. Jamaica's shoulder involuntarily jerked up to wipe her face dry.

"Well, then, is there something I can help you with?" Sherley dragged himself back behind his desk.

Jamaica couldn't quite look him in the eye either. Luckily, her right eye was crossed ever so slightly. Besides endowing her with the perpetually quizzical expression that was useful to her as a reporter, her wandering eye allowed her to stare at people's noses while giving the impression that she was looking directly into their eyes with great sincerity.

She began with a rush of words. "I have this idea for a story. Actually, it was my husband, Sammy's, idea. Anyway, it's not really an official idea yet because I haven't discussed it with Henry, yet, Henry Frank. You know him? He's my editor. He's got me running around doing half-assed 'portraits of power,' he likes to call them. I go in and talk to some movie director or politician for a couple of hours and then write something deep and insightful and utterly ridiculous about who they really are in twenty-seven inches or less."

"Um, yes, of course, I see," Sherley said sympathetically, fingering his bow tie. "It's much the same in my line of work. I try so hard to choose just the right sorts of letters to run in the paper, a mixture of serious commentary and amusing observations. So often I find myself being criticized for not tipping the balance toward well-known authors, when clearly they are the most tiresome with their self-important blather."

"Exactly my point," Jamaica said triumphantly. "Who are the most intriguing correspondents? The people who have no reason to write at all. No obvious reason, I mean. The ones who aren't grabbing power like politicians or grubbing for money or fame like journalists. They are humanity, the collective spirit, Everyman, Everywoman."

Though Jamaica wasn't quite sure what she was saying, she liked the sound of it. She turned up the volume. "They are the ones who teach us about who we are, where we come from, where we are going. They are the best of us and the worst of us. They will set us free."

Sherley looked baffled. "I see."

Jamaica realized she hadn't told him her idea yet. "So what do you think about an article about who these people are? The chronic letter writers. I thought maybe you might have noticed a pattern."

A faint trace of pink broke through Sherley's pallor.

"Marvelous, marvelous. Permit me to help you. I have been preparing for this moment for quite a while, although I didn't know precisely what form it would take."

He puckered his glistening lips at Jamaica. "And what a lovely form it is. Oh, this is grand."

"Where do we start?"

"Why, my dear, just look around you."

Jamaica had been so transfixed by Sherley, she hadn't bothered to notice his surroundings. In general, she found scenery distracting and was forever having to telephone people she'd just interviewed to ask them the color of their hair, whether their eyes were steely blue or warm and brown, what was the shade of the suit they had been wearing (although she could never understand why it mattered whether pinstripes were gray or navy). The copy desk, however, wanted to know. The nitpickers never asked whether someone's mouth was cruel or if the interview subject kept his finger jammed up his nose. When she included this pertinent information, it was always deleted.

She had simply assumed that Sherley's office looked like all the others in this building. She'd become inured to the grand blandness of the place; she never bothered to glance around once she stepped inside the building.

The walls of Sherley's office were lined floor to ceiling with white filing cabinets, dozens of them. They were nondescript, like all the "contemporary" office furniture the company supplied. What did Sherley expect her to see in these metal boxes? They had no oak, no finely wrought latches, no hints of crinkly pieces of parchment containing the key to lost treasures or disappointed dreams, no little boxes filled with perfumed letters or long-hidden diaries.

"Very nice," Jamaica said glumly, after a brief look around. "It was nice meeting you, Mr. Thompson."

"Don't you want to take a look at what I've got here?" Sherley asked.

"What have you got here?" Jamaica was getting snitty with impatience.

He started to get up from his chair and sank back down. "I'm feeling a bit fatigued, my dear. Why don't you open a few drawers and then I'll explain my system to you."

Jamaica walked over to a cabinet and pulled open a drawer. It was stuffed with folders packed tight with pieces of paper of all sizes and colors.

"Go on, pull out a folder, but mind where the place is," Sherley said, smiling slightly.

"No, wait, don't choose from that drawer." He paused and looked around the room, waving at different cabinets as though ticking things off on some mental checklist.

"Try that cabinet over there, the third—no, fourth—drawer, I believe."

Jamaica idly rubbed her hand along the cool, smooth surface of the cabinets as she walked by. She opened the drawer that Sherley had indicated.

"Do you see the little markers on the side of the folders? Look closely. I suspect you'll see the one I want you to take a look at."

Jamaica quickly flipped through the stack, reading off the names printed neatly, by hand, on the sides of the folders. They all seemed familiar. "Jackson, Jannsen, Jergens, Jenson—whoops, that one's out of order—Jihan, Jolson, Jottney, Julmeyer, Just. Just?"

"That's your file, my dear. Those are all the letters to the editor we've gotten on your stories. Four years' worth."

"I thought I always got all the letters from my stories. I'd always get them in interoffice mail packets. But I never knew about you. There would just be these unsigned notes: 'Thought you might be interested in these.'"

"You get the letters I decide you should get," Sherley said. "Don't look upset. It's my job to decide what gets printed in the letters column and what doesn't. After that, I can do what I want with the letters— burn them, build a squadron of paper airplanes, turn them into landfill.

"I disapprove of waste, you see, particularly the waste of history. It's so fleeting, isn't it? Most of us don't have very much of it, although there are those, I suppose, who have more of it than they know what to do with. It seems to me you can appreciate that, my dear."

"Does management know about your system?" Jamaica asked.

"Oh, dear, no. They have no idea. But no one bothers with me so long as I keep the letters column filled. Every now and again I requisition a new cabinet from purchasing and a few weeks later one shows up outside my door. Generally, I'm left quite alone to go about my business."

"This is amazing." Jamaica ran her fingers across the tops of the letters in her file. "It'll be pretty hard for me to figure out who the regulars are though, won't it?"

Not at all, my dear. I've unwittingly been your errand boy." Sherley giggled a bit. "You see, these files over here are the by-line files, the ones I've set up for the paper's reporters. Over there are the files for outside contributors—regular free-lancers and people who write for the opinion page. Over there are the unofficial regular contributors, the unacknowledged ladies and gentlemen of the press. They are a select crew, you know, because as you yourself have ascertained, they get nothing out of their endeavor in the ordinary sense."

"You wouldn't by any chance recognize the name Jules Marlin, would you?"

"Ah, Mr. Marlin, of course! A great favorite of mine. He's a fan of yours, I've noticed, although he doesn't like you quite as much as he detests Archie Cornwall, if one measures emotional depth by the number of lines written." Archie Cornwall was the paper's resident "radical." His politics were hardly revolutionary but seemed so when compared with the libertarian *Observer*'s reactionary editorial policy.

"Who else is there?" Jamaica could barely contain her excitement. She was experiencing firsthand the phenomenon of the lucky reporter. This is the cub who covers for the poor schmuck who's been diligently attending school board meetings for fifteen years, week after somnolent week, listening to endless debates on whether or not to retile the art department, on new libraries versus new gyms. One night, the first time in those fifteen years, the regular reporter calls in sick and the cub is sent in. This is the night some drugged-out kid, enraged because he was cut from the football team, pulls out a gun and blows away the school principal, right there at the meeting. For the first time anyone can remember, the school board meeting makes the front page. The cub is promoted to Metro, where he'll be the one on duty for the plane crash of the decade, for the prison break of the century, for the fire bombing that wipes out an entire neighborhood. Disaster follows him like a faithful dog and makes him famous.

"Well, there's quite a number of them. Do you have the time?"

Jamaica glanced at the tiny clock on Sherley's desk. "I'd better scoot pretty soon. Tell me a bit about them and I'll come back later." She sat down in the chair near Sherley's desk.

Sherley cleared his throat and pressed one hand against his head, as though conjuring up the spirits he had tucked away in his files. He began with Congressman Unglemeyer, the Bronx Democrat who sent a letter every single day. The congressman was aware that his drab and uninfluential district elected him because he represented it so well; he had long since ceased trying to speak in the House, knowing, as he did, that his speeches were considered a sure cure for insomnia. He sat on no important subcommittees. In a town infested with eager young politicos, he had to pay a premium for aides. It wasn't that he was disliked. He was simply boring. So he wrote long, chatty letters to the paper about what was up in Washington. They were dreadful things, full of misspellings and impossible sentence structure, but

Sherley, out of pity, would search for and snip out grammatical excerpts periodically and publish them in the letters column.

Then there was "Lt. Col. Alan Williams (Ret.)," formerly of the Air Force, now of the Sunset Retirement Home out on the Island, a specialist in military affairs and street crime, and Miss ("don't call me Ms.") Frances Walker of Greenwich Village, whose subjects were art subsidies, health care, and pornography. Jules Marlin required no elaboration. And, oh yes, Dr. Arthur Crightendon, the neurosurgeon with a carefully elucidated opinion on almost everything.

"Shall I go on?" asked Sherley, who was wheezing uncontrollably by then. He apologized, saying he couldn't remember the last time he had talked this much.

"No, no, I can see you need a rest. This is certainly enough for me to propose a story. I am curious about one thing, though. How did you happen to select these people?"

"Quite simple, my dear. As letters arrive here at the office, I divide them by topic. You know—nuclear war, abortion, landlords, Frank Sinatra, and so on. Periodically I go through all my files to discover repeat authors. When I collect a dozen or so from an individual within a year's time, I set up a separate file."

"Can I ask you one more question, and then I really must go?"

"Of course."

"Why do you do this?"

Sherley's pallid face with its girlish lips looked blank. "If I don't, my dear, who will?"

Later that day Henry gave Jamaica the go ahead, even though his enthusiasm for the piece could most favorably be described as muted. He explained to her that he was willing to coddle her on this one because she'd had a pretty rough few months, even if the anxiety she'd been dithering about was entirely of her own creation. He elaborated: her office was a fucking mess and she wasn't looking too terrific either. What was her problem? Most of his reporters were dying for a little attention. Who cared what kind of response your stories got, as long as they got a response, shook people up a little? Her biggest failing as a journalist (and as a functioning human being, she could see he was thinking) was her insistence on taking everything so personally. Enthusiasm was fine, but her job, for God's sake, was to write stories, not to live them. Luckily, she was pulled together enough, or glued together enough by that husband of hers, to keep cranking 'em out. He wouldn't like to have to fire her.

Jamaica listened to Henry's little speech impassively. She couldn't figure out why the thought of pink-slipping her, or anyone, would disturb the imperturbable Henry. Maybe she underestimated him. Or maybe Henry still remembered his confession to her years back about the woman he'd left alone with her unwanted pregnancy. Maybe even Henry hadn't rid himself of all guilt.

Her first stop for this story was Miss ("don't call me Ms.") Frances Walker. The foyer of the slightly seedy tenement was dimly lit. Jamaica could barely read the names scrawled on the bits of paper taped by the buzzers. She felt queasy, the way she always did before an interview. It was all so presumptuous, this business of playing the snoop-cum-sociologist, legitimizing her nosiness by transforming it into pop profundity. What was the name of that young woman who'd scored big headlines, gotten onto TV talk shows by disclosing that the man she'd successfully accused of raping her seven years earlier was innocent? Instant oblivion followed instant celebrity, and what had any of it meant?

"Journalism is history on the run," she'd dutifully scribbled in a notebook once. Journalists were no longer the fleet-footed historians her professor had been talking about; where could you find anyone comparable to a Liebling or a Rebecca West? If Hunter Thompson and Tom Wolfe had once seemed egocentric iconoclasts with their personal, gonzo style, they were still writing about *somebody else*. Television had put an end to that. The reporters weren't mere observers anymore, they were participants. They had become the stars in the improvisational theater of life.

If Miss Walker had any qualms about subjecting herself to probing questions, she masked them well. The thin, quavery voice that had invited Jamaica for tea seemed quite unshaken by her request for an interview, as though Miss Walker routinely took telephone calls from reporters. Why shouldn't she feel that way? Look at the dozens of magazines piled up at newsstands, listen to all-news radio, look at events passing by twenty-four hours a day on cable TV. Ordinary lives did appear to be interviews waiting to happen. Perhaps Miss Frances Walker would consider dying without having been interviewed a mistake, a cruel joke. Perhaps life had become so incomprehensible that it needed to be explained all the time, every minute of the day. Or had it become so confusing because it was always being explained?

Miss Walker hadn't even inquired as to what the story would be about. It was enough for her that Jamaica said she was interested in some of the views Miss Walker presented in her letters to the editor.

What seemed like several minutes passed before Jamaica's buzz was answered. She identified herself, although she wasn't quite sure if that's what the garbled voice crackling through the ancient speaker phone wanted to know. A sharp, piercing noise unlatched the front door. She entered the building.

Peering into the dark hallway, she saw the stairway. Miss Walker had warned her the building had no elevators and she lived on the fourth floor. "Oh, no problem," Jamaica had gurgled in her cheeriest voice. "My husband and I live on the fif—"

"I'll see you at four o'clock on Tuesday," Miss Walker had interrupted.

A surprise greeted Jamaica when the door to 4A creaked open. There was a small, elderly woman, limbs awry, slumped in a wheelchair. Her legs hung like wooden sticks from her plumpish torso, her twisted right arm fluttered in the air as she reeled it in from its excursion to the doorknob. Behind thick, black-rimmed glasses a pair of striking violet eyes gazed at the visitor.

"Miss Walker?"

"I certainly am. And you are Miss Just, I imagine."

Jamaica quickly reached forward to grasp the hand making its uncertain way toward her. Miss Walker held on while her sturdier left hand wheeled her chair backward, drawing Jamaica into the room. Drafts blew through the cramped quarters, spreading around the smell of violet sachets and unwashed linens. There was a clear passageway from the door to the cot in the corner. Another led toward the back, where, to judge from the odorous currents, there was a bathroom. The passageways, just wide enough for the wheelchair, were carved from between piles of newspapers and magazines, and the dozens of little lacquered boxes that were strewn about.

A small television set rested on a low table by the cot. A pot of tea, two cups and saucers, and a plate of broken shortbread cookies had been arranged on a tray balanced on top of the TV. Some light leaked in from behind the one window's drawn blind. Most of those faint rays were absorbed by the apartment's murky green walls. As Jamaica's eyes adjusted to the dimness, she could make out dozens of drawings taped to the walls. Most were tiny etchings of miniature flowers and insects.

"You didn't have to bother." Jamaica nodded toward the tray.

"I invited you to tea, Miss Just. The girl arranged things before she left for the day."

"The girl?"

"The young black woman the city sends over to help me out. As you can see, I have some difficulty getting arou—organizing things."

Jamaica walked over to examine the etchings on the wall. "These are amazing! Where did you get them?"

Miss Walker wheeled over. "I did them, before I got the disease. My hands are too unsteady now. You really like them?"

"Very much." Jamaica was fascinated by the painstakingly crafted renditions of tiny cockroaches, minuscule azaleas.

"I used to display them every year at the Washington Square art show. I had my little booth set up and had a loyal following." She laughed. "Of course, there wasn't a lot of demand for these little fellows, but oh, my, I had a wonderful time with them.

"That's been the worst part of this MS. The way I slur my words is bad enough—"

"No." Jamaica interrupted.

Miss Walker jerked her hand in the air impatiently. "My hearing is fine. I slur my words. But I miss my art, and I miss going out, and the damn—pardon my French—city bureaucracy won't do a thing. That's when I started writing to the papers, I figured I'd get some results that way."

Jamaica interrupted again. "Do you mind if I take out my notebook?"

Miss Walker talked nonstop all afternoon, and Jamaica listened. Afterward, she hurried back to the office, as though her notes would spoil if they weren't immediately transferred into her computer.

An unexpected voice startled her.

"How's it going, babe?"

Periodically, Henry dropped by the newsroom to demonstrate his concern for his reporters. These brief, unscheduled appearances always left him feeling warmly self-satisfied because they required a great deal of effort. Nothing had pleased him more than the installation of the computer system that had put a stop to most human contact, setting things into neatly impersonal order.

"Great, Henry. I think this is going to be a great story. I had my first interview today with this amazing lady, Miss Frances Walker. She's incredible. She's all fired up about what's going on in the world, and there she is with multiple sclerosis, hasn't left her apartment in eight years, since she was sentenced to wheelchair confinement. And—"

"That's nice, dear. Sounds good. Do me a favor, though. Do yourself a favor. Don't get too involved with these people. I don't envision this piece as a downer. Keep it light."

Henry patted Jamaica on the head and winked.

Jamaica smiled sweetly. "You asshole," she thought.

However, Jamaica, too, wanted to keep it light. This time she was not going to delude herself into thinking that a story was anything more than just a story. She wasn't going to take it personally. If a sketch of the Miss Walkers and Dr. Crightendons of the world added a little perspective, or offered a small diversion to the readers of the *Observer*—whoever they were—that would be enough. No matter what she wrote, she wouldn't make Miss Walker ambulatory again, or cure Jules Marlin's loneliness. In turn, they wouldn't help her right the world's wrongs, or even understand them.

To keep her distance, she arranged to meet Sherley's cast of characters one by one in a series of lengthy but contained interviews. In other words, she wanted enough time with each subject (better to think of them in clinical terms) to jot down the pertinent details and to make them comfortable enough to reveal the source of their need for public expression. All she wanted to know was this: how did they remain engaged in this aimless era? Were they the last civilized voices left on earth, or were they bonkers, one foot out the door onto the street with the rest of the wigged-out mutterers, the loony-tune protesters?

10

The Field Correspondent

She called Jules Marlin the day it was reported that Josef Mengele's moldering bones had been exhumed in Brazil. To her surprise, Jamaica wasn't relieved to hear that Mengele might be dead. For years she'd followed the pursuit of Auschwitz's traffic cop of death, the man who had made sure no gridlock fouled up the steady march to the gas chambers. Only now she realized that Mengele had become the crusading Jew's best friend. An enemy in the flesh was far easier to hate than the goose-stepping ghosts preserved on film.

Finished with the distressing details—the convincing dental records, the X-rayed proof that the skull and cross-bones belonged to the bad doctor—Jamaica set the paper aside and dialed the number she'd pinned to the cloth surface of her little cubicle. There was no one left to call on her list, except for the shrinks, and she didn't need them until the end. They were merely wrapping paper. Her notebook was filled with colorful detail and vivid examples of compulsive letter writers, whose similarities and differences she hadn't begun to analyze. She'd listened politely to letter-writing hobbyists and to fire-breathing proselytizers; to people barely eking out a living and to fat cats; to the overeducated and to the barely literate. Because these were people desperate to be heard, she listened to things she didn't want to hear. It was as though her notebook were a confessional and she'd met up with a busload of devout Catholics who hadn't unloaded in weeks. Tales of adultery mixed with harangues at the national debt; blacks hate whites, whites hate blacks, and everyone fears the Japanese. Jamaica scribbled and traveled, by train to Long Island, by bus to New Jersey, by subway everywhere else. Henry was asking for the story already, and she still hadn't called Jules. Mengele was dead.

Maybe.

The telephone rang five, six times. Finally, just as she was about to hang up, relieved, someone picked up.

"H'lo." The voice was gruff and suspicious.

"Hi. May I speak to Jules Marlin, please?"

"I . . . he don't want no magazines, no insurance. None of that stuff. He's very busy."

"No, I'm not calling to sell him subscriptions to anything. I want to talk to him."

"Who is this?"

"My name is Jamaica Just. I'm a reporter for the *Observer* and—"

"Well, now, a reporter. Jamaica Just. How about that? Did you ever get that letter I mailed you? You wrote some nice articles there. Real nice. What can I do for you?"

"Is this Mr. Marlin?"

"Who did you think it was? Where did you get my number? Out of the phone book? Where are you? Manhattan? Wait a second. I'll go turn the TV down a little. The connection must be bad. I don't hear you so good."

Jamaica waited. The cuticles on all the fingers on her left hand were bitten bloody, her leg was shaking so violently her computer terminal was vibrating. She felt giddy, as though the cracked voice muttering at her in a strange blend of Eastern Europe and western Queens belonged to a prospective lover, not an old man she knew was probably unbalanced.

"Miss Just? How can I help you out? I'm not a movie star or a welfare cheat." A chuckle accompanied these gentle digs, so Jamaica plunged ahead.

"I'm sorry I never got back to you. Your letter . . . Usually I respond to everyone who writes, but I was so busy and—well, never mind. I was wondering if you had time to meet for an interview for a story I'm doing about people who are news junkies (she remembered he'd described himself that way once, in one of his letters)."

"Oh yeah?" His tone brightened. "I figure I'm a news junkie, all right. It isn't bad for my health. I could take drugs or cigarettes." His voice was wonderfully expressive, lacking any vestige of subtlety or the falseness born of overcultivated manners. Now there was an unmistable darkening. "Cigarettes. You don't smoke do you? You sound clean."

"Oh, no, I don't smoke, Mr. Marlin. I never have. When I was five I ate a package of cigarettes and then I threw up and—"

"Good, you don't smoke. Smart girl."

"So. Were you glad to hear about Mengele?"

"Why should I feel glad? Of course that wasn't him."

"But the dental records, the doctors."

"Look." The voice was now registering exasperation. "The heat got too tough so they had to make up some story about him dying. You think those Nazi bastards are stupid? They want us to let things lie, forget about punishment. I figure we were getting too close to him, so they came up with this story, a bag of bones."

"Right, yes. You could have something there."

"Of course I have something there. I know the way those bastards think."

"Yes. Of course. Do you think you might have time for a chat? About the news, I mean. The letters you write to the papers."

"Let me see what I'm doing. Where do you want to talk to me? In person?"

"I think so. It's much easier, don't you think? I could come out there, if that's more convenient for you."

There was a long pause.

"Maybe I'll come into Manhattan. I haven't been to the city in a long time, when I used to go down to Fifty-second Street to Roseland to the dances. You know Roseland?"

"Fine. Would you like to have lunch, or dinner? What would be best?"

Jules shuddered as an uncontrollable desire for companionship came over him. "Do you know the Hungarians?"

"Pardon?"

"The Hungarians. The restaurant up on Third Avenue in the Seventies."

"The Red Violin?"

"Yeah, that's the one. You ever been there?"

"Not in a very long time," Jamaica said slowly.

"Can we meet there, maybe on Sunday?"

"I'm going away for the weekend, to my mother's house. How about next Tuesday? At seven? I'll make a reservation under Just."

"Thank you very much, Miss Just. Bye."

As Jamaica put the phone back in its cradle, she felt the urge to go home, to her mother.

That weekend, as they often did on sunny summer weekends, Sammy and Jamaica visited Eva in Connecticut. They would wake up on warm Saturday and Sunday mornings to the smell of onions simmering, the same smell that had greeted Jamaica and Geneva early every morning of their childhood. Onions were the basic grammar of Eva's cooking, as necessary, she felt, as nouns and verbs were to a sentence. The rest was modification.

Back in Harmony, all life eventually spiraled back to the kitchen. That was where the Just family convened nightly at five-thirty for dinner, which had to be consumed by six o'clock so Dr. Just could get back to his patients. There was nothing relaxing or soothing about the preparation of dinner at the Justs'. It more resembled a form of guerrilla warfare, a hastily put-together military operation. Generally, the only thing that was ready at five were the onions that had been prepared in the morning. Eva would screech into the kitchen and begin opening, stirring, pouring, and salting. "I must be in love," she'd giggle, serving her thirsty family their oversalted dinner. (In her endless lexicon of axioms, salt was a sign of love, as well as something to throw over one's shoulder to prevent a *nehora*, Eva's variation on the Yiddish *kineahora,* a magical phrase chanted to ward off the evil eye. According to Eva, a *nehora* was a jinx born of overoptimism, of forecasting sun on a day scheduled for the beach, or declaring—instead of hoping or praying—that Geneva would marry the man she was dating this month. *Nehoras* could be offset in a variety of ways: throwing salt over the shoulder, knocking on wood, spitting three times—a nasty preventative that had been modified. It was permissible merely to mutter, "Puh. Puh. Puh.")

By the time she'd finished, pots and pans and containers of Morton's salt were scattered across the counter, where globs of paprika matted into the liquid that had dripped from exposed chicken carcasses and their sticky brown wrapping paper. Jamaica and Geneva would pause from setting the table to watch with fascination as their mother charged around the kitchen with one eye on the clock. Promptness was absolutely necessary. If evening office hours started late, they'd go beyond eleven and Dr. Just would miss the final edition of the news.

No matter what the weather, Mrs. Just would present her family with great rolls of cabbage stuffed with rice and chopped meat, enormous dumplings embroidered with fried bits of bread, goulash, paprikash, all of it meant to stoke the fires of hungry peasants on a cold winter's day. She served these vast, leaden platters on July evenings, when people in Harmony sweltered on their porches and muttered, "It ain't the heat, it's the humidity."

After her children bravely gulped down what their mother gave them but refused seconds, she would ask, looking gravely disappointed, "Don't you like it?"

"Oh, it was wonderful, Mommy, the best. Let's have it again tomorrow."

After her husband died, Eva salted less.

Indeed, the dinner she prepared for Sammy and Jamaica's arrival that weekend after Mengele allegedly was unearthed was almost bland.

Late Saturday morning, Jamaica and Eva sat on the lawn by the public tennis courts waiting for an opening. The courts lay in back of a baseball field and in front of a playground, yet Eva took care to dress appropriately in a flouncy white skirt and panties embossed with two pink tennis balls.

"Jamaica, dear, what happened to those nice shirts I gave you? When did you wash that T-shirt?"

"I'm saving it for a special occasion, Mom." They were both smiling. The sun was warm, the battle was old.

"Can I ask you something?"

"Of course, darling."

"What do you think about Mengele?" She smiled as she remembered Jules Marlin's tirade.

"About Mengele? He must have been very old now. He was a young man when I knew him. Good-looking. In his early thirties."

"You *knew* Mengele?"

"Well, yes. I was at Auschwitz, he was at Auschwitz. Everyone knew Mengele." Eva paused, and tilted her face toward the sun. "He saved my life."

"Hello?" Jamaica sucked in air.

"Yes, he saved my life. As we all came in from the trains to Auschwitz, Mengele decided who would live and who would go to the gas chamber. He saved my life."

"Yeah, but Mom, I guess you could say he killed your mother, then."

"That's right, dear. He saved my life and he killed my mother." Eva's tone was not much different than it had been a few minutes earlier, when she had told Jamaica about the trouble her friend Lucy's husband was having with his business, or than it would be later, when she would complain about her serve. It was what one might call a pensive tone, the voice of someone slightly bemused by the horrible details of the story she was hearing, even though she was the one delivering the news. Detached, yet involved, the field correspondent.

"But I didn't hate him for that. When I saw the way we had to live there, sleeping twelve women on a bunk, our heads shaved, I knew my mother would never survive. She was a lady. Climbing up and down into those bunks, the latrines, she couldn't have taken it. I was glad Mengele killed her right away. He did her a favor. I felt grateful to him."

Jamaica propped herself up on her elbow. The sun was scorching her cheeks and nose. Splotches of red and freckles erupted. She glanced aimlessly at the courts. A mother was patiently tossing balls across one net at her small son, who slammed every one of her gentle throws against the back fence. Two paunchy men were batting the ball steadily back and forth, right down the middle line, and discussing real estate. A young man and a young woman paused between every volley to meet at the net for a kiss. A pair of high school boys played a cutthroat game. A dog ran across the baseball field in the distance.

Her mother's voice seemed to float lightly through the baking air. "I didn't really hate him until later. He would come into our barracks for the *appel*. All of us would strip down and stand there while he examined us for signs of disease. There was a girl in my bunk who was from Just. She was there with her mother and her sister. Her name was Judy, and she was a beautiful girl with a fresh face. She reminded me of Maureen O'Sullivan when she used to play Jane in the Tarzan movies. Remember?" Eva tossed her daughter a small smile as she recalled the way Jamaica used to crawl up right next to the television set on Sunday afternoons when she was small and watch Tarzan movies very attentively. Jamaica raised an eyebrow. Eva looked skyward again.

"This girl was not just pretty, she was nice and so clean. After all the rest of would come in from the latrine, she would stay outside to give herself an extra wash. I remember watching her scrub herself so hard, as if she could wash away every particle of Auschwitz that clung to her. Hers was the only skin that still looked pink. The rest of us were gray or, God forbid, yellow." Eva inspected her own arm, broiled to a glossy bronze.

"Three days a week they gave us a pat of butter, margarine probably. Judy rubbed hers into her face. When one of the women yelled at her for wasting precious food, Judy looked at her and said, 'I'm preparing myself for when I leave this place. I want my skin to be smooth.'

"One day, Mengele came around to look us over. He stopped behind Judy. I remember her standing there like a statue, certain that nothing was wrong with her. In German, he said, 'This one has sores on her back. Move her out.' I understood him, although I pretended not to. As Judy walked past me, I looked at her back. There was a tiny rash, no bigger than the birthmark on your tushie." Eva jerked upright, jarring Jamaica.

"Come on, darling. There's an empty court. Let's go." The two women scrambled to their feet. Jamaica touched her fingertips to her mother's now toasty arm.

"What happened?"

Eva opened the swinging metal fence leading to the tennis courts and pulled the tab off the new can of balls she'd bought for Jamaica's visit. She squeezed one of the neon green balls, then bounced it on the brick red, year-round surface. She said: "Within a week after Judy was killed, her mother died and her sister went mad. That's when I started to hate Mengele."

11

Driving Lessons

Sammy and Jamaica had rented a car instead of taking the train that weekend. From time to time they liked the chance to listen to AM radio and to enjoy the sense of freedom a car allowed, though they rarely deviated from Interstate 95. Much as she loved being a passenger on the subway, Jamaica also loved to drive. They were entirely different adventures. One tested her resourcefulness, the other her control.

As she slid behind the wheel Sunday night, her muscles tensed in anticipation of forbidden thrills—reflexes left over from her hot rodding days. Those days were behind her, yet the mere acts of accelerating and braking, turning on the blinker, peering into the rearview mirror, all of it still had the tantalizing prohibitiveness of a furtive enterprise. The highway to Manhattan was crowded, but traffic moved steadily. Jamaica kept her left hand on the wheel and her right hand next to Sammy's on the seat. They listened to oldies but goodies on WABC.

"God, this music takes me back," said Sammy. "When you were a kid, did you and Geneva sit in the back seat and listen to the radio?"

"Oh, yes," said Jamaica. "We had some fine times in the car." She shook her head slowly. "Fine times."

For the longest time, the Justs had been the only one-car family in Harmony, or so it had seemed to Jamaica and Geneva when they were growing up. Everyone else's mother had some independent mode of transportation, a car or a pickup truck, except for the mother of their friends Sarah and Rebecca. She had epilepsy. The girls found it a matter of some embarrassment to see Eva walking the half-mile uptown on the cracked sidewalks that only kids used, and even then on bicycles. Eva strolled along in her high-heeled shoes, stopping to chat with the old ladies perched on their front porches. The main street of Harmony, the one on which she promenaded, was called Main Street. In those days the trees lining the street were kept neatly trimmed and the houses were all painted fresh and white. A kind of genteel shabbiness pervaded the town, which had never really seen better days. In a good year, unemployment dropped to 15 percent; when times got tough, which was almost always, nearly a third of Harmony's residents were on the dole.

The girls didn't understand why Eva didn't press Dr. Just for a car after they started to accumulate savings. This was in the sixties, when even rural folk with a healthy resistance to government interference, good or evil, signed up for Medicaid and Medicare. Suddenly a huge proportion of Dr. Just's previously nonpaying patients were able to cough up some cash. Even when it had become clear that President Johnson had made a dreadful mistake in Vietnam, the Just family would defend him. He'd helped the poor help themselves, and the Justs, too. Only once did the girls hear Eva suggest that Dr. Just let her keep his old car instead of trading in his custom-built Oldsmobile for a newer version of the same model. He looked at her sadly. "I'll take you wherever you want to go," he said with such hurt in his voice Eva never broached the subject again.

Instead, she arranged matters so that she could do the right thing, the practical thing, without upsetting her husband. She had her friends teach her on the sly. After Geneva was enrolled in grammar school, Eva would leave Jamaica with a stack of Golden Books and a big basket of lace doilies and Dr. Just's cotton broadcloth shirts—they required cuff links, their gleaming white elegance was frequently remarked on in Harmony—at the small clapboard house of a silent, birdlike old woman the girls knew only as "the lady who irons." For hours, Jamaica sat propped in an overstuffed forest green chair reading; across the small, overfurnished room, the lady who irons ironed. Eva would take off with Wilma or Ivy or Mabel for Cincinnati, which was two hours away, for shopping trips or the movies. "The girls," as she called them, were delighted to take part in any conspiracy designed to thwart the intentions—good or evil—of any one of their husbands. Although they were women in their thirties and the town's respectable matrons, they liked nothing better than to bomb around the county's perilous roads at reckless speeds, or to shuck their prim dresses and heels and put on shorts and halter tops and dance to Elvis Presley records until they were sweaty and giggly.

As Dr. Just's practice expanded, Eva had less time for these outings. She had taken over the office's business affairs, for which her husband was grateful. He always found excuses not to charge people for his services. Back in New York, he had refused to charge former residents of Just; once word circulated in the refugee community, his various practices were so laden with freebies it was no wonder they failed. In Harmony, his gratis list included ministers, teachers, and the families of his children's friends, whenever he found out who they were. When Eva took charge of billing, the matter was out of his hands. Money started coming in. With the government reimbursements, the paperwork became complicated. The family began eating every meal in the kitchen, face to face with the carnage of preparation, because the dining room never emerged from beneath the piles of forms that preoccupied Eva until well into the night.

If she had taken the time to think about it, Eva might have recognized her husband's paradoxical nature. His generosity was limitless, as though money meant nothing to him. (Although Eva was familiar with this expression, its meaning was almost incomprehensible to this daughter of successful merchants.) Dr. Just's quiet tenderness for his daughters, when he expressed it, never failed to move her. Every night, she'd lift her head from her paperwork to hear Dr. Just enter the girls' bedroom down the hall and listen to them murmur their prayers:

Now I lay me down to sleep, I pray the Lord my soul to keep. Guard me through the starry night and wake me safe with sunshine's light. God bless Mommy, Daddy, and Geneva (or Jamaica) too, and make all his kiddies honest and true. Amen.

"I love you, Daddy," the children would say, as their father bent down to kiss them good night, to tickle their feet.

Every morning, from the kitchen, Eva would gaze at his lovely back silhouetted against the filmy curtains draped across the glass pane of the living room door. He stood there, his hands clasped behind him, until he could no longer see a trace of his daughters as they walked, hand in hand, to school. Later, she would tell the girls how she longed to press her face against his white shirt and tell him he reminded her of Gregory Peck, he was that handsome, but she didn't dare. There were only a few things in life that Eva considered unapproachable. Her husband was one of them.

Periodically, black moods would overwhelm him, and in turn, the entire family. Deep silences or horrible rages would erupt over matters seemingly so small and inconsequential Eva couldn't even identify them. She spent a great deal of time trying to anticipate these tender areas so she could avoid having them irritated by her or by the children. This constant striving for peace, to keep the girls from accidentally enraging their father, often conflicted with her desire to help them grow up normally, or at least the same as other kids. In the children's eyes her unarticulated peace plan made their mother seem as unpredictable and irrational as their father. Geneva took the passive road. She simply acquiesced to all her parents' demands and soon became better at sidestepping arguments and scenes than Eva. For example, she never mentioned to her parents her brief religious conversion in high school. For a time, she considered herself a born-again Christian. She believed that she had been saved. She almost had no choice. Two of her best friends were ministers' children, and she would accompany them to revival meetings on Wednesday nights, telling her parents they were all studying together. Every night, she would add a silent prayer to the one she said aloud to her father, begging her Lord Jesus to forgive her parents for not recognizing the meaning of what they had suffered. These prayers would torment her later, after her father died and she had long since converted back to Judaism. Eventually, she rejected all organized religion.

There had been a great deal of unstated jealousy between Eva and her elder daughter, who had learned to pacify Dr. Just better than anyone else. While they were snapping beans or peeling potatoes, Eva in a confiding tone would tell Geneva about the "special relationship" she'd had with *her* father. "He never talked to any of us," she said. "But he'd look at me with a certain look in his eye that said everything I needed to know." Over time, Eva learned to use Geneva's favored standing. If there was bad news to deliver—unexpected company, say—Eva would pass off messenger duty onto her daughter. "You tell Daddy, darling," she said. "He'll take it better from you. You're his little girl." Only later, when she offered this story to her psychiatrist, did Geneva recall the edge in her mother's voice.

Jamaica, however, insisted on protest. When Dr. Just walked in the door, Geneva was up in a flash, throwing her arms around him, kissing him hello. Jamaica would continue to read or to watch television until the end of a chapter or a commercial. "I never contradicted him," Geneva would explain later, trying to give her little sister the benefit of her expensive analysis. "You would just wait. I never knew if you were really so absorbed in what you were doing or if you were just bidding for any kind of attention, good or bad." When the two girls were grown, Geneva forced Jamaica to look at old photographs. Dr. Just had taken hundreds of snapshots of his wife and their children. All of them were the same. Geneva and Eva smiled gaily at him. Jamaica gazed absently at the ground or the sky.

For her inquisitiveness she was rewarded by her mother with spankings and screams followed by teary reconciliation, and by her father with long, cold-shouldered spells finally broken by lengthy, self-abnegating letters of apology from Jamaica. "Dear Daddy, I don't know why I insist on irritating you all the time. I try very hard to do the proper thing, but no matter how hard I try I manage to upset you and hurt you. I'm not really a bad person, although I realize sometimes it seems that way." These notes droned on in this self-pitying way for several pages. Dr. Just never mentioned them. He simply resumed conversation.

When Geneva was fifteen, she took driver's education at school. "Don't tell Daddy, dear," Eva advised. "Keep it a little secret." The Just children were used to keeping little secrets, like the one about the bottles of Mogen David wine hidden in the hall closet behind the good linens, or the one about the candles the family lit in the master bedroom on Friday nights. They kept secrets about trips to synagogues in Cincinnati on Yom Kippur and secrets about the Hebrew lessons they learned from Berlitz records. Jamaica figured their parents didn't want them to feel embarrassed in front of their friends, but later Geneva's shrink would say they were being prepared for another Holocaust. When Jamaica told Geneva she thought psychiatrists were full of shit, Geneva replied sweetly: "It doesn't matter if you don't understand yourself if you're happy with things. It doesn't matter how sick you are if you're contented. It only matters if you're unhappy."

Eva borrowed cars from her friends so she could take Geneva out for practice drives after school, with Jamaica tucked away in the back seat. The girls adored these secret outings with their elusive mother, who rarely had time to spare from business.

Geneva took easily to driving. It suited her cautious yet persevering nature. As this slight, pretty girl would calmly propel them about the winding roads of the countryside, she and her little sister would listen dreamily to their mother chatter about their father's nurses—also called "the girls"—the complexity of Medicaid billings. What did they think about remodeling Daddy's office? She always spoke to her children as though they were adults, from the time they were quite

119

small. American children seemed so bright and precocious to her, which was the reason she always gave for her failure to tell the girls— her girls—about such basic matters as menstruation.

During one of these drives, a large truck came careening around a hairpin turn on the wrong side of the road. Geneva's reflexes were remarkably well honed for such an inexperienced driver. She managed to swerve off the road in time to avoid a head-on collision. The car slammed against the side of a ditch as she braked to a stop. Within seconds, the terrified screams and screeches had given way to startled silence. The only noticeable sounds were distant moos from a nearby pasture and loud, jerky breathing. Jamaica huddled on the floor of the back seat sucking her thumb. Geneva touched a sore spot on her fore-head, which had been bashed against the steering wheel. Her finger came away bloody. She looked at the passenger seat and felt sick. It was empty. The door hung open. Slowly she started to get out of the car.

"Don't move, darling." Eva was walking back toward her daugh-ter from the road. The truck had disappeared from sight before she had a chance to take down its license number.

"What are you doing, Mommy?" Geneva was disoriented. Her mother was gently sliding her across the seat and moving into the driv-er's position. Now her mother—her mother who walked to town be-cause she couldn't drive—was confidently starting the engine and eas-ing the car back onto the road. And now this same mother—the mother who explained to her children that she didn't drive like other mothers did because their father could take them wherever they needed to go— was steadily cruising around difficult bends. Geneva sank into her seat, clutching her mother's handkerchief to her head.

As Eva headed toward the county hospital, she glanced at her watch. With any luck, Dr. Just would be finished with afternoon rounds. She could call Mabel to come to the hospital and they would pretend she and the girls had been on an outing with Mabel when the truck ran them off the road. In some ways, she thought, it was lucky that idiot driver hadn't stopped. Less explaining this way.

She guided Mabel's car into the parking lot by the emergency room and turned off the engine. She turned toward Geneva, slumped down in her seat, and touched her face. "Come on, Geneva. I'm taking you and Jamaica into the hospital to make sure everything is all right. Do you think you can walk?"

Geneva sat up and reached for the door handle. "Sure, Mommy."

Eva propped her knees up on the seat so she could more effectively lean over to retrieve Jamaica from the back. This maneuver left Eva's backside carelessly thrust into full view of anyone meandering across the parking lot. There it hovered for many, many seconds, maybe a minute, as she pulled Jamaica's thumb out of her mouth—"Don't be a baby, darling. Upsy daisy"—and hoisted her into the front seat. Busying herself with her girls, wiping the blood off Geneva's face, pushing Jamaica's recalcitrant hair out of her eyes, Eva reached awkwardly behind her with her free left hand for the door handle, and touched air. Someone had opened her door from outside.

"Oh, could you help me with the girls, we've been in an accident," she said as she turned to greet whoever had arrived to help her. Relief lasted as long as it took her to complete the turn and for her brain to register that Dr. Just's rounds had lingered well into the afternoon and that, even though he might not have recognized Mabel's car immediately, he had memorized the contours of his wife's shapely bottom long ago and was curious to know what it was doing hanging in midair in a car in the hospital parking lot in the middle of the afternoon. A second later, she registered additional information. Judging from the extreme agitation of her husband's mobile brow and the bleak, stony set of his darkened face, she saw that his emotions had sprouted quickly and fiercely from the indifferent seed of curiosity that had pulled him over to inspect that familiar piece of anatomy. As he approached, his clinical training took over and fear flowered as it became clear that this car had been in an accident and those doll-like and wan children were his. Then, with barely time for a growing pain, rage overtook fear when he realized that it was his wife—by now sitting upright—who must have been driving.

Without a word he grabbed Jamaica from Eva's arm and stormed (a silent storm expressed only by the frantic pace, the black face broken only by the thin white line that was his lips) around to the other side of the car to collect Geneva. Hugging them close, he almost ran into the hospital. Eva remained in Mabel's car, unable to move, shaken with the knowledge that she had casually violated the invisible pact her husband had given her to sign. Maybe it had been foolish for her to agree to a contract she wasn't allowed to read, but she had agreed after all, and she was known as a woman of her word, even if she had to lie to keep up appearances. She continued to sit there numbly as her husband cheerily greeted the emergency room staff and cracked jokes with the nurses who helped him examine his daughters for signs of serious injury (there were none). She sat there as her husband ignored his children's question: "Where's Mommy?" She sat there all afternoon, as her husband quietly tended their children's cuts and bruises, herded them into his Oldsmobile, and drove them home.

121

For a week the Just family sat down to meals uninterrupted by a single word from the head of the household. He ate silently and slowly, studying the food on his plate as if it were a specimen he was trying to diagnose. He seemed absorbed in thought, not anger. Still, the girls remained quiet, too. Their meek attempts at conversation fluttered like dying moths in the air. Eva remained in motion, shuttling between the stove and the table.

At the end of the week (the number of days required for sitting *shivah*, Geneva would later point out to Jamaica), a second Oldsmobile appeared in the Justs' driveway. And when it came time for Jamaica to drive a few years later, it was Dr. Just who taught her how.

12

Soul Mates

As Sammy and Jamaica crossed the New York border on the drive home, they heard another news report on Mengele. Jamaica turned down the radio.

"Do you think it's him?" she asked Sammy.

"Hmmm?" He'd dozed off. Rubbing his eyes, he asked, "By the way, how's your story going? You haven't mentioned it all weekend."

Keeping her eyes on the road, Jamaica explained that she'd been trying to keep the letter-writers story at a distance, to keep it as light as she could. She admitted that Jules's pull was hard to resist. His accent, everything about him seemed familiar. She couldn't wait until Tuesday night and the heated, enlightening exchanges they were bound to have—about the nature of truth, whether God exists, and other vexatious subjects.

While Jamaica was maneuvering between the other cars and trailer trucks on I-95, Jules Marlin was clearing away the pots and pans he stored on top of his bed and laying out all his suits and jackets. The dark blue one his sister, Erzsi, had bought him to wear to *shul* was too somber. This wasn't a funeral after all but a meeting with a young girl. Of course, he didn't know if she was a girl or an older woman. All he had to go on was that high, childlike voice. He thought of her as young, though, tall, with long hair, like those girls in the advertisements on TV. He never understood American women, cutting their hair to look like boys, dressing in clothes that obscured their bodies, ruining their figures by dieting obsessively.

Jamaica Just. She had a good vocabulary. He always underlined lots of words in her stories. He thought she was too soft on deadbeats and welfare cheats, but she seemed to have a sense of humor. That story she wrote about the Holocaust had been real nice. Funny, he would meet her now. She was the only reporter he'd ever written a letter to. Usually he only wrote letters to the editor.

Jules's taste in clothing ran to the dazzling. He avoided garish colors but managed to put together combinations so complicated and oddly coordinated they boggled the eye. His favorite jacket, composed of a chemically produced fabric, had a deep green-and-white houndstooth pattern and lapels wide enough to hide behind. He liked to match this up with a blue-and-white checked shirt and a red-and-white-striped tie. Afraid of appearing too flashy, he completed the ensemble with brown slacks and oxblood wingtips. By Sunday afternoon, this was the outfit he had pulled together for his date, his meeting on Tuesday evening. He carefully folded a towel over the back of one of his rickety metal kitchen chairs and arranged his shirt and suit jacket across the towel to keep them from wrinkling. He repeated the operation on another chair for his slacks. As he ate supper that night, his eyes kept alternating between the television set and the clothes. Occasionally he would leap up from his chair and tug at a sleeve here, a pants leg there, trying to straighten out almost imperceptible creases.

When the telephone rang, he turned the TV volume down a bit so he could hear what Erzsi was saying. He knew it would be her; she always called on Sunday afternoons. He immediately launched into a vehement denunciation of the building superintendent, who had neglected to repair a leak in his bathroom. His voice boomed louder and louder as the conversation wore on until the background drone of the television set was punctuated by headlines: "*Israel has agreed to enter into . . .*"

"Shhhh, Erzsi, wait a second."

He listened intently to the news brief, forgetting about his sister holding the phone in Florida.

A round of faint chatter drew his attention back to the phone. "Oh, sorry there, Erzsi. What is it? You have to go now? To play bridge? Me, I don't have time for games like that. Well, if that's what you like, why not? Yeah, yeah. I'll talk to you next week. Right. Bye-bye."

He slowly put the phone down, his fingers reluctantly letting go of the smooth earpiece, already missing and forgetting the sound of his sister's voice. It was a little past four, time to start preparing dinner. Every night he ate his supper at five, his eyes fixed on the television set, the conversation supplied by Chuck or Sue or Tom, whoever was anchoring the evening news. They were great company, the newscasters, and he hated to eat alone. They were never reproachful of him; they told him interesting things about the (deteriorating) world out there; they didn't mind if he interrupted them.

Jules was a plump little bulldog of a man who almost never resisted the urge to snarl at strangers and friends alike. Over the years, his snarl was received more and more by strangers, as his friends aged and forgot how to forgive his quirks, his unthinking cruelties. They ran out of excuses for him.

"What should I make for dinner tonight?" He heaved himself with some effort from his bed, carefully avoiding the stack of cereal boxes piled at the foot. There were similar piles of packaged footstuffs throughout his L-shaped studio apartment. The head of his bed was flanked by twin peaks, a mountain of matzoh boxes, another of canned peach halves and fruit cocktail in light syrup.

He lived in what used to be called an efficiency, and he used the space efficiently indeed. The living room, the long arm of the L, was filled with appliances packed in cardboard boxes. Food processors, pots and pans, irons, small vacuum cleaners—Jules had collected this bounty over the years from banks back when banks were giving away prizes to new depositors. In his thirty years of employment as a refrigerator salesman and repairman, Jules had saved a sizable nest egg. He spent hours figuring out how to parse it into portions that would generate the greatest number of "free" gifts over the shortest period of time (the banks required the money to be left on deposit for a set period; the bigger the present, the longer the duration). He never sold nor did he open the boxes that were delivered to his apartment. He just added them to the stacks.

Pots and pans were strewn across the white nubby bedspread; at night Jules stowed them under his bed. Every morning he dragged them all out again, even if he had no plans to use them. He regarded the pots and pans as evidence of the bounty of capitalism and his own shrewdness. The daily display had become a ritual as impossible for him to abandon as the prayers he chanted every morning, the glass of slivovitz with which he said amen.

In the kitchen, he pulled a can of vegetable soup from a cabinet, a roasted chicken leg from the refrigerator. Before shutting the door, he scanned the refrigerator's contents with pleasure. The shelves were jammed with jars and plastic containers, remnants wrapped in aluminum foil and Saran Wrap, bottles of seltzer and prune juice, celery, tuna, sour cream, cottage cheese, half-eaten pieces of cake. He knew the contents of each container and when he planned to eat them. The thought of these future meals gave him a sense of well-being.

As he waited for the soup to warm, he glanced through the newspaper. Later, when the television news—the local news, the network news, the analysis on public TV—was over, he would read the articles whose headlines attracted him. He read the papers holding a pencil. Words he didn't understand he underlined, then looked up their meaning later in the dictionary. International news, local crime—these were the stories he liked the most. He glanced up from the newspaper and saw a group of women dancing in skimpy spangled outfits cut high above their thighs, way up to the middle of their taut bellies. They high-kicked and waved their hands at him, and jiggled their behinds and their creamy white chests, which appeared slightly green on his imperfectly tuned set. They all smiled joyously and opened their mouths to sing. He supposed. After the news he turned the sound off so he could read. The soundless flickering images kept him company until it was time to go to sleep. Sometimes he would chat with the women he'd see there on the television set: Weren't they tired from all that dancing? Were they tired from smiling so diligently? Could he caress one of their friendly cheeks? Now the dancers had formed a circle by clutching one another's hands. They were bobbing up and down, flashing their backsides in his direction, up and down, up and down. If he stood next to one of those leggy women, the top of his head would barely reach her breasts. He blushed at the thought of those gravity-defying breasts resting gently on top of his head like two inflated yarmulkes. What he really wanted was just to talk to one of them. He hadn't had a woman to talk to in a long time.

Years ago, he and his friend Willie used to go to the singles dances at synagogues, in hotels. They'd read the ads in the Jewish paper: "Singles! Thirty and Up! Dancing!" The women there were never thirty, they were always "and up." He didn't mind that so much. He wasn't a spring chicken himself. It was the smoking. He would fix himself up in his houndstooth jacket, striped shirt, navy blue tie, douse himself with Old Spice cologne, smooth back the few strands of hair left on his freckled, balding head. His nice smell and clean clothes would get ruined by that smoke at those places, those women sitting around filling their lungs with that black junk. Just thinking about those women, from five, ten years ago, made him angry. Who wanted to dance with those women? What kind of women would they be, killing themselves, making him smell bad with their filthy habits?

One day, Willie married one of those women, who understood

enough Hungarian to translate Jules's opinion of her. The word she understood meant "pig."

Willie wasn't sorry to end his friendship with Jules. Neither was Jules, he told himself on lonely Saturday nights.

He hadn't thought about those women for a long time. Now he was even thinking about the woman he'd once loved. For the first time he could remember, he didn't care if he missed the evening news. He turned the heat off under his soup and walked slowly into the living room, eased himself into the Barcolounger, and rested his head in his hand. Having broken his routine, he had no defense against the years of memories that began to assert themselves in the vacuum. He sat there shivering.

He blushed red with shame. "I remember how it felt, watching her laugh and dance with the man she loved. Her husband. I probably wasn't much to her, but she . . . I remember talking to her about my studies, and the way she smiled. It lit up the town, that smile. The women here, what do they know about being a woman?"

Wearily he went to the bathroom to wash his face. Back in the kitchen, he rekindled the flame under his soup.

No one could remember much about Jules as a child because there weren't many people left who had known him then. His family was modern, middle class. They'd owned a pastry shop and a wood-cutting mill. His older brother, Miklos, was charming and lovable, the idol of their two sisters, their parents. Jules, it was said, was born cranky, came spinning out of his mother's womb bellowing with rage.

"It was the Cossacks," his sister Erzsi in Florida would say. "When Mother was pregnant with Jules, there were rumors that the Cossacks were coming to town. That was before my time, but the parents used to blame the Cossacks for everything. Anyway, my mother and father decided to move to another town for a while, until the scare passed. They traveled with a horse and wagon, got caught in an unexpected storm, and my mother got chilled. Her knees swelled to the size of squashes, because she was pregnant. She never walked the same after that. She would tell Jules that story when he was small and whiny."

The Marlins sent their children to public school, not *cheder*, the Jewish school. That made them modern Jews in Just, slightly suspect.

The Marlin girls and Miklos were liked by everyone. They helped out in the family café, were known around town as bright and dependable kids. Not so Jules, who had little patience for the weakness of others. The early maturing of Jules's unsociable behavior left him with plenty of time to study. He was about to enter the university, to study medicine, when the war came to eclipse his young manhood.

After dinner, Jules wrapped up the chicken bone, the empty soup can in newspaper and carried them out to the incinerator. He dreaded bugs. When he returned, he stood in front of the bathroom mirror and was surprised to realize that he had gotten old. His face was splotchy with age spots, lined. His sideburns and the few lone hairs he had left were brittle and gray.

He pulled off his shirt and stood there in his thin undershirt. He opened the medicine cabinet. There was an ancient bottle of Loving Care hair color mix, medium brown. He hadn't used it in years, since he'd stopped scavenging at the singles dances. Mechanically he reached under the sink, put on the yellow rubber gloves he found there, and began to splash the murky brown contents of the bottle onto his hand. He rubbed the Loving Care into his sideburns, stroked his wisps of hair, massaged his head, even at the risk of adding artificial splotches of brown to the ones already occurring naturally there. He purred at his own touch, at the surprising reassurance of human hands. He sat on the toilet to wait until the dye took hold.

As he waited, he thought about the nice lady—clean-looking, no tobacco stains, crisp white apron—in the deli where he bought his roasted chickens. She'd told him to get a dog, a companion for the long walks he took every day.

"Maybe for some people a dog is all right," he told her. "I don't like having animals in the house. I'm allergic to the smell of them. You don't know him, but I used to have this friend, Willie. He had a dog. Every time I went over to his house, I noticed that funny smell there. I got a small apartment. I don't need no dog."

The other night, though, he saw a television show about police dogs. He started thinking. "If I got a dog, one of those big German shepherds, maybe it wouldn't be such a bad idea. I could walk over on the other side of Hillside Avenue where I don't like to walk now. All those blacks and other people moving in there. A big, mean German shepherd would keep the muggers away. I could train it to leap at their throats and tear them apart. Leap at their throats. It would be better than a gun or a knife. The dog would be at them before they could blink." He chortled from his belly, a substantial chortle then, at the thought of the throatless mugger, lying at the feet of his trustworthy pet, dead perhaps, bleeding.

"But what would I do with it when we got back from the walk? I guess I could put it down in the basement there where the furnace and the pipes are. Yeah, it wouldn't bother nobody down there."

With some effort—his thick buttocks had spread comfortably around the edge of the toilet seat—he stood and stared at his splotchy reflection. Dripping dye had stained his undershirt brown.

"No, I wouldn't want the animal," he said to the mirror. "I like the idea of it for the muggers, but the smell. I can't get used to someone else around me. A woman maybe I could stand. If she could cook."

Jules went to sleep trying to remember the face of the woman he'd once loved.

Jamaica had no trouble sleeping Sunday night and stayed in bed Monday morning, finally dragging herself into the office late that afternoon. She was so tired because every time she left Eva alone up there in Connecticut, she felt like a deserter; inevitably, she and Sammy left much too late Sunday night after prolonged good-byes.

She flipped through the telephone messages scattered about her desk. There were calls from flacks and friends, and a message from Abraham Palermo. It took her a minute to connect this odd yet familiar-sounding name with the movie-producing commodities trader she'd written a story about months before. He'd actually been nice, she recalled, despite the custom-built limo and custom-made silk suspenders and the silk socks he'd worn backwards. He couldn't possibly be calling to complain. The piece she'd written was short, sweet, and long gone. Curious, and unwilling just yet to start rummaging through her notes for her story about letter writers, she dialed the number on the yellow slip of paper. A voice barely audible against a cacophonous background snapped at her.

"Palermo? Yeah, yeah. He's here somewhere. Ya wanna hold on there?"

It occurred to Jamaica that Mr. Abraham Palermo must be down at the commodities exchange since he wasn't likely to be loitering in a subway station, the only other place she could think of that could generate so much noise. She'd been under the impression that he'd given up trading when he went Hollywood; however, whatever impressions of him she still retained were rather vague. Most of the people she interviewed vanished from her memory the instant they hit type, as though this minor feat of immortalization relieved her of the responsibility of thinking about them anymore. They were available on microfilm.

A deep voice, the kind that could be heard droning learned introductions to classical music on public radio, resonated in Jamaica's ear, drowning out the din. "Hello, Jamaica? This is Abraham Palermo.

You may remember me as the subject of one of your articles awhile back. I'm back in New York and I was wondering if you'd like to have dinner some evening to talk about show business some more. I pick up the *Observer* out on the coast from time to time, and I've noticed that you've been writing about Hollywood."

Jamaica had nearly drifted off to sleep to the sound of his soothing, soporific voice. What had he looked like? He had a nice mouth, and he hadn't been the jerk she'd expected him to be. She couldn't envision his face, only his disembodied mouth and suspenders and socks. What was he talking about? Show business stories? God, no. Her brief bout with celebrity features had been, she hoped, somewhat akin to the German measles; brief, relatively painless, and nonrecurring. There was really no reason for them to meet again.

"That sounds nice," she said politely. "This just isn't a good time right now. I'm in the middle of a big story and . . . well, I'm in the middle of a big story."

"I understand." He sounded so disappointed Jamaica wanted to comfort him, even though she could barely remember him.

"Maybe later," she said as a sop to that appealing voice.

"Great!" He was so enthusiastic that she was sorry she hadn't accepted his invitation.

Sammy worked late again that evening. Jamaica read the printouts of her notes and tried to picture Jules—and, oddly, Palermo. When Sammy finally came home, she reminded him that her dinner with Jules was scheduled for the next night.

Tuesdays were Sammy's card nights. He and his friends had started this routine in college because they thought it fit the image of young men about town. They played poker, did lots of drugs, and told coarse jokes about girls. As they grew older, they substituted beer and Scotch for drugs and joked less, gossiped more. Although none of them smoked, they all immediately lit cigars the minute the game started. Sammy, who otherwise kept his emotions on a deliberately even keel, stumbled home Tuesday nights bleary-eyed and stinky with cigar smoke and beery sentiment. Jamaica encouraged Sammy's nights out with the boys. She liked to imagine the dangerous secrets they revealed to one another, free from the probing ears, the jealous hearts of their wives and lovers. She was certain that he kept the delicious details of his poker evenings to himself because he didn't want to hurt her with his dear, wistful memories of lurid sex and achey romance or to make her jealous of the vibrant wit only male companionship could kindle. In fact, he was utterly candid. "What did you do?" she'd ask sleepily when he came home. "You know, sit around and play cards and drink beer and reminisce. Cut people up," he'd answer.

Tonight she tried pressing him for details again, and instigated one of their rare arguments. Sammy simply refused to fight; he didn't even like to discuss. His parents had been married for nearly forty years, happily, a situation they attributed to a few simple rules: Never go to sleep angry. Don't dwell on minor irritations. Save arguments for the privacy of your bedroom, then forget them. His father was a gentle, patient man who lavished attention and gifts on the woman he would always think of as his child bride, and she rewarded him with three sons who were exactly like him. The Feins weren't immune from life's pricks and pratfalls: their parents died of old age; they themselves endured with bravery and good spirits a heart bypass here, pneumonia there. Their lives marched forward with the optimism born of the predictability they and their parents before them had worked long hours to ensure. They had been born in the Jewish section of Kansas City and there they would die. It would change only by becoming a nicer, more affluent, more comfortable ghetto, and they would change not at all.

"C'mon, Sammy," she wheedled, "tell me what really happens when you go out with the boys? What do you guys talk about? You can tell me."

He cut off her teasing probe about poker nights. "You live in a dream world, Jamaica. I don't," he said in an unusually exasperated tone. "Why does everything have to be romantic or meaningful? Why can't it just be a poker game?"

This rather insulted Jamaica, who considered her search for truths (the ones she cared to acknowledge) and deeper meanings (the ones that didn't hurt too much) an intellectual, not a romantic pursuit.

"Who lives in a dream world, Sammy, Mr. Let's Build the Perfect City on Paper? I'm the one who's out there in the streets every day. And I don't even have me for comic relief."

"Is that what you think you are to me? Comic relief?"

"Do you have a better idea?"

Sammy looked at his wife and burst out laughing. She did look slightly ridiculous standing there half-undressed, her skinny legs poking out from *his* T-shirt (why did she always put on his nicest one?), blue cotton panties, and a pair of furry slippers.

"Friends?" He seemed troubled as he lightly touched Jamaica's hair and tapped the bump in the middle of her nose. Jamaica quickly considered the alternative to remaining friends (and trying to think of herself as family) with a calm man like Sammy. Even as she ached with passion for her childhood—and for something else—she remembered the fearsome price she had paid for that exhilarating, agitated love. She remembered sitting on the closet floor listening to the anguished Hungarian screams and the slamming doors, eating meals so quiet the sound of a knife cutting a chicken leg made her fillings rattle, crawling into the dark calm of Poochie's doghouse to avoid the disappointment on her father's face.

"Never go to sleep angry," she said, lifting her face to Sammy's.

The Red Violin

Jamaica didn't much believe in karma or any kind of spiritual communion, yet she had felt a pull—a kind of familiarity—toward Jules Marlin from the moment she had first clipped one of his letters. As her taxi approached the Red Violin, her chest tightened with the palpitations that usually preceded visits with her mother and sister. They knew too much about her, making her love for them a drought-proof well of joy and pain. Her love was constricting and expansive, euphoric and harsh. It almost crushed her sometimes with its weight of memory, and the responsibility of judgment and forgiveness. Neither husbands nor lovers could ever fully penetrate their cocoon. Geneva and Jamaica had always regarded each other's friends with suspicion; it had taken years for Geneva to warm to Sammy. "I felt you'd betrayed me," Geneva confessed to her sister one day. "I felt we were here in this world together."

It was Jules's choice of the Red Violin that had cracked Jamaica's dam this time. The palms of her usually icy hands were sweating and her eyes filled with tears. Jamaica had always thought of this Hungarian restaurant, with its folklorish decor, its authentic cuisine, its mawkish gypsy music as an example of her father's cosmopolitan flair. She couldn't have known it was every Hunky immigrant's favorite paprikash joint. On their yearly New York vacations, Dr. Just would steal an evening from the relatives and take his family out for a gut-stuffing evening at the Red Violin, or the (now defunct) Budapest, or the Magyar. He would beckon the inevitable strolling violinist and have him play "Az a Szep," and then "Sunrise, Sunset." Listening to the sentimental lyrics, the Justs would stare at each other moistly, overcome with nostalgia for the moment even while it was taking place. The girls would beam as they listened to their parents order dinner in Hungarian, as though their ability to speak their native tongue was a miracle. They would eat mountains of nockele and chicken paprikash and veal cutlets and palacscinta and agree that the cook couldn't hold a candle to Eva. Not enough salt.

Until much later, New York for Jamaica was the Red Violin and the beach, and crowded apartments in Queens filled with familiar strangers babbling in Hungarian. And Radio City Music Hall. Dr. Just took his children and all of his relatives' children there every year. On those days he was charming and expansive. Strangers would turn to look at this tall dark man herding a dozen or more small children into the vast theater. He supplied them with armloads of expensive soda and candy. He distributed boxes of miniature Almond Joys and Reese's Cups—whose prices would have infuriated Eva had she been there—with a wide smile on his face. That smile caused Jamaica's cheeks to flush as she sat in the dark air conditioning, sucking through the bittersweet coating of the Mounds Miniatures until she reached the coconut center. At peace, she watched the Rockettes strut and kick in the dazzling unison she preferred to notice, and ignored the occasional wandering gam.

Gypsy music still oozed out the front door of the Red Violin. Jamaica gave her name to a woman wearing an embroidered skirt with suspenders. She followed this Upper East Side peasant to the table where her dinner companion was already waiting.

Jules had arrived twenty minutes earlier, a full half-hour before the appointed time. He felt uncertain about the whole enterprise. What was the code of etiquette; should he shake her hand or merely nod hello? On television they didn't do restaurant interviews. The reporters usually sat on couches or stood in front of buildings. He'd studied the menu and come to terms with the shocking inflation in prices. Years of eating supper while watching television enabled him to butter his third fragant slice of dark peasant bread without breaking his vigil of the aisle leading to the table. The meaty blond woman who'd seated him—a well-preserved fifty-year-old, a full-bodied Hungarian dumpling—approached. Behind her trailed a young woman who seemed to rattle around in a baggy black jacket that was pulled off to the side of one shoulder by the enormous canvas bag hanging there. Her eyes peered out from a shaggy mass of brown hair.

Jules stumbled to his feet. "Miss Just?" Their eyes didn't meet as they awkwardly shook hands. Her jacket slipped over her knuckles. The white table cloth, tangled in his belt, rose with him.

Jamaica assumed her cheeriest, most professional manner. Except for the absence of the first-person plural, this pose was not unlike a hospital nurse's hearty jocularity. "So, how *are* you this evening, Mr. Marlin? I've really been looking forward to meeting you." Her stomach turned as she listened to the squeaky overeagerness in her voice.

She needn't have worried. At this moment she could have recited the alphabet and Jules Marlin would have smiled at her dreamily. The candlelight flickered and the music poured over them like honey. Jamaica was an attractive young lady, a little bony for Jules's overripe European taste, but attractive. Her voice chattered on with girlish vibrancy. There was nothing overtly sexual in his response to her. What excited him was the notion of being the special guest, live and in color.

He couldn't remember the last time he'd eaten in a restaurant. In the fifties he and Willie used to come here with whatever women they could find and they'd eat well, slip the violinist a buck to come over and play something schmaltzy, get the girls in the mood. Some evenings he'd end up stuffing five, ten dollars into the gypsy's belt, but it was almost never enough.

He noticed that Jamaica was smiling at him expectantly. "No, no. I waited only for a few minutes," he said. "How did you come here? By bus or by cab?"

They stuttered through a few more minutes of introductory pleasantries, then ordered. Jules noted Jamaica's command of the Hungarian menu. She asked him if she could place her tape recorder on the table to enable them to talk freely without pausing for her to take notes. Generally she avoided tape recorders. Notebooks seemed more trustworthy and personal somehow. Tonight, though, she wanted to study the nuances of Jules's voice, the pattern of his remarkable storyteller's gift—more of a preacher's gift, actually, the smooth incantations of a holy roller whose gospel was the news.

It soon became clear that despite his preoccupation with current events, Jules was a man who lived in the past. Not, as she suspected, the distant past of the Holocaust. For Jules, on that night at least, history ended in 1979; American politics began and ended with Jimmy Carter. The grinning peanut President represented for Jules all that was wrong with America today. Starting with the cucumber salad sprinkled with paprika, right through the goulash, the Bull's Blood wine, and the apricot palacscinta, Jules blasphemed the name of the president who had denied haven to the shah of Iran, thus opening up the Middle East, and possibly the world, to the evils of Islamic fundamentalism.

He thundered out monumental declarations and whispered rhetorical questions. He traced the welfare state, hostages, international terrorism, inflation, and the country's overall moral decay back to the ineptitude of Jimmy Carter, and Miss Lillian, and Amy. He spoke as though there had been no other presidents, except for a brief (favorable) mention of Harry Truman ("There was a man with guts. He let the Japs have it. He wouldn't put up with no Ayatollah Anyone") and Richard Nixon ("I guess we seen that all those guys were crooks, not just old Tricky Dicky").

Finally, he paused. "Do you like your dinner there?"

"Oh, yes, delicious," she said quickly, before he had a chance to start up with poor Jimmy Carter again. "But tell me one thing, Mr. Marlin. Why do you think you are a news junkie?"

This remarkable fount of information needed no time to reflect. "It goes back to before the war. World War II. In those days, Jews didn't concern themselves with politics. Who needed to know what was going on in government? Czechoslovakia, the country I was from, was a democracy, just like here. With voting, the works. No Jew I knew paid attention to any of that. That was for the *goyim*. You understand what I mean, *goyim*?"

(Jamaica thought of the time she told her mother about a girl she'd met at college who had had her own father arrested for trying to molest her. Eva had interrupted Jamaica in a worried voice: "They were *goyim*, weren't they?")

Jules tapped his knife on the table. "Next thing you know, Hitler and his gang are in power and we were wiped out. Finito. You got the picture?" He waited until she nodded. "The Jews in America were no better. You think they said anything to FDR? Franklin. Delano. Roosevelt." Tap. Tap. Tap. "He had to wait until the Japs bombed out Pearl Harbor to realize the Germans were *tsutcheppening* over there in Europe." Tap. Tap. "You know what means *tsutcheppenish*? You don't speak Yiddish? *Tsutcheppening* is what a guy does who's a bully but doesn't want to admit it. He pushes and pushes until he provokes some kind of an action. Or like a wife who nags and nags and nags until finally her husband smacks her a good one."

He laid down the knife. He stared directly at Jamaica; she had the sense that he didn't see her. "To get back to your question: When I got to this country, I figured the Jews better get informed about what's going on. So when Walter Mondale—not Mr. Walter Cronkite, a good man—I mean Walter Mondale, says he wants more responsibility working as vice president for Jimmy Carter, he can't a few years later run for president and pretend he wasn't there."

He cleared his throat. "But what I want to explain to you is that I gotta be involved to protect my own skin."

Jamaica was woozy with Bull's Blood and sympathy and remorse, as she gazed in a candle-lit fog at her squat dinner companion. The only context she had for him was the picture shimmering on the wall just behind him. She didn't know the name of the town he was from, who his parents were, what he had dreamed. She glanced at the scene of Hungarian peasants frolicking in a hayfield. Why hadn't she steered Jules away from Jimmy Carter early on? This was purely a rhetorical question. Clearly, Jules traveled on automatic pilot.

"Have you always lived alone, Mr. Marlin?" she ventured.

He stiffened. "Why do you want to know?"

"I was just curious."

"If you want to have a serious discussion with me about news, young lady, I am happy to go along with you. My private life is my business. You know what I mean? What do you want? To invite *shvartzehs* over to my apartment and have them rob me? What?" His voice had harshened so rapidly Jamaica flinched. Instinctively, and miserably, she drew back into her chair.

"What's the matter? Don't you feel well?" Jules asked with some concern. He was oblivious to the effect his burning words might have had on Jamaica, scorched white. He had grown accustomed to flinging his most abrasive opinions, his keenest insults at the ever-forgiving television screen.

"No. I'm sorry. I didn't mean to pry. I was only trying to understand how the war left you?"

"Oh, why didn't you say so? The war." It was Jules's turn to settle deeper into his chair. For once, words failed him. How had the war left him? He tried to turn his mind to this question, but his memory was rusty from disuse. After all these years of moving on, with no one minding much what road he took or where he had come from, someone was urging him to look back. But look what happened to Lot's wife. He thought briefly about Mrs. Lot, an exquisite, frozen pillar of salt, doomed to gaze forever at the charred remains of her hellish home town. Who needed that? Still, he wanted to help Miss Just out, to give her the kind of story that would restore the color to her ashen face.

"I remember one thing that happened that's kind of personal. I'm telling it to you because you're a reporter and you have to know these things. Okay? I don't want you to get the wrong impression, but it's a true story and maybe it'll explain something about human nature."

In the candlelight, his face appeared to be a distant planet, an orange surface divided by the deep-set craters of his eyes, the shadings of age spots and wrinkles resembling faraway rivers and mountains. A map from a a third-grade science book. An orbital sphere containing the mysteries of the universe, as the earnest textbook writers would describe it.

Jules fixed his hollow gaze on the empty wine bottle and began to speak in a quiet monotone.

"When the Nazis came into our town, my father pushed me to run away. I was twenty-one at the time and working in his business. I had been in medical school to study for a doctor, but when the Nazis came in I left Prague to go back to my home town. We had almost made it to the end of the war—"

"What year was it?"

"Nineteen forty-four. We had almost made it to the end of the war when the Nazis decided to make a final push through Czechoslovakia. 'Where shall I go?' I asked my father. 'Toward the Russian border,' he told me. In those days we were allies with those Soviet bastards. Jimmy Carter didn't do a goddamned thing when they marched into Afghanistan. I tell you—"

In a panic, Jamaica yanked him back. "You said you were heading toward the Russian border?" Her mind filled with shadowy scenes from half-remembered war movies, men dressed in black head to toe, crawling on their bellies through forests, whispering.

"I went over to the train station. A friend of mine—a *goy*—was the station manager. He let me hide in his office until the night train for a town near the border was scheduled to leave. He told me the train would make a few stops before we pulled into the next station and that I should jump off during one of those stops out in the country."

Jamaica waved away the waitress hovering by their table. There was something hypnotic about Jules, about his ability to unreel political rhetoric or personal history on cue. Living life undistracted by ordinary tasks—the humdrum of "Good mornings" and "Good nights," schedules—had invested him with a remarkable single-mindedness. From what she could gather, Jules Marlin had no time-tables to keep, no pleasantries to maintain, no one's tears to dry except his own. He was not accustomed to adjusting his antennae to pick up the wounded quiver in another's voice. In turn, he sought no affirmation of himself in anyone else's eyes.

"I got on the train the way that he told me to. I hopped on just as the train was about to leave the station. I rode between the cars like some kind of human hook. Do you know what I'm talking about? The ground was moving a few feet below me. The air rushed by with such force! Like a river torrent. I knew if I moved one way or the other I was a goner. I wasn't brought up for this kind of thing, believe me. I was going to be a doctor, like I told you. We weren't peasants in my family. Educated people."

Jules chuckled heartily, not with bitterness. "Let me tell you something. I was lucky the train made so much noise because I was breathing hard enough to create my own windstorm, a tornado maybe. The noise! You wouldn't believe how loud that train sounded to me that night, like Times Square with all the trains coming and going all at once. You ride the subways, right? You know what I mean.

"I feel the train slowing down and, brother, am I scared. I'm not crazy about heights and I don't like to jump. I'm not exactly what you would call Olympic material." He patted his round belly. "I feel myself starting to sweat, but I realized that this was a life-or-death situation. Life or death. Black and white. A situation where I had to take action, not like Jim—"

Jamaica was ready. "And did you jump?"

"Jump? I flew off of there like a bird. I didn't feel my feet hit the ground until I was a hundred yards away from the track. You know what it is to be high, Miss Just? I was high, like they call it here. Without drugs or cigarettes or alcohol. I was like a bird. One of those Australian birds—what is it? The ostrich. A bird on the ground. Believe me, I was hoping I wasn't going to lay an egg. Do you know the joke about the egg?"

Startled, Jamaica nodded.

"You do?" Jules sounded disappointed.

"No. I mean, no."

"One man—a *Yiddele*—says to the other one, 'I've got such *tsuris*. My son thinks he's a chicken.' His friend says, 'Your son thinks he's a chicken? Why don't you take him to a psychiatrist?' 'We would,' says the father. 'But we're afraid he might get cured.' '*Noch*,' says the friend. 'That's the point. You want your son should spend the rest of his life thinking he's a chicken?' 'No,' says the father. 'But we sure will miss the eggs.'"

Jamaica was wound so tight any release was bound to start her bobbling. She laughed until tears rolled down her face and her shoulders shook. She snorted and whooped until her cheeks glowed quite pink.

Jules was pleased at this unexpected response. "I heard that one on the *A.M. New York Show* the other morning. Good, no?"

"Good, yes."

For the first time all evening, they both relaxed at the same time. They left Jules's story dangling out there in the Czechoslovak countryside while they idled a few moments, chatting about Hungarian restaurants, the healthful benefits of long walks, Sammy's job. Idle is as idle does, and this idle chatter served the valuable purpose of giving Jules a chance to recharge his memory. Jamaica changed her tape. They sat quietly for a minute.

"Do you mind finishing the story?"

"No, no. Where was I? Running away from the train. It was dark and I really didn't know where I was. We didn't travel too far away from home then like people do nowadays. Fifty miles, that was a big trip.

"I got to a road and followed it to the edge of a town. I didn't want to go into any town. I don't know what made me do it, but I stopped at an old house set back from the road and knocked on the door. No one answered, so I knocked again."

Jamaica cupped her face in her hands and propped herself against the table top with her elbows. The only thing she was aware of was the dramatic rolls and pauses of Jules's story.

"An old woman—Who knows if she was really old? The women in those days didn't take such good care of themselves. They didn't have all those products I see advertised all the time. These health and beauty aids."

Jules adopted the pitchman's tone. "Take ten years off your age! The older you get, the better you look!" He shook his head, smiling. "Those things."

After a pause, he returned to the past. "She opens the door and asks me what I want. I tell her I'm with the Czech underground and, if she doesn't let me in, my comrades will come along and they'll kill her."

"'Are you a Jew?' she asks me."

"'No,' I said. 'I told you. I'm with the Czech underground.'"

"'If you're a Jew, you're lucky my son isn't home,' she says, like I hadn't said anything. 'He's with Hitler. He used to stand in front of the mirror practicing how to throw his arm straight up in the air. Sieg Heil! Sieg Heil! Sieg Heil!'"

"She looked like a ghost, her eyes rolling, her mouth screaming: 'Sieg Heil! Sieg Heil!' She had on a white nightgown and a white shawl. I remember that shawl because it was real nice and thick, made from good wool. My mother had one just like it."

He touched the man-made fabric of his jacket thoughtfully.

"I was getting ready to get out of there when she pulled that shawl around her real tight, like she was freezing, and waved her hand that I should follow her. She led me behind her house to a pile of sticks, maybe for firewood, I figured. She starts digging around in them like some kind of crazy woman. I could see the white of her nightgown in the dark. The moon—there was a moon. She doesn't say a word. Finally, I see why she's digging. There's a door in the ground. She had hidden there a cellar, a place to keep food cool. She lifted the door and told me to get down there and to keep my mouth shut. There would be food and water, she said.

"I didn't know whether to believe her or not, but what choice did I have? I was tired and hungry. My feet hurt. I climbed down into that cellar, where I discover right away that she already has other people down there. A family. A man and his wife and their little daughter, a girl of about eleven or twelve.

"We couldn't see each other. It was pitch dark down there. I mean pitch dark. I know you probably know that expression—"pitch dark"—but I bet you never really got to experience it. Here in the city you don't feel black like that. There's always light coming in from somewhere, even when you don't want it. I mean it was blacker than the inside of your head when you close your eyes in the dark. Blacker than Africa. Blacker than sorrow. Do you know what I mean? Black! Black!"

Jamaica knew it must only be the shadows cast by the candlelight, but she was sure she saw black in Jules's eyes. Not knowing what else to do, she nodded and waited for him to continue.

"We introduced ourselves to each other in whispers. Our real names, we told. I guess we figured if we weren't Jews or something why would we be introducing ourselves in the dark in a cellar in the middle of the night. I didn't realize that in the middle of the day it would be just as dark down there."

"We lived down there together for three months. That tiny room—about eight by eight—was everything for us. Do you know what I'm saying to you as politely as I can? Our bedroom, our dining room, our bathroom. Do you know what I'm saying to you? Every day the old woman came at night and dropped food and water down to us without saying one word. Among ourselves we didn't talk much. We were afraid they could hear us outside."

Jules inhaled deeply and averted his eyes, which had been peering intently into Jamaica's.

"What I want to tell you is that there's something in us humans that still is like the animals. We have our animal instinct that goes very deep into us. Do you understand what I'm telling you?"

"Not exactly."

"I'm telling you this because you're a reporter. For the record."

Again, Jules cleared his throat. "This man and the woman, his wife, were people in their late thirties, I guess, maybe a little older. Educated people. He was an engineer, and she had gone to the university. These were not some kind of bums. Educated people."

"Every night when they thought their daughter and I were asleep, they would behave like a husband and wife, right there next to us. Sometimes twice in one night. Can you imagine? The animal instinct." His voice shook with outrage and excitement.

"For three months I never got a full night's sleep. I was very careful that they shouldn't know I was awake, and that took a lot of trouble. To keep my breathing very even, while next to me the two of them were panting and groaning and . . . behaving like a husband and a wife."

Jules shifted uncomfortably, as though the regurgitation of this well-digested memory was causing stomach pain. He seemed perplexed over the memory of his confinement. What bothered him wasn't the remembered terror, the fear that each crack of moonlight that slipped through when the cellar door was opened at night could have been the herald of doom. He simply could not comprehend what could drive two civilized, *educated,* almost middle-aged people into each other's erogenous zones when they might be killed at any minute. It didn't occur to him that perhaps they were combating fear with the best, the only weapon they had available.

"How did you get out?" Jamaica asked gently.

He looked at her with some surprise, even startled to see her there.

"One day, the old woman didn't come. We waited until the next day and the next. Funny how we knew when one day came to replace the one before it, but we knew. I saw on TV where they do experiments with monkeys to find out about what they call internal time clocks." He fell silent, then sighed. "Internal time clocks."

"We were parched and hungry. Finally, the husband couldn't stand it anymore. Not for himself, but for the child. She was whining. I couldn't stand it either, the whining, but I thought we should wait. He'd had it, though. When he sensed it was the time the old woman normally would feed us, he sneaked out in the dark, into her house. Later, he told us he found her sitting in the dark in the parlor, rocking back and forth in a chair."

"'Where have you been?'" he asked her.

"She looked at him like he was *meshugge,* a crazy man. "'Why, the war is over,' she said to him."

This time Jules's laugh was bitter. "Can you imagine? 'The war is over,' she said. 'The war is over.'"

The violin wailed. Jamaica blinked.

"Whatever happened to those people?"

"Who?"

Jamaica grimaced. "The people you lived with in the cellar."

Jules shrugged. "I heard after the war they moved to New Jersey. I know people who know them."

"Did you ever visit them or see them again?"

Jules looked at her with curiosity. "What for?"

14

Back to the Cocoon

It was fairly late, ten-thirty or so, when Jamaica and Jules emerged from the hypnotically mawkish environment of the Red Violin. Outside they found a hot town. Fine-looking men and women sporting deep tans and white shirts paraded by, stopping to admire exquisite window displays of designer chocolate chip cookies and pasta. Among these fashionable denizens, this odd pair—the rumpled, tall American woman and her short, obviously foreign companion—mingled, strolling down Third Avenue to Fifty-third Street.

"Are you coming down?" Jules asked when they reached the subway station.

Jamaica hesitated, glanced longingly down the steps and shook her head. Sammy didn't like her to take the trains at night.

"I'll walk you downstairs," she said. When they reached the token booth, Jamaica shook Jules's hand firmly. From the turnstile she watched him go down the escalator, then break into a waddling run toward the front of the train, where the policemen ride at night.

Heading back up toward the street to hail a cab, she idly rewound her tape recorder. ". . . like animals," Jules's voice droned somewhat indistinctly, muffled by the clatter of dishes and background hum of voices and violins. She zipped her bag shut and thrust her hand into the air. Within seconds, a cab jerked to a halt next to her. Her hand shook as she opened the door, and she wished she were safe on the "E" train instead. Stirred up as she was, she couldn't bear the thought of a terror trip in a cab. In general, she hated being at the mercy of the city's army of demented drivers, all of whom appeared to be devout believers in hara-kiri. Taxis forced her to think, to consider life and all its sorrows—because it seemed about to end soon.

Settling in the reasonably clean back seat, she absent-mindedly complimented the driver on the tidiness of his car.

"Thank you, miss," he said. "It's my own. Took me a long time to save up for it."

"Yeah, I imagine a car like this costs a lot," Jamaica said agreeably.

Inexplicably, the driver took her idle pleasantry as an affront. "Listen, lady," he hissed. "Don't fuck with me. I don't ask you no personal questions and you don't ask me none. Who the hell do you think you are, getting into my own stuff? Shut up, okay?" He turned the radio up to its loudest amplification:

Israeli troops massed at the Lebanese border in an attempt to ward off attacks from terrorists. Shiite Moslems claimed responsibility for the murder of two Israeli officials in the northern settlement of Ramat Harara . . .

"Do you hear that?" screamed the driver. "Why don't the Israelis pick on someone their own size, like the Russians? I'm sick of Jews and their Holocaust. I heard on the news the other day there ain't never was no Holocaust, no six million dead. Get off my back with this shit."

Jamaica was terrified. She feigned a fit of coughing.

"Excuse me," she gasped, hacking loudly. "My allergies! I have to get out in the fresh air at once. Pull over here, please."

His sudden stop threw her forward. Though she was ashamed that she hadn't confronted him directly, she took her revenge; making a quick calculation, she left only a 10 percent tip.

Luckily she had to walk only a few blocks to the subway, where she had some control. If provoked there, she could move to another seat. And, especially at night, there was an endless supply of distraction from the turmoil above ground, the chaos in her head.

Safe behind the closed doors of the subway car, Jamaica sought a friendly face with which she could communicate silently, a diversion from immediate contemplation of the taxi driver—and Jules Marlin. Her pupils shrank from the white glare of the overhead lamps as she glanced around the car. Across the aisle, a drawn woman stared at her lap. There her fingers were caressing the ends of her extremely long mane of hair, which in kinder light would surely glisten. Strawberry blond. Those lights were so cruel to women. No makeup could bring a glow to cheeks unfairly thrust under a harsh fluorescent gaze. This woman with the fluorescently faded strawberry blond hair was hunched over in her seat. Jamaica wanted to tell her, kindly of course, that she would regret her poor posture in a few years, when she wouldn't be able to straighten up again. Regarding that long, horsy mane drawn back into a pony tail, Jamaica briefly understood the fascination some men had for women with Rapunzel-like hair. What desirable objects, these women who could occupy themselves for hours brushing their tresses, parting them, braiding and unbraiding them, wrapping them in chignons on top of their heads. They would have no time for neuroses or job insecurity or memory or self-absorption. They would have time only to be beautiful, and to be loving and giving to whoever found himself wrapped up in that comforting mass of hair. As Jamaica dragged her fingers through her own unmanageable mop, she thought about the joys of living secluded in an unreachable tower, lowering her overgrown braid for the occasional visitor.

The woman sitting across from her dropped her mane onto her bare knees. She was dressed not like a fairy princess but like a professional hiker, in multipocketed khaki shorts, a khaki T-shirt, and low-top boots. Glancing Jamaica's way, she quickly turned her attention to her backpack. After rummaging furiously for a couple of minutes, enough time for Jamaica to tighten with apprehension, she withdrew a small object. She lifted her hand, and Jamaica gasped.

"What's your problem, lady?" the woman snarled, as she began to brush her teeth furiously with her Py-co-pay.

Jamaica shrugged—for her own benefit; no one else was paying attention. She closed her eyes and thought about Sammy playing poker and about how much he loved her. Often he implied that he loved her as much as humanly possible.

"How much do you love me?" she would ask.

"How much is there?" he would reply.

She wondered if he loved her as much as Dick Diver loved Nicole in *Tender Is the Night,* or as much as F. Scott Fitzgerald loved Zelda in real life. Did Sammy mean, when he said he was "in love" with her, that, like Dick, he felt a "wild submergence of soul, a dipping of all colors into an obscuring dye?" Did he have "certain thoughts" about her, the way Dick had had about Nicole before he stopped loving her, which would make Sammy feel physically sick? "Certain thoughts about Nicole," she muttered, quoting a favorite passage, "that she should die, sink into mental darkness, love another man, made him physically sick." The questions were, did Sammy love her that much, and if he did, did she want him to?

"Yes and no," Sammy had said, when she had once posed the first of these queries. He hadn't actually read the book, but he had seen a PBS dramatization on television, and Jamaica kept thrusting pages she had marked by turning the corners (in the paperback edition she carried around with her, not the hardcover on her shelf at home) in front of his face. "I love you as much as any healthy mortal man could. But Dick's love for Nicole was sick, as I read it. She was not a normal girl. Granted, you aren't normal, God forbid, but you aren't schizophrenic no matter how hard you try. Your father didn't fuck you when you were a teen-ager either."

Silence.

"I'm sorry," Sammy said. "I didn't mean to be so blunt. But that was the problem wasn't it? She was screwed up because her father molested her and then she threw Dick over. Didn't he end up a big nobody in some small town somewhere?"

As the train paused for a few minutes between Twenty-third Street and Fourteenth, Jamaica thought about her own days on the Riviera with Sammy.

They had honeymooned on the Côte d'Azur. Jamaica took careful notes during the trip in her journal, which was chock-full of amusing little anecdotes about the charming restaurants they ate in and endearing encounters with friendly natives. Amidst these pages of tour-guide descriptions, she slipped a reference to her marriage: "A record of our honeymoon, eh?" she wrote. "Oh, yes, well, I finished school and began work and moved into a new apartment and two days ago, Sammy and I formalized things. It was a swell party." This segued into starry-eyed accounts of the Mediterranean, the winding roads, the indescribably delicious food. Several pages later, she noted: "Sammy and I have been married a week now. Still don't feel like a married lady, but then, don't know how one of those is supposed to feel. Weddings and honeymoons with Sammy are swell!"

A month after they returned, they dropped in at a party on the Upper West Side. This was in the days before the area had become infested with stylishly-clad young adults in feverish search of the perfect pesto or mesquite or whatever was in fashion in a given week. Back then—and in these escalated times, "back then" could be as recent as five years ago—one was far more likely to meet earnest feminists at Upper West Side parties than investment bankers.

"Don't you feel that marriage has altered the world's perception of you?" a woman asked Jamaica in an accusatory tone.

Jamaica nervously glanced around for Sammy. It had been his idea for them to get married at a time when no one they knew considered marriage a reasonable way of life for people in their twenties. Sighing, she formulated an answer.

"I don't feel less liberated because of my attachment to Sammy. All marriage means is that we are more vital to each other in a public way."

That didn't sound right. She tried again.

"We are growing up together. That's what I meant."

The vicious stranger smiled cruelly. "Well, maybe when you reach 'up,' you won't want to be together anymore."

When Jamaica told Sammy what the woman had said—she often told Sammy more than he wanted to hear in those days—he snorted. "She's just jealous. A fat, ugly, unpleasant hag like that won't ever find anyone to marry her."

To wipe away Jamaica's scowl, he offered an outstretched hand and began to dance with her. "Spin, spin, spin!" he shouted, lifting his arm so she could twirl around. His shiny cheeks and freckles twinkled. And Jamaica did spin, and they wept with laughter and the premeditated madness of the moment. They would never grow up, that's all, she told herself.

Yet the reason Jamaica had anchored so quickly in the safe harbor of Sammy's arms was precisely because he had seemed so grown up at eighteen, so self-assured, so imperturbable. He knew who Jackson Pollock was and that a young man could go anywhere in a blue blazer and khaki slacks. He knew exactly which courses he should take to prepare for the career he had already chosen, and he knew—he always said—that Jamaica was the only girl for him. On their first date, as he walked Jamaica back to her dorm, he talked about the plays they would go to see, and the concerts they would listen to, and the trips they would take, the two of them. He listened attentively to everything she said, and he sobbed at the sad movie they saw that night. By their third date he could already imagine what their children would look like, and how Jamaica would fill their tiny souls with the sensitivity born of suffering, and how he, Sammy, would balance all that with common sense and cheery optimism.

Sammy listened to her moan about the blank spaces she hadn't filled, and about her conviction that the promise she thought she'd had was a fib. The overachiever's lie. He didn't try to understand all those feelings, he simply admired her for having them.

The train jerked forward, causing Jamaica's memory disc to skip back to the most often played groove, back to Harmony.

Geneva's shrink said that the Just family had lived in hermetic conditions, there in Harmony, and that this had contributed to the girls' uneasy transition to adulthood. They were the outsider's outsiders, he said, educated, Jewish foreigners hiding out among Gentiles, and even less at home when they mingled with what were supposed to be their own kind in Cincinnati at the fancy temple Dr. Just joined when Geneva started to date. The four of them against the world—or above it—was the way the family saw it. For better and for worse. They were a romantic quadrangle with their flare-ups and emotional heats, their teary reconciliations and their euphoric reunions.

For weeks after Geneva deserted, which is how Jamaica viewed her departure for college, the younger sister wept for hours every afternoon after school. She ached with the tormented grief of an abandoned lover. Nothing, she knew, could ever fill that great gaping hole left by Geneva, whose vacated bed became a kind of shrine. Jamaica would sprawl on Geneva's bed, day after day, scribbling woeful dirges into her diary about her sadness, her loneliness, the futility of a life that could so casually untie the knot of such a paramount friendship.

Had she been equipped to examine the already well concealed innards of her young soul, she might have connected her tears with the terrible responsibility she was now left to carry alone. Their parents were hers now, and she was only thirteen. There was no one with whom to huddle when the Hungarian screams started, when Dr. Just accused Eva of trying to prevent him from instilling Jewishness into his children. There was no one left to clap a warning hand over her mouth the way Geneva did when their father careened around dangerous curves at 90 miles an hour. This freed Jamaica to scream, "Are you trying to kill us?" Dr. Just would slam the car to a stop by the side of the road and they would sit there, he and Eva and Jamaica, in silence charged with uncertainty. Finally, he would reignite the engine and resume more slowly. Jamaica could feel him staring at her in the rearview mirror.

"I think my father was too good for this world," she told Sammy when they first met. There were deletions from the record: the purple passions and red-hot fights that would distort the warm hue she cast on the pastoral scene of her early youth as she presented it to the outside world, and that included her husband. Instead, she told him how her father bought her carnations on every birthday—one for each year—and cyclamen for Geneva. "He taught us how to waltz in the living room, and he was the handsomest man in the world, and a war hero—he nearly died in jail because he treated an English flier, not because he was a Jew," she confided.

Sammy listened with sympathy and awe for hours and weeks and years about this man who defied description, he was that fabulous. He studied pictures in photo albums, where he saw a tall, good-looking foreigner with a distant smile. He knew he could never compete with this dead stranger, but he would do all he could to make his life with Jamaica as perfect as her childhood.

Jamaica's musings were brought to an abrupt halt as the "E" train pulled into her station. She headed home at a half-run, filled to bursting with the excitement of the evening. She couldn't wait to tell Sammy all about Jules Marlin—the real Jules Marlin—and wondered how she'd contain herself until he got home from his poker game.

She didn't have to wait long; the door was unlocked.

As she walked into the apartment, Jamaica tossed her bag on a chair, and blurted: "Sammy, what are you doing home already? Your game break up early? Jules Marlin is more amazing than I could have imagined."

Without pausing, she continued, talking faster and faster. Her cheeks were flushed, her hands acting as visual aids. "His head is spinning from the mixed-up things he sees in the world around him and he's a war hero. Sort of. At first I thought he was lonely, but maybe he's found peace out there in Queens, on television. I think—"

"Jamaica, please. I'm too tired."

Jamaica clutched her stomach and stared at the pale face glaring at her from across the room, where Sammy was sunk deep into the fat pillows of their big pink sofa. Squashed against the velvet material, his face looked distorted, like a stuffed animal that had spent the night jammed under a kid's arm. His eyes and nose seemed peculiarly close together.

"Do you have a fever? Should I call Geneva?"

"I'm just feeling a little down, that's all. Don't make a production out of it."

Jamaica laughed. "I get it. All right, Sammy. What did you lose?"

Sammy shuddered. His right eye began to tic, just like his father's did when he was tired or nervous. His voice was anxious, the way he sounded when he called to explain why he was going to be late. "What do you mean, what did I lose?"

"At poker, sweet boy. You must have really dropped a bundle."

"Not really." Sammy shrugged. "Just more than I'm used to."

Jamaica tossed her jacket on a chair and walked over to the couch. The cat jumped up to perch on top of one the pillows and curled up tightly until she resembled a fuzzy slipper with eyes. As the cat looked on without much interest, Jamaica shook her husband's shoulders and began to rock him back and forth. She felt mildly giddy at the power she felt in her hands. At that moment she understood what drew Sammy to her, the potency of being a healer. With some difficulty—Sammy was lying on the couch with the irresoluteness of a very large sack of potatoes—she continued to push and pull at his shoulders. Soon she would levitate him, not literally, of course, but lighten him enough to make him dance, the way he exorcised her dybbuks through exercise.

"Jamaica!" He cried out.

"Yes, Sammy, my sweet, sweet boy?"

"Are you trying to break my fucking back, or what?"

Jamaica giggled and nuzzled his cheek. "C'mon, don't you want to dance?"

"No I don't want to dance, and I don't want my shoulders cracked either." Apologetically and somewhat weakly, Sammy tousled her hair. "Let's go to sleep."

"You go ahead. I want to play with the cat awhile. I'm sure *it's* interested in hearing all about my interview with Jules Marlin." The latter was whispered into the cat's warm gray fur, where Jamaica had buried her nose as Sammy shuffled off to the bedroom. Jamaica settled into the sofa's pillows, which retained Sammy's warmth, and pulled the cat on top of her like a tiny comforter. They had never intended to keep the cat, which had shown up on their windowsill one stormy night, and so had never bothered giving her a name. By the time they'd owned her—or it, since Jamaica felt uneasy bestowing gender on a neutered animal—for several years, "the cat" seemed the best name of all. Since there were no other cats in the apartment, they weren't likely to confuse her with anyone else.

Jamaica listened to Sammy clear his throat, and to the sound of his belt buckle hitting the wooden floor with a small thud. Odd, she thought. Sammy usually folds his clothes so neatly at night. For a few minutes there were more throat clearing sounds and rustlings and squeakings as Sammy sought out a comfortable sleeping position. He would wind up on his back and start to snore. Jamaica sleepily wished that Geneva lived closer by, to make sure Sammy was all right. He didn't seem to be sick, but then why didn't he care about her meeting with Jules? She glanced at the clock. It was too late to call Geneva. *She'd be interested.* As Jamaica stroked her cat's fat belly, the animal's purring lulled her into a cozy daze. She forgot about Sammy—and even about Jules. When muffled honks and whistles finally emerged from the bedroom, Jamaica dug her fingers into the cat's flesh in shock. "What was that?" she hissed. The cat jumped to the safety of the couch's arm, from where she stared at her owner reproach-fully.

Jamaica often gave the impression that she was childlike because she was so easily distracted. She would wander alongside office build-ings to caress a granite facade, or squat on the sidewalk to examine glass bricks wedged into the pavement. "Isn't it beautiful?" she would sigh. Sometimes the object of her momentary affection might be a sliver of moon hanging magically by the Art Deco spires of the Chrys-ler Building. But it might just as easily be an underwear ad at a bus stop that brought a gleam to her eye.

What people didn't understand was that Jamaica had never thought of herself as a child when she was one. The innocence she must have been born with seemed to have vanished almost immediately. "She's like a little old lady," Eva used to say when her daughter was very small and would pipe up with unchildlike pronouncements on the sit-uation in the Middle East or grammar or civil rights or the Holocaust. The only person Jamaica truly trusted was Geneva. When their father pointed out the Big Dipper in the sky, Jamaica turned to Geneva: "Is that true?" When he kissed them good night and said he loved them, Jamaica waited until he closed the door behind him, then whispered, "Is that true, Geneva?"

Geneva left. Dr. Just died. After that, Jamaica began to cultivate the naiveté most of her contemporaries seemed eager to lose. While her friends nurtured skepticism, Jamaica affected credulity. Let others hack at memory in search of the splinters they called the truth. Jamaica layered on the paint and the polyurethane. Intuitively she grasped the value of the white lies her mother told her.

Look what happened when she unshuttered the facts. She ended up breaking young girls' hearts, not to mention her own. When Ge-neva offered this explanation for her sister's periodic bouts of disillu-sionment, however, Jamaica scoffed.

"That man"—Jamaica thought of her sister's psychiatrist as a harmful intruder into their past—"is taking your hard-earned money to turn you into an old crank. It's just hormones."

"When Mommy says that, you fly into a rage," teased Geneva. "And you know very well my psychiatrist's name is Elliott."

"When Mommy says that, she's wrong."

Jamaica passed a rueful moment thinking about that conversation. Then the phone rang.

It was Geneva. "Jamaica? It's me. Why are you laughing?"

"I was just thinking about our talk the other day and here it's you on the telephone."

"And you're laughing because—"

"Mommy always says she can will one of us to call just by think-ing about it very hard."

Jamaica and Geneva rarely saw each other; they talked regularly on the telephone, however. Their conversations moved in shifting pat-terns that sounded jagged and nonsensical to outsiders but made per-fect sense to them. From sentence to sentence their roles would change. Jamaica at times played the worldly younger sister, whose job was to keep her cloistered, somewhat academic doctor-sister in touch with the goings on in the big world out there. Then a phrase or frag-ment of a thought would be their cue to reverse roles. Geneva would become the wise commentator, whose job it was to press a mirror to her sister's face and force her to acknowledge the presence of an adult on the glistening surface.

"How are you?"

Jamaica unloaded her evening with Jules onto Geneva, who was an appreciative audience.

"You went to the Red Violin?" Geneva's voice quivered. "Do you remember what it was like when we were little, maybe the most glam-orous place in the world? What did you eat?"

Jamaica told her, and about the stories Jules Marlin had to tell. After she finished, and Geneva made the appropriate empathetic noises, they sat quietly for a minute or two, enjoying the sound of each other's breathing.

Then, Geneva remembered why she'd called.

"What do you think of me buying a house?"

"Why not? You can afford it. You could unpack."

"That isn't funny."

The family couldn't help but think it was funny the way Geneva had lived out of suitcases ever since the year she had lived in New York after she'd graduated from college, the year their father had died. "I simply don't have time," she explained throughout medical school and her four years of residency. "I'm waiting for the right place," she explained in the years that followed. Her dinner plates were neatly stacked in boxes. Her living rooms in the five or six apartments she lived in during those years always appeared to be in transition. A pic-ture would hang on a wall, slightly askew. The sofa and chairs were littered with hammers and nails and yardsticks, all lying in wait for the moment when Geneva would unroll her posters and set up the stereo she kept meaning to buy.

Eva didn't object to her elder daughter's transitory living condi-tions. If she settled in alone, there would be no reason for her to marry.

"What does Mommy have to say about it?"

"'Vat do you mean you are buying a house?'" Geneva mimicked their mother's accent. On cue, Jamaica laughed hysterically.

"Why have you waited so long, Geneva? You always seem so organized about everything else."

"I guess I didn't want to give up the dream." Geneva sounded somewhat embarrassed.

"What's the dream?" Jamaica loved to hear Geneva tell her about the dream. She turned on her side and drew her knees close to her chin.

"You know, the dream of the perfect home with the mother and the father and the two children. They would sit in their big house and eat supper together and they'd have Tupperware containers to put the leftovers in instead of cottage cheese containers with lids that don't fit so everything gets coated with freezer burn and you have to throw it away."

The girls regularly inspected Eva's refrigerator on their visits to Connecticut. It was crammed full of bottles containing small amounts of mysterious leftovers, whose identities were obscured by green and gray mold. Because she had never learned to cook small portions, her freezer was a study in Eastern European culinary anthropology. Hidden beneath shimmering ice crystals were frozen rolls of rice and ground meat, wrapped in petrified leaves of cabbage. Peering out from ripped pieces of aluminum foil were the rigid forms of buttery yeast pastry stuffed with nuts and preserves. Thawed, it all tasted roughly the same, slightly nauseating, like tepid, unseasoned oatmeal. The girls stocked Eva's cabinets with fresh rolls of plastic wrap and aluminum foil, which she would nod at approvingly as she continued to store things in used (and often ripped) plastic bags, and aluminum foil that had served time in the oven.

Geneva's voice lightened and became more girlish as she continued.

"The father hugs the mother and never leaves her and the children and they light the candles together on Friday night and they are very happy all of the time. Elliott says this dream is childish and unrealistic and it would be good for me to move into a house. I'm a doctor and can afford it and if I unpack it will be this incredible act of independence, not that he's telling me what to do. My friend Sally is thirty-eight and she owns her own condo and she's been unpacked for years. She has good silver and everyday china and fine china. She has a lettuce spinner. Now she's moving into a house."

Jamaica filled the silence. "That sounds great. Houses are such a good investment, aren't they? There won't be more real estate. Isn't that what Uncle Zollie always said?"

Geneva's voice wavered even more. "It seems so lonely in a house," she said in a rush. "All those pipes that can leak and empty rooms to fill."

Unable to think of anything to say, Jamaica changed course. "Are you thinking of getting married?"

"To whom?" Now Geneva sounded cool and professional.

"I don't know. To George or Henry or Jon or any one of the doctors you've dragged down to New York for us to meet at one time or another. They all seemed fine."

"They are all fine. They just aren't fine enough. Do you feel at home in your apartment?"

Jamaica always set up housekeeping the minute she moved in anywhere. On her first lonely day of college she painted her room in warm yellows and plastered the concrete walls with photographs. She covered her bed with a quilt one of her father's patients had made for him, and spread her collection of stuffed animals on top. Later, when she and Sammy married, she bought only old furniture, massive stuff that couldn't be budged and looked like it had been passed down from generation to generation. Yet, whenever she passed a travel agent's office she felt the urge to buy a ticket and never come home again.

"Don't tell anyone, Geneva, but you know when I feel at home?" Jamaica lowered her voice and glanced at the darkened entryway to the bedroom. "When I get on the subway and the doors close behind me. I feel like that's my world and it's as comfy as it was when we used to lie in bed on Sunday mornings with Mommy and Daddy. No, not as comfy, but somehow my family down there doesn't demand so much."

She wound the cord around her hand. "Why are you moving into a house if you're afraid of leaky pipes?"

Geneva hummed tunelessly for a minute or two. The Justs all seemed to be congenitally tone deaf, though they all loved music. She began to talk in the patient, disembodied voice that used to tell Jamaica stories at night. As she talked, they felt themselves drifting far away from New York and Boston, snuggled deep into their twin beds at home in Harmony, listening to the occasional car burn rubber in the parking lot in front of their father's office.

"Do you remember when you were a little girl, no more than two or so? You used to make me read you the story of "The Three Little Bears" every night?"

"Uh-huh." Jamaica felt the same eagerness she'd felt all those years ago, when Geneva was about to unravel some great puzzle, like how a Nancy Drew mystery ended, or how to tell time.

"You loved that book so much, you used to caress the pictures of Goldilocks and all the bears. I read it so often you memorized the words that were on each page, even though you hadn't learned to read yet yourself." Geneva laughed.

"One day I heard someone talking in the bathroom. I walked in and there you were, propped on the edge of the toilet looking like you might fall in at any moment. Your little legs were just dangling in the air and you looked so serious; it seemed like nothing in the world could distract you. You were reciting "The Three Little Bears," and as you finished each page, you tore the page out of the book and dropped it on the floor. You didn't pay any attention to me standing there. When you got to the end you looked down at all the pages on the floor and seemed absolutely shocked to see them there."

There was a catch in Geneva's voice.

"The next thing I knew you were sobbing, as though you'd lost your best friend."

For what seemed like a very long time, the two sisters clutched their separate telephone receivers, the way they used to hold onto each other's hands, trailing behind their parents.

Finally, Jamaica coughed and asked. "What does that have to do with leaky pipes?"

Geneva's voice was very soft. "I can't remember."

"I love you, Geneva."

"I love you too."

15

Lady of Letters

Jamaica arrived at work to find the message light on her computer flashing. It had taken her six months to learn how to use the machine and another six months to warm to it. When the computers were first installed, she'd taken the required operations course along with everyone else. She had rebelled quietly by writing her stories in longhand before entering them into the machine. Her objections began with the terminology. "Entering," for example. Despite its sexual overtones, "entering" suggested an impersonal act bound to procreate only the kind of unheartfelt messages that clogged her mailbox every day: "Dear Resident: We regret to inform you that your electric bill is overdue." "Writing," on the other hand, conjured up all kinds of romantic imagery: Emily Dickinson scrunched over the backs of envelopes, Melville scratching away with his fountain pen. She couldn't imagine old Herman entering "Call me Ishmael" into a computer terminal. What if the machine responded, "Hello, Ishmael. I am waiting for your command"? No. *Moby Dick* would never have been written had Melville been born in the computer age, Jamaica was sure of that.

She also resented the computers because they represented Henry's victory, technocracy over humanity.

One day, though, she'd had a deadline to meet and there wasn't time for her writing two-step. Reluctantly she began to compose directly on the computer. Soon she was having a grand time, whipping her cursor up and down the screen, blanketing entire paragraphs in green with the tap of a key and whisking them somewhere else in the story with the tap of another. "Joanne!" she'd shouted, swiveling her chair from side to side as her fingers flew over the keyboard. "Isn't technology wonderful?"

Now she entered and transmitted without a thought; she even hyphenated and justified with ease. She pressed the "MSG" key.

Within seconds words formed on the screen. "Just, Jamaica. How is your letter writers story coming along? Could you come up and talk? Cheers, Hen."

Immediately Jamaica swiveled around to her desk and began gathering her notes into the folder she'd placed on top of the stack of magazines she'd been rummaging through earlier. Then she reached into her desk drawer and pulled out a bottle of contact lens solution and a lens case. Poking a finger in her eye, she shuddered slightly at the moist, pulpy feel of her eyeball as she grasped her contact lens. Balancing the filmy speck of plastic on her finger, she doused it with cleansing solution, then dropped it into storage. Her work world blurred as she repeated the ritual with the other lens, then came back into focus when she slipped on her tortoiseshell glasses.

Appearances meant a great deal to Henry, so Jamaica always carried an armload of papers into meetings with him. And ever since she'd overheard Henry tell someone he thought Jamaica looked smart but vulnerable in eyeglasses, she made a point of wearing spectacles around him.

"How do I look?" she asked Joanne, whose cubicle she passed on the way to the elevator.

"Like a fifties prom queen who really wants to be Miss All-Around Student." Joanne's desk was bare except for the neatly arranged copy of the story she was editing and a tube of lipstick. "The plaid skirt and cardigan sweater are bad enough, but tortoiseshell glasses and an armload of files? You meeting with Henry?"

"You got it."

"You look perfect."

Henry's office never failed to astonish Jamaica, with its elegant Victorian antiques, thick Oriental carpet, a Baccarat decanter. A fierce-looking turn-of-the-century gentleman surveyed the room from a portrait mounted on one of the paneled walls.

"He a relative of yours?" Jamaica had asked Henry on her first visit.

"Um, no. He was a Princeton trustee. A founding father of the eating club I belonged to."

"Oh," she had said. "Of course."

Henry had furnished his office at his own expense. The only evidence that a newspaperman worked there was the 1940 Corona typewriter propped up like a trophy on a fragile end table and the framed copy of the First Amendment hanging by the door.

Jamaica settled in the high-backed chair Henry pulled alongside his handsome mahogany desk, and looked at him expectantly. He drew a thin cigar out of an engraved silver box, then offered her one. (Henry often dated women who smoked thin cigars, an affectation he liked because he felt that only a rake would tolerate such behavior. A WASP rake.)

"You look terrific, kid," he purred. "Smart, but vulnerable. That's good for a reporter. You're doing a terrific job. We haven't had a chance to talk in a while."

"Right." Jamaica couldn't resist. "Well, I guess there hasn't been much need to since we put in the computer system. We can just flash messages back and forth."

Henry pulled his eyebrows together to form the mournful expression he used to convey hurt.

"I meant talk about things in general, not just stories. All work and no play and all that, you know." Henry leaned back in his chair, crossed his legs, and inhaled.

Jamaica began to worry. Either he was going to kill her story or impose some impossible deadline. If she'd been a better math student she would be able to graph the coordinates of Henry's affability and his demands. The more he wanted, the less direct he would be.

"Tell me, hon, what do you think about alternate-side-of-the-street parking?"

This was a curve. Jamaica simply smiled.

Henry began to talk, with a certain amount of passion. "I think it's just a way for police to harass local residents. Look, by making people move their cars from one side of the street to the other every morning, isn't the city discriminating against people who don't live with housemates who can spend an hour sitting in the car each day? Why don't they do it the way it's done in Paris—fifteen days on one side and fifteen days on the other."

Jamaica interrupted. "Why do they have alternate-side-of-the-street parking?"

Henry looked at her pityingly. "I told you. To harass local residents. Oh, they say it's to clean the streets, but look at the streets. Do you buy that?"

Jamaica hadn't seen Henry get so excited about anything since his Princeton reunion. His agitation seemed genuine as he puffed vehemently on his Cuban cigar.

"I get so irritated when I see these out-of-town cars parked in spaces in my neighborhood, making the whole situation even more difficult. You get up in the morning to move your car to the other side of the street and there's no spot. There's a Valiant from Pennsylvania, or a Chevy from Jersey. Just sitting there smugly, without having paid a dime in taxes. Really!"

As she observed the glower in Henry's dark eyes, Jamaica envisioned herself trooping around the Upper West Side asking men and women on the street their deepest feelings about alternate-side-of-the-street parking.

The thought pressed her lower in her chair, while Henry drew himself up straighter in his and beamed. He lowered his already silky soft voice conspiratorially. "You know when we had that big storm last week and the city took down all the wire garbage cans along Central Park West to keep them from blowing away? That left me without a place to deposit those disgusting little plastic bags I use to carry my dog's turds back from the park. You know what I do with them now?"

He whooped gleefully. "I just leave them on the hoods of the out-of-town cars."

"That's disgu—great, Henry." Jamaica paused as she tried to picture Henry skipping up Central Park West in his three-piece suit, dropping turd-filled plastic bags on cars. She laughed only when she remembered that Henry had been fined $100 last year for neglecting to scoop up after his dog, an elegant and mean-spirited Afghan.

"I guess it's tough to find parking spaces," she said with what she hoped sounded like sympathy.

"Oh, I don't have a car," said Henry. "It's the principle of the thing."

Blood leaked inside Jamaica's mouth, as she bit her lip to plug the shriek of laughter ready to explode in Henry's pious face. Pain settled her into a watery calm. Jamaica took off her glasses and dabbed at her eyes with her shirt sleeve.

"So, Henry."

"So, Jamaica. I had lunch with Ed Findlay the other day. It turns out he's in a bit of a bind for the magazine, week after next. A feature spread he'd assigned to a free-lance about best friends fell through. Brilliant girl, but a bit of a flake. Couldn't separate her work from her social life."

"Who is she?"

Henry reddened slightly. "Marcy Williams."

Jamaica shook her head. Marcy had been Mindy's replacement.

"Anyway, hon, this cloud has your silver lining. I mentioned your letter-writers piece to Ed, who was thrilled. He can give you lots of space, pictures, side bars, the works—a lot more than we could have gotten on the regular features pages. You have until a week from today to deliver the whole package."

The room seemed to tilt a little as elation crowded out Jamaica's sympathy for Marcy. "It could have been worse," Jamaica thought. "Henry might not have dumped her." Pushing against the arms of her chair, she stood up.

"That's great, Henry. I had just about all I need for the piece except a deadline and some enthusiasm from you, and now I guess I have both."

"You're such a card, hon. You know I always loved this story. I told Ed how I've been behind you on it all the way. Now, go to it, babe."

For the rest of the morning Jamaica pored over the piles of articles she'd clipped on the subject of loneliness. She was looking for some insight into the people she'd been interviewing for the past few weeks, but mostly what she needed was names of reputable, quotable psychologists or psychiatrists. The *Observer*'s editors scoffed (wisely, Jamaica thought) at the notion of hanging every social phenomenon on a psychological frame. All the same, they insisted on quotes from experts. The theory went that readers distrusted reporters but respected experts and were too stupid to figure out that the experts served as the reporters' dummies, their Charlie McCarthys. To keep up the illusion of objectivity, reporters often had to spend weeks sifting through experts until they found one or two whose version of the truth coincided with their own personal opinions.

One name kept reappearing. A Dr. Carla Miller had become the Will Rogers of loneliness. Her credentials were impeccable; *Newsweek, Time,* the *Washington Post,* and even the *New York Times* had on various occasions described her as "loneliness expert Dr. Carla Miller." Her brief but cataclysmic pronouncements had shown up in articles on loneliness and the business traveler, loneliness and the divorced mother, loneliness and teen-agers, loneliness and your pet. Much of what she said didn't hold up well under close examination, but what counted was the conciseness and authority with which she said it.

"Loneliness is a state of mind," according to Dr. Miller in *Newsweek.* "Think happy and you'll be happy."

"Sometimes you think you're lonely when you're just plain hungry," according to Dr. Miller in the *Ladies' Home Journal.* "Next time you feel that pit in your stomach, try a hamburger and fries."

"The end of loneliness could be only ten days away," according to Dr. Miller, in an ad for Nirvana Ten-Day Beauty Creme.

"I'd like to speak to Dr. Miller," Jamaica said to the celery-crisp voice on the phone.

"I'm sorry, the doctor's very busy. Are you a patient?"

Before Jamaica could answer, the voice pattered on. "Dr. Miller doesn't have any free time for three weeks except for regular appointments. Her TV schedule is so demanding, and there's the radio spots and speaking engagements. Let's see, now, if you're lucky I think I can squeeze you in first thing next month, three weeks from the day after tomorrow. That's a Friday."

"Wait, I'm not a patient exactly, I'm, well, you see, I'm . . ."

"You want to become a patient? In that case I'll have to get more time. The doctor requests all new patients to undergo a three-day series of tests before she accepts them. She doesn't have time for . . . ordinary cases that could be handled by just anyone. Are you recommended by someone?"

"Am I recommended? No, I'm not recommended. I'm not a patient and I don't want to be a patient. I'm . . ."

"Well, what do you want, dear?" Jamaica hated to be called "dear," a term of affection that had somehow come to mean bothersome tool or bitch.

"I'm a reporter with—"

"A reporter? Why didn't you say so? I'll buzz you right in."

"I thought you said the doctor was busy?" she said to an empty phone line.

A creamy yet authoritative voice broke in. "Hello?"

"Dr. Miller?"

"Yes. I'm sorry, I didn't catch the name of the publication you're with."

"The *Observer*. My name is Jamaica Just, and I'm doing a story about compulsive letter writers. Not to friends but to newspapers. I'd like some insight into what would make these people spend their time this way, what kind of people they might be, what their motives might be."

"You mean you'd like some quotes?"

"Not if you don't want to be quoted by name."

"Don't be foolish. I'm proud of my quotes. Ms. Just, is it? What's your number? I'll call you back in ten minutes."

Jamaica contemplated the silent telephone receiver and shook her head. She wanted to call Geneva and tell her to stop seeing her shrink immediately; however, she had to keep the line open for Dr. Miller.

Exactly ten minutes later the phone rang.

"Ms. Just? Carla Miller here. I think the compulsive letter writer must be a lonely person filled with rage or disappointment that he or she can't express in any other way." Jamaica copied down these words entering her ear slowly and distinctly as Dr. Miller read them to her with studied precision. Dr. Miller left nothing to chance. She took care to write her quotes before she handed them out so she could examine how well they resonated in print.

"These are people who live alone, either physically or spiritually, or perhaps both. Writing letters to newspapers is a way of avoiding looking inside themselves. Rather than looking into their own souls, they take refuge in the idea of the world around them. They aren't likely to venture out there themselves, but they will happily comment from the sidelines. This affords them the fervor and certainty that elude those caught up in the middle of the shifting, elusive morass we call life."

She paused. "Is that enough, or would you like some more?"

Jamaica scribbled feverishly. "Could you hold on a second?" Glancing over the doctor's stock of glib quotes, she shook her head and grinned. Put this lady in the Henry Frank grudging admiration society. What she does may be distasteful, but she does it well.

"What would you say if one of the letter writers had survived something horrible, like the Holocaust?"

After only a breath of a reflective beat, Dr. Miller was ready. "I would say that writing letters would be that person's way of gaining control. You could call it "undoing," performing a meaningless, purposeless ritual that is meant to erase guilt but that doesn't really accomplish anything. It's on the neurotic, not the psychotic end of the spectrum."

Jamaica's hand ached from writing so fast. "Thanks, Dr. Miller. This is just perfect. I couldn't have said it better myself."

"All right, then. Call me anytime." Dr. Miller then sent this afterthought over the wire. "And remember, loneliness isn't a cure for anything, but there are a thousand and one cures for loneliness."

"Right, yes. I'll keep that in mind." Jamaica spent the next few minutes crumpling the edges of Dr. Miller's Nirvana Beauty Creme ad. She gazed thoughtfully at the glossy picture of the smooth skin and slightly crinkled eyes of the elegant woman wearing a neat maroon suit and holding a jar of Nirvana in her well-manicured fingers.

"Joanne," she yelled from her chair. "Lunch?"

"Just a second." Jamaica heard the muffled murmur of Joanne's delicate voice wrapping up a telephone call. The reassuring echo of

Dr. Miller's prepackaged truths lingered in Jamaica's ear, as tranquilizing as the purr of a smooth-running train.

Joanne was amused by Jamaica's story about Dr. Miller. "My father used to talk like that." She swallowed her hiccuping aftershocks of laughter along with her grilled Swiss. Joanne ate the same lunch every day. It gave her a sense of continuity, she said.

"He wasn't quite that original, though. He was the only person I've ever met who actually spoke in homilies." She coughed. "'Half of life is if,' he'd say when I'd talk to him about missed possibilities. 'There's no fool like an old fool,' he said when my mother left him for another man."

"When did he stop? Did he go to a shrink?" Jamaica chuckled.

"Well, no. He stopped because he died."

Stunned, Jamaica pulled at the strand of cheese dangling from her mouth. She'd known Joanne for four years. They'd consumed pounds of melted cheese together. She knew the maximum number of orgasms Joanne had mustered on a single night, and she knew the embarrassing sobriquets Joanne conferred on her lovers' penises. She'd heard all about Mr. Robbins's coldness and alcoholism, but she hadn't heard that he was dead. How could she not have known?

"It didn't mean that much to me, when he died." Joanne flicked a cigarette ash. With her free hand she fiddled with the spigot of the sugar container.

"You must have been quite young."

"Twenty-three or twenty-four."

"It must have been painful."

"No. I can't remember his face. I can't remember the sound of his voice or what he smelled like. I barely have any memories of him at all."

Jamaica didn't believe her. How could she? Almost every day she confronted her father's face, slapped up like a poster in the front of her brain. Every day was Father's Day and Dr. Just was leading the parade. For a few years she'd managed to keep him at bay. He'd disappear until a holiday or a birthday, when he'd rear his handsome head. Ever since she got married, though, she'd had a hard time shaking him. She didn't know what his expectations were for her, but she was certain she wasn't living up to them. She licked her lips and tasted salt. That was the flavor of love, at least the kind of love she had for her father. High-sodium love—always served with a splash of tears. It's gone so fast; you know it was there only by the aftertaste.

Jamaica genuflected at the altar of her father's memory. Dr. Just embodied all the qualities she thought a prince among men should have. Except maybe understanding. Except maybe compassion. She'd worked hard to make up for his deficiencies by becoming so tender she'd wince in pain when a match was lit at forty paces. Sudden loud noises set off an immediate vibration of fear that knocked the wind out of her. The mere thought of sadness—anyone's sadness—made her chest ache and her eyes water with sympathetic congestion.

Her cockeyed stare and round cheeks gave her thin face the appearance of composure and warmth. Joanne reached across the table and lightly touched Jamaica's hand. "You are the dearest friend. Nothing ruffles you, yet I can tell you care."

Joanne's cool fingers dissolved the fog that had crept over Jamaica, who smiled blearily at her friend and drank some water.

"Oh, I almost forgot to tell you," Joanne giggled. With her immaculate blunt hair cut and tailored yet feminine silk dress, she looked misplaced behind the peeling Formica table, her slender hand maneuvering between the ketchup bottle and sticky salt and pepper shakers to reach the ashtray. "I've almost decided to marry Matthew. I've decided we're meant for each other after all."

Jamaica bit into an ice cube and gurgled. "Why now?"

"The other day I was crying about something awful he said to me. He said I only dated him because he didn't want to have children, so I knew he'd never tie me down. I went over to the mirror to fix my makeup and I was bowled over by how green my eyes were. Everything else was a mess, but my eyes almost meowed they were so cat-like green against my tears." She paused and leaned slightly forward. "They were almost as green as Matthew's eyes."

Jamaica examined Joanne's eyes. They were hazel with a few flecks of olive.

"Well, that's it." Joanne settled back in her seat with the self-satisfied look of a debater who's made an irrefutable point. Jamaica didn't know what to say, as she often didn't, and so simply waited for the torrent of words that was bound to come to fill her silence. People generally took her slow response time as an appeal for elaboration. They thought she was peering directly into their hearts, when in fact she didn't quite catch what they were saying.

"It just hit me that we were simply meant for each other. You know how you can look at yourself standing next to somebody in a picture and you realize you could be his sister? There's something so familial that you might as well not bother explaining. And Matthew is so stable; he understands my need for a house with trees and a view of the sunset."

As Joanne paused to pull on her cigarette, Jamaica thought about how, as long as she had known her, Joanne had refused to leave Manhattan for more than a few days at a stretch. When she returned after two weeks at the beach or in the country, she sighed with relief the minute her feet struck concrete.

"All right, Jamaica. Don't give me that look. How did you know?"

Jamaica sucked another ice cube from her glass. "Know what?"

"About Barry."

"Who's Barry?"

"He's this artist I met at my pottery class last week. I like him because we are so much alike. He understands I am a frustrated artist and that I'm only shuffling paragraphs around here because I have to earn a living." Joanne's co-op was fully paid for, and she went for weeks without ever picking up her paycheck. Jamaica had always assumed Joanne's father underwrote his daughter and, as it turned out, she was more or less right. Trust funds and other legacies darted through her mind as she raised her hand for the check.

But she didn't have time to dwell on these thoughts; she had a story to do, a deadline. Her lunch with Joanne was the last time she would come up for air until her story was nearly finished.

Sammy barely caught a glimpse of Jamaica for the rest of the week. By the time he'd awakened, she'd quietly have slipped out, leaving behind a trail of bran muffin crumbs, coffee on the warmer, and a barely legible note: "Am at office if you need me, sweet boy. Hope the Atlanta project is moving along. Home late. J." Night after night she crawled into bed, already half-asleep. The cat got diarrhea from polishing off the half-eaten peanut butter and jelly sandwiches Jamaica left on the counter.

At work, the floor of Jamaica's cubicle disappeared under a carpet of notes. Joanne peered in occasionally to watch her friend crawl around the floor, searching out a quote. Jamaica glanced up and squealed. "Dr. Crightendon hates his patients. That explains it!" She began to write excerpts as she went along, little vignettes that would be waiting for her in the computer when she was ready to sew it all together.

She neatly trimmed the afternoon she'd spent with Dr. Crightendon in his office into a soap opera episode; his was the kind of domestic woe that kept readers hooked. She wrote:

Dr. Arthur Crightendon, an eminent neurosurgeon, began writing his immaculately typed letters four years ago, after his wife left him.

"My personal life was in a shambles," he says. "I turned my attention to the world around me and found it was in a shambles, too."

Dr. Crightendon had been extremely ambitious, he says. From the moment he entered the prestigious Columbia University Medical School, he pointed his feet at the academic track. After graduation, he moved his wife from city to city, university to university. He played the game.

"The pawns," he says, "were my wife, my patients, and eventually me."

The upheavals of the sixties passed him by, as did the uneasy readjustments of the seventies. In 1980 he found himself with all he'd been working for—a university chairmanship, renown as a neurosurgeon, a lovely home, and a beautiful wife.

Then it all fell apart. "My wife ran off with a social worker," says Dr. Crightendon. "A nobody who made $16,000 a year. 'I don't care,' she told me. He's involved with other people. He isn't a grubbing careerist.'"

Shortly thereafter, the neurosurgeon says, he began to take note of the world around him and was appalled by what he saw. He expresses his carefully articulated rage in well-researched letters and Opinion Page pieces that generally concentrate on medical issues such as the Right-to-Die movement (he's for it) and the Right-to-Life movement (he's against it).

Lately, Dr. Crightendon says, he has cut back somewhat on his written work since he began participating in TV call-in shows. "I can reach a larger audience if my call is taken on, say, The Phil Donahue Show," *he explains. One such program elicited a telephone call from his wife, whom he hadn't spoken to in three years. "She called to tell me she was getting married again," he says.*

That done, Jamaica was ready to go home, exhausted yet oddly fulfilled by the silly little anecdote she'd filed for later use. Jamaica had once tried to analyze for Sammy the charge she got out of clipping and sorting masses of information into the shape of a story. Self-delusion didn't explain it; she didn't think for a minute she was creating art or even history on the run. The momentum that swept her along grew from having a sense of purpose—even the limited purpose of producing a story, some photo captions, a couple of side bars. For that period of time there was just one riddle to solve. Nothing else mattered. The world shrank to the size of an outline; philosophy shriveled to a good quote. On this scale things were manageable.

Before she left for the night, she set up a special computer file for the "expert commentary." There was David Lumpner, a sociologist working for something called the Institute for International Urbanism; he'd spent the last three years studying the relation between urban violence and the availability of twenty-four-hour news on television as well as radio. She loved his quote: "You may not know where Angola is, but it sounds sinister. Most of all, it's frustrating. You can't do anything about that, so if you have the time and the verbal skills, you protest about what's happening in your home town."

Jamaica "entered" Dr. Carla Miller's smooth pap, then came to her favorite, Joel Bregman, a specialist in pathological behavior at the Rappaport Psychiatric Center in Manhattan. He'd interrupted their interview three times to take calls from his mother. This is what he had to say about compulsive letter writers (which, she suspected, was the same thing he had to say about almost everyone): "Some people become so aware of injustice it becomes a kind of paranoia. They don't really know that what they're doing is trying to make their mothers love them."

As the deadline approached, the main piece still lay in fragments in her computer's brain. The side bars, however, were nearly finished. Her favorite was the "explainer," a generically solemn, authoritative essay studded with what Henry liked to call "factoids," bits of free-flying information that serve no useful purpose except to make you go "ah" when one of them pops up before your eyes. There were explainers for hijackings ("The first known hijacking occurred during the Roman Empire," the story would begin) and plane crashes ("The stabilizer design of the Boeing 747 has long been debated by aerodynamics experts) and Miss America scandals ("The pristine image of the Miss America contest was first clouded back in 1954, when one of the candidates was accused of padding her bathing suit. Since then . . . .)

Jamaica's explainer was about the mechanics of letters to the editor pages. *Observer* readers would learn that their newspaper received about 14,000 letters a year, compared with 12,000 for the *Herald* and 17,000 for the *Tribune*. The *New York Times* declined to disclose how many letters it receives each year. A spokesman said only that each letter was "given careful consideration."

Jamaica cited rules on what kinds of letters were printed, and how many from one person per year. The only letters the *Wall Street Journal* wouldn't run were those that seemed to be part of an organized campaign, like the October the paper received one hundred yellow postcards a day denouncing a subtle shift in the way the money supply was measured. The only letters the *Post* would run were those that "expressed strong personal opinion"; she didn't cite her suspicion that "strong personal opinions" were those that coincided with the *Post's* screeching editorials.

She produced statistics that answered questions few people would ever bother to ask: How many letter writers were regulars? How much postage revenue was generated by letters to the editor nationwide and in the New York area? How much newsprint did letters chew up, and how much money did newspapers spend on personnel and letter openers? What percentage of readers turn to the letters column (a) first thing, (b) right after the front page but before the editorials, (c) after the editorials, (d) not at all? (Someone in the circulation department had actually bothered to ask the last question after the *Observer's* publisher once mused whether anyone actually read the letters to the editor. They'd discovered the letters weren't the first thing anyone read, but they were more frequently read than the editorials.)

She was about to start writing when the phone rang. Paper scattered like dust balls as she scrambled to dig out the phone. "Gee, hi, Mr. Palermo . . . Abraham . . . Tomorrow night?"

She tried to mask her impatience. "Gosh, I don't think so. I've been working on that piece I told you about all week and I'm supposed to have a draft due tomorrow . . .

"What's my lead? You really want to hear it?"

Whatever annoyance she felt at being interrupted vanished. Jamaica's anxiety that people would laugh at what she had to say was always doing battle with her eagerness to be heard. She was grateful for Abraham's—anyone's—interest, so grateful that she violated the paper's policy against letting outsiders have an early look—or listen, in this case—at a story. She'd been fiddling around with a catchy opening anecdote and was glad to try it out on someone. She began:

Every day George Percy Adams writes three or four letters to Jerry O'Reilly, the man in charge of the New York Herald's *Letters to the Editor section. Each letter is precisely three pages long; "precisely" because Mr. Adams begins typing at the top of page one and doesn't stop until the bottom of page three. Each letter is on the same subject: international terrorism. Of the approximately 1,100 letters Mr. Adams writes to the* Herald, *exactly none get printed.*

She paused. "You liked that? You want me to go on?" With his go-ahead, she continued to read the green words on her screen.

"One day I'll get it just right," shrugged the affable Mr. Adams, a night watchman for the Brooklyn Gas Company. Mr. Adams, for-

merly a political science professor at an upstate college, left academia five years ago to write what he calls "the definitive work" on terrorism, past and present. So far, though, he's only written the prologue. "I keep getting distracted by news begging for commentary," he said. "If I can just get one letter printed, I'll be able to move on."

Jamaica deepened her voice, to seem more the authoritative narrator.

In some ways Mr. Adams is a throwback to the days of Pompeii, when every hovel was the Fourth Estate, when publicly posted missives from ordinary citizens functioned as newspapers. These days, most newspaper and magazine readers are passive. They are content to respond to bad news with a cluck and a sigh, and to good news with a smile. Once every decade or so something will hit them where they live and they'll fire off a letter to the editor.

She giggled. "You like 'cluck and a sigh?' Not too folksy? God, this is so nice of you."

Mr. Adams, however, belongs to an elite corps of readers. The Herald's Mr. O'Reilly calls them the "Irregular Regulars." Others call them armchair activists. Still others call them screwy. Who are they? They are habitual writers of Letters to the Editor.

"Nope, sorry. That's all I've written. Which is why I have to get off the telephone. This thing really is due tomorrow. Thanks a lot for listening . . . You mean that?" Jamaica was embarrased to feel the blush crawling up her neck. "You really think it's good?" She hesitated just a second. "Listen, about dinner tomorrow night. Could we play it by ear? See if I'm coherent by the end of the day? I can't thank you enough for your encouragement. I feel ready to forge ahead."

Without pausing to consider why she'd changed her mind about dinner with Palermo, Jamaica cleared her computer screen. She kicked her piles of notes against the walls of her cubicle, then reseated herself in front of the terminal. Its blank face now seemed combative. She tried to picture what would follow her lead, how the anecdotes would coalesce into a story on the screen. The computer defiantly presented her instead with the image of a gnarled old man huddled by a subway entrance. Jamaica squeezed her eyes shut, then slowly reopened them. The monochrome monitor hadn't released the distracting image. The old man floated there, a blur of gray thrust into relief by his bright red sweater, which sparkled in the early autumn sunlight. He gleamed like a polished apple on a plate. Inexplicably, Jamaica felt a joyful moment of revelation, the way she felt when she glimpsed humanity corraled in the confines of a great work of art.

She wasn't really surprised to see the old man's image dancing on her computer screen. There was something mystical to her about writing, a process she would never fully comprehend. She hadn't conjured up the old man; he'd been hanging around the subway entrance on her way to work that morning. She flushed, remembering how she'd looked directly into the dissipated old man's shifting eyes that morning and seen the ghost of something that had made her smile. Her delight was fresh, unspoiled by even a trace of moldy pity.

The old man had jerked his head up off his chest.

"Thank you, Miss Sunshine," he had yelled. "Thank you for that smile, I feel blessed today."

Jamaica had nodded at him before he disappeared behind a mass of briefcases and legs; an "E" train had just arrived in the station. She'd bolted up the street, exhilarated by her contact with the man she'd already designated a good luck omen.

"There is hope for the future," she'd thought, even as she sidestepped the Vietnam vet—labeled as such by the sign dangling around his neck—who was slumped cross-legged, as always, near the entrance to the *Observer*.

Now, faced with the blank screen and a deadline, she knew she couldn't rely on magic. "Okay, Saint Just," Jamaica muttered to herself. "Think about your lead." Who were these people she'd been interviewing and interviewing? "People with a lot of anger about something they don't want to confront head on," one of her experts had said. "It's easier for them to rant at the world. They want to talk, but they don't know how." Mechanically, Jamaica ordered the computer to display her original story proposal. She reread her own, unfamiliar words, and sent them back into the computer's memory, which was far more precise and obedient than her own. Without consciously processing the anecdotal material stored in her brain, she pressed "enter" and began to write.

For several hours she was locked in a trance with Jules Marlin, Miss Frances Walker, the elusive Congressman Unglemeyer. She took special pains to include a trenchant quote from Sherley, and to balance the anecdotal material from the *Observer* with stories and facts from other newspapers.

Jamaica filed the story in her computer without bothering to reread it. She was exhausted. She pushed back her chair and stumbled out into the deserted newsroom to check the time. It was ten-thirty. She stared at the darkened partitions and briefly noted that they were perfect hiding places for a murderer or rapist. Shadows danced on the walls and ceilings; maybe they were reflections of the dim, flickering fluorescent night lights, and maybe they weren't.

"Shh, don't be a baby," her mother would whisper to her daughter when she cried out in the night. Eva would slip into Jamaica's bed and promptly fall dead asleep, leaving her terrified daughter wide awake in the dark with her demons and with no room to move.

"Don't be a jerk," she now said to herself, as she pinched the flesh of her own left cheek very hard. Her legs refused to move toward the door. "Now I know what those trashy mysteries mean when they talk about the heroine being 'frozen in terror,'" she thought. The numbness of exhaustion gave way to the clammy palpitations of dread.

"Miss Just?" a voice called out softly, menacingly.

Still unable to move, Jamaica squatted, grabbed her knees with her arms, and bowed her head. She had no desire to stare death in the face. Let it stab her in the back.

Finally she felt the expected touch on her shoulder, and she began to weep.

"Don't cry, Miss Just," the voice said. "I wouldn't leave without saying good-bye to you.

Was the Angel of Death from the Bronx? This voice sounded familiar. Jamaica risked a glance upward. She was blinded by an explosion of light. Her pupils contracted, then widened. A fuzzy silhouette came into focus as Stanley Portnoy, the copy boy.

Copy man, really. Stanley had worked at the *Observer* for eighteen years and six months. He updated Jamaica on his tenure every day when he dropped off the mail. Not all of Stanley's wires were plugged in, as Sammy liked to say. There was something comforting about him though: about the way he appeared at the entrance to her cubicle every morning at exactly ten-fifteen, the way he tapped exactly twice on the edge of the opening before he came in, the way he always asked her for a light even though she never had one, the way he propped himself up on the edge of her desk and asked her if she actually got paid for making up stories, the way he asked her if she'd ever seen the pictures of his daughters, and the way he showed them to her every day.

Stanley was a fixture in the place, like tickers and typewriters.

"What the hell are you doing?" Jamaica shrieked.

Like typewriters.

"Did you say 'leave,' Stanley?"

"Yeah, Miss Just. They told me I've been . . . wait a second." Stanley pulled a crumpled piece of paper from his pocket.

"We regret to inform you your job's been obsolesced," he read with some difficulty. "The mail delivering function will be handled by Triton II, the new robot delivery system from BMH."

"I'm sorry, Stanley."

"I got this last week and I kept waiting for a good-bye party. I guess they forgot."

"Stanley, if I'd only known."

"Oh, that's okay, Miss Just. I went out this morning and bought a big good-bye card and I took it around to everyone at the paper to sign. I'm going to make a scrapbook. That's why I'm taking pictures. I kept coming by here but you were in front of the computer and I know better than to disturb you at work."

She remembered all the times she'd yelled at Stanley for bothering her, and winced.

He handed her an oversized greeting card. A group of cartoon characters waving tennis rackets danced under the word *Congratulations*. Jamaica opened the card. Inside, dozens of tennis balls rushed toward a single cartoon character cheerfully holding up his tennis racket.

"You've got the world by the balls," it said.

She noticed that many of the autographs were addressed to "Sam," and a couple to "Sandy." Right in the middle was Henry's farewell, written in bold, black strokes. "You're a good man, Stanley Portnoy. Cheers, Henry Frank."

"Here, Miss Just. I saved you a spot right up on top. I'll miss you."

"I'll miss you, too, Stanley. Do you know what you'll do next?"

"Oh, I'm not worried. There's lots of things around for a guy like me, don't you figure?"

"Where do you want me to sign?"

"Right up there."

Jamaica gave Stanley her best wishes in writing, looked at him in the eye and did something she would never do deliberately. She lied.

"I figure there are a million things around for a guy like you, Stanley. You want to walk me down to the subway?"

16

Passion

Remarkably cool and clear air slapped Jamaica awake when she stepped out of the subway station. The autumn night was brisk and reassuring, like a British schoolmistress.

When had autumn arrived, she wondered?

Tired as she was, Jamaica was reluctant to leave this chilled night, which she longed to press against her cheek like a bottle of champagne. Writing all day—and, yes, her unexpected interlude with Abraham—had revived the sparkle of promise she hadn't felt in a very long time. She was afraid to go home and face the distance she'd inserted between herself and Sammy.

What used to be the neighborhood *bocce* court appeared on her right as she ambled up the street. She paused to sit awhile on one of the new benches the Parks Department had recently deposited there. The benches seemed forlorn, out of place on the asphalt that had been spread over the courts a few months earlier. She felt nostalgic for the *bocce* courts. They had been used only once a year for a tournament sponsored by Sambuca Romana and were obliterated after the neighbors complained about the dog shit that piled up on the dirt courts in between tournaments.

She much preferred autumn to spring; the lyricists' favorite season had always struck Jamaica as rather a sad time—all that fragile new life struggling to survive. She felt anxious peering at the raw earth, wondering if this would be the year that the grass simply wouldn't return. The promise of spring made her nervous because it carried with it the potential for failure. Autumn, on the other hand—at least autumn in Harmony—had always been thrilling. All along the country roads clipped fields and bales of hay offered evidence that the long, toiling hours of summer hadn't gone to waste. With the harvest came relief.

Jamaica remembered the autumn calm that followed the death-defying nights of summer, when she used to sneak out of the house in the middle of the night and go drag racing with the boys. Other girls would display the hickeys on their breasts when they congregated in the locker room before softball games. Jamaica would smile slyly, and think instead about how she'd outstripped all the guys out there on Route 47 on nights so sticky her bare legs could have been lined with gum, the way they stuck to the vinyl car seats.

Terrified and exhilarated, she'd do ninety-five on the curves between Harmony and Peach Nook, whipping past the signs that said "Dip" and "Curve" and "30 MPH." She'd keep her accelerator foot pressed pretty near the floor no matter what, egged on by Jimmy Ebberly, whose yellow MG she was usually driving. Jimmy wasn't from around Harmony. He was an Army brat whose dad had decided to retire to the country.

The Ebberlys lasted only three years, long enough for Jamaica to learn how to drive a stick shift and how to make out around one, and for Jimmy to die with a telephone pole wedged between his eyes.

Jamaica stopped hot rodding after that, and she was the one who shinnied the hundred feet up to the top of the town's silver water tower with a can of red spray paint. "Long live Jimmy Ebberly," she wrote above and below the black letters that spelled out "Harmony." She was a senior in high school then, and she sat up there on top of the tower for a very long time, staring out over the scattered lights sparkling in the blackness that was Harmony at night. She sat up there and sobbed as she thought about what a fool Jimmy was and how her father would kill her if he knew where she was, which made her half-inclined to tell him.

It broke Eva's heart to watch Jamaica mope around the house after Jimmy died, wearing ragged shorts and dragging around a beat-up copy of *Moby Dick* and asking unanswerable questions.

"What was Captain Ahab after, Mommy? The meaning of life? I bet whales feel stupid, don't they, with those little eyes that see sideways. They see so much peripherally and miss what's right in front of them, huh?"

Eva was sorting out Medicaid forms on the kitchen table. Jamaica was silhouetted against the window. Eva patted a new bloom on the African violet on the ledge, then reached up to smooth Jamaica's hair; its unruliness was exacerbated in those days by its waist length.

"Remember Gregory Peck in the movie, darling? We saw it together on *Saturday Night at the Movies*?"

Jamaica leaned against her mother's chair and began to cry. "Why did Jimmy have to die, Mommy? He didn't hurt anybody. What's the point?"

Eva continued to stroke Jamaica's hair with one hand and shuffle papers with the other.

"Darling, sometimes I don't know what the point is. To tell you the truth, I never feel like I'm part of it. In that camp I felt like I was floating above it all, like I wasn't there."

"Did you get used to seeing people die?"

"In Auschwitz I didn't see dead people. They just took people away and disposed of them in the crematorium." She paused. "We could smell them," she said absently.

Jamaica grabbed her hair out of her mother's hand.

"Could you bring the wastebasket over here, dear?" Eva had a pile of empty envelopes to throw away. Jamaica brought the trash can to the edge of the table. "I didn't see dead people until we were liberated," said Eva. She dropped a handful of paper into the trash. "On both sides of the roads we saw bodies of German soldiers. We didn't know who killed them or how they got there. I just felt happy to see them dead."

Jamaica forgot her tears for a moment. "Didn't it give you the creeps? All those corpses?"

Eva ripped open another envelope with her fingernail. "I'd never seen a dead person except before the war. A Gentile woman we knew died, and they showed her. She looked so peaceful."

She studied the form she pulled from the envelope.

"Why don't you go rest with Daddy in the den, darling. You'll feel better."

Mournfully, Jamaica went into the family room, where her father had taken to reading Hungarian poetry in the afternoon instead of going on house calls. She slumped on the sofa and slung one leg over the arm.

"Why did Jimmy die so young?" she asked Dr. Just accusingly. "He was just a kid out for a good time, and God knows, he wasn't the first person in this world to drive too fast."

Dr. Just didn't tell her to sit up straight. He pulled his maroon cardigan sweater tighter around his ribs—when had he gotten so thin?—and took off his black-rimmed eyeglasses. The snap was out of him. He looked small sitting there in his big reclining chair.

"You can't explain God's ways, Jamaica." His voice was thin too.

"Do you believe in God, Daddy?"

He glanced at the book tucked under her left arm. "What was that passage you read from your book there at dinner the other night?"

Jamaica raised her head in surprise. "You were listening?"

Dr. Just ignored the question. "Read it to me."

Jamaica thumbed through her book, then read quietly.

Is Ahab, Ahab? Is it I, God, or who, that lifts this arm? But if the great sun move not of himself; but is an errand-boy in heaven; nor one single star can revolve, but by some invisible power; how then can this one small heart beat; this one small brain think thoughts unless God does that beating, does that thinking, does that living, and not I. By heaven, man, we are turned round and round in this world, like yonder windlass, and Fate is the handspire.

She paused and looked at her father, who was gazing at the ceiling.

"But do you believe in God, Daddy?"

He hesitated and pressed his fingertips together.

"The laws are all there, in the Bible," he said slowly. "God told Moses to deliver the Ten Commandments to the people. It must have been God, or some kind of . . . what is the expression? . . . higher being. That *Moby Dick* paragraph makes sense. And maybe it's better not to ask too many questions."

"What kind of religion is Judaism, anyway?" Jamaica was crying again. "This Jewish God is so tough. There isn't any rest for the weary, Daddy. There isn't any forgiveness. There isn't even heaven. What are you supposed to look forward to?"

Dr. Just was ready for that one. "You're supposed to look forward to life on this earth. Do your best on this earth. Be a good girl on this earth."

Jamaica responded with a whine of fiery impatience, the kind that comes only from the daringly foolish mouths of the self-righteous, or teen-agers.

"But do you believe in God, Daddy?"

"I believe you have to learn that death is part of life," he said deliberately. His fingertips, still pressed together, were white. "Knock on wood, you have a long life in front of you and . . . and death is part of life. Your friend Jimmy just learned that a little early."

Jamaica jerked upright, tears running down her face.

"You can be so cruel, Daddy," she said. "Was Jimmy not good enough for you to care about because he wasn't a Jew?"

Without a word, Dr. Just put his eyeglasses back on and resumed reading. His face contorted slightly, as though he'd unwittingly gulped a slug of milk that had gone sour. Not very long afterward he was dead, and the dismay on his face at that moment would haunt his daughter's dreams.

Jamaica's tears still ran, all those years later, as she sat on a bench in an asphalt park, formerly a Greenwich Village *bocce* court. When she finally went home and slipped into bed, she told Sammy she'd almost finished her story, and that she might have dinner with Abraham Palermo the next night, since it was Sammy's poker night.

"That's nice, dear," he murmured. "Take a cab home and make him wait until you get in the door in case the game runs late and I get in after you."

Jamaica pressed her face right up against Sammy's. His soft lips trembled as he blew even snores into her mouth.

Lying sleepless in bed, she realized with a shock how long it had been since she had paid attention to the man whose outline loomed next to her in the dark. She suspected that in every marriage there comes a time when you stop paying attention. That's the moment when you think you know exactly what a gesture means, or a silence, and you don't bother to ponder it too deeply—if you consider it at all. There is great comfort in that heartbreaking, liberating moment when you are freed from the consuming uncertainty of fresh love and can pay attention again to the world, to work, to everything that exists outside of passion. The passion hasn't died, necessarily; it has simply matured from the wailing urgency of a child's "I want's" to the measured reasoning of an adult.

She didn't feel very grown-up just then. She felt exhausted, far too weary to keep her anxieties from free associating. Pulling the quilt over her head, she wondered what was wrong with her. She had the best kind of husband, a man who only wanted her to be happy. He never complained about her demanding working hours or the demands she put on herself. Don't take it all personally, as Henry said. None of it's real. A hijacking here, a blast of terror there. Our job is to tell it like it is, and move on.

Move on? To where? And who's arguing on the other side? What kind of debate is it, where everyone agrees? Who's saying—besides the cranks and lunatics—that the Holocaust was a good thing? All right, the cranks and the lunatics and the otherwise normal people who might whisper words to that effect late at night in their bedrooms in Berlin, or Philly, or think such things quietly across the lunch table. "Only 12 million of 'em left around the world. Shut up, Jews! We're sick of you and your bedraggled tale of woe."

Jamaica's frenetic musings were momentarily quelled by a thud.

The cat had settled in on the portion of quilt covering Jamaica's head. Jamaica stuck a hand out to rub her pet's fur. But hard as she tried, she couldn't doze off. She was wired.

How do you invest life with tautness and urgency? she wondered. Look at Mommy, she thought. Eva's the last living heroine, isn't she? She's the only reminder we—I—have that survival can be a form of hope. She isn't like Jules Marlin, burying himself in the "reality" of the news while he hides out from the world. Yet how can you look at life objectively without worrying about getting pushed onto the sub-way tracks by a recently released mental patient, or being murdered by an upholsterer with a rap sheet long enough to cover a couch? And what if you can't escape in dreams?

Still, Jamaica thought, trying yet another sleeping position, she'd be damned if she'd sink into the anomie that had consumed her gen-eration. Even in literature. Henry had deleted her ideas on the subject from an acerbic piece she'd done on postmodernist fiction, of which he was a great fan.

"Anomie will be the death of literature," Jamaica had written. "Aren't we getting a little tired of characters who stare at each other blankly as they casually dispense with death and despair? Aren't we getting bored with passages like this: 'I loved him once,' she thought. She bit an apple. She forgot his face. She forgot his name. She went to sleep.'"

Was she, Jamaica, really content to think of passion as something "adult" and "reasonable?" No, she realized, as she lay there tor-mented by wakefulness. She wasn't so different from Jules Marlin, finding passion in the terror stoked by fear. How could she rely on something, someone as sustaining, as settled, as *safe* as Sammy? He could lull her into feeling secure, a delusion far more dangerous than danger itself. What if, as Geneva once had said, another Holocaust was just around the corner? Or was she afraid of something entirely different?

From this jumble of thoughts emerged one final question, as she drifted off to sleep: When had Sammy stopped listening to her and why hadn't she noticed? How long had she been sailing without her anchor?

17

Unhinged

Tuesday Jamaica jumped out of bed, pumped up by the insomniac's jitters and the press of final deadline. She passed the morning in a tinkering frenzy—tightening sentences, rearranging paragraphs. She grew dizzy from scrolling her words up and down her computer screen, reading and rereading her story as she tried to come up with the catch phrase Henry wanted for her epistolary subjects (finally settling on "the Irregular Regulars"). By the time she'd massaged the main piece to her satisfaction, it was already afternoon, leaving her just a few hours to work up the Jules Marlin side bar ("Holocaust Survivor: Pen Mightier than Sword?"). It was a trick to insinuate the anecdote about his anxious nights in hiding, listening to his cellar mates make love, but she managed, all the while berating herself for leaving so much until the last minute. In the end, she thought she'd stitched together a nice piece of handiwork that portrayed Jules as the last angry man, the seeker of truth. Finally, exhausted, she tossed in a last tidbit to balance the piece, to give it the air of objectivity: Dr. Miller's observations on why a Holocaust survivor, in particular, might become a letter-writing addict.

As she transmitted the story and side bars to Henry's computer, her phone rang.

"There's a Mr. Palermo here to see you," said the security guard.

"Who?" Then, remembering, Jamaica pulled out the compact her mother had bought her when she got married ("I want you to look healthy in the pictures," Eva had said). She was very pale.

"Could you put him on the phone?" she asked the guard.

She listened to Abraham explain, a little nervously, that he happened to be in the neighborhood and wondered if she felt up to dinner. Remember, she'd said she might, after her story was finished?

"Gee, I don't know," she said, brushing pink powder on her cheeks until she looked rather feverish. She surveyed the mess in her cubicle, then thought of going home to an empty apartment and spending the evening waiting for Sammy to come back from his poker game.

"You know what?" She paused, as though she herself wasn't sure what she was going to say next. "I'd love to have dinner, if you don't mind spending the evening with someone who's a little bedraggled."

On the elevator ride to the lobby—after stopping in the ladies' room to pull herself together—Jamaica began to feel revived, even enthusiastic.

A much thinner man than the one she remembered was waiting by the guard's desk.

"Mr. Palermo? Abraham? Jamaica Just here," she said heartily, thrusting her hand forward.

"Yes, I remember," he laughed. "How are you?"

"Exhausted."

"I'm sorry. Would you rather do this some other time?"

"Oh, no. I didn't mean exhausted. I meant tired. Tired of work. Not tired of work, I like work. I meant tired of working on this specific story. No. Dinner, that would be great. Fine."

With some amusement Abraham watched Jamaica pull on her hair and rock from one foot to the other. His eyes were startlingly green, the same color as the type on the computer screen. Joanne should meet this guy, Jamaica thought. He'd fit in her family album.

The limousine wasn't waiting when they arrived on the street.

"I've gotten past that," he said when she asked him what happened to it.

They went to dinner at the Russian Tea Room. Jamaica was a sucker for this gaudy show-biz eatery, where it was Christmas all year round. She wasn't put off by its red tackiness even though it had been the site of many a vapid celebrity interview. Press agents would call her and tell her their clients absolutely loathed interviews, and being gawked at, yet, inevitably, they congregated at Elaine's or the Russian Tea Room. How many times had she listened to the bored and the beautiful explain with false earnestness their never-ending search for "serious" roles that had "relevance" in today's world. Once they were box office gold, they'd stop making sequels of tired pap, they'd never prance as nudie-cuties again.

Abraham set the basket of pumpernickel bread on Jamaica's side of the table.

"You've lost a lot of weight, haven't you?" Jamaica ventured, as she idly tore a piece of bread into crumbs and dropped them on her plate.

"Yeah, I went to one of those fat farms out in California," he said a bit sheepishly. "Me and the girls. At least I didn't have to get the bikini waxes."

They drank vodka and he told her about the Sephardic origins of his peculiar name, about how stupid Hollywood executives are, and about the director of the latest Palermo production.

"He's a nice guy, but he always says the wrong thing. The first thing he says to me when I get back from the fat farm: 'You put on weight?'"

Abraham gestured for the waiter.

He picked up his story. "I tell him, 'I just lost twenty pounds.' "So what does the *putz* say to me? I've practically fed him his next line. 'Wow!' he says. 'You must have really ballooned up since I saw you.'"

They drank more vodka. Jamaica felt a little wild, as intoxicated by the close attention Abraham seemed to be paying to her words as by the Stolichnaya. She was accelerating into high charm, encouraged by Abraham's acquiescent smile. Eva had always told her girls that none of the Just women were exactly what you would call gorgeous—in the *conventional* sense. However, she assured them, they radiated an innocent energy that, in the right reflected light, attracted people in a way mere perfect features couldn't. Sober, Jamaica thought that was just another way of saying her right eye was slightly crossed and that she had a small bump on her nose. Drunk, Jamaica discovered that Eva's wisdom could pass for truth.

She began telling war stories. Her mother's war stories. "She'd been moved from Auschwitz to Tzittau some months earlier, as the Russians advanced. When she woke up that morning, the seventh of May, 1945, the Germans were already gone. The day before she'd been a prisoner, listening to the Russians shooting Stalin candles in the distance. In the morning she was free.

"You can imagine, people went wild. They'd been starved and now they were free. The food bins were theirs. My mother and her friend Bella caught a chicken."

Jamaica lowered her rather squeaky voice and assumed an exaggerated Hungarian accent.

"Pretend I'm Eva, *draga*—that's "darling"—okay?"

Abraham wiped his mouth and nodded with a giggle.

"I said, 'Geve me a good knife.'" She winked conspiratorially, the way Eva would. "I remembered the way the *shochet* did it."

She shrugged her shoulders, like Eva. "Vell, the knife vasn't a sharp knife. I know I'd vatched the kosher butcher turn the neck of the cheecken up and take out a few fedders and just keel it. Boom! Vith a sharp blade."

Jamaica chugged the rest of her Stoly.

"I took that cheecken over the toilet and I couldn't keel it. I kept hacking and hacking and it vas just skvirming and skvirming, skvawking like a *meshuggeneh*."

She grabbed the edge of her napkin and shook it above the table, as though to strangle it, then threw the wrinkled linen on the plate of bread.

"Finally, I held its body on the ground vith my foot and slammed the knife down vith all my strength. The head came off and I stepped back. The next thing I knew, the cheecken's body was racing around and around in a circle, spraying blood from its neck. Round and round like a sprinkler, covering all of us vith blood."

The silence that followed Jamaica's overexuberant rendition of this gory anecdote was broken by a swarm of red and green brocade. Waiters converged on them; china clattered, silverware clanged. When the bustle stopped, Abraham was grimacing. On the plate in front of him rested a tidy piece of chicken Kiev, its chest pierced by a knife. Butter dribbled onto the plate.

He looked at Jamaica's crimson face, and at the chicken. Gingerly, he slid out the knife, sliced a bite of meat, and waved his fork in the air.

"To liberation!" he cried, toasting Jamaica with the dangling chicken flesh.

She raised a glass of water, gratefully.

"To liberation."

They ate their platters of rich Russian food and drank more vodka and talked until the tables around them emptied and the waiter placed the check on the table.

They kept on drinking and talking. Jamaica felt as though she were watching Abraham through a pane of very clear, hot glass. He asked her what she was working on so hard, and as she told him about her story, she realized how much she had to say. She explained how the letter-writers story had taken on some irrational importance to her that she herself didn't understand and that Sammy didn't want to hear about.

"Sammy?"

"My husband, Sammy."

"You're married?"

Jamaica leaned back a little unsteadily. The vodka was taking effect.

"Yes, I'm married." She waved her left hand in the air. "What do think this is? My high school ring?"

Abraham laughed a little crazily.

"Of course you're married. A girl like you, who's good-looking, accomplished and so . . . I don't know. Adult. You seem to have a grip on what you're doing."

"Me?" Jamaica shrieked. "You think I have a grip? I seem gripped? Oh, my God. Excuse me."

The shock of hearing an attractive stranger volunteer this extraordinary view of her acted as a catalyst for the chemical reaction already occuring between the vodka and the mushrooms stroganoff. Jamaica stumbled halfway to her feet, then leaned over the table and threw up, vigorously and substantially. Horrified, she watched her vomit splash across the white tablecloth and engulf the check. She collapsed weakly in her chair.

By the time she'd mustered the courage to raise her mortified head, Abraham had gathered the four corners of the tablecloth together and tied the whole soiled mess—dirty dishes and all—into a neat packet. He motioned for the waiter.

"Would you mind writing us up another check?" he said calmly. "I don't think we'll be wanting any dessert, thanks."

Jamaica shrank back as Abraham walked around the table to her chair.

"I'm sorry," she blubbered. "Maybe you should just leave me here. I'll get a cab home."

Abraham chuckled. "What is wrong with you? You aren't the first person to lose her cookies after too many laughs mixed with too much Stoly." He took hold of her arm and led her to the ladies' room.

"Anyone in there?" he called out, holding the door open with his toe. When no one answered, he pulled Jamaica inside, bent her over a sink, and gently washed her face with cool water. Holding her at arm's length with both hands, he inspected her, then dabbed some water on her sleeves, which had gotten caught in the line of fire.

"You aren't mad at me?" Jamaica asked in disbelief.

"I'm only mad at myself for not having met you sooner," Abraham said. He didn't miss Jamaica's grimace.

"Not a very good line, huh?"

Jamaica grinned. "You think I'm going to criticize your dialogue after this?" She pointed vaguely at the tiled walls.

Abraham steadied her by the arm. "You feeling well enough to go?"

"I'm fine, thank you."

The dining room was quiet except for the occasional clatter of dishes. Only two other customers remained, a couple huddled in anxious conversation in a booth along the wall. She looked distantly familiar, someone who had perhaps appeared in the back section of *People* magazine, once.

Abraham briefly studied their second check.

"What do I owe you?" Jamaica asked, unclasping her bag.

"You don't have to pay for your dinner," he said. "You didn't even get to digest it."

"Oh, no, I always pay my own way. It isn't political. I mean, it was my father, not Gloria Steinem, who told me not to let anyone take care of me. Financially."

Abraham regarded her fondly. Despite the mess Jamaica had made of the evening, he seemed infatuated enough to want to find out more about her perfect marriage—enough to run the risk of becoming her friend if he couldn't be her lover.

"Fifty-five dollars should do it."

"Fifty-five?"

"Hey, they make you pay for it whether you keep it down or not."

"I like your style, Palermo."

When Abraham dropped her off in front of her building, he kissed her on the forehead. "What I meant to say back in the bathroom was that I have a knack for being in the wrong place at the wrong time. I hope you feel better in the morning."

Jamaica drifted up the stairs in a pleasant fog. As she reached the third-floor landing, her cat's hungry whines echoed two flights down. Jamaica picked up her pace; she was out of breath by the time she walked into the dark apartment. She flicked on the light in the kitchen, then opened a can of Meow Meat, flinching at the coarse smell of the "by-products" the label said were ground together with the liver and egg stew. The cat leaped at this foul meat with the exuberance a gourmand might display for blini and caviar. Something jerked inside Jamaica, as though her stomach were gasping for air. While the cat greedily slurped, Jamaica thumbed through the mail. There was a huge bill from American Express itemizing lots of restaurants she didn't recognize. Must be business, she thought, tossing the bill on the "keep" pile. There were lots of flyers with coupons; these she carefully ripped out and stored in a large envelope stuffed with three years' worth of unused coupons. There was her weekly edition of the *Smith County Defender,* the paper she used to read as a girl in Harmony and still subscribed to. She scanned the front page, which listed the week's divorces and arrests. The Gilmore boy had been fined for letting manure seep into his milk tank. (The Gilmore boy was now thirty but would be known as "the Gilmore boy" until his parents died. Then his son, now known as "the Gilmore boy's boy" would become "the Gilmore boy." Jamaica was still referred to as "Doc's daughter," even though more than a decade had passed since either Doc or his daughter had lived in Harmony.)

Jamaica stuck the American Express bill in a drawer and scribbled a good-night note to Sammy. She wandered into the bathroom and splashed some water on her face, then smeared thick cream around her eyes and mouth, and on her neck. In the magnifying mirror she held inches from her face, the pores of her skin yawned like murky potholes. She washed her face again, this time with a steamy hot washcloth followed rapidly by handfuls of icy water. The shock clamped the pores shut.

She taped Sammy's note to the toilet and crawled into bed.

At Loose Ends

As if by silent agreement, Sammy and Jamaica didn't display much interest in each other's Tuesday night out, although Jamaica did mention she'd thrown up.

"Anxiety, I guess," she shrugged.

"Yeah," Sammy answered. "Okay now?"

When Abraham called to see how she felt, she was friendly but a little cool. There were lots of last-minute details to check, editors to haggle with over the final version of her letter-writers "package." It was scheduled for Sunday's paper.

Sammy worked on Saturday, so Jamaica had a quiet day reading and watching part of *Wuthering Heights* on television. That evening they caught a double feature at the Theater 80 near St. Marks Place, ate dinner at one of the cheap Indian restaurants on Sixth Street, and walked around the East Village, holding hands, waiting till the time came to pick up the first edition of Sunday's paper at the big newsstand over by West Fourth Street. Jamaica refused to open the newspaper until they were safely home, where she could alternately admire and cringe at the final product in private.

Sammy, who in the past had been her most eager reader, skimmed the piece before offering his perfunctory congratulations.

But Jamaica was so busy analyzing every inch she barely noticed his lack of interest.

Monday morning she walked into the office feeling both charged up and let down. "The throes of postpublication," Joanne explained, adding mischievously. "Kind of like the throes of postorgasm. You get all heated up and concentrated and then the very thing you've been grunting and groaning to get at comes—pardon the expression—and breaks your concentration. You've got what you wanted and what's left? Relief, yes, but a sense of loss too."

"Joanne, you are perverse," Jamaica laughed. "Pretty accurate, but perverse."

Shortly after she settled in at her desk, Henry called.

"Congratulations, hon. Great package yesterday. Everyone's delighted."

"Why, thank you, Henry. That's very sweet of you to call."

"No problem, hon. No problem at all."

"Okay. Well, thanks."

"Jamaica?"

"Henry?"

"Remember that little conversation we had week before last about the parking problem on the Upper West Side?"

Jamaica was out of the office for the rest of Monday and most of Tuesday interviewing car owners. "Just a quick 'n' dirty," Henry had said. A little filler for Thursday's paper, a little wrapper for Friday's fish.

This trifle was welcome. Foolish as she felt on assignments like these, she preferred the minor anxiety of approaching strangers on the street to the strain of waiting for the telephone to ring in her cubicle.

On the way downtown, she had the opportunity to change trains at Thirty-fourth Street, switching from the BMT to the IND. Jamaica particularly liked this station because it offered a choice of stairs, an escalator, and a ramp that made a sharp forty-five-degree turn. The escalator was old-fashioned with wood handrails, like the escalators in old department stores, and it was just wide enough for one person. This eased the rush-hour crush, since you could only be pressed from above and below, not on the sides. Much as she liked these slim, friendly escalators, Jamaica generally trotted down the ramp in a sort of half-skip. She'd never mastered skipping.

A frantic looking woman with a mop of uncontrolled red hair paced on the edge of the platform.

"Do . . . you . . . know . . . which . . . train . . . goes . . . to . . . Washington . . . Square . . . Park?" she said very slowly, leaning close to Jamaica's face.

"Sure," said Jamaica cheerily. Giving directions gave her a heady sense of power.

"Oh! You speak English?" The woman straightened up.

"Sure."

"What a relief. I've been asking everyone I see how to get to Washington Square. I have an interview at NYU, and everyone is Spanish or Chinese or German or Italian—"

"Isn't it wonderful?" Jamaica interrupted.

"Huh? Wonderful? No, it isn't wonderful. I haven't been able to get a simple answer to a simple question and I'm late."

"Well, it is a simple answer. Take any train that comes, and get off at West Fourth Street."

The woman leaned over the edge of the tracks. Jamaica wondered what kind of job she was seeking. Her clothes were odd: black stretch pants tucked into paisley boots, a red leather jacket with hulking shoulders and fur trim.

She glanced back at Jamaica. "Do you think I can make it in seven minutes? I better be on time. I'm interviewing to be the receptionist at a law firm and they're kind of stuffy."

"No." Jamaica was a little miffed the woman hadn't thanked her for her clear directions. She softened when she saw the woman's panicky gaze. "Maybe twelve minutes, if the train comes soon."

Suddenly the woman's face cleared, and she clasped Jamaica's hand.

"You know, it isn't your fault if I'm late. Really, it isn't."

The end of her sentence was swallowed by the rumble of an approaching "B" train. Jamaica watched her disappear into the crowd spilling out through the half-opened door. What had she meant, it wasn't Jamaica's fault? Of course it wasn't her fault that the woman would probably be late for her interview. But, as Jamaica stepped into the first car of the "RR" train, she felt fretful. "What if she doesn't get the job?"

Leaning against the clattering doors, she reached in her bag and pulled out her paperback copy of *Ellis Island*, Mark Helprin's collection of short stories about immigrants. A tall black man, modestly but well dressed, peered at her through eyes that were nearly clamped together by lids swollen as if they'd been stung by bees.

"You sure seem interested in that book. What is it? A love story?" Even though he was shouting, his voice was a dim echo, barely audible through the old train's insistent yelps and moans.

Jamaica glanced up at him and decided his interest was genuine (by the absence of a smirk, the plaintiveness conveyed by the slits that were his eyes).

"Oh, no. They're stories about newcomers to the United States."

She paused, trying to think about how to describe appropriately the fantastic tales about men who looked at naked women and saw butterflies and swords.

"It's about the way someone can come to this country full of expectations and hope and find a place that fulfills those expectations in some way, but crushes them in another. By its weirdness. America's, I mean."

He shifted from foot to foot, balancing in rhythm to the train's rocking.

"That's true, that's true. But I figure America's still the best place to be. I met a woman the other day from Germany, and she told me how in Germany the women and children are starving."

He shook his head. "Terrible. Terrible."

Jamaica nodded, then started reading again.

"You born in America?"

Jamaica let her book dangle between her thumb and forefinger. "Of course."

"You know, I was in Turkey in the service."

"Istanbul?"

He looked at her with surprise. "Yeah. Istanbul. I was in Istanbul for three weeks, and let me tell you, that's a mess over there. I was never so glad to leave anyplace in my whole life."

Jamaica shouted. "How was the food?"

"Oh, man, you couldn't eat that shit, let me tell you. They'd give you things to put in your mouth that you'd actually be afraid to step in." He grabbed at his stomach, looking pained at the memory. "So what do you think about New York?"

"I love it. Look around this subway." They were riding in one of the decrepit old cars of the BMT line. The graffiti was thick and so was the air, with the heat of too many bodies pressed together. At that time of day—midday—there was no majority. After dusk fell up aboveground, the whites would gradually disappear, but in the dark underground daytime democracy ruled. "You can go all around the world without leaving this car, in a sense."

He whooped. "I sure never quite thought about it like that, but you are absolutely right. But you don't find it too fast?"

"The subway?"

"No. New York." They were both growing hoarse in their attempts to be heard above the heaves and wheezes of the old rattletrap. Jamaica detested the BMT. It was slow and junky.

"Not really." she yelled. "I don't feel the fastness, you see, because I watch people rushing all around me and I get very excited thinking about where they might be going. Stimulating, you know?"

A middle-aged man dressed in a business suit watched Jamaica talking to her subway mate with undisguised disapproval. She glared at him and placed her index finger below her left eye, tugging gently on the skin. It wasn't a genuine evil eye—she didn't feel she had the power to turn him into a worm or a moth. At least she let him know he was misinterpreting a pleasant chat between short-term commuters.

"Yeah," said her companion. "I feel New York is the fast lane. You can't live in this city unless you're willing to move quick, get in with the flow. The money's better here, but not that much, and it don't go as far as it might other places. Opportunity, though. There's lots of opportunity here to make something of yourself if you want to."

"Are you from around here?"

"No, I came up here from Florida. Different pace of life."

"What line of work are you in?"

He leaned against the clanging doors. "Maintenance."

"Where?"

"Subways."

Jamaica startled him with her shriek of delighted surprise. "You work in the subways! How neat! That must be amazing, and scary, working down here in the tunnels. Are you afraid?"

He eyed her to make certain she wasn't mocking him. When he saw her interest was genuine, he straightened up. "No, no. I don't work down in the tunnels. I work with a partner out where the subways are kept when they aren't working."

"Where's that?"

"Long Island, or Jamaica, depending what shift I'm working on. There's nobody around. Yeah. It's a pretty interesting job, I guess. I hadn't much thought about it before."

"You ought to go see this new French movie about the Paris Metro system. The whole thing takes place underground in this allegorical underworld."

"Um, yeah. Well, I don't get out to movies too much. I'm going to another job right now."

"You have two jobs? What's the second one?"

He smiled broadly. "I supervise four women."

"Doing what?" This time, Jamaica's innocence wasn't feigned.

"Maintenance. I make sure they do the job right. Listen, next stop is mine. It sure was nice talking to you." He looked as his shoes.

Jamaica opened her book. "It was nice talking to you, too."

He repeated. "It sure was nice talking to you."

She glanced up from her book and nodded. "It was nice talking to you, too."

"You have a name?"

"Jamaica. What's yours?"

"Jamaica! I'll be. Mine's James. How about that. Hey, Jamaica. You have a phone?"

The train began to jerk into the station. "I have a phone. And a husband."

He shook his head. "A husband?"

"Yep. Package deal. Phone. Husband."

The doors opened. As he stepped out, James's pleasant face contorted into a snarl. "Why are you wasting my time, bitch?"

Jamaica's face was still red when she got to work. She spent the next couple of days out of the office on the trail of Henry's parking offenders. It was Friday before she had a chance to look through the pink message slips piled up on the corner of the desk: Abraham Palermo. Frances Walker. *Good Morning America*. Dr. Carla Miller. Someone from something called Scribes Anonymous. The flack from Hallmark Cards. More flacks. Friends. But nothing from Jules Marlin. Maybe he didn't know if it would be appropriate to call, she thought anxiously, praying that he wasn't going to be another Lonnie.

Caressing the message from Abraham, she punched his number. She felt eager to see him again; there was something enormously appealing about the way he'd popped up out of nowhere after meeting her such a long time before. She felt oddly comfortable with him, perhaps most of all because he didn't seem to need her. They agreed to meet for dinner the next Tuesday. One by one she answered the rest of her calls. *Good Morning America* wanted to get in touch with everyone she'd interviewed for a segment on compulsive letter writers. Hallmark was thinking of using one of her subjects in an ad campaign. Frances Walker was delighted to report that she was going to be on *The Phil Donahue Show* the next week; Phil's crew was prepared to hoist her and her wheelchair down the stairs. Scribes Anonymous, a club of chain-letter writers, wanted to know if she'd like to write a story about them.

By the following Monday Jamaica was surfeited with congratulations. Her head couldn't have felt lighter if she'd eaten a pail of sweet whipped cream.

"Sammy?" she said excitedly into the telephone. "I'm sorry to bother you at work, but I wanted to tell you how terrific things are going. I kept it light enough, I guess. Let's go out and celebrate tonight, okay?"

As she listened, her features drooped. "Oh, sure, I understand . . . No, I won't wait up for you. I know you have your meeting . . . Right. Bye."

"Joanne? You busy?"

"Not for you. Come on over."

Joanne was the picture of professionalism, a muscular calf neatly crossed over a smooth knee, a cigarette caught lightly between two fingers.

"Joanne, would you say I have a hard time expressing myself?"

"What are you talking about? Look at the way people respond to your stories."

"No, I mean in real life. Out of print. Interpersonal relationships."

Joanne sucked on her cigarette and leaned forward with great interest. "Is something going on with you and Sammy? Has the perfect duo had a fight?"

"Don't be ridiculous. Sammy and I never fight. Sometimes I wonder if . . . well, no, never mind. It isn't important."

"Come on, Jamaica. Out with it."

Jamaica bit a ragged cuticle. "Do you think I don't pay enough attention to Sammy?"

"That's ridiculous. You're the best listener in the world. What's brought on this little bout of self-criticism? Has Sammy said something to you?"

"Oh, no, no. He hasn't said anything. Not anything at all. Thanks a lot, Joanne. For your help."

"Are you sure everything's okay?"

"Oh, sure. Perfect."

Joanne's face frosted over and she cocked her head. "Excuse me? Can I help you, sir?"

Jamaica turned her head just in time to see Sherley step gingerly into Joanne's cubicle with the concentration of a child trying to form perfect footsteps in the snow.

"Sherley, how nice to see you," Jamaica said with relief. "Do you known Joanne Robbins, one of our editors here?"

Sherley snapped his feet together and presented Joanne with a half-bow.

"Delighted to meet you, lovely lady."

"I'm delighted to meet you, too, Sherley. Jamaica told me all

about you. I'd love to come down and see your operation someday,"
said Joanne coquettishly.

Sherley's cheeks flamed like a campfire against the wintry pallor
of his face. His sharp little upper teeth clamped fiercely onto his plump
lower lip.

He turned to Jamaica. "I called earlier this week to offer my congratulations on a story well done."

"I know. Thank you. I got your message and was calling everybody back this afternoon. Henry sent me out—"

"Yes, yes. No need to apologize. I saw your little piece about the
cars and the dog doody in the computer system. But wait. I nearly
forgot." He pulled an unopened envelope from his back pocket. "This
letter to the editor arrived today from Mr. Marlin and I brought it
directly up to you, since I reckon it is probably for you anyway."

"Thank you very much, Sherley. And thank you for all your help
on my letters story. I couldn't have done it without you."

"Yes, well, Miss Jamaica, the real reason I am here in your domicile—pardon, the lovely Miss Joanne's domicile—is that I have come
to bid thee farewell. As of next Wednesday I will cease to be an employee of this noble institution."

"Oh, no! Sherley!" Jamaica felt her chest constrict. "What happened?"

"Well, my dear, your story was quite charming and accurate.
However, the powers that be were apparently quite disturbed to learn
of my filing system. The powers that be apparently aren't concerned
at all with history, which I find utterly shocking for the proprietors of
a news organization." Sherley tossed his head back dramatically.

"But what happened?"

"Well, they—they being the illustrious Mr. Frank and his superiors—showed up at my figurative doorstep the other day and ordered
me to clean out my cabinets. Imagine! They said they could see no
need to keep letters for more than a month, and they ordered me to
turn in all my filing cabinets save one."

"Those assholes," Joanne muttered.

"I quite agree with you, Miss Robbins," said Sherley, who hadn't
managed to look Jamaica in the eyes.

"But, Sherley, what happened?" sniffed Jamaica.

He forced himself to direct his gaze at her, and to pat her hand.
"It was quite simple, my dear. I offered my resignation. They wanted
to reduce my occupation to glorified scutwork. I had created a magnificent world, a preservation of contemporary voices, and all they

could see was a silly old man confiscating a few extra tin boxes. I had no choice."

Jamaica was forlorn and immobile. "Sherley, I am very, very sorry."

"Don't be, my dear. It isn't your fault."

Jamaica began to laugh hysterically. "So I've already been told once today."

Joanne stood and put one arm around Jamaica and the other around Sherley. For several minutes, the three of them stood in a tiny circle, pretending they didn't hear the clicking of computer keyboards and the muffle of voices pondering tomorrow's news.

Sherley lifted his moist face. "This is a bright spot, though. When will I ever again have the opportunity to have my poor brittle arms wrapped so tightly around not one but two pretty girls? Things aren't so bad, then, after all, are they?"

Jamaica shook loose from Sherley's grasp and took two swift steps to Joanne's phone. "I've had it," she said, firmly pressing the buttons of Henry's extension.

"What do you mean he isn't in?" she shouted into the phone. "I'm sorry, Madeline," she said in a chastened voice. "I didn't mean to raise my voice at you. Could you please tell him Jamaica Just called?"

Sherley had tightened his hold on Joanne's silk blouse and was smiling somewhat dreamily as his fingers rubbed her firm biceps through the tantalizing smoothness. Joanne settled into his caress naturally, without flinching, without any more thought than a cat gives to curling up on a pillow. If Joanne understood anything, she understood the comfort of bodily contact. After years of aerobics and psychotherapy and self-help books, she could handily touch her emotions if not get hold of them.

It was Sherley who stepped away from Joanne and laid his hand on Jamaica's rigid shoulder.

"Miss Just, my dear. Jamaica. Don't do anything rash. No, let me revise. Don't do anything at all. I was in full complicity with you on the story about letter writers. I, too, was fascinated by them, long before you came on the scene. All you did was help me find a way to do something useful with what had become my life's work. Truly, you did. You mustn't take my departure to heart. Truly, my dear. In some ways my parting with the *Observer* comes as a relief. I feel as though my mission is over here and I must move on to some other endeavor. I might have died down there amidst my filing cabinets and letters, and no one would have understood what I was trying to accomplish there, in my small way. You, at least, tried."

Joanne and Jamaica looked at the tears in each other's eyes, and Jamaica was moved to put her arms around Sherley, somewhat awkwardly, since she found it difficult to publicly display physical affection of any sort to anyone besides Eva or Geneva. When she and Sammy walked hand in hand, she could never tell who was keeping whom from slipping away.

"Good luck, Sherley," Jamaica said. "You'll keep in touch?"

A twinkle flickered in Sherley's black eyes. "Why, of course, my dear girl. I'll read your stories and write you letters." With that, he slipped out of Joanne's cubicle and disappeared around the corner.

Jamaica's phone rang. She waved at Joanne and ran around the partition to answer it.

"Oh, hi, Henry. Madeline said I called?" She took a deep breath. "Oh, yes, I called. You guys had a hell of a lot of nerve firing Sherley. He wasn't hurting anybody—"

She listened numbly as Henry interrupted her and explained how her story had simply offered management an excuse to do what it (as though "it" had nothing to do with Henry, the master of depersonalization) had "needed" to do for a long time. She heard him explain that management had tolerated Sherley's idiosyncratic behavior far longer than most tightly run organizations would have.

"Calm down, Jamaica," Henry said in closing. "And thanks for the alternate-side-of-the-street parking story. You did a swell job."

Before she could reply, the line was dead.

"Are you okay, Jamaica?" Joanne called out.

"No problem, thanks," said Jamaica, biting her lip. She pressed Sammy's number. When she heard his voice she hung up the phone.

She stared at the single framed photograph on her desk. It was a rare family portrait. There was a tall man wearing a white shirt and dark slacks and dress shoes. He was standing very straight. Next to him a small, pretty woman leaned over a pretty little dark-eyed girl, instructing her, it seems, to smile at the camera. The little girl wore shorts and a jaunty hat; the angle of her head and her half-smile indicated a desire to obey her mother. Another, smaller girl—turned completely away from the camera—seemed to be on the verge of leaving the scene. One foot was in the air. She too wore shorts and a hat identical to her sister's.

It was early autumn. They were standing in front of a tree burning with color. They were eating apples. It was a pretty picture. A day in the country.

When Eva handed Jamaica this picture a few years ago, shortly after the Just family's belongings had arrived in Connecticut, Jamaica remarked, "Isn't that an attractive family?"

Eva glanced at the photograph. "The most attractive part is gone," she said curtly. Suddenly she exclaimed loudly. "Oh, my God!"

"Mommy, what is it?" Jamaica grabbed her mother's hand.

"Look at Khruschev."

"Huh?"

"On the television." A documentary about the Cold War had been running silently behind Jamaica's back. Eva brushed past her daughter and turned up the volume and stared at the screen with delight. "What a live wire he was! Banging his shoe on the table at the UN."

The memory dissolved. Jamaica settled into her chair and felt paper crinkling in the pocket of her skirt. It was the letter from Jules Marlin. She studied the neat block lettering on the envelope and ripped the corner. Instead of removing the letter, however, she tapped her head with the envelope, then tossed it on her desk. She didn't need any more nasty surprises just now. Tomorrow would be soon enough to see what Jules had to say.

A numbing loneliness crept through her body as the realization took hold that her latest diversion had run its course. There would, of course, be another, and another after that. The thought occurred to her that she might consider what it was that she was diverting her attention from.

19

Dining Out

When she got home, she chose her clothes for her evening with Abraham with unusual care. A mass of dull colors greeted her when she opened the closet. On the top shelf, however, was one of the packages from Mrs. Fein. Inside—folded in tissue paper, tags intact—lay a deep purple dress with lovely lines. It was the kind of dress the ladies' magazines said had "presence," which was precisely why it had remained hidden in the closet for close to a year. Giggling a bit, she shook the dress out and ripped off the tags with her teeth. She felt slightly embarrassed at the small thrill generated by this unfamiliar act of girlishness. The cat watched quizzically as Jamaica dropped her sweater and skirt, slipped on the deep purple, and sashayed across the room on her toes. From the bottom of an old music box her father had given her for her twelfth birthday (it played "Londonderry Air," his favorite song), she pulled out an old strand of pearls.

Showered, powdered, and deodorized, she stood in front of the bathroom mirror in her slip, applying makeup as though her cheeks and eyelids were mined and the slightest deviation would cause a violent explosion. An artificially bright face looked at her from the mirror. Almost unconsciously she opened a drawer and removed her diaphragm from its case. She flushed as she filled its rubbery insides with contraceptive jelly and slid it inside her.

"You look absolutely wonderful," said Abraham, when he met her downstairs in the vestibule. "Your color has improved greatly."

Jamaica lowered her lashes, flirtatiously, she hoped.

"Do you have something in your eye?" he asked.

She sighed. "Where would you like to go for dinner?"

"Someplace where we can talk. Any ideas?"

To his surprise, she took his arm. Last time they'd seen each other, she'd cringed if their coats had so much as brushed together.

She mentioned a small restaurant in Tribeca; a recent, favorable write-up in the *Times* had been confirmed by Joanne. The dark streets were nearly empty; the trucks that rumbled through this warehouse district had already made their passage through the Holland Tunnel, and the night was too cold for most casual strollers.

Abraham's conversation was alternately amusing and densely revelatory. He was in his mid-thirties and had lived what seemed to Jamaica an exotic life, filled with tumultuous relationships with women and brushes with professional failure and success. His childhood had been placid until, when he was seventeen, his older brother quit MIT to go to Vietnam instead of accepting the deferment his parents had arranged for him. He didn't die, but the deranged hulk that came back didn't resemble the ambitious engineering student who had left. Abraham hadn't seen his brother in a dozen years, not since he'd pressed a knife to their mother's throat before taking off for a mountain cabin in Montana. Their parents divorced shortly after that.

"You must have an unusual marriage," Abraham said after they were seated at the restaurant, a small place decorated in muted colors. They'd almost missed the dark entryway, tucked in between the giant closed doors of two large trucking garages.

"Why do you say that?"

"Do you mind if I smoke?"

Generally, Jamaica was repulsed by cigarette smoke. "No, not at all," she said, quite sincerely.

When Abraham tipped the pack toward her, Jamaica drew out a cigarette.

"Do you smoke?" Abraham asked with some surprise.

"No," said Jamaica, tapping on the table with the cigarette. "Sometimes I like something in my hands when I talk, and it's wasteful to crumple up bread." (She'd been thinking about the pile of pumpernickel she'd left behind at the Russian Tea Room, last time they'd met.)

Abraham drew deeply on his Camel Lite. "When I was married, my wife was horribly jealous. If we'd go to a party and I'd so much as talk to another woman, I could feel daggers in my back. Things got much worse when we went to Hollywood. My hours were erratic, and we had to go to a lot of parties."

"Did she have cause to be jealous?"

"No, not a bit. I loved her, or thought I loved her. She was a beautiful woman."

Jamaica put her elbows on the table and leaned forward. "What did she do?"

"Actually, she'd been a reporter for the Commodity News Service. I met her when I was still trading futures for a living. She thought I was a genius, the smartest man she'd ever met, she told me. I was fat then, and flattered by the attention she paid me. You have to understand what she looked like. She was tall and always wore spiky heels and skirts slit up the side. I didn't know she walked the way she did just to keep her balance, but the effect of it was to get every guy on the floor of the exchange so hot there'd be an exodus for the bathroom when she left."

Jamaica made a face.

"Sorry." Abraham smiled wryly.

"She was sweet, too, and Jewish. When I took her to meet my mother, she told me she couldn't imagine what Evelyn saw in me. Good old Mom." A shadow fell on his amiable face.

"When we got to Hollywood, she decided she should become an actress. She was prettier than most of the starlets we'd see at parties, and movie acting wasn't much—so she thought. I arranged a screen test, then another and another. Poor Evelyn. She wasn't just bad; she wrote a new definition for awful."

Jamaica peeled the wrapping off the cigarette in her hand. "Why didn't she go back to journalism?"

"Two reasons, the biggest one being that she didn't believe she was bad." Abraham cracked his knuckles over his head. "She started to imagine that I'd set her up for a fall because I didn't want her to succeed in my business. I tried to get her to talk about why she felt that way, but she didn't want any part of that. 'If you truly loved me, you'd understand how I feel without me having to spell it out for you,' she'd tell me."

"And the second reason?"

"She was a commodities reporter for a wire service. Her credentials couldn't get her across the street much less a job."

Abraham fell silent, then he began to chuckle.

"Why are you laughing?"

"Did you notice, I asked you about your marriage and I've told you about mine. Nice trick, Jamaica."

Hesitantly, she laid her hand on his arm. "It wasn't a trick. Honest. What do you want to know?"

"Why does the word *perfect* invariably come up when you talk about your childhood and when you talk about your husband?"

"Does it?"

"Don't be coy, dear."

Jamaica's voice cracked. "Because it was. I mean, because it is. Sammy lets me do whatever I want to for work, and he believes me when I paint a lovely picture for him about who I am. You don't understand." She sounded defensive. "His family was everything mine wasn't. They were what we were trying to be but . . . Don't you understand?" She forgot she was talking to a stranger. "Sammy loves me no matter how unworthy I seem."

Abraham looked at the tobacco and cigarette wrapping lying in a pile by Jamaica's butter dish.

"Need another cigarette?"

"I must be overwrought. I don't know what I'm saying." Jamaica rubbed her eyes with the back of her hand.

Abraham dipped his napkin into his water glass and wiped her smeared mascara. "I think you know very well what you're saying," he said. "Self-awareness raises its ugly head in the strangest ways."

"Did you go to a shrink when you and your wife broke up?" Jamaica asked suspiciously.

"As a matter of fact, yes. Why do you ask?"

"You sounded like my sister."

"Is she a therapist?"

"No, she's a therapee."

"What do you mean by unworthy?"

Jamaica whimpered, "Abraham, do you mind if we don't talk anymore?"

They'd been at the restaurant an hour and hadn't gotten beyond their drink orders.

"Would you like to leave?" Abraham asked.

"Yes, but I don't want to go home."

Without looking directly at her, he asked. "Is that a proposition?"

"It is, but a different kind than I thought it was going to be." Jamaica squirmed in her chair, wondering if he could discern the diaphragm simply by looking at her.

They walked through Wall Street and gawked at the skyscrapers jammed haphazardly together like the gleeful concoction of a child handed a boxful of Legos. She remembered the way Sammy and she had felt—or said they felt—when they'd first craned their necks at those buildings. They wondered if they'd ever lose the urge to stare upward in disbelief or if they'd always feel like rubes. What Jamaica never expressed, directly, was how much she wanted to be an American rube, a gee-gosh, ain't-it-grand kid like Sammy, full of optimism and enthusiasm. Only once did she hint that her father might have run away, that the only place he could survive was in a bramble patch like Harmony.

"How can you talk about your father like that?" Sammy had said disapprovingly. From that moment on, Jamaica spoke more carefully.

She and Abraham wound their way to the tip of Battery Park and looked out over Ellis Island and the Statue of Liberty glimmering like crystalline shards of memory in the reflected glow of the moon.

"My dad was a superpatriot," Jamaica mused as they leaned against the cold metal guard rails. "We flew the flag on every holiday. When Geneva came home from college wearing a black armband to protest the war in Vietnam, he didn't say a word about it. Just stared at her the whole weekend like she'd wrapped that armband around his heart tight as a tourniquet. Poor Geneva. That was her big rebellion. Everyone else was mangy, wearing torn jeans. She'd still dress in Bass Weejuns and plaid skirts and nice sweaters, and a black armband."

There had been strained arguments in the Just household about Vietnam and the way the world seemed to be crumbling around them, much like the discussions that were taking place in other households around the country. Dr. Just and Jamaica would fight less about intangibles like U.S. foreign policy and more about specifics like young men sprouting beards, and students refusing to study.

Jamaica still treasured the letter—one of three in a lifetime—she'd received from her father on that subject. Her parents had shipped her off to a kibbutz the summer after her junior year in high school, to fill in the gaps in her Jewish education. Jamaica and Eva corresponded three times a week; Dr. Just would scrawl "Love, Daddy" at the bottom of Eva's (poorly) typewritten letters. One day, however, an entire letter written in that familiar scrawl arrived.

"Jamaica, dear," it said:

I just wanted to let you know that my car broke down the other day in the middle of nowhere. I was late for the hospital and very upset because I knew my patients would be waiting. A truck came along and two young fellows got out with long hair and beards. I didn't want their help, but they insisted. In fact, they were very nice, responsible young men and they had interesting things to say about the war in Vietnam. One of them was a veteran. I decided I was wrong about the beards. Love, Daddy.

Jamaica turned to look at Abraham.

"You are a funny girl," he said. "You have so much sympathy and empathy for everyone else—that shows up even in your newspaper stories—yet you are cruel to yourself. Why don't—"

She cut him off, screaming. "Why don't I what? You're just like Sammy. 'Jamaica, you're so wonderful, you're so perfect, you're so this, and that.' Don't you understand, any of you? I'm a nothing, a cipher. You think I could have lasted a minute in Auschwitz? I'm a weak-kneed lily-livered nothing."

She began to pace up and down the deserted boardwalk, jerking her hands stiffly, methodically, as though she were conducting the symphony of her own words. "I've tried so hard to buy into the normal world, to be pretty and sleek and well dressed and well postured and groomed, but the elements fight against me. I'm a congenital mess. It's a struggle to get my hair in order."

She yanked on the ends of her hair. "You tell me I'm sympathetic and empathetic but what I really am is an idiot savant of the emotions. I have eyes that can see right into a person's soul, but so what? I don't have an inkling about what it is that I see."

Her carefully regulated emotional sluices were flooded. She was gushing words. "You ask me about my perfect marriage and I tell you I wonder how I can trust someone, some man, who could love me completely. What kind of person could be satisfied with me, who is willing to take all the guff I dish out? Sometimes I think I'm looking for trouble, as my mother would say. Looking for someone who will hurt me, who will give me what I think I deserve."

Her breath came in deep, short spurts. "Sammy and I have worked very hard to show that we can love more than anyone, play harder, be more thoughtful. But he isn't talking to me very much anymore."

"Why is that?" Abraham asked softly.

She looked at him with curiosity, as though she didn't recognize him, and continued talking, faster and faster, as though she were working against the clock.

"Because I'm too wrapped up in my own concerns. Look, if I weren't Jewish, I could be convinced the prophecy of Revelations is coming to pass. As much as I remember."

She paused reflectively, gazing out over the harbor. In a monotone, she began to recite:

And the kings of the earth, and the great men, and the rich men, and the chief captains, and the mighty men, and every bondman, and every free man, hid themselves in the dens and in the rocks of the mountains, and said to the mountains, and rocks, 'Fall on us, and hide us from

*the face of him that sitteth on the throne, and from the wrath of the
Lamb: for the great day of his wrath is come; and who shall be able
to stand?'*

Abraham whistled admiringly. "Where did that come from?"

"Mr. Rainey, tenth grade composition. He never made us write a
single paper. All we ever did was memorize passages from the New
Testament and recite them in class." She shuddered.

"Pretty rough for a Jewish kid, huh?" said Abraham.

She continued, "Have you been watching the news, for God's
sake? Every night Tom or Mary Alice or someone presents me with a
bouquet of death and destruction, and the sports. Mudslides, earth-
quakes, volcanic eruptions. Every day thousands of people are being
whisked away by God."

Exhausted, she sat down hard on a park bench. Abraham quietly
took his place next to her. Jamaica gave a short laugh. "Sing ho for
the simple life."

He put his rather long arms around her and pulled her close to
him. She turned her white face and slightly blue lips to his. She felt
excited as a teen-ager who's allowed herself to be coaxed into the
backseat of a car—heart pounding, face flushed, the works. Yet when
Abraham began to answer her invitation with a kiss, she started to cry.

"I'm sorry," he said. "That was out of line."

"Don't apologize," she said, shivering. They sat in silence. Finally, she looked at him. "You are a kind man and I am a basket case."

"Ah, but there are a lot of interestingly colored eggs in that basket," he said.

They both smirked good-naturedly.

"I think I'd better go home," said Jamaica. "It's late."

They retraced their steps in a silence that was not uncomfortable
as each of them considered what this night of laying themselves open
might mean, if anything. When they finally reached Jamaica's door,
she stuck out her hand.

"Is this party over?" Abraham asked, forlornly regarding this formal gesture.

"Don't worry, pal. I'll give you ninety-days' notice," she said,
and quickly left him standing in the vestibule.

20

Home Alone

She nearly ran up the stairs, eager to hold Sammy close and to reveal to him what she had told Abraham, and to have him tell her that he loved her no matter what. On the third landing, however, a shock of fear overcame her. Had she shut the drawer holding her empty diaphragm case? What if Sammy had come upon this evidence of her faithlessness, however unconsummated, and (the horrifying thought occurred to her) had that been her intent?

Grabbing onto the bannister, she hoisted herself up the final two flights. Clutching her keys in her hand, she froze. The thought of opening the door and facing Sammy's reaction—hurt, anger, or disgust—made her physically sick. She sat down on the top step, breathless from running up the stairs and from fear, and shame. She remembered how, in the months after she'd met Sammy, he had worked so diligently to make her whole again, to show her she could go on living after her father's death. On her first birthday away from home, at college in New England, she'd felt a great emptiness. Dr. Just had always awakened her with kisses and flowers on her birthday, and Eva would sing, off key. Glancing around her cinderblock dorm room, she'd pulled on her jeans and sweatshirt and told herself she was too old for such childish celebrations. As she walked to class on the far end of campus, people she barely knew stopped her and said, "Happy Birthday, Jamaica." Puzzled, she lifted her eyes from the ground. Finally she noticed. Nearly every tree and telephone pole on campus carried this posting: "Today is Jamaica Just's birthday!" When she returned to her dorm later that day, a dozen red roses were waiting outside her door. Overcome with happiness, she'd greedily grasped the flowers by the thorny stems. Her hand bled as she let herself into her room and called Sammy to thank him.

For more than half an hour Jamaica set on the steps reflecting on the scope of her ingratitude. She imagined Sammy on the other side of the door, weeping silently, or in a drunken sleep of despair. The sound of a ringing telephone penetrated her numbness. It kept ringing. Unable to ignore the sound the way Sammy apparently was, she quickly got to her feet, unlocked the door, and retrieved the phone just in time to hear Geneva's high-wire voice.

"Thank God! You're alive."

"Geneva, what is the matter with you?" Jamaica realized this was a foolish question to ask someone who never failed to record flight numbers and departure times every time anyone close to her took a trip so she would know instantly if they became crash victims.

"Where have you been? Do you know it's four in the morning and I've been calling you every half hour since 1 A.M.?"

"Four in the morning?"

"Where have you two been?"

"Poker. It's Sammy's poker night, and I was out with a friend." Where was Sammy? she wondered a little frantically. "Is anything the matter, chum?"

In a much deescalated tone, Geneva sighed. "Chum. God, it's been a long time since we called each other that. Are Hekyll and Jekyll still on television?"

"I don't think so." Jamaica held the phone numbly. Why didn't she tell Geneva how she'd driven Sammy away? But then Geneva would never marry and that, too, would be on Jamaica's conscience.

"Now I'm embarrassed to tell you why I called."

"Out with it, Gen." Jamaica was speaking by rote. She slumped into a chair, staring blankly around her apartment while her sister prattled on.

As part of her teaching fellowship at one of the big New England medical centers, Geneva was doing a tour of duty at a state hospital, whose patients included a small but significant population from the state prison system. In general, the practice of medicine among urbanites in the eighties had failed to bring her the adulation it had brought her father in a small town fifteen years earlier. The vague sense of disappointment she felt when examining decent folk from Brookline and Wellesley was brought into keen relief when examining convicts for whom she had a difficult time invoking an urgent desire to heal.

She still strongly resembled the slight, dark-eyed child whose picture hung on Sammy and Jamaica's bedroom wall.

For the past two months she had been amusing Jamaica with anecdotes about a schizophrenic patient who had been placed under her care because he claimed his chest was in a perpetual state of constriction. Repeated tests revealed only a slightly elevated blood pressure, but the requisites of Hippocrates and malpractice kept him under observation for a period of time. Besides, he was a good specimen for a teaching hospital, providing classroom material for both the psychiatric and the cardiac doctor-professors.

Geneva hadn't lost her power over her sister—or her storytelling gifts. Sammy—and Abraham—dropped out of mind as Jamaica got caught up in Geneva's tale.

The patient was a large, muscular man with a handsome face and the elocutionary elegance that graces many schizophrenics. When Geneva had first stopped by his bed, he'd allowed her to press his flesh with her fingers. However, when she began to ask him questions about his breathing patterns and the exact nature of the pain in his chest— this in front of a half-dozen medical students—he had angrily shouted, "Could you please turn down the intensity of your eyes, Dr. Just?"

Geneva didn't want her students to see the flush on her neck, so she quickly thanked the schizophrenic for his trouble and moved her brood along.

This exchange was the first in a series between the attractive woman doctor and her overbearing patient who spoke to her with such unqualified confidence she kept forcing herself to check the diagnosis—"forty-year-old paranoid schizophrenic"—on his chart to remind herself that he was mad.

"I know those interns you sent down here the other day were really from outer space," he lectured her sternly after she'd absented herself from his bedside for a couple of days. "I'd appreciate it if you wouldn't allow them to beam their laser beams on me again."

In her most authoritative tone, Geneva assured him that those were indeed interns who had examined him, and she simply walked away when he accused her of lying.

On the day she telephoned Jamaica, it was evident that the schizophrenic had been waiting for her to appear by the way he slumped back against the pillows when she arrived with a young woman intern in tow.

"You aren't really a doctor, I know it in my bones, *Dr.* Just," he sneered, and jerked his head toward the intern. "Neither is she. Don't come around here anymore with your intellectual medical talk. I know the truth about you."

Shaking, Geneva quickly examined him without saying a word. She moved through the rest of her afternoon rounds in a daze, and excused herself from the weekly meeting of the ward staff to go to the gym for a workout. By late evening she was exhausted, and dropped off to sleep during the news.

"You poor thing," clucked Jamaica. "What woke you up?"

"I dreamed I'd been exposed as a fraud," Geneva sobbed. "Everyone at the hospital finally realized that I wasn't a doctor at all and neither was my intern. We'd lied and lied and lied, and everyone had believed us and this lunatic exposed us for what we were. Frauds!"

"Then you woke up?"

"No, no. I woke up after we were fired and sent off to work in a butcher shop cutting up meat. Jamaica, four years of medical school, four years of residency, and I'm nothing but a meat cutter," Geneva wailed.

Jamaica couldn't tell if she was choking back tears or laughter.

"You're kidding, aren't you, Geneva? It was only a dream. Please don't be upset. You are really a doctor. I promise. I was at your graduation. I saw them give you the diploma. You are a wonderful doctor."

Angrily, Geneva snapped. "If I'm such a wonderful doctor, then why did I believe Mommy when she told us Daddy had a fungus on his lungs?"

"You were only in your first year of medical school. You didn't know anything."

"Don't be a ninny, Jamaica. I remember calling home and asking Mom how he was feeling and she said, 'Oh, he's fine. He just has a little fungus on his lung. Don't worry. There's a 15 percent cure rate in Japan.' 'Oh,' I said, with relief. Relief! Did I bother to consider that she was saying that 85 percent weren't cured in Japan? More to the point, I didn't bother to ask what happened to the 85 percent who weren't cured."

Jamaica exploded. "And what if you had considered it? Would you have been able to save him, or make him feel anything but weak and helpless?"

There was silence. "I'm sorry, Gen. Is that why you didn't cry at the funeral?"

"I cried at the funeral. Didn't I?"

"Sure you did, chum. I'm all mixed up. It's late. Do you think you can go to sleep now?"

"Yeah. I think I'll heat up a little milk."

"Old doctor's cure?"

"Right. Go to sleep, kid. I love you."

"I love you."

As she put down the receiver, a pleasant dullness rolled over Jamaica, a sensation not unlike the way she felt after she'd had her wisdom teeth pulled—four at once, two impacted—and drifted in a Tylenol-codeine daze for two weeks. The mild narcotic distanced the pain boomeranging around her poor mouth, bouncing off her violated gums. The pain still existed, but she no longer cared.

She slipped out of her clothes and tugged on her red flannel pajamas from L. L. Bean, one of Sammy's heavy sweaters, and a pair of knit booties. In the bathroom she crouched on the toilet and sent a finger in rueful search of the slippery rim of her diaphragm. She washed it carefully, then patted it dry and glanced at the open drawer. The empty case was in clear view. Quickly she dispensed with her nightly cleaning rituals and padded into the living room, where she curled up on the sofa to wait for her husband. The apartment was dark except for a thin beam of street light that squeezed in through a crack in the blinds.

21

The Confession

Jamaica's arm flopped over the side of the sofa. "Daddy?"

She moaned and grunted in disgust, as she emerged from the netherworld of her dreamy half-sleep.

"Daddy, indeed. Daddy's dead and your husband's gone. Happy now?" She said these words aloud, with sarcasm. The room undulated in the eerie light of early dawn, when even the furniture seemed to lose its inanimate certainty. This was her home, yet she took no comfort from the floor-to-ceiling shelves jammed tight with books, artfully jumbled to give the place a literary appearance. In Harmony she'd been content to read books, then return them to the Bookmobile in exchange for new delights. Here she felt a compulsion to have the volumes on hand, in case she was overcome by a sudden urge to reexamine a passage from Proust, so she told herself. Sammy liked having the books there too. When his mother redecorated their family room, the interior designer had filled one wall with books, all chosen for the colors of their matching leather jackets. The Feins had four complete sets of the works of Shakespeare—in rust, forest green, amber, and black.

Jamaica got up and walked slowly to the window. The street below was empty. It was almost six in the morning and Sammy hadn't come home yet. The realization sank in that he might not come back. With the empty diaphragm case—the screaming beacon of her presumed infidelity—she might finally have gotten his complete attention. She remembered Joanne telling her about the way she slept with poor Matthew. Every night she'd lecture him about crowding her, and warn him not to trap her under his arm. Even in sleep, Joanne wanted it to be clear that Matthew had no hold on her. Obediently he would curl up on his side of the bed, his back toward her. During the night, Joanne, half-asleep and cold, would edge closer and closer to him. Desperately afraid of losing her, Matthew—aiming to please—would inch away every time she drew near. Finally, he would drop off the edge of the bed onto the floor.

Disgust and fatigue overwhelmed Jamaica. She stumbled into the bedroom to change into jeans and a heavy, oversized sweater.

"Sammy, please forgive me," she scribbled on a note pad, and stuck the message to the refrigerator door with a magnet shaped like a banana. The radio alarm went off in the bedroom: "*Seven-forty and snowing in New York . . . traffic snarled on the Triboro . . .*" Jamaica slammed the door and trotted down the stairs. She hurtled up the street, bending her head against the forceful sheet of snow flapping against her. She didn't know where she was going, but she knew she was getting there by subway.

She felt somewhat calmer only when she sat on the orange plastic seat characteristic of the "E" train. The car was fairly full; rush hour was about to begin. At Fourteenth Street, a roly-poly blind man with large, deep-set eyes boarded the train. He was accompanied by a well-built German shepherd with a blinking light strapped to its back. The man carried a ghetto blaster that had a microphone attached to it. As man and dog patrolled the center aisle, the man spoke into the mike with the authority of a professional fund raiser.

"It's been your help that's allowed us to develop this inner light." The dog's back glowed and faded, glowed and faded, as the light flashed on and off. "With your continued support we can develop new and better methods of helping ourselves at the Inner Light Institute."

He flipped a switch, and music poured out of his box. He began to lip synch: "*Why do the birds go on singing? . . .*" His presentation was quite polished, and the passengers responded accordingly.

Jamaica contributed too—two quarters. She was impressed by the response the man was drawing. This was a perfect example of the power of organization, how eagerly people hopped on a bandwagon pulled by officials, any officials. There was something comfortingly aloof about his plea and its association with an "institute," and his audiovisual aids. He wasn't merely begging, he was offering his contributors a chance to participate in research, to put their money to good use that would benefit mankind, not just one poor blind man.

He got off at Twenty-third Street. As the train grew more and more crowded, Jamaica felt herself sinking into a state of terror. "You like to think you're going mad," Sammy would tease her when she fell into these dark moods, but Sammy wasn't there, and she didn't like whatever it was she was feeling at all. She couldn't bear to look at anyone around her. The subway—her refuge—teemed with hostile strangers. Every pair of lips seemed to be damming up shouts of outrage, every pair of eyes seemed rimmed with tears. Jamaica felt overwhelmed by the discomfort they must be feeling, jostling up against one another, squirming away from an unwanted touch. Her fellow passengers looked like the gaping fish at the fishmonger's in Chinatown, crammed so closely together they were barely able to open their fins. There were few sights more pitiful than those ignorant, doomed fish choking down their last, watery breath. Scanning the harried faces, Jamaica couldn't find a single person to talk to. She wanted out.

At Fifth Avenue, she allowed herself to be swept onto the platform. In a daze, she moved with the crowd up the escalator and out onto the street. She shrank against the wall of a building, shocked by the purposeful crowds and the fierce wind buffeting her with icy rain. Miserable, she began to walk down the street, uncertain of her destination. Reaching a phone booth, she called the office.

"I won't be coming in today," she told the receptionist. "Yes, yes, the flu that's going around. Right. Lots of fluids. Thank you."

It was far too cold to continue wandering aimlessly. She picked up her pace, concentrating on the cracks in the wet sidewalk, only dimly aware of the huffing of buses, the mellifluousness of the rainfall, the seemingly endless stream of trench coats passing by. Her own footfall was distinct, somehow isolated from the mélange of noise around her. The gargantuan granite blocks of Rockefeller Center rose up from the concrete with impossible confidence, a reminder of a more innocent time when the Western world conned itself into believing that the very existence of these giant buildings would inspire progress. The bronze statue of Atlas, casually balancing the world on his shoulders, was luminescent, even in the sleet. The Gothic spires of St. Patrick's Cathedral materialized across the street out of the gray. Somewhat guiltily, Jamaica brightened at the prospect of stopping for a while in the giant church. She'd always envied the Catholics their gorgeous edifices that hinted at the glory of the afterlife. She envied them their ornate masses and the forgiveness implied by the wooden confessional booths she'd gazed at longingly. She had always thought that these high-priced monuments to God were borne on the backs of peasants around the world. Still, the concept of a higher authority was an idea she could believe in when she came face to face with the glory that was stained glass and marble and absolution.

What did Judaism offer? Rational thought. Morality. The common-sense way. There was good and there was evil. No rapture. No redemption. No chance just to confess Abraham Palermo away. These laws and principles, such dandy guides for day-to-day living, were lousy when it came to explaining irrational phenomena, like the Holocaust, say, or like why she fucked everything up. At least Catholics could make a bid for a second go-round; they could dream of nifty sing-outs with Saint Peter.

Slowly she climbed the steps and found herself up against a pair of massive doors. Her eyes met a bronze carving of a graceful bird, curving its neck and dropping nourishment into the beaks of her three babies. Jamaica's eyes watered at this tender scene. A group of worshippers or tourists exited. Jamaica slipped in through the open door without actually touching it.

There was only a handful of people scattered about the cathedral's vast interior. Jamaica was comforted and terrified by the hushed darkness, broken by the light filtered through the stained-glass windows and the flickering glow of votive candles. A man stuffed a dollar in the collection box near the entrance. "For the poor of the world," it said. He dipped his hand in a nearby marble basin and made the sign of the cross. Apprehensively, she mimicked him; dollar in the box, hand in the basin. She hoped no one would notice the symbol she drew in the air in front of her chest was the Star of David.

There was a bulletin board next to the information desk. "Confessions," it said, "after each morning mass and from 12 to 1." Morning masses took place at 7, 7:30, 8, 8:30. "Excuse me," she whispered to the man who had just made the sign of the cross, and remained standing nearby. "What time is it?"

"9:05," he said.

Rows and rows of small silver bowls spread out before her. Hesitating, she grasped a long wooden stick—one of the designated votive lighters—and lit a candle, and prayed her mother would never find out. In the southeast corner of the church, the gift shop was doing a brisk business selling statues of saints and crucifixes.

She began to wander around the perimeter of the church's interior, clutching the pamphlet she'd picked up at the information desk. The pews, upholstered in red, seemed endless and nearly empty. The seating capacity, the pamphlet said, was 2,500. There were a few worshippers. A man was kneeling, his head in his hands. A few rows up, a woman with hair that looked like a bright, orange tumbleweed rubbed her chin and crossed her legs.

Jamaica walked up the north side, examining statues of saints, running her fingers across marble. Her boots hit the stone floor with a distant thud. She lit another votive candle. Her eye was caught by a series of bas-reliefs that struck her as terribly sad. Poor Jesus, staggering under the weight of the cross. A civilian muscled him, a Roman guard hassled him. As the scenes progressed, Jesus grew weaker and weaker, until he fell to the ground.

She moved on until she arrived in front of a giant organ, its wood carved into a mass of curlicues until it resembled the castles she and Geneva used to make with drizzles of wet sand. Jamaica imagined the explosive sounds this organ—with its nine thousand pipes, according to her pamphlet—could issue to the farthest corners of this vast building. Her head filled with the memory of the Hallelujah Chorus from Handel's *Messiah* as she continued her tour. Under a marble cupola, a pretty statue of father and child was illuminated by electric lights. There was a helpful sign. "Saint Joseph, husband of the Blessed Virgin and foster-father of Jesus." Jamaica lit another candle.

In the far northeast corner there was another densely carved wooden structure. A mustard yellow velvet curtain hung over a doorway. There was a doorbell. She heard the murmur of voices. A woman emerged from behind the curtain and quickly turned her eyes to the floor when she saw Jamaica. Jamaica touched the curtain, then released it as though it were on fire. She turned and nearly ran to the opposite side of the church. Trying to calm herself—her breath was growing short—she fixed her gaze on the stained-glass window above her. It depicted some sort of battle scene. In the center, a king oversaw the scrimmage taking place around him. Men were piled up on one another; a purple arm there, a bright green legging there. Seeking clues for what she was looking at, Jamaica found only a small blue square that said: "Gift of Henry J. Anderson." Way up above, the church's highest windows beckoned, kaleidoscopes of blue, blue, blue fractured by a flash of yellow—a halo—an outline of red. Exhausted and overwrought, she felt barely conscious.

She was knocked out of her torpor by a birdlike woman in a faded cloth jacket, who whizzed by quietly in her Adidases. A thick wool cap was jammed over her brittle yellow hair. She swiftly padded around the pews; her patrol seemed endless. When she came around again, Jamaica saw she was a hag; her face resembled ancient parchment. The expression on her face, though, was curiously childlike. When she drew near, Jamaica tapped her on the shoulder.

The woman stopped immediately and waited.

"Excuse me," Jamaica said. "What's that over there?" She pointed at the wooden structure in the far corner.

"The confessional, miss," the woman said. She spoke with the attentive nervousness of a well-bred child.

Jamaica nodded.

"How does it work?"

"What do you mean?"

Jamaica hesitated. "How do you know when it's open for business?"

The woman looked across the way. "He's in there now." Then she took off, even faster than before.

Jamaica went back and stood in front of the yellow curtain. It was silent. Who wants to talk to a priest? What are they anyway? A bunch of faggots, she thought. Immediately, she asked God—her God, any God—to forgive her for referring to homosexuals as faggots (it was only a figure of speech) and for insulting priests. Hadn't Bing Crosby played a great guy of a priest in *Going My Way?*

She slipped inside and knelt. It was so calm and quiet there, like all the dark spaces in which she'd found refuge: the closet, the dog-house, under her desk at work. The grill separating her and the priest slid open, just like in the movies.

"Bless me, Father, for I have sinned," she began, hoping that the Hollywood script writers had at least gotten that much right. "It's been . . . a very long time since I last confessed."

She fell silent, and felt overheated and cold all at once. Maybe she was sick. What else could explain her position, kneeling in the dark, in a Catholic church, even thinking about laying bare her soul to a priest? She shut her eyes tight, and saw a burst of yellow stars.

"What am I doing?" Her voice startled her. "Listen, sir, Father, please don't take offense. I have no right to be here."

A voice that was elderly and friendly, that sounded, in fact, the way God should sound, made its way into her darkness.

"What do you mean, my child?"

Jamaica breathed deeply. "I'm Jewish."

She heard a cough. "Is this a prank?"

"No, sir, not at all." She began talking very fast. "I needed someone to talk to and I came into the church and I saw a woman come out of this booth and . . . listen. I'll go. I didn't mean any disrespect. Believe me."

She yanked on the curtain.

"Wait a minute." The voice was compassionate—and curious. "You don't have to go. I have time for lost souls."

"What do you mean, lost souls?" Jamaica asked suspiciously.

"That's just an expression, dear."

Slowly, she pulled the curtain shut. "Oh. Okay. The first thing I have to confess is that I don't have the foggiest idea how to do this. Do I just talk, or what?"

He chuckled. "That's pretty much it. Since you probably don't know what's a sin and what isn't, why don't you just start with what's bothering you."

"I know what a sin is," Jamaica said indignantly. "I sinned the sin of thinking about cheating on my husband."

"And did you cheat on your husband?"

"Not really."

"What do you mean, 'not really'?"

"How technical do you guys get?" She quickly added, "Oh, I'm sorry. I didn't mean to be disrespectful."

There was another cough. "You can be as technical as you want."

So Jamaica told him about her evening with Abraham and about the diaphragm, and about Sammy's disappearance, even about the men who had abducted her when she was a teen-ager.

"Did you ever tell your father about your encounter with those men?" The priest's voice betrayed no sign of boredom.

"I never got the chance. He died the next year."

"Oh, I'm sorry."

"Father, sir, I am sorry, too. I am so, so sorry. Is it a sin not to realize someone you love is dying? What is the penance for . . ." Jamaica began to sob. The grating slid open and a tissue dropped out.

"I'm sorry, sir." She gulped and snorted into the tissue. "I've taken up a great deal of your time. I probably should go."

"Why don't you stay awhile," said the kindly voice. "What exactly happened when your father died?"

"The truth?"

"Try," he said.

The death scene had been a long act that seemed quite brief because it had been kept a secret right up to the melodramatic finale. Only recently, she told the priest, had she discussed it with her mother.

"He brought it on himself," Eva had said with disgust, furiously kneading yeast dough for the long loaves of nut and raisin pastry that were her specialty.

"You mean because he smoked?" Jamaica kept an eye on the number of egg yolks her mother was dropping into the thick batter.

"No, no no," said Eva impatiently. "He was so jealous and angry at me because Wally was over in the afternoon for some advice."

"What are you talking about?"

"Remember Wally Snider, Betty's husband, the lawyer?" Eva didn't break from her rhythmic thumping.

"Of course I remember Wally. He came over all the time to borrow your *Wall Street Journal* and to bug you about the stock market. Drank a lot. Did Daddy think he had the hots for you?"

"Daddy was extremely jealous."

Jamaica shrieked. "He was?"

Eva dug her thumb into the dough. "Well, is it such a shock?"

Jamaica waved her hands. "No, don't get me wrong. You know I think you're beautiful, Mom. I guess I never thought of you and Daddy as thinking of each other that way."

Eva sprinkled more flour onto the wooden board on which she was working. "Didn't you hear us arguing?"

"Sure." Jamaica idly pressed a J into the dough with her fingernail. "And you told us that Hungarian was just a loud language."

"And you believed that?" The question came with an unfamiliar layer of sarcasm. "Then why did you hide in the closet?"

Eva wiped her doughy hand against her forehead, leaving behind a pasty smudge.

"I thought you were yelling about me." Jamaica put her finger to Eva's mouth. "Lick," she said. She wiped her mother's forehead clean. "What does Wally and all this have to do with Daddy's death?"

Eva's eyes grew watery. "I wish I were dead," she muttered.

"Mommy, how can you say that?" Jamaica was shocked.

"I didn't say it," Eva said. "That's what he said. Daddy said it. 'I wish I were dead.'"

A tear dropped into her dough. "I wanted to scream at him, to tell him to shut up. It was evil of him to even think that. What a *nehora*. What a *nehora*!"

In the confessional, Jamaica dropped her head, just as she had back then to lean against her mother's shoulder.

"What did you say to him?"

Jamaica's head dangled as her mother shrugged. "Nothing," Eva said. "I put the news on."

What Eva didn't know at the time of Dr. Just's outburst, she told her daughter, was that he had gotten back the proofs of pictures he had taken of his chest. When it came to X rays, he was no amateur photographer. Unlike the albums full of off-kilter likenesses of his pretty wife and their adorable daughters, this picture was starkly clear. There was an unmistakable shadow on his right lung, proof that the pain he'd been feeling for the past few weeks was physical. It wasn't, as he'd hoped, a recurrence of his chronic, crushing fear of never escaping the past.

He sent the X rays around to specialists in Cincinnati, Columbus, the Mayo Clinic. They confirmed his diagnosis. In February, he quietly told Eva that he wouldn't be going on house calls in the afternoons anymore.

"That's wonderful," she said. "It's Jamaica's last year at home. Maybe the two of you can find some time to talk, maybe play some chess."

Without looking directly at her, he explained that he would be driving into Cincinnati four afternoons a week for treatments.

"What treatments?" She reached up to hold his face in her slender hands. Her nails were deepest red that day.

"Evakem," he said, his voice breaking over the term of endearment. "I have cancer."

For the next six months, four times a week after morning office hours, Eva rode with Dr. Just for the two-hour drive into Cincinnati. She waited while chemicals were pumped into his bloodstream for an hour, then drove him home, almost unable to look at his twisted face. They agreed to keep those trips a little secret, and were always home in time for dinner. Dr. Just made a special effort to show interest in Jamaica's progress with college applications, and never missed a single night of work.

There were two Just households during that period. In the one to which the girls had access, there was a becalming wind. The mad Hungarian storms virtually ceased, and Dr. Just seemed far more interested in reconciliation than confrontation. The girls assumed it had to do with Jamaica's impending departure for college. On Geneva's increasingly rare visits home, she was so fatigued from her medical studies that she spent most of her breaks sleeping. Jamaica was preoccupied with drag racing and dreaming, and avoiding the thought of what the future would hold for her in the East. She was pleased that her father had begun to reveal to her the sentimental side that he usually reserved for Geneva. Still, she was mystified by the fuss he kept making over her high school graduation. He kept saying over and over how glad he was to watch her pass this milestone.

Only Eva and Dr. Just were privy to the other household, a frantic bedlam filled with doctors sadly shaking their heads at their colleague's obstinacy. Dr. Just simply did not want to die. He did not want to believe that the cure he'd read about in the *New England Journal of Medicine* didn't apply to his case, or that the crack cancer team in Rochester couldn't do something for him. After years of doubting his right to live, he vehemently protested his death sentence.

Later, Jamaica and Geneva would try to explain to themselves why they hadn't noticed the weight loss, the slowed gait, the slightly bent shoulders, the absence of temper. "He was so tan. He worked so hard. He ate," they said. He continued to drive at reckless speeds, and he continued to suddenly bring the Oldsmobile to a screeching halt and order everyone out of the car when his eye caught sight of a pink sunset in the rearview mirror. He would throw his arms around Eva and the girls and, gazing up at the miraculous colors streaming above them, he would say, softly: "You see, girls, there is a God." And even though the girls were nearly adults at that time, he didn't forget to roll down his window as they drew near to the farm with a penful of peacocks near the road. Without braking a whit, he nodded his head toward the back seat.

"Ready?" he said.

The girls, who were young women, really, tensed up and leaned their heads out the back window on the right-hand side. "Help! Help! Help!" they screamed, before collapsing into giggles.

In the distance, they heard a faint response that they interpreted as "Help! Help! Help!" And, as always, by the time they got to their knees and peered out the back window, the peacocks had disappeared from view.

"Why didn't you tell us?" Jamaica asked Eva years later.

"He didn't want it, that I should." Eva's locution warped when she was pressed too closely for unpleasant details.

"Why?"

"Why? Why? Your father was proud. He didn't want to seem weak to his patients, or to you girls, I think."

"Didn't he think about how we would feel after he died?"

Eva smiled. "Don't you understand, *draga*? He didn't think he would die."

In keeping with that sanguine outlook, Dr. Just and Eva had decided to reward Jamaica with a lavish high school graduation gift. They arranged a trip to Australia, where she would stay with Vera Stern, Eva's oldest friend from Just, and her family. There was an ulterior motive. Jamaica had been corresponding since she was a small child with Vera's younger son, Martin, and the two families hoped the youngsters might marry someday. The geographic distance was problematic, but they were both Jewish. So much in common.

Jamaica fell silent.

After a moment or two, the priest broke in. "Is something wrong?"

She looked up in the dark toward the opening that led to his voice. "No, I was just thinking about how often my parents talked about 'things in common.' How important that was. And here I am, telling this story to you."

"Is it too difficult? Do you want to stop?"

"Do you want me to?"

The silence now was his. "No."

Jamaica expelled her breath, gratefully. She resumed her story, smiling as she remembered the pleasure Eva took in preparing for Jamaica's trip. Together they studied the statistical tables in the world atlas, and copied data such as the population and longitude and latitude of Australia's major cities. They read the *Encyclopedia Britannica* entry on kangaroos, and looked at the pictures of the outback in an old issue of *National Geographic* Eva had saved for just this occasion.

Right before Jamaica boarded her plane, she hugged her father close, even though she hadn't quite yet forgiven him for his callous response to Jimmy Ebberley's death, which was still fresh in her mind. "Bye, Daddy," she whispered in his ear. "Yell at the peacocks for me on the way home."

Sydney had appeared to Jamaica like an opal Oz, rising up white and sparkling from the shores of the South Pacific. Vera's family lived in a modest, pleasant home with a terrace that looked down on a vast, sloping incline of terra cotta roofs. Across the bay, the modern spires of Sydney twinkled in the bright June sky of early winter. She was eager to be dazzled, and so she was, by the city's endless supply of Chinese restaurants and the rough-edged Australian accents. The only kangaroos she saw were the ones at the Sydney zoo. That didn't dim her enthusiasm. At seventeen, she retained the blush of girlhood even as she teetered on the edge of adulthood. She longed for exoticism and adventure almost as much as she dreaded growing up.

She told the priest about her disappointing romance with Martin. To please their parents, they nuzzled each other, only to find the spark that jumped out of their letters snuffed out on contact.

She told him how her sleep had been ruptured night after night by the same troublesome dream. Jamaica suspected she was suffering internal disturbances from having passed through the International Date Line. In her dream it was spring. The Just's back yard was overgrown with thick blades of deep green grass. Trees bowed under the weight of leaves that had overmetabolized to enormousness. Rain covered the landscape, as it did in reality, with the warm, syrupy wetness that shrouded southern Ohio in the spring. No bones were chilled there in the dream world of Harmony.

The rain had interrupted a family picnic. Dr. Just was standing, lazily waving at someone from his post by the barbecue pit. One of Eva's frilly aprons shielded his white shirt and dark pants from the splatter of fat and barbecue sauce. Eva reclined on a chaise longue, laughing and talking. Some neighbors tossed beach balls to children, and bit into succulent burgers dripping with relish and the juice from thick slices of tomato. A burst of rain scattered this jolly assemblage. They dispersed languidly, as though they were floating in a large aquarium.

Jamaica dreamed she saw herself lingering behind, watching the others disappear into the house. She lifted her face skyward and let her tongue loll out of her mouth. The raindrops she caught tasted fresh and pure, like water from a well, or from a New York City tap. A ferocious thunderclap sent a shiver down her back. The telephone wire strung up by the birdhouse perched on a tall pole near the tool shed snapped and drifted slowly, slowly toward Jamaica's transfixed body. She reached up and grabbed the wire. All sensation left her. She lay there in the warm, wet grass, unable to move or to speak. Helpless, she watched her parents sobbing silently in the distance. Three mornings in a row she woke up to find her pillow drenched with her tears, and the fear of spring rain and death.

As she recalled that dream she could barely hear the priest's comforting hmmms and yesses. For the first time in years she thought of those days—no, felt herself reliving them with awful clarity. Though she could hear a sound that resembled her voice, she had drifted far, far away from the confessional booth. Her cheeks felt warm; she was sitting with Martin on the terrace in Sydney, enjoying the late afternoon sun.

"You are quite pale, Jamaica," Martin informed her on the fourth day of her visit. "Hasn't the jet lag worn off yet?"

They were resting after an organized day of sightseeing that had begun after the breakfast clean-up.

"I feel fine, thank you, Martin." Jamaica tipped her face toward the sun. "I'm still adjusting to the change of atmosphere. I have the feeling I'm hanging upside down."

Martin lifted his sunglasses and glanced at her quizzically.

"Just kidding." Jamaica smiled reassuringly. "Down under? Get it?"

Jamaica adored Sydney for its beauty and cosmopolitanism and simply for where it sat on the globe. Still, she couldn't wait for the end of the second week, when Martin and one of his friends were going to fly with her to a sort of camp on the edge of the outback. They would hire a guide and take a jeep into a nature preserve where koalas and kangaroos ran free, and the wilderness stretched out endlessly. Even though the trip had been arranged by a travel agent, the whole enterprise resounded with a satisfying ring of adventure.

The night before their outing, Jamaica fell asleep clutching the safari cap Vera had bought her for the trip. It was the first time since she'd left home that night brought peace. She sank almost immediately into blessed unconsciousness.

She woke up to find Vera's arms around her. "Is it time to go?" Jamaica blinked sleepily. "It's still dark."

A strange man came into the room and handed her a pill and a glass of water. "Here, dear, have a go at this," he said.

"What's going on here?" Jamaica demanded, setting the water on the night table. Shaking off Vera's arms, she unwound her hair from the orange juice can on her head. It had escaped its mooring of bobby pins and was dangling over her forehead. She jerked her head toward the stranger. "Who is he?"

"That's a neighbor," said Vera. "Dr. Klein."

Jamaica anxiously looked around the room and noted who was absent. "Oh my God," she said. "Has something happened to Miklos, or Martin?"

Miklos spoke from the shadows. "No, Miss Bright Eyes. Jamaica. We're all fine. The problem is at home."

A hoarse scream cut through the polite stillness with a force so raw and terrible it ripped the nerves of those who heard it. As the last echo subsided, a mesmerizing, distressful chant began:

"Dad-dy, dad-dy . . ."

"Do something!" Vera screamed at Dr. Klein and her husband. As though breaking out of a trance, the doctor grabbed Jamaica. She was rocking back and forth, immersed in her Mourner's Kaddish. With one hand he squeezed open her mouth and tossed in the tranquilizer. He forced her to swallow it, gagging, with water. He nodded at Vera.

"Your father's in the hospital," she said quietly. "Geneva is on the phone."

Jamaica stumbled out of bed and groped her way to the hall phone, snorting like a terrified animal. "Hello!" She yelled into the telephone. "Gen? Is that you?"

She heard the faint semblance of her sister's voice. "Jamaica, hon. Daddy's in the hospital. Mom and I think you'd better get home."

"Is that the truth, Geneva? Are you telling me the truth? He isn't dead?" Jamaica twisted the telephone cord tighter and tighter around her wrist, and banged her head against the wall. "I know he's dead," she wailed. "How did he die?"

There was no response.

"Is he dead, Geneva?"

Geneva's voice came faintly. "I can't hear you, chum."

Jamaica shouted. "I said, are you telling me the truth?"

Another pause. "Jamaica, have I ever lied to you?"

Miklos removed the phone from Jamaica's hand and untangled her wrist from the cord. He spoke briefly to Geneva about plane connections and tranquilizers. Then he carried the nodding Jamaica—eventually granted a few hours of chemically induced sleep—into her room.

Of course, Dr. Just was dead when Geneva made that telephone call. She had come home for summer vacation shortly after Jamaica had left, with three of her medical school friends in tow. The city slickers were impressed with Harmony's quaintness and the natural beauty of the surrounding countryside, and admiring of the large number of cars and trucks that crowded the parking lot outside Dr. Just's office every day. Geneva had never seen her father as charming and outgoing as he was during that brief period. Over dinner he was full of questions about their anatomy and physiology classes and expansive reminiscences about his own medical school days. He even talked at length about the curious virus that had kept him coughing for months. For the most part, though, the young people kept to themselves, and Geneva was delighted to see how well her new Jewish friends from New York adapted to her home town.

The night before he died, Dr. Just undressed for bed with a great deal of difficulty. His joints seemed rusted, Eva would tell the girls later, much later.

"Are you all right, *draga*?" Eva asked him, as she watched him struggling with his blue-striped pajamas.

Sitting on the edge of their bed, his back toward her, Dr. Just murmured. "You know, I don't regret living here in Harmony. I think the girls have grown up well."

Eva didn't answer. For the first time, she tried to imagine the years stretching out before her without Dr. Just. Every time a picture started to form in her mind, it was eclipsed by the long shadow of denial.

The next morning Dr. Just remained in bed. He asked his wife to tell his patients to go home. By noon, his fight was over. Later, Eva explained to the girls how lucky he was that the embolism brought things to a quick end. And even later, when Jamaica heard herself repeating that ameliorative distortion to the priest, her throat felt thick, as though she were choking something back.

"God help me, I don't think he was lucky," she finally confessed on that sad, rainy day in November. "*Avinu Malkeinu.*" She chanted in Hebrew long-forgotten prayers. "Our father, our king, we have sinned the sin of being stiff-necked. *Avinu Malkeinu,* we have sinned the sin of calumny. *Avinu Malkeinu,* I have sinned the sin of selfishness. Father, please forgive me, for I have sinned."

Exhausted, Jamaica crouched in silence.

After a few minutes, the priest spoke. "Do you have anything more you'd like to say?"

Jamaica straightened up. "No, thank you." She hesitated. "Don't you have anything for me to do? Some Hail Mary's or a couple of rosaries?" Silently, she thought, "What about absolution?"

"I do have something for you, my dear." The grating slid open and a card dropped onto Jamaica's knee. She opened the curtain a crack so she could examine it in the light. "Interfaith Counseling Service," it said. Several phone numbers and locations were listed.

Jamaica was shocked. "You're sending me to a shrink?" She huddled in the corner of the confessional as she imagined her voice reverberating to the corners of the cathedral. That was the final blow to her collapsed expectations. She'd come for a quick fix, to throw holy water on the guilt aroused by her contemplated infidelity. Instead, she'd been tricked into opening the floodgates of shame and sorrow, the Catholic's burden.

Weary and disappointed as she was, her Midwestern upbringing didn't fail her; she didn't want to appear ungracious.

"I'm sorry," she said. "I guess I thought I'd get something else from you. Something spiritual."

"I can't give you that." The priest sounded sad. "I think you could use some guidance. From a professional. Then who knows? Maybe faith will follow."

Jamaica wanted to console him. "Listen, I appreciate it. Thank you for taking the time to listen to an infidel."

"God be with you," the priest said as the curtain opened and the sound of Jamaica's boots faded into the distance.

Losing It

There was nowhere for Jamaica to go but home. It was well past noon when she put her key into the apartment door and found it was open. Various emotions—primarily relief and apprehension—presented themselves to her as she stepped across the threshold; once she saw Sammy's troubled face, only apprehension remained.

Before he could say a word, she rushed over to him. "Please forgive me, Sammy. It wasn't anything like what it appeared to be. Nothing happened. I swear to you on . . . on whatever you want."

From his post by the window, he stared at her blankly. "Don't do this to me, Sammy," she cried. "I've felt so distant from you lately. Sometimes when I talk to you, I see the words vanish into the air before they reach your ears. I guess Abraham flattered me. He made me feel . . . ," she paused, trying to remember, "as though I really existed."

Sammy, usually well groomed to the point of fanaticism, was unshaven and smelly. His eyes were open but he seemed unconscious.

"What are you babbling about?" His voice was flat.

"I'm trying to explain why I was out so late last night and why you found my diaphragm case open and empty." Jamaica was the picture of earnestness.

For the first time since she'd stepped into the apartment, Sammy focused on his wife.

"Jamaica. For once in your life, open your eyes." Sammy spoke slowly and distinctly, as though talking to a recalcitrant child or a deaf person. "I don't know what you are talking about. I wasn't here last night."

Jamaica drew back her hand and slapped Sammy's bristly cheek, hard. A searing red mark appeared immediately. "Oh, my God," she gasped. "I've never hit anyone in my life. How could you make me do this?"

Sammy pulled her close and began to cry. "How could you make me do *this*?"

Overcome with confusion and anguish, they swayed against each other silently, afraid to speak the words they knew would give form to their turbulent emotions. All future joy or pain, whether it greeted them together or separately, would be diffracted through the dolorous prism of this moment.

They broke apart in tandem.

"Where have you—," said Jamaica.

"What did you—," said Sammy.

"You go first," said Jamaica.

"I love you," Sammy said forlornly.

"This must be awful." Jamaica was finding it difficult to breathe. She sat down. "Talk, Sammy. Where were you?"

"Do you know how hard I've tried to make things right for you?" Sammy pushed Jamaica's hair out of her face. "I'm thirsty. Would you like a soda?"

Jamaica shook her head and drew her knees to her chest.

Sammy carried a can of Diet Coke from the kitchen. "Don't put your shoes on the couch," he said automatically. He exploded. "Jesus, Jamaica, don't look at me like that! Stop acting like a child."

"Me!" she screamed. "Who's the child? Who goes off to play with his little boyfriends and then comes dragging in here without calling all night? You could have been dead."

Sammy swallowed some Coke. "That's right. I could have been dead, and I'd be shocked if you'd notice. I see the way you look at me, Jamaica. Like I'm not there. Good old Sammy. Picks you up when you're down and not worth blinking at when you're up." Jamaica flinched at these unfamiliar notes of bitterness.

Sammy sat on the chair opposite Jamaica and rubbed the back of his neck. His voice was soft.

"I don't know why I wanted to take care of you so much. From the moment I met you I thought to myself, 'This girl needs me.' You were so pathetic and funny and—I don't know—different. I won't say you were everything I'd dreamed of because I'd never thought of meeting anyone like you. You were special. If you were mine, I'd be special, too."

Jamaica protested. "Sammy, you were special without me."

He shook his head. "No I wasn't, and you didn't believe that either. I knew why you would never tell me you loved me. How do you think I felt when you kept telling me you were flying away, that this house never felt like your home?"

"I didn't think it made any difference. You never said a word."

Sammy sighed. "I didn't want to drive you out. You're always so distracted by your stories, by the people you pick up on the street. I thought I was boring you."

"Sammy," said Jamaica. "Where were you last night?"

"Don't take this the wrong way." Sammy looked miserable.

Jamaica began to tease. "Did you kill somebody, or what? C'mon, Sammy. It can't have been that bad."

He scrutinized her with disbelief. "Jamaica. I spent the night with somebody else. Another woman."

She started to get up.

"Where are you going?"

"My hand is bleeding." She held up the evidence. When she'd clenched her fist, her nail had gone right through her skin.

Sammy didn't move. She returned, a Band-Aid covering her flesh wound.

The knowledge of Sammy's transgression had metamorphosed her guilt into gall. "Do you love her, too, Sammy? Did you want to take care of her, too? Does she have big tits?"

Jamaica began to cry. "Is she pretty? Is she calm? She's practical, isn't she? How long has this been going on? I can't stand it. Sammy. This is like a B-movie. Couldn't you have done better than this? What *is* this?"

Sammy stayed put. "I don't know what it is."

"Don't make me drag it out of you," Jamaica sniffed. "I'm not the prosecutor."

He shrugged. "I met her at work a couple of months ago. She's in my project, a structural engineer. I guess it was about when you were starting to get all hyped up about that story about letter writers, after all that *tsuris* with the welfare mother story."

After a pause, Sammy continued. "Jamaica, you exhaust me. I'd been banging my head against the wall trying to cheer you up, and you never seemed to notice. Out of one thing and you were ready to fling yourself into something else. All I wanted was a little love and affection. I have feelings, too."

Jamaica had grown calm. She nodded. "So, I guess this person met you and told you how wonderful you were, and carried on with a lot of PDA." Public displays of affection, Jamaica had told Sammy early in their relationship, were not part of her repertoire.

Sammy smiled reluctantly. "Well, sort of. I don't know, Jamaica. She thinks I'm smart and funny and sophisticated. Maybe she's faking it, but it seems like she can't listen to me enough."

A thought occurred to Jamaica. "Where did all this talking take place?"

Sammy looked surprised. "I don't know. Restaurants, mostly. At first."

"I'm glad to see your ethics are still intact," she said huffily.

"I don't get it."

"You paid for dinner on your own American Express card instead of billing the client. Nice touch."

"Since when do you look at the bills?" Sammy seemed pleased, the way he always sounded when he noticed Jamaica's feet touching the ground. He was eager to latch on to something prosaic.

Jamaica exploded again. "I look at bills when my husband's playing poker, or fucking some stranger, or whatever he's doing on Tuesday nights."

He was wounded. "You don't know what it's like for me to have someone look at me the way she does. Like I'm fascinating. The way I listen to you."

She started to reach for him, then pulled back her hand. "I'm sorry, Sammy."

"Don't turn this around on me, Jamaica. I made a mistake. It's my mistake and my guilt." He shook his head. "It isn't yours."

She gave a short laugh. "It could have been."

He looked at her quizzically.

"I was out for a little fling, myself," she said airily, but precisely. "Only I remembered what these vows were all about." She yanked at her wedding ring, but couldn't slide it over her swollen knuckle. "I'll get some soap. That'll do it," she muttered.

Sammy walked over to her chair and put his hand on hers. "No theatrics. This isn't one of our games."

"Fine. You tell me what to do, then." Her eyes looked like empty sockets; her face a blank wall. "Do you want to get a divorce? It's not a tragedy anymore, right?"

His hand remained on hers. "I think it would be a tragedy."

She brightened. "You do?"

"Yes, I do," he said. "But we both need some time to figure things out for ourselves."

"That's so of-the-moment," she said sarcastically.

"Don't slam that shield down on me," Sammy cried. "I want to love you, Jamaica, but I can't live with you until you learn how to love yourself."

"That's absurd," she snapped. "I don't know what you're talking about."

He became deliberately cool. "Figure it out," he said. "I'm leaving."

"Where are you going?"

Sammy had already figured out his part. "I'm going down to Atlanta for a while. That way I won't have to fly back and forth."

With difficulty, Jamaica asked, "Is your engineer friend going to be with you?"

He patted her head. "No, she isn't. She's staying in New York. I want to simplify things, not complicate them."

"How do I know you're telling the truth?" For the first time, she noticed the packed suitcase by the front closet.

Sammy kissed her on the forehead before she could turn her head. "You're going to have to trust me."

Numbly, Jamaica answered. "Right. Well, you have a good trip, or . . . whatever."

He started to say something, then walked out the door.

The cat padded over to Jamaica and sat at her feet, looking up expectantly. Jamaica leaned over and picked it up and buried her face in the cat's warm belly.

"Ouch!" Jamaica dropped the cat, and touched the scratch it had left on her cheek. "Where are you, you little creep?"

She looked around the room and spotted the cat plunked down on the rug in front of the television set. The animal cocked its head toward Jamaica, as though encouraging her to take comfort from whatever idiocy the box offered at what must be an unprofitable hour. Jamaica flicked on the switch with some effort. It was as though the emotional fever that had brought her to this sodden state had finally infected her bones. Utter depression accomplished for her what years of yoga couldn't manage. Gravity took hold and pulled her unresisting form to the ground.

"*IS IT FOR REAL?*" Jamaica's half-closed eyelids flipped open. The jocular voice continued at a slightly lower volume. "*That's the question we ask OURSELVES and YOU, THE AUDIENCE, every morning on* IS IT FOR REAL?'' Without moving, Jamaica listened with revulsion as the announcer explained the premise of the program. It purported to offer portrayals of slices of life, peopled by . . . well, real people. To be "real" enough to qualify for this show—since "realness" has become such a staple of television fare—it appeared one had to be extremely bizarre or, better yet, pathological.

"TODAY'S FIRST SEGMENT," screamed the invisible announcer, *"WILL TAKE US INTO CATTLE COUNTRY."* A herd of cattle appeared on the screen. "Git along Little Dogie" played on the harmonica, sounded in the background. The cattle grazed peacefully, occasionally bumping heads.

The camera zoomed into the middle of the herd and settled on the face of a man of medium build, wearing denim and a goofy grin. His eyes were dark and slightly bewildered looking, his mouth a gallery of empty spaces where his teeth should be.

"THIS," boomed the announcer, *"IS LONGHORN JOE. HELLO, JOE."*

"Hi, there," Joe said to the wrong cameraman, thus giving the audience the impression that he was staring off into space. He cocked his head, apparently receiving instructions, then swung around to the right direction.

"Hi, there," he repeated, now looking at the audience.

"TELL US ABOUT YOURSELF, LONGHORN. HOW YOU GOT YOUR NAME."

Jamaica watched with disbelief as the man explained that he had changed his name to Longhorn Joe because he likes to sleep with cows. *"Cows are better than people,"* he explained. *"They didn't put me into an orphanage when my parents died, people did."* He began to sob.

"Oh, my God, get me out of here!" Jamaica pulled herself up from the floor, forcing the cat to leap to its feet. Jamaica switched the dial.

DON'T BE A NOBODY FOR THE REST OF YOUR LIFE. LET ABC TECH SHOW YOU THE WAY. COMPUTER PROGRAMMER, TELEPHONE OPERATOR. WE CAN TEACH YOU A SKILL. CALL . . .

Next channel.

PRAISE THE LORD, SINNERS. ARE YOU TIRED OF WATCHING OTHERS SUCCEED WITH GREED AND EVIL IN THEIR HEARTS? LET BROTHER BOB SHOW YOU THE WAY TO GLORY—

AND, YES, EARTHLY GAIN, THROUGH THE BIBLE. YOU THOUGHT THE BIBLE WAS JUST FOR SUNDAY? NO! BROTHER BOB CAN SHOW YOU THAT PROFITABILITY AND BELIEF IN THE LORD ARE NOT INCOMPATIBLE. TRUST IN GOD AND GOD WILL GIVE YOU YOUR JUST REWARD.

"What have you got for me, Brother Bob?" Jamaica couldn't take her eyes off the white-haired man on the screen.

BROTHER BOB HAS THOUGHT HARD AND STUDIED LONG ABOUT HOW TO KEEP THE FAITH IN THESE TROUBLESOME TIMES," he answered. *"YOU CAN SHARE HIS KNOWLEDGE AND WISDOM BY SENDING $15—A SPECIAL PRICE—FOR HIS NEW BOOK,* YOU CAN LOVE GOD AND YOUR MERCEDES TOO. *DIAL NOW, 1-800-GOD-GAIN, TO TAKE ADVANTAGE OF THIS SPECIAL OFFER.*

Jamaica turned off the set. "No thanks, Bob. God's already given me my reward, and I didn't pay a cent."

Redemption

That evening Eva called. Jamaica managed to cheerfully discuss movies and salad bars—her mother's latest obsession. As they were ready to ring off, Eva asked, "How's Sammy?"

"Fine," Jamaica said lightly. "He's going to be down in Atlanta for a while."

"Is anything the matter?"

Jamaica sighed. "No, nothing's the matter. He just needs to spend a bit of time down there for the big project they're working on. I told you about it."

Eva hesitated. "You don't mind him going off by himself? You know, you never tell me much about what goes on with you two."

Jamaica exploded. "I never tell you what goes on in *my* marriage! What about yours?"

"What's the matter with you? What do you want to know?" Eva's voice broke. "What do you want to know?"

Jamaica felt panicky. She never pressed her mother for details, always afraid of what would emerge if she pried open Eva's box of secrets. Did she want to destroy her mother too?

"Nothing, Mommy. I guess I feel just a little lonely, that's all. Don't worry. You understand?"

"Of course." Jamaica could hear that Eva had already sprung back. "Give Sammy my love when you speak to him."

"I'll be sure and give him your love. Good night, Mom."

"Good night, dear."

Jamaica kept her hand on the receiver a long time after she hung up. She started to call Abraham, then thought better of it. Instead, she stood on the couch and reached up for her copy of *The Bible as Living Literature* and went to bed. She fell into a deep sleep halfway into one of her favorite love poems, the Song of Songs.

The next morning she took special care to dress in lively colors and to apply blush-on. The sun was insolently bright, the air so clear that the buildings she passed on the way to work seemed etched into the sky. She planned to fritter away the morning with busywork. Thumbing through the mail on her desk, she noticed among the preaddressed mailing labels a carefully lettered envelope from an L. Williams. Could it be from Lonnie? Months had passed since their last meeting, when the young black girl had walked out of the room. Jamaica's fingers were so icy she had some difficulty tearing open the flap. The letter inside was written in painstaking script.

Dear Miss Just,

Remember me? You probably thought you would never ~~here~~ hear from me ever again. I felt myself hurt bad when I read my story in the newspaper. You were so nice to me I thought you would write up a nice story, like the kind they do on tv. I looked at the story you wrote and I got scared. It said to me, Lonnie, they aren't any dreams. That broke my heart. I hated you cause you ~~was~~ were the one that did it.

Then the lady at the Institute she tell all of us that the story only ~~say~~ said what ~~be~~ was true. We got it hard having babies and all and just being young girls ourselves. We ~~ain't~~ have not had much luck in our lives. But you said in my story that we be trying.

Jamaica read the rest of the letter through a mist of tears. Lonnie told her how hurt and angry she had been at Jamaica's presumption—so angry, in fact, that proving Jamaica wrong had become a full-time job for Lonnie. She'd finished her high school equivalency course and had begun to work mornings at a day care center, where she could bring her child. She was going to secretarial school in the afternoons; her grammar had a way to go, but her typing was impeccable.

Things are not easy but I got hope and maybe that be better than dreams. I want to let you know I don't hate you. When I got more hope maybe we can see each other again. Be good.

Sincerely . . .

Automatically, Jamaica called her mother. "Mom? I found something out today. Something wonderful—"

She picked up after Eva's interruption. "Really? That's great . . . You made five thousand dollars? . . . On paper? . . . Congratulations.

But listen to what I discovered . . . We can't all be physicians, now, can we? We can't all find affirmation of life in the giving of it to others."

Eva broke in. "That's what I tell you all the time, darling. The truly great ones don't weep and moan about what they haven't got. They move forward. They let their feet take them forward bit by bit and are only happy they don't sit on their heels." She paused. "What happened, *draga*? Did you win a prize?"

Jamaica laughed. "In a way I did. Do you remember the story I did in Harlem, about the girl with the baby?"

"*Nu*? How could I forget? You were so upset."

"She wrote me a letter. She's going to secretarial school."

Eva's response was triumphant. "What did I tell you! If life doesn't move exactly as you'd like, it's moving well enough. And far more interesting than you would have imagined. I find this is so."

"Mommy?"

"Oh, dear. I must run now. My tennis partner is driving up."

Jamaica smiled and shook her head. "Have a good game." She was still smiling as she laid the phone back on the receiver.

Jamaica's state of grace lasted long enough for her to throw away most of the rest of her mail. Then she noticed the letter from Jules Marlin that lay waiting, unopened, by her Rolodex. Without thinking, she picked it up. After a quick scan, her reaction was fierce and vocal.

"My God, Jamaica, what's wrong?" Joanne ran around the divider separating them and shook her sobbing friend.

"Look what I've done." Jamaica waved the crumpled letter in the air. "I can't take any more."

Joanne took the letter from Jamaica's hand and began to read:

Dear Miss Just,

I cannot tell you in words how angry I am with you. We went out together and had a nice dinner and I tried to be frank with you about the subject of your story, which was why do intelligent people like myself get involved in the news. I tried to explain it to you, how important I feel it is for Jews particularly to keep in touch.

I was very surprised, you can imagine, to see not an objective story about people in the news but garbage about "compulsive letter writers" and "irregular regulars." Like a laxative commercial! The worst thing was to see an article about myself that indicated that I am some kind of nut. Who was that woman doctor to call me a neurotic? I seen her on television and thought she was pretty smart but now I see something else.

I just wanted to let you know I am sorry I ever met you. Don't publish this letter. I'm cutting your paper off my list.
> *Sincerely,*
> *Jules Marlin*
> *Kew Gardens, Queens*

Joanne tossed the letter back onto Jamaica's desk. "This guy's a lunatic. C'mon, Jamaica. Don't let this crackpot get to you. He is some kind of a nut. It was a great story."

Jamaica's face was wet and red. "Listen, Joanne. Thanks. I've got to make some calls."

"You aren't going to call this Marlin character, are you?"

"Of course not. Don't be silly." Jamaica smiled damply. "I'm fine. Promise."

She waited until she heard the clicking of Joanne's computer keyboard before flipping her Rolodex to the M's and picking up the phone.

"Hello? Mr. Marlin? Jules?"

Jules growled. "Who is it?"

Jamaica hesitated. "It's Jamaica Just. Listen, we have to—"

Jules slammed down the receiver.

Every half-hour for the rest of the day and into the night, when Jamaica went back to her apartment, this wounded flirtation was repeated. She called, he hung up. He didn't, as he could have, take the phone off the hook or simply let it ring. As the half-hour approached— and she knew he could measure the passage of time easily by the endings and beginnings of his television programs—she could imagine his eye drifting warily to the phone. When the expected ring came, he would set his lips into a posture of ferocity, to steel his will against that winsome voice. Each half-hour Jamaica reset the oven timer so she wouldn't forget to phone. As the evening wore on, she noticed, more and more time elapsed before the hang-up. She'd gotten as far as "I'm sorry you misinterpreted the story." At eleven-thirty, she decided that Jules could wait in vain for her call. Jamaica was obsessive, not rude.

Without compunction, she called in sick the next morning. She *was* sick, she told herself. Chronic contrition. She refused to allow herself to think about Sammy; the thought of him actually leaving was too terrifying to contemplate just then. First she had to set things straight with Jules; after all, Lonnie had shown her that not everything she touched had to turn to sludge.

Jules waited vainly by the telephone the next morning. At noon, as he shambled into the kitchen to investigate what he needed to buy for dinner, the downstairs buzzer rang.

"Who's there," he barked into the intercom.

"It's me, Mr. Marlin. Jamaica. Can I come up?"

"Who told you where I live?"

"The telephone book."

"What do you want from me?" he asked. "Did you come all the way from Manhattan?"

"Yes, I did."

"How'd you come? By subway?"

"That's right, Mr. Marlin." Jamaica's teeth began chattering. It was cold in the vestibule.

"What's that noise."

"My teeth."

"What's the matter with them?"

"Cold."

She could sense Jules's finger wavering between the button that would cut her off and the one that would buzz her in. It was only twelve-thirty, and she knew that he was unlikely to have much planned for the afternoon.

"Number 4B," he mumbled.

"Excuse me?"

"Come up to 4B. I'll buzz you in."

They met each other with uneasy glances. Jules motioned Jamaica inside without a word.

Jamaica pulled off her hat and coat. Observing the boxes stacked up around the small room, and the bare walls, she asked, "Did you move in recently?"

From behind her, Jules said. "No. I've lived here twelve years. Why do you ask?"

"Oh. No reason," she stammered. "The paint looks fresh."

He looked pleased. "You think so? That's real nice. I thought maybe it was a little dark in here."

The Venetian blinds completely covered the windows facing onto the street. Light came through in narrow slits. Two newly washed tea-cups were dripping dry on the flowered plastic tablecloth Jules had hastily spread over the Formica table.

"Want a cup of tea with lemon?" He spoke uncertainly. It was clear from his nervousness that guests were rare.

"That would be lovely." Jamaica, too, was uncertain of her next move, now that she was here. Making amends was never an easy affair, and things weren't made easier by the inexplicable pull Jules exerted on her. For all the clutter, the studio didn't seem inhabited. There were no mementos except a pair of bronzed baby booties resting on top of the giant color television set that dominated the room. Jamaica shivered. The place was eerie, like the lair of a human grasshopper who foraged not just for food but for small appliances. Although Jules had mentioned something about bank prizes at dinner, she wasn't prepared for this. There was enough stuff to supply a dozen bridal showers, to which Jules wasn't likely to receive invitations. Clearly, he was preparing for Armageddon. He couldn't fiddle while the world burned—there were no signs of musical instruments—but he could make waffles with his never-used waffle iron, or toast in one of his four toaster ovens, or popcorn in his electric popcorn maker, also unopened. If the networks were still broadcasting, he could watch the final meltdown on one of his three television sets—two of them kept unused in their boxes—or listen to the last protesting screams on one of his five digital clock radios.

Jules poured water over the tea bags he dropped into the cups.

"Were those your baby shoes?" Jamaica forced herself out of her gloomy meditation.

"Huh?" Jules turned his eyes in the direction in which Jamaica pointed.

"No, no. Those came as a bonus prize with some cereal coupons." He set the teakettle back down in the kitchen, then brought the shoes over to Jamaica.

"Look there on the bottom." Turning the toddler-sized shoes upside down, she read the inscription: "Jules." Jules chuckled. "They did it for free."

They blew at the steam rising out of their cups, and sipped their tea in silence that began to seem companionable as the minutes ticked on.

Finally, Jamaica ventured to ask exactly what it was in her story that had wrenched such a hostile reaction from Jules. He widened his sorrowful eyes.

"You still don't get it after what I wrote to you in my letter?" His tone was exaggerated, appropriate for the stage, perhaps, not for a tiny studio apartment. "I know you aren't a stupid girl, Miss Just. You tell me."

Gamely, she presented him with the theory she had worked out the previous sleepless night and refined on the subway ride over.

"You think because a psychologist was quoted using words like *neurotic* and *psychotic* in an article about you, the article gave the impression that you were mentally unbalanced." She looked up in time to catch him nodding angrily; her analysis was reviving his grievance.

"I guess you also think that the articles were trying to make fun of letter writers because their reasons for writing letters sound odd when you look at them—those reasons—in black and white in newsprint. Am I right?"

He was nodding more vigorously. His entire body quivered; the table shook.

"But the impression I was trying to convey—and I believe the impression people took away from the thing—was that you and the others seem odd to the rest of the world only because you are still capable of feeling outrage. You haven't pulled the covers up over your head and gone to sleep."

Jamaica was trembling with passion. Jules became very still as he watched her promulgate her fervent defense. His already weakened fury died as he saw that her pain was genuine. He couldn't quite follow the hurly-burly of her polemics, but it became quickly apparent that malice didn't lie at the bottom. Something long forgotten asserted itself and lingered in his heart's conscience. Though this odd sensation from a faraway past had occasionally sprung to the surface before, it had always vanished before he had a chance to examine what it was. He couldn't find a definition in his usual glossary for this resurrected emotion; it was neither anger nor hate nor fear nor remorse. The word that eluded him was compassion.

His features slackened as suspicion relinquished its grip. "You weren't trying to make fun of me?"

Jamaica's pupils had grown so wide her eyes appeared black. "Make fun of you!" Her voice was shrill. "I wanted to understand you because you meant so much to me."

Jules was nonplussed. How had this strange girl inserted herself into his placid existence? He looked down at his bloated belly resting on his lap and at the age spots on his hands. Involuntarily, he grazed the smooth skin of his head with his finger. Surely she wasn't infatuated with him. Years of living alone—barricaded from the past and at a safe distance from the present—hadn't prepared him for this meeting.

Feebly he asked, "Why do I mean so much to you? We only met one time."

Jamaica shook her head. "No, no. We'd met before . . . No, I'm not crazy, don't be scared. Remember? I'd read your letters. And you'd met me, in a way, through my articles. You told me so."

She had him in her sway. She continued.

"I can't explain what it is exactly. There was something exhilarating about your high dudgeon, your conniptions, your rage toward everything you thought was wrong. I felt some kind of kinship with you, even when I thought you were crazy."

He twitched.

Jamaica shook a finger at him. "Don't act like I put a pea in your shoe. I mean crazy as in 'I don't agree with your opinion,' not crazy as in nuts, bonkers, cracked, wacko, squirrely, bananas, *meshugge*."

Jules scratched his face and broke into a smile. He felt himself becoming a spectator again; the role was familiar, even if the sport was not.

"Where do you get those words?"

Jamaica was startled. "What words?"

He waved his hand. "I don't know. 'Bonkers.' 'Squirrely.'"

She rubbed her chin on her shoulder. "I read a lot, I guess," she said uncertainly. "Most of them stay in storage until I start foaming at the mouth."

The room fell silent again.

"Would you like more tea?" Jules asked.

"No thanks," she said.

A few minutes later he hauled himself up out of his chair and huffed his way to a closet barely visible behind a stack of boxes. His fat man's waddle made him resemble, from the rear, Charlie Chaplin swollen out of focus. He had been struck with an urge to examine the contents of the one box that hadn't required a deposit of funds into a bank. He exhumed it from its hiding place behind the Electrolux vacuum cleaner and a pile of old coats, and brought it back to the table.

"Ugh," he said. "Look at this filth." He wiped the dust from the cardboard flaps.

"What is that?" Jamaica noticed a warning label. "Fragile: Glass." She said hurriedly. "You don't have to give me anything."

He tugged at the flaps. "No, no. The teacups came in this box a long time ago. I want to show you something."

He reached into the box and drew out sheafs of yellowed paper. Jamaica felt her throat tighten with excitement.

"Can I look?" Her voice quavered.

"Sure, go ahead. I told you I brought these things to show you." He emptied all the papers in the box on the table.

The paper was brittle. Jamaica gingerly picked up the top leaf. It was a clipping from a Hungarian newspaper. Underneath was another clipping, and another one. Some of the papers were written in English, others in Hungarian, others in Yiddish.

"What are all of these?" she asked. Jules sat down.

"I used to save articles of interest," he said. "Before I started writing to the papers I collected the things I thought were valuable—"

She interrupted. "Don't you save your letters when they're printed?"

He shook his head and looked somewhat bemused. "No. Why would I save them? I know what they said. I wrote them."

"Why did you stop gathering clippings?" She nodded at the papers spread out in front of them.

He struggled for a moment to remember.

"You don't have to tell me if you don't want to," she said hastily.

"No, no. I would tell you if I could. I just don't remember," he said, feeling as though he had failed her in some way.

Jamaica began to read some of the articles in the English papers. There were several chronicles of Truman's election to office, and a number of accounts of the Korean War and McCarthy's rampages. More surprising were numerous gossip columns detailing the activities of Elizabeth Taylor and Marilyn Monroe as well as society matrons Jamaica had never heard of.

"How did you happen to decide what to cut out?" She asked this as she lingered over a faded photograph of Liz and Eddie Fisher. He reddened when he saw what she was looking at.

"Who knows?" He shrugged his shoulders. "I was working then, and I didn't have a lot of time to keep up with things. I didn't have nobody at home . . . Who knows?"

Languidly she turned her attention back to the old newspapers. They were only thirty or forty years old, yet they seemed ancient, withered documents from a dormant civilization. She began to read one of the Hungarian newspapers out loud. Her pronunciation was nearly perfect, her comprehension nil.

Jules was delighted. "Where did you learn to read Hungarian? Oh, I remember. Your parents were from the old country."

"What are these clippings about?" Jamaica asked. Most of the Hungarian papers were dated 1946 and 1947.

Jules looked them over. "Not much. Mostly stories about who was here from my town, what they were doing." He thumbed through the pile. "Look at this," he chuckled. He placed a photograph under her nose. She peered at a large group of mostly young people assembled awkwardly before the camera. The men seemed lost inside suits with heavily padded shoulders; they stared at the camera with the fear and defiance commonly reflected in old photos. The women smiled brightly, their chins in the air, their legs delicately posed one in front of the other.

Jamaica gazed benevolently at the picture. When she remained silent, Jules prodded her. "Look closer."

She bent closer and began to examine each face carefully. All at once she gasped.

"You saw me, heh?" Jules chuckled. He saw that she had grown quite pale, the way she'd looked that night in the restaurant.

"Do you eat fruit?" he asked.

Jamaica composed herself. "So, who are all these people?" she asked as calmly as she could.

Jules translated the caption. "These are survivors from Just," he explained. "This is the Hungarian Jewish paper."

He chuckled. "See how much thinner I was there." He pointed to a suspicious looking young man with thinning hair and already substantial proportions.

"You look quite nice." With forced casualness, Jamaica pointed to a fiercely dark man with an unruly crop of thick hair. "Who is that?"

"Oh, you like his looks?" The razzing was good-natured. "That was Dr. Pearlman. Good-looking man. He was my brother's best friend."

Jamaica thought she was going to faint. It wasn't the shock of hearing her father referred to as Pearlman. Eva had explained the origins of their family name to them when they were quite small. The girls had accepted the story the way they accepted everything Eva told them—warily but without contradiction. What choice did they have? They had relatives named Pearlman. None of them ever indicated that the Justs had ever been anything else.

"What happened to him?" She couldn't take her eyes off that smooth yet troubled face. "God," she thought proudly and sadly, "was he handsome."

"I don't know," Jules said. "I heard he was over here after the war, but we never got together. Someone told me once he moved out west somewhere, to Idaho or Indiana. Someplace like that."

"Oh." Jamaica became agitated as she tried to think of a way to pursue the inquiry without unmasking her relationship to the man in the photograph. For reasons she couldn't explain to herself, she knew Jules mustn't know that Dr. Pearlman was her father.

"He was quite a man." Jules had drifted off into his own meditation.

Jamaica trod carefully. "In what way?"

Jules exited momentarily, then returned with fresh tea bags and more hot water. He prepared the hot drinks and resumed his seat with the settled air of someone preparing for a marathon entertainment.

The shadow of a remembered hostility skimmed along his face. "This is a story between you and me. Not for the newspaper."

Jamaica gulped her tea, then pressed her cold fingers to her burnt lips. "Of course," she whispered. Soon she was caught up in the narcotic enthrallment of Jules's story.

"You have to understand what kind of a town Just was before the war," Jules began. It was a bustling community in southeastern Czechoslovakia where Jews and Gentiles coexisted separately, but more or less equally, particularly during the democratic period between the World Wars. Just's Jews more closely resembled and identified with their urbane coreligionists in Germany than the ghettoized Jews of Eastern Europe. They derisively referred to them as Polacks and Litvaks, almost spitting out the harsh consonants that made the very words seem ugly.

The picture Jules painted of prewar Just was very different from the one that Jamaica had conceived. Her view was obscured by the death camp photos and *Fiddler on the Roof*. In her mind, European Jews were huddled and fearful. They dressed like peasants. Though she knew her mother had seen a lot of American movies as a girl, she had never associated the stylish thirties' dresses and brisk mannerisms with her parents. Yet here was Jules, reminiscing about after-dinner strolls on the promenade in town, when the girls would put on their best dresses and parade in front of eager suitors. His sister Erzsi created a bit of a scandal when she wore a two-piece bathing suit to the beach; Jules admitted he was a little ashamed.

What was on the minds of most Jews in Just in the prewar years wasn't the occasional horror story that filtered in from Germany. What worried people in those days was the depression, which had severely strained the local economy. A number of young Jews emigrated to Palestine in the late thirties simply because they couldn't find work. For the vast majority who stayed behind, however, life was comfortable despite the pressure of lighter pocketbooks and rumblings of war. Jewish children were permitted to advance in the state school system. There were quotas in the universities of neighboring countries but not in Czechoslovakia; bright Jews were encouraged, in fact, to become doctors and lawyers.

Jules met Dr. Pearlman shortly after the young doctor arrived in Just in 1940 with a great deal of fanfare—and noise. He was unmarried, an attribute almost as attractive as a medical degree in a Jewish community long on daughters. Even before they were exposed to his easy charm, the Jewish matrons of Just had forgiven him for roaring into town on a motorcycle. He was extraordinarily handsome.

He spent his first few months working long hours in his rapidly growing practice, and playing cards with Jules's brother and their friends well into the night. They invited Jules to join them, but he refused to set foot into the tavern where their games took place.

"It was like a chimney in there," he said, recalling the curls of cigarette smoke with disgust. "I don't know how they stood it. And that Pearlman was a doctor." Jamaica winced.

One day Jules noticed a huge crowd of people gathered in front of his family's cafe. As he drew closer he saw they were gaping at a car: a highly polished yellow Oldsmobile from America. In the entire town of Just there was only one other automobile, and it was a Tatra, a Czech car owned by the local lumberyard man. Even Jules was struck by the Olds's singular beauty. It was like a motorized reflection of the sun's rays, a sign from God of how far a Jew could go in the modern age. He had seen nothing more stunning, not even in a movie. He watched the crowd separate, like the waters of the Red Sea before Moses. Enviously he watched Dr. Pearlman—who also seemed to gleam in the sunshine—tip his hat at the onlookers and climb into his new car. He didn't recoil from the attention. Indeed, he welcomed it.

"The funny thing is," Jules mused, "he wasn't from a wealthy family at all. No one knew much about his background, except that he'd been poor. His parents were farmers and had a lot of children."

"Seven," Jamaica thought silently. "And his rich aunt and uncle paid for him to go to medical school." She remembered how her father had forbidden Eva to force them to eat carrots when she and Geneva were small and found orange food repulsive. He told them how he had been afraid of insulting his aunt, so he had eaten the carrots—which he too hated—first thing when she served them. She kept refilling his plate and he kept eating them until the only thing he'd had for dinner was carrots. He'd never eaten a carrot since.

The sight of a pretty young Jewish woman—a different one every night—in the passenger seat of Dr. Pearlman's yellow Oldsmobile soon became a familiar sight. He represented the best a Jewish man could become in a democracy. He could be as debonair as a *goy*. One day, though, Jules heard from one of the ladies at the cafe that Dr. Pearlman's bachelor days were numbered. The talk had it that a perfect match was about to be made: the handsome young doctor and the beautiful daughter of a rich Jewish man in town.

"No!" exclaimed Jamaica involuntarily. "That isn't possible." She combed her memory for the details she knew about the past. There weren't many, but one of them blazed clearly: her parents were married after the war.

Jules looked at her curiously. "What did you say?"

Jamaica shook her head and said haltingly. "I only meant, how sad for the other girls."

Jules laughed. "You sure are talking!"

"What was her name?" Jamaica asked, using all her will to control her voice.

"Ilana. Ilana Zisovics." Jules seemed momentarily moonstruck.

"Why do you look like that?" Jamaica snapped.

"I was remembering Ilana. What a gorgeous girl." Jules shook his head and seemed on the verge of smacking his lips.

He resumed his tale. Ilana was a beautiful girl, tall and slightly *zaftig*. She had masses of reddish hair that was kept in place with large ivory combs. Her father owned several blocks of local real estate. Not a great intellectual, she was bright in every other sense of the word. Like many attractive and beloved daughters, she gave off a glow of well-being that drew people to her. Her generosity of spirit deflected whatever resentment might have built against her comparative wealth and good looks.

Their wedding took place in 1941 and was remembered by all who attended—and survived to remember—as one of the few moments of hope in an increasingly desperate situation. Because of its proximity to the Russian border, Just and the surrounding countryside had been able thus far to sit out the war. Occasionally, though, a young man was enlisted for "work camp." A local resistance movement was formed. Dr. Pearlman was the medic.

Life continued in a weirdly normal fashion, even as reports of deportations became as much a fact of life as food shortages. Dr. Pearlman and his bride quickly rose to the top of local Jewish society, and they happily accepted their symbolic, glamorous role. They never failed to appear at Saturday night dances, which began after Sabbath when the sun went down. They waltzed like lovers and danced the *czardas* with a wildness bordering on frenzy. One day, in a daring act of modernism, Dr. Pearlman taught Ilana how to drive. At first the matrons clucked and gossiped rudely when they saw her steering the always polished Oldsmobile down the street. Soon, though, they were encouraging their own daughters to marry men who would be self-assured enough to give their wives the gift of freedom. Years later, the memory of Ilana grinning behind the wheel of that large car brought a smile to Jules's face. More than ever, she was everyone's dream girl.

When the golden couple had their first child, two years after they married, Jules overheard the rabbi offer Dr. Pearlman condolences along with his congratulations.

"The next one will be a boy," the old man said.

"I don't care if they're all girls," Dr. Pearlman replied. "It's a new world."

Jamaica interrupted the narrative. "Do you know what the little girl's name was?"

After a moment of reflection, Jules shook his head. "I think maybe Sarah, but I'm not sure.

Relieved and disappointed (how much worse, or better, if her sister—her *sister*!—had borne Geneva's name, or Jamaica's, as if that could have been possible, those names in prewar Czechoslovakia), Jamaica nodded for him to continue.

Around Dr. Pearlman the old world had sickened and was dying. The once distant and rather vague reports of deportations could no longer be dismissed as hearsay or housewives' tittle-tattle. It was 1944, and not even the blessed quirk of geography that had protected Just until then could keep out the rottenness in the air.

Jules and his brother were in Dr. Pearlman's squad. The underground parroted military organization as best it could with members of entirely civilian background. Listening constantly to BBC broadcasts, they became aware of a horrible irony. The tide of war had turned against the Germans, and that ebbing tide was going to suck up the citizens of Just. Their underground contact from the west warned them to prepare for the German onslaught.

Jules confessed that the rest of the story was based on secondhand information. It had been confirmed and enhanced many times by people he'd met after the war in those initial bursts of reminiscence that preceded decades of silence.

Dr. Pearlman decided that Just had grown too hot for his wife and their child—at least that was the consensus among those who'd been closest to him. Ilana's parents had already decamped for her aunt's house in a town that sat almost on top of the Russian border. He would stay behind with his raggle-taggle troops, and they would reunite when the war was over.

One night they packed the yellow Oldsmobile with as many of their belongings as they could: the baby carriage from America, his medical school diploma, her lovely custom-made dresses that she was finally able to wear again after months of reducing. A neighbor told Jules after the war that she would never forget the confident smile on Dr. Just's face as he stood in the street at dusk the night Ilana drove out of town. Long after the car was no more than a yellow speck on the horizon, he remained standing there, his arms held up in triumph.

The neighbor remembered the words he shouted, too: "We've beat you, you bastards."

Ilana's victorious journey was brief. Less than five kilometers out of town, a patrol of Nazi flunkies, Hungarians, halted the big yellow car cruising through the night. There were no friendly witnesses to this encounter; later Auschwitz survivors from Just said they dimly remembered the young mother clutching her child at the camp entrance.

Jamaica and Jules sat quietly in their private lachrymose meditations. Shock and horrow and pity froze her very senses, yet as these anesthetics wore off, Jamaica began to feel strangely free.

"You were in love with her, weren't you?" She caressed the top of Jules's head. His hands covered his face.

He nodded miserably. "I haven't told this story in thirty years."

Jamaica started to tell him who Dr. Pearlman was, then thought better of it. "I'm sorry if it hurt you."

He lifted his face from his hands. "No," he said. "I wanted to remember." He wiped his eyes and peered at the digital clock across the room. "Well, Miss Just, I don't want to be rude, but it's almost time for the five o'clock news."

24

Considering How to Run

It was well into the dark of an early winter's evening when Jamaica emerged from the West Fourth Street subway station. Maybe I'll call Sammy, she thought, trying to remember his number in Atlanta. She stopped at the first pay phone she came to. Out of order. She'd try again later. Around her, the street peddlers had set up their blankets on both sides of Sixth Avenue. There were the Senegalese hawking carved wooden elephants and giraffes, and the tall Black Muslims in their flowing robes and down coats waving sticks that sullied the air with the treacly odor of incense. Less exotic street vendors displayed seasonal offerings; woolen scarves, sweaters, and mittens were out in abundance. The sidewalk was crowded with holiday strollers. The lights on the Empire State Building were still in their garish Thanksgiving hues of orange and yellow.

Jamaica meandered through this carnival atmosphere in a state of near obliviousness, pausing only when she reached the giant Christmas tree set up in front of Washington Square Arch. The arch, now protected by graffiti-proof paint, glowed like a pharos for the lost souls who gathered nearby murmuring, "Loose joints. Loose joints."

A boisterous voice penetrated her oddly tranquil castle building. ". . . of the season shouldn't allow us to forget *the poor, the needy, the suffering*. Ladies and gentlemen, gentlemen and ladies, the time is *now!*"

Jolted into consciousness, Jamaica sought out the speech maker. A raggedy man who was part scarecrow, part Lincoln, swayed in the shadows beneath the arch, his hands lifted to the sky, his wild and

257

mangy head rocking to some private beat. Sensing Jamaica's eyes upon him, he waved at her. "Come closer, my child. My message is for you." He spoke the truth, as all other passers-by made a point of circling wide around him.

Obediently, Jamaica drew near. He bent down, so his face was very close to hers. His breath reeked of liquor and poor health; the deep lines springing out from his eyes and mouth were caked with dirt and dried spit.

"The end of the world is drawing nigh," he said in a stage whisper, rolling his eyes hypnotically. "Look around you. Drugs, despair, vagrancy." The Christmas lights twinkled red, green, and blue above Jamaica's head. "You think all is well because you have comfort, a warm coat, a nice apartment to go home to. But you have *forsaken God*. You have *forsaken the Lord*. You dwell *in the House of Self-Love*." Jamaica jerked her head back; her feet remained firmly planted in the circle of his spell.

His voice fell again into soft persuasiveness, his fixed gaze was unrelenting. "Give up your evil ways, my dear. Turn aside from your earthly concerns. There will be no peace until people *like you* take refuge in the Lord. The misery of the earth is on your shoulders. *You are a sinner*!"

Jamaica trembled from the force of this powerful shout. The world around her dissolved into the mist swirling around the haunted outline of the prophet standing before her.

"*Well*?"

She shook her head.

"*Well*?" He repeated.

The scene around her sprang into clarity. She became aware of the hat thrust in front of her, demandingly. As if by rote, she began to rummage deep into her bag for her wallet. She drew out a five-dollar bill and held it above the hat.

She looked once more at the man staring deep into her eyes and she saw a derelict, not a sorcerer. A roar burst out from somewhere deep within her. She thrust her finger in his startled face.

"You don't know what you're talking about," she shouted. "I may not be noble and I may not be pure, but I'm no sinner either. If you want to buy a drink, then say so. Don't play on my guilt. *It's not my fault*!" She was giddy with exhilaration. "*It's not my fault*."

Ignoring the curious stares she was attracting, Jamaica stuffed her five dollars into her pocket, turned on her heel, and marched toward the eastern rim of the park in triumph. If it hadn't already been dark, she'd have faded into the horizon, resplendent with conviction. She listened with joy to the confident thump of her boots on the sidewalk.

At the corner of the park, however, she hesitated, then shot a glance back over her shoulder. The man she had conquered was slumped against the arch. He was pathetic. Jamaica turned and marched back. She pulled the crumpled bill from her pocket and dropped it into the hat dangling from his outstretched hand. Just in case.